TRIALS & TRIBULATIONS

Book 1

By

C. B. R. Davidson

PART 1: TIMES OF CHANGE

"WE CANNOT BECOME WHAT WE WANT BY REMAINING WHAT WE ARE." —MAX DEPREE

THE WOMAN WHO FORGOT

It had been snowing for hours. Winter came fast and harsh and the villagers had barely enough time to prepare. Wood was chopped, animals hunted before the blizzard, and pelts sold out before noon. Each night a glowing fire could be seen in each house, the smell of roasted meat and boiled vegetables strong enough to make anyone hungry. It did not help that Farren *was* hungry and had yet to eat that day. It had been a long day of running errands for her uncle only to return home to decipher her father's scribbled notes. Being the only woman in the family with the ability to read took its toll when her uncle needed to understand her father's harsh writing. Her father's business was something she took pride in even if she were a silent employee. Her Uncle Theron would often remind her of that fact when she was ushered out of meetings and told to make tea for their clients. A medical sales business, something that should make them rich, yet every time Farren translated her father's figures it got worse and worse.

As the snow worsened she shook her head. The crunch of her boots flew behind her as she ran back to the house. It was a respectable size, a snow covered garden arched around the side. Her mother's rose garden was barely distinguishable from the herbs and peonies that brought colour to the pale, blue house. In the summer the house didn't look so dull but as snow continued to fall the stone mimicked wet cobbles instead of the early morning sky. It was a miracle the building was not seized the moment her father took out his third loan. There was no grounds-keeper, only her mother to tend to the garden and the upkeep of the house. There were cracks in the paint, broken steps that lead to the front door and windows that often rattled in the wind despite their thick glass. A merchant would often be respected, often be someone with riches that made their lives comfortable but fate was a lot harsher than people spoke about. Where was her Father's good fortune?

Where was their security? Why did her Mother have to sell her cooking skills just so *they* could eat the next day?

Farren rushed up the gravel path, past the tarp-covered carriage that was older than she was and through the wooden door. The smell of wet dog greeted her and soon two large hounds followed. The elder of the two: Baltar –named after her father's favourite ale- sat and wagged his tail with all his might, the other, less docile dog placed her two front paws against Farren's stomach and wagged her tail in a fashion that matched her brother's.

"Down, Damera," she chuckled.

The dog did as she commanded but neither moved from her path until sufficient hugs and pets were given. Their fur was damp but not recently so, meaning their evening walk was taken care of and the two could lounge by the fire in peace, and hopefully so could Farren. It also meant that her father was home from her uncle's, or as they called it: work. They likely argued for a few hours then wound down with a drink or two. Her suspicions were confirmed as she and the dogs walked into the kitchen. Sat at the table with a glass of amber liquid in his hand was her father. His face was tired and he stared into his glass like it held the answers to the Universe. More than one drink then. He was happy none-the-less, at least that's what was pretended. The longer they lived in the beautiful house, the higher their debts rose which was not helped by the 'business expenses' Theron demanded each month to keep the business afloat. She didn't see him struggle to keep his large house or his many servants. Farren often wondered if the day would ever come that her uncle was brought to his knees, begging for help and she hoped that she would be there when the day arrived.

"You're home late. Did the snow keep you?" Jessibelle Attarah was as beautiful as she was an expert cook and was stood, spoon in hand, a colourful apron around her waist and a worried crease to her brow. The usual look of a mother who awaited her only child to return.

Farren smiled, "no; Aunt Eydis refused her medicine for an hour." It was hard talking about her aunt, it always sucked the life out of the room when she was mentioned, but Farren thought she saw improvement. 'Hoped' was a better word for it. There was more clarity in her eyes, but perhaps that was just wishful thinking because it took her and two maids to hold her down to take her medicine.

Farren pulled out a chair and sat. The coat and gloves she had yet to take off were strewn on the table next to her father's pile of papers. Lines of numbers were crossed through with thick lines of ink. It was mostly in her uncle's handwriting but the scribbles on the side and at the bottom were distinctly her father's. Farren lifted her eyes to the man in front of her but handed her a separate parchment. A sigh escaped her as she read the paper. More empty ships turned up in Altin with no explanation from the merchants. Just as many ships were lost in the Dark Sea. It was not named as such because of its calm nature. Those ships were lost because of her uncle's arrogance because *his ships were the best.* No ship could survive those Pirate attacks, he truly was an idiot.

Farren refrained from crumpling the parchment and handed it back to her father, "does he know?"

"He knows we're in trouble," he took a sip of his drink.

"Then let me help." She leant across the table and her mother clicked her tongue, waved her spoon and Farren sat back in her chair with a huff.

The room fell into silence save for the crackling fire and rustling papers. The hounds did not move from their cushiony beds by the curved-back couch. Snow continued to fall outside whilst her mother pulled a meat pie from the oven; Farren felt her stomach rumble. She pressed her hand to the plane of her abdomen and smiled as the dish was placed on the worn wood of the table. Steam rippled from the bowl of vegetables which were covered in oozing butter and the pastry crunched beneath her mother's knife.

"I can talk to Uncle Theron and explain the papers to him, show him how foolish the Dark Sea ventures are."

Her father blew out a breath, "you know he won't listen to you, no, Farren."

Farren shifted in her seat, "if reason fails then I can threaten him with the loss of money and possibly his business, that should make him understand the stupid, reckless-"

"No more business talk at the table," her mother insisted.

Farren made to protest but a short glare had her mouth clamped shut and her fork stabbed a carrot. The papers had been moved to the chair beside her Father which allowed Jessibelle to sit at the head of the table. Her hands were clasped in front of her as she watched her family devour her food. A mumbled compliment from her husband made her smile and she dug into her own plate. Dinner was short and her parents spoke about their day. Farren drifted in and out of the conversation, her mind still on the papers. Perhaps a visit to her uncle was necessary but if she spoke too much out of turn she would lose her place in the business... what place she had. She chewed on her lip which caused her mother to tap her hand with the back of her fork. She refrained from rolling her eyes. Once dinner was over what was left on their plates –a few strips of pastry and sprinkling of potatoes- was scraped into bowls for the dogs whilst her father went back to agonising over the papers. That left Farren to check the windows and doors and stoke the fire. Each entrance had to be locked –many with more than one- and the thick glass that acted as their windows was enough to keep anyone –*anything*- out, even if they did rattle.

4

All the village funds went into building and renovating houses that would keep everything out and possibly *in*. It was why the rabbit meat and pelts were sold so desperately at markets, it was the only worthy export from the village. It was not often that something broke into the houses but it was expensive enough that when it did, the village would pay it off for years.

A shudder ran down her spine at the thought of the village's Night Creatures. They skulked in the shadows and hunted any animal that dared leave their homes. She imagined they looked like overgrown wolves or perhaps they were simply the village men excusing themselves for murdering their wildlife. There were no solid reports, rumours and old stories from the elderly about how they were once friendly. Despite these stories, the Night Creatures were still a danger to those who lived there. It was why Baltar and Damera had their walks earlier in the day. The Night Creatures slipped in and out of the Veil as they pleased. They preyed on livestock and sometimes humans whether it was for sport or for food she did not want to know.

"How is Eydis?" her mother's voice floated through her thoughts, to where Farren stopped half-way up the stairs.

It seemed their previous conversation was not over. She shrugged and braced her hand on the cracked banister. Eydis was Jesibelle's older sister and someone who didn't deserve the hand she'd been dealt. Eydis never wanted a part of her husband's business and made it clear even before her condition worsened. She was a complete contrast to Theron: she was soft-spoken, caring and timid; she was a dutiful wife to him, and Theron was not cruel to her, not as cruel as Farren saw the village cattle-herder be to his wife. He loved Eydis in his own way, just not in a way Farren ever wanted to be loved.

"Today was a good day." Because most days it was not.

Eydis slipped away bit by bit; the Healers never found a cause. They continued to work dutifully; they checked on her and ran test after test to see

5

why her mind was deteriorating like an old woman. Some days she was lucid, she would remember her family and on those days she painted. Her studio looked over her gardens, nearly identical to theirs. Paintings of all sizes filled the walls of their house; paintings of roses, lilies, unknown wild flowers, trees and small creatures brought their house to life. Even the winter landscapes were full of brightness. A painting she received for her fourteenth year hung above Farren's bed proudly. Her uncle never commented on her painting but every time she worsened, he blamed the King, he blamed the Night Creatures that terrorised the village; he blamed anything but medicine; he blamed anything but her own mind.

A far look entered Jesibelle's eyes as she fiddled with her fingers. She casted her eyes to the painting on her right. It was portrait of Damera and Baltar with their collars glittering in the fire behind them. It was painted last winter and there had been few paintings since. With a deep breath Farren continued up the stairs to check the locks in the bedrooms. That left her mother at the bottom of the stairs, a look on her face similar to Eydis'.

Farren's window clicked closed with a quick flick of her wrist. That left her to stare at the rolling hills covered in snow. The cold seeped through a gap in the window frame and she pressed a hand to the chilled pane. The white land glowed as the snow lessened before her eyes. The white specks danced in the wind and Farren found herself smiling. It was so beautiful yet so cold. The thought had her changing out of the woollen skirts into her thick leggings but as she made to turn to her dresser, a speck of blue caught her eye. What raced across the hills was a streak of blue so fast she could not make out the figure beneath the colour. The moonlight bounced off the figure. A glow of silver and she realised its eyes were on her. It made her heart thrum in her chest but just as suddenly, those eyes moved to the forest.

On slow feet she continued her task; she unlaced her heeled boots, unbuttoned her skirts and pulled on fitted, fur lined trousers. The blue shirt

6

she tucked into her skirts was snug in the waistband of her trousers. The sword pinned to the bottom of her dresser was belted around her waist as she kept her eyes on the window. The discarded boots were pushed from her path and she treaded out of her bedroom, new boots laced around her shins. Farren's steps paused; silence ran through the house. Damera and Baltar remained docile, quiet. There was no-doubt about what streaked across the countryside and she attempted to memorise its features for future reference. As she continued down the hallway there was a tap at the window and she refrained from unsheathing her sword. A small raven perched in the cold, its feathers fluffed and a note tied to its leg. It sat preening itself as she untied the note with a smile.

You are late.

Farren chuckled and tucked the paper into her pocket. A jar of treats sat in her room. They were the ones she snuck the hounds but she jogged to the jar and offered a biscuit to the bird. He took it gratefully and flew away. Speed was needed if she was to leave without being attacked by whatever ran across those hills. She rather liked her limbs attached to her body and not in the belly of a Night Creature. With a shake of her head she followed the raven out of the window, down the snow-covered pipes and into the cold night.

On the outskirts of the village stood an abandoned Church that had not been used in centuries. The roof remained intact which meant the village children had yet to destroy it. Meeting at night was her only option lest the villagers realise how she spent her spare time. Not that it was any of their business but her parents would be hassled to no end. Theron would hold the shame over their heads for years. An icy wind bit at her cheeks as she trekked to the Holy ground. It was muscle memory that lead her to the Church, the moonlight aided her eyes. Torches flanked the large iron doors and she could see the flickering flames behind the boarded windows.

The closer she walked, the clearer the voices filtered from inside. They were both male and very unimpressed, so she slowed her steps with the hilt of her sword sat beneath her hovering hand. Trees and dead grassland surrounded her for many feet, no chance of hiding behind foliage. Her prints in the snow were the only giveaway that she was there.

The metal of the door bit against her hand and she unsheathed her sword slowly. The slow scrape of metal sounded. Both voices ceased; at the end of the bare room stood two men. One man she knew: Argen Bray, who was better known as the Commander of the Village Guard. The stranger's back was to her, though his fine clothes told her enough of whom he might be. Said man turned at her entrance with his arms folded across his chest. Her fingers tightened around the hilt of her sword at the sight of his dark eyes. She straightened her spine as her uncle looked her up and down, and she nearly did not lower her sword. He slowly looked between her and Argen and kissed his teeth at the two of them. A raise of his brows was sent to Argen and he sauntered toward her, the points of his boots nearly touched hers. The way he looked at them screamed judgment. There was only one reason that would jump into Theron's mind and her hand twitched at the thought: he assumed they were an item, two people who met in secret, two people who spent most of their days together already. It was only logical that he thought as such. It was also a better alternative to the truth. He hummed and she moved, gave him a sickly sweet smile and refrained from plunging her blade through his neck. Somehow she doubted that would go over well with her aunt, or her parents.

Theron rolled his eyes, "you can do better than a King's Guard, Farren."

"Is Argen not a suitable enough man?" She tilted her head. "He has a King's title, respect in the Capital and in this village." She glanced at her childhood friend. "He is handsome and kind and has long protected everyone's interests in this village, yours included. You should be happy, Theron, that I am spending my time with a man who treats me well and satisfies my... whims."

The grin on Argen's face was a sight to see. His hands were folded against his chest and a dusting of pink adorned his cheeks like a smattering of roses. His shoulders hunched forward to hide his chuckle as her words echoed in the small Church. The sound was not as well hidden as he hoped because both Farren and Theron turned to him. The older man scanned him from head-to-toe. Farren's sickly-sweet smile remained but it soon morphed into a genuine one as she locked eyes with Argen. "I'm sorry," Argen covered another chuckle with a clear of his throat, "if you do not approve of our relationship Theron, but I hope that you can see I want nothing more than to keep Farren safe."

Theron sneered, "just keep it out of the public eye." The merchant's face was stone when he left.

Both Farren and Argen burst into laughter, doubled-over and wheezing as they replayed the interaction in their head. Farren nearly fell to the floor at her uncle's disgusted face but it was Argen's pink face that was a true struggle to hide her snort. They composed themselves after a few indulgent minutes of laughter.

"You handled that well," Argen complimented.

She physically shook off her laughter but continued to grin at him. The amount of sleazy suitors her uncle found for her over the years still made her roll her eyes. Many of them were much older than her and were either merchants or other businessmen Theron deemed worthy of his time. Each of them wanted a young bride capable of bearing lots of children and making them feel younger. Prized trophies to compete with their friends. *Better than a King's Guard* indeed.

"What *was* my uncle doing here?"

Argen straightened his back just as she had and pushed his hands into his pockets. He swapped his usual uniform for a similar outfit to her own though his was compiled of warm shades of brown. His mousy hair was a pile of curls atop his head which matched the short beard that curved around his jaw. When he stood in front of Theron he seemed so short but in reality he was a few inches taller than her. He had grown into an attractive man which was hard to believe considering Farren remembered when he was a short, chubby child with hands that liked to play in the dirt.

"He followed me here."

"And you didn't know?" she was quick to ask. He raised a brow and stepped toward her. Of course he knew; her uncle wasn't nearly as stealthy as he liked to think he was. Whether they conversed about business, taxes or the weather, Theron always found a way to corner the Commander into an unpleasant conversation. At least he believed she whored herself out to Argen and not that she sought his training, his guidance. She sheathed her sword and walked around the edge of the room. The walls were bare stone, the coloured windows nothing more than boarded up holes. Yet the smell of incense remained. The raven from before sat on the mantle of the fireplace and he let her trail a finger down his soft feathers. "You know," she turned from the raven but continued to stroke his head, "I don't need you to summon me, I was on my way."

He chuckled, "you're here aren't you?"

She barked out a laugh and scanned the expanse of the room as she began to stretch. Bare wooden floors that her body knew all too well were smooth beneath her boots. Many bruises littered her back, arms, legs, basically any working part of her body because of that floor. There was still a large purple bruise on her hip after Argen knocked her down with the hilt of his sword. A cheap shot but an effective one.

Without another word he gestured to the middle of the room and walked slowly over to a particularly worn area. His sword remained at his side as he shifted his feet, twisted his side and held his palms in front of his shoulders. His hands were wrapped in bandages, thicker than when they first started training. They alternated between hand-to-hand and swordplay. The former was her preferred method of combat. She blew a few stray hairs from her face and copied his stance so the session began: double punches, swift kicks, cross-punches. She landed nearly every blow she aimed at him but when he swerved to the side she was unprepared which forced her leg to twist awkwardly beneath her. If his arm had not grabbed her waist she would have fallen flat on her face thus sending a diminishing blow to her pride. She huffed and righted herself. Offence was always easier than defence which soon became painfully clear. His eyes were focused as he sent kick after punch after kick her way. There was a breath and Farren's legs trembled from the ducking and diving.

"Have you been practicing at all?" he asked as she thumped to the floor again.

"Funny," she replied and flung her left leg out from under her, directly into his own.

The sweeping motion had him on the floor with her. She grinned at him and stood, her hand reached down to help him. He glared playfully but took her hand anyway. Their sparring resumed for another hour before he called a time-out. The bag he brought with him sat near the raven who looked to be dozing in the dim light. Farren nearly didn't see the skein thrown her way. She unscrewed the cap and sniffed. "It's water don't worry." That might be true of her skein but what of his?

When he noticed she hadn't taken a drink he gestured with said mysterious skein. The cool water slid down her sweat drenched throat and she had to stop herself from draining the contents. The sweat that covered her body was like a second skin and she yanked at the fur-lined material which clung to her body.

"Let's get ready for round," he paused, "what number are we on?"

She swallowed her water, "was I supposed to be counting?" The reply died on his lips as a low grumble shook the floor of the Church. Farren's eyes shot to Argen as the grumble turned to a growl. The village trembled at the sound, the stumps outside shook and any forest animal ran in the opposite direction. The boarded-up windows left little room for anything bigger than a mouse to enter the building. The doors were the only thing which stood between them and the un-earthly growl. "You don't think..." her whisper trailed off.

Argen did not answer but he knelt and pulled his sword from beneath his jacket. The long-sword glimmered in the light and he pointed it at the doors. The raven was at his shoulder, eyes sharp as though the bird would fight alongside him if need be. She unsheathed her own weapon but it dangled at her side as she listened for more sounds. The wind blew but silence hung around the Church. It was the calm before the storm as the growl sounded again. Farren started as Argen shot into action. He checked the locks on the door where there turned out to be none. A curse flew from their mouths. She started muttering about how to survive, if there was something she read about battling Night Creatures, if there was anything in her arsenal that could protect them.

"We're going to be fine, Farren."

A look of disbelief and Argen pushed her behind him. The Guards were trained to hunt thieves and murderers; there was nothing in the handbook that told them they had to fight Night Creatures. Though there was no-doubt any man in the village would happily do so. The growl turned to a low whine. It was nothing like the supernatural growl they heard moments ago. It was just like Damera or Baltar. It sounded again and she shot past him. Whatever compelled her to move had her opening the doors and she peered outside. The snow fell once again, the slippery ice covered in thin layers of it. Her companion cursed at her, asked if she'd gone mad, and tried to grab the back of her shirt. Everything became a blur as she stared at the mighty creature before the Church. It was a beast of winter, like snow atop a frozen lake formed a living, breathing thing. Its scales were a pale blue, almost white, its tail nearly as long as its large body. Its ears were flat to its head and its snout was covered in scales. Its claw-tipped paws were as big as her torso, but that was blood that trickled down its side. It was as red as hers or Argen's. It wasn't until its eyes –pure orbs of silver- looked at her did she realise she'd seen the beast before. It was the creature from the rolling hills. It growled again as she stepped from the threshold of the Church. The wind bit at her flushed face and bare hand as she held it before her. Argen continued to curse behind her but moved so that his silhouette framed the doorway. No more moves were made to pull her back inside; he thought better of it with the sword in her hand. Said sword was placed slowly to the floor. Her eyes never left the creature. With Argen in the doorway, the light was limited and her own shadow stretched toward the creature's lowered head.

"It's injured." It wasn't a question. Her boots dug into the snow as she stopped mid-way between the Church and the Night Creature. Its eyes followed her every move, as wary as they were in pain. The even rise and fall of its chest meant the wound likely missed any major organs. Something tightened in her chest as she watched the liquid flow freely from its host. Deep scratches ran beneath its ribs. Whatever did that to the Night Creature was stronger, bigger, and meaner. A shudder ran down her spine but she took a step forward. Another growl. She stepped to the side and leaned in to get a better look at the wound but with the darkness and the way it shifted away from her, she could only see the claw marks.

"Can you understand me?" The Night Creatures had been known to talk to humans. Sometimes they sat and listened or sometimes they taught them their own language in return. These were the creatures that did not hunt, that didn't hate humans. That was before the First Great War and before the humans learned to fear their own shadows. It was a long-shot but with Argen stood behind her and the creature as injured as it was, communication was the safest option for everyone involved. Slowly, almost imperceptible, the creature nodded. A breath escaped her which formed a swirl of mist in the air. She kept her face as open as possible as she took another step.

Argen called her name as she was pinned to the floor. Silver and blue flashed in her vision before one of those claw-tipped paws added pressure to her chest. The wind flew from her as she landed amongst the ice. Both her hands gripped the scales that held her to the ground. Her eyes were wide as she stared at the snout that was too close to her face, her neck. Drool hung from its sharp teeth and the smell of uncooked meat wafted up her nose. She dug her nails into the creature's scales and huffed. She wanted to yell, to curse at the creature but with its claws so close to her heart she only took as many deep breaths as she required. She was faintly aware of Argen's yells but she tilted her head back to find he remained in the doorway, horror on his features, his lack of magical training evident. His raven flapped relentlessly on his shoulder.

Farren rasped out, "I was trying to help." Her voice sounded distant and she grunted against the weight on her ribs. Just as the picture of them cracking in half fluttered in her mind, the pressure was gone. The Night Creature stepped back which allowed her to breathe easy. Dangerous it was, but vicious it was not. She pressed a hand where that foot had been and gulped down breaths. She didn't go for her sword like she originally planned but instead she used her free hand to try and peel her damp shirt from her back. The snow melted beneath her and the soggy mess that was her backside made her shiver.

Argen finally stepped into the outside world, his sword pointed at the beast whose stare was no longer on her but on him. With its teeth bared it growled for the umpteenth time that night and limped forward. His limbs shook but Argen held his ground. *Ever the dutiful guard.* The menacing staring match did not last because the creature tilted on its feet then collapsed to the cold ground. No movement suggested it would attack her again so she manoeuvred around the large legs toward the gore at its side.

"Argen I need your pack," her eyes remained on the wound.

A thud sounded to her left where he threw the heavy satchel. There was no hesitation. She rifled through a set of clothes, small weapons, food and finally she reached his medical kit. It was mandatory for every guard to carry one no matter where they were. A cry from Argen paused her movements. Slowly, she lifted her eyes to meet his across the walkway. There was no room for argument, no room for him to try to stop her. It was Theron who taught her 'the stare' and it was one of the only useful things her uncle taught her. It was a stare that sent lesser men scurrying.

15

With the same slow movements she returned to the pack. Copious alchemic vials and tonics looked up at her along with arm-ties, bandages, scissors and a needle and thread. Her gaze swapped between the tiny needle and the bulk of shredded flesh in front of her. With a shake of her head she moved to the vials, each labelled with neat writing. She nearly laughed; Argen's handwriting was far more feminine than her own.

"Farren, what are you going to do if you heal it? Suppose it attacks us?"

"I'm going to have to hope it doesn't." There was a glimmer of humour in her eyes as she gazed into shining silver.

A short huff came from the creature as though to say *'silly human doesn't know what he's talking about.'* She crouched at its side, her back to the warm snout but her hands worked quickly as she poured tonic after tonic on the exposed wound. Hisses and growls emanated behind her but she ignored them and focused on keeping her hands steady. There were just enough bandages to cover the wound. A short glance over her shoulder at Argen's pale face quickened her pace. If he got more impatient he may try and kill it. The Opioids in the last potion she doused on a few of the bandages. It would stop the pain and hopefully prevent infection. She shuffled back to survey her work; it was not aesthetically pleasing, just like the blood that stained her hands, but the injury was covered and the creature breathed easily. Swiftly, it jumped to its feet and stood tall once again. There was no malice in its gaze and the pain in his eyes ebbed away slowly. Her body caught up with her mind and she blinked owlishly at the magnificent creature.

"I hope that helps," she didn't know what else to say.

The world slowed as the great winter-creature lowered its head, eyes slipped shut as it bowed before her. She lowered her head in return and when it straightened she thought she saw a grin before it leapt off into the dark, away from the village and across those rolling hills once again.

"A Night Creature just bowed to you."

"Yes it did."

Sunlight shone through the frosted windows. The kitchen of Theron's estate was warm and bustled with cooks. The smell of roasted rabbit and boiling fruits filled the room, making it that much more cozy. The stone worktops and wooden cabinets were that of the old estate but one step outside the door and you were transported to a high-ceiling foyer. Farren breathed in deeply as she turned the page of her book. The worn pages turned with ease and as she absorbed the familiar words, she found her legs curled beneath her in the lone armchair designated for the Head-Cook. A smirk graced her features as she heard the older-woman yell at one of the servers. Her eyes lifted from the book to the plump woman who took her frustration out on a fresh batch of bread. The server scurried out of the kitchen.

"That was awfully harsh, Lyla," Farren commented.

"Do you want to run this kitchen for a day?"

She licked her lips with a laugh. "I think I'll stick to my job thank you."

Lyla stopped her movements for a second but she narrowed her eyes on the bookworm. "What job?"

Farren's eyes flicked to the dough beneath her friend's hands. "Tasting your food of course."

The vein in Lyla's head was nearly visible as her words processed and the kneading returned with vigor. Farren continued to smirk but cast her eyes

17

back down, the story of a banished prince and his loyal lover stared up at her. The peace did not last long as the doors slammed open, her uncle marched in. Everyone in the room paused, backs straight and eyes downcast. Theron rattled off his requests, namely what to have for dinner and at what time etc etc. Farren stopped listening until his eyes fell on her. Her teeth clenched but he only rolled his eyes and stalked back out. She kissed those teeth as he left, shot a glance at Lyla whose own gaze warned her not to do something stupid and jumped up. The book was placed on the vacated armchair. Servants moved from her path as she rushed after Theron and she weaved in between them to call out her Uncle's name. The set of papers in his hand were deemed more important that acknowledging her yell, so he continued to read as he walked throughout his house. She caught up to him with a huff, "did you not hear me, Uncle?"

He looked at her with a raised brow, "you would think someone who spends all her time with the Commander would be in better shape."

Farren wasn't sure his comment was entirely necessary but she responded, "running in heavy skirts around servants is much different than the clothes and activities when I am with Argen," Theron's lip curled in a disgusted sneer and he looked down his pointed nose at her, "I need to speak to you, it's urgent."

"Well?"

She blinked and felt her eye twitch as he looked back at his papers. It was likely the only time he would give her so she straightened her spine, clasped her hands before her and stared him in the face even if he did not give her the same courtesy."We are losing too much cargo, too many ships and-"

"You have done your research eh?" she nodded, "when you have your own business you can advise me on how to run mine."

She refrained from rolling her eyes. "Whether I run this business or not, the medicine is becoming too expensive to restock and our ships are few and far between. You cannot tell me honestly that the business is doing well, Theron."

The slow movement as he lowered his papers was threatening beyond anything he could have said to her. His eyes lifted from those papers and there was a glint in his eye that had her step back. He was *livid*. The papers finally rested at his side, the figures on them nothing more than smudges of ink as she quickly glanced at them. "You suggest we do what exactly?"

A blink, then another and she opened her mouth like a gaping fish before she replied, "stop travelling the Dark Sea, take the longer route, we'll get our supplies and less men will die at sea which means less funeral costs. The medicine will actually make it to its destination. Yes, it will take longer but we will lose fewer ships –which are expensive- and we will have the cargo rather than losing it to a deadly body of water!" It tumbled from her mouth like the words were vomit so much so her voice increased in volume.

The shock from being asked her opinion made her heart pound against her chest as she awaited his reaction. The poorly veiled accusations were not lost on either of them. Each word was like a weight from her shoulders. Mutterings sounded from downstairs, the clang of pots silent. They had an audience. Farren risked a glance behind her to find Lyla at the head of the nosy group. A nod and two thumbs up was all the cook offered. Farren turned in time to see Theron walk away. With a click of her tongue the young woman scrambled to catch up, her brows furrowed.

"What part of what I said was not true? Why won't you take anyone else's advice but your own?" The last question was more to herself than it was addressed at him.

He rounded on her and used the papers in his hand as a pointing mechanism. The bob in her throat was indication enough that she was prepared to listen. "Let me ask you something, Farren: Where do you suppose we get the money to pay for this longer shipment? Where do you suppose we find the money we lost in the Dark Sea? Where do you suppose we get sailors who will want to work with us after finding out their friends died on our vessels?"

There was only one answer she could offer but she kept it locked in her head. If she suggested he used his own finances she would be thrown from his house. The words that wanted to fly from her mouth, the blame she'd throw on him, caught in her throat as he walked off again.

"We have to do something-hey!"

"Go home, Farren, or do whatever it is you do with your abundance of free time."

The thought that she could easily kick his ass crossed her mind for a fleeting second, and then she blew out a breath and relaxed her back. That time her deflated form did not follow and he did not turn back. A hand scrubbed through her hair and snagged on some of the tangles. She turned to leave with a sigh and the servants bustled back. Noise returned to the kitchen and her Uncle's footsteps retreated upstairs. Lyla remained with that knowing look on her face ever present. Farren waved to the cook who left her to seethe and walked toward the doors.

Hours later the village bustled with people hauling goods to and from the square. Jessibelle was likely teaching the village kids how to knead bread or exchanging recipes with the baker who lived on the other side of the village. Farren crossed the rolling hills that sat behind Theron's house, the same ones that flanked her parent's house, and shoved her hands into the pockets of her grey coat. Her skirts dragged against the ground but she paid the frayed edges no mind. A dagger was strapped to her thigh beneath the heavy material but as the village bustled and the Night Creatures hated the day, she felt safe within the confines of the trees. The sunlight filtered through the canopy and drenched the floor in a cool light. Regardless of her safety she kept her steps light and avoided the winding paths that lead deeper into the forest. She peered at the leaves above her; the sun turned them a deeper green. The pad of her glove brushed over the veins and watched the light ripple. It was a leaf similar to a fir tree that started her uncle's fortune: a leaf that when crushed and mixed with certain tonics could ease a headache. It was something Farren would need a bucket full of when she was finished with Theron. With a sigh she pulled the leaf from its branch and continued walking. By the time she assessed what went wrong with her argument she had been walking for a while. The only reason she stopped was because she kicked something solid.

There was neither a rock nor a twig but there her boot was, pressed against something so hard it bent her toes back. The more she stared the more solid the object became. It rippled with colour against her boot. The colours travelled skyward, past the trees and beyond. She followed it back to her boot, her head tilted to the side. She moved backward then she pressed her foot against it again. Not a hallucination. Her attention was pulled from the beautiful colours to a shadow just beyond. It was like looking through frosted glass as the silhouette moved beyond the barrier; strands of hair framed the person's face and tickled their jaw, the clothes they wore were fitted and they held themselves in such a way that drew Farren closer. The person paused their pacing and turned their head ever-so-slightly to the side, their chin pointed in Farren's direction. The slight glow of teeth greeted her as the person smiled. Their head bobbed for a moment and then they turned fully. Their hands were in their pockets but they stepped forward so that their boot also touched the barrier, mere inches from where hers remained.

"Hello?"

The person shook their head. A poor visual and even poorer sound quality. For a moment she stared down at their boots pressed so closely to one-another, the upturned leather the only sign that she had not lost her mind. She clicked her tongue and pressed her foot harder against the shimmer. The colours returned and both she and the person opposite watched as they danced. Then, Farren lifted her arm, palm flat and ready to press against the barrier in front of her before a hand seized her wrist and pulled her back. She stumbled. Wide eyes met concerned ones and the curly hair was wild atop the man's head.

"Argen you scared me half to death!"

"What about you, I thought I was going to find your body disintegrated next to the Veil!"

"Never mind that did you see…?" She trailed off. Farren's finger remained aloft as she stared at the space where the silhouette once stood. The thundering of her heart died down as the empty space before her did nothing but shimmer with remnant colour.

"What are you looking at?" Argen sidled his way behind her and peered over her shoulder like a puppy. He raised a brow as they both continued to look at nothingness.

Farren shook her head, glanced down at her boot that was back on solid earth then lifted her eyes to Argen's. "Do you think we could just," she made a vague gesture toward the Veil, "walk over?"

Argen stared at her like she'd grown several heads, "no, Farren, I don't think we could just walk over!" He blew out a breath. "Not that any of us should want to anyway," he said it pointedly enough that she rolled her eyes.

"I knew there was a piece of the Veil nearby but to have it this close to the village," she pushed her hair from her face and smirked at him, "must make your job a lot more unbearable," she nearly laughed at Argen's pout, "but honestly Argen, if you were that worried that I would disintegrate then shouldn't more people know it's here? Wouldn't the past village guards have told you, told the people that there is a very alive barrier of magic near where they sleep? This Veil has to be what, three hundred years old, give or take?"

"Give or take," he agreed, "it was created after the First Great War I think, a solution for peace or some such bull." Farren thought she could read the thoughts in his head: *what good that peace did when the Night Creatures still run rampant, when Magic-Users still breathe.* "I only found out about it a couple of months ago," at her bewildered blink he continued, "it was just as much of a shock to me! I was on patrol with Ritrio and we happened upon it. We thought it was the best course of action to not tell anyone outside of the guard. The villagers would demand we move the whole village." He laughed at his own joke then quieted as he looked back at where the Veil stood. "I forgot it was even here and obviously nobody else has found it; people don't usually stroll into these woods and those that do see how dark it is even in the day and turn back." His lips twitched in amusement. "Of course you were the one to find it after me."

"Well I was going to find out about it eventually, after my trial of course," she smirked.

It was a comment that made Argen state, "I'm speaking with the guards tonight, that will give them a chance to think of whatever cruel and unusual training they wish," they both chuckled, "nobody has raised any concerns so far, your trial might go more smoothly than mine."

The trial was a test of will and of skill; it was to prove to everyone that she could become a King's Guard. When she told Argen her plan he grumbled and told her it was ridiculous. Only one woman completed the trial and no-one heard from her since then, but Farren broke his resolve, she begged and begged until he agreed to train her. That was so long ago. Her eyes lit up as he told her every detail he could about the trials his friends undertook in the Capital. If the trial was not completed in the Capital the King left it to his Commanders and their colleagues to determine the contents and timetable. What never differed was that those who completed it successfully heard the Prayer of Loyalty and Courage when the King anointed them. It was something Farren would hear no matter what.

"So what are we betting, three on one sword fight? Maybe four on one? Or will they have me run laps and cut down a tree?" the snort that escaped her at the thought echoed around them.

"Enrys will definitely want to take you on," the laughter was still in Argen's voice, "but Ritrio will want to be the mastermind. Don't forget," something mischievous twinkled behind his eyes, "I get to help them plan."

"Ah." There was a pause. "So I'm just going to be handing you your ass in the Church?" He shoved her lightly. He looked so young, not like a

Commander of an entire village, not like he had to protect their lives every day. Farren's chest filled with pride the longer she stared at him. The flutter in her chest made a grin burst onto her face. They both allowed themselves one more glance at the faded Veil and he followed at her side, his hand relaxed on the hilt of his sword. She glanced between him and the path in front of her. "It's all well and good that I didn't get disintegrated or spirited away but, how did you know where I was?"

The brunet scratched the back of his neck and kept his eyes forward. A muttered response followed but she furrowed her brows. She made to ask him again but the hand that was behind his neck moved to his cheek and he sent her a sheepish grin. "I've been keeping an eye-" she opened her mouth to protest, "after the other night I wanted to make sure the Night Creature wouldn't come back or bring friends. It's not that I don't think you can take care of yourself. I do! You just do not seem very concerned that you healed a creature that belongs to the other realm."

Farren sighed, her previous indignation faded like the Veil behind them. "I want to be perfectly clear, I can take care of myself."

A smile graced his features. "I know," there was silence before he continued, "I wanted to ask you something about that night, actually. Why did you help the Night Creature? It was double your size Farren and when it pinned you to the ground I thought I was going to keel over! It was bleeding, sure I understand that, but they are not for us to meddle with. They hunt this village and yet... why?"

Farren stared at the tree canopy above them. "If I were injured I would like to think someone in that Realm would help me." Argen's face told her the likelihood of that. "And I don't know, it was hurt, it wasn't being aggressive;

25

I walked away without a scratch on me. Do you not ever wonder what it would be like if we weren't so afraid all the time?"

"The only way that will happen is when the Night Creatures are dead and that Realm stops being connected to ours."

An absent minded hum from Farren and the conversation was complete. The two of them walked in companionable silence before they reached the edge of the forest where it met the hills beyond. The wet grass squelched beneath their boots and she looped her arm with his. He coughed at her sudden touch and her hold became that little bit tighter as they walked.

Farren steered Argen toward the center of the village and his brows rose. Farren, the woman who caused a riot every time she opened her mouth, wanted to socialize with her fellow village-mates. He nearly scoffed at the thought, but it soon turned to a reality when they made their way from the forest and toward the heart of Bentham.

"You-" Argen's eyes were wide. "You want to go into the village with me?"

Farren practically skipped as she said, "there's a travelling market arriving today and if I turn up with a King's Guard we might get free food."

He said under his breath, "that makes more sense."

She stopped and turned on him with a cheeky smile. "What did you say?"Argen scratched the back of his neck and repeated what he said only louder. "Oh yeah? For that comment I'm not sharing."

"Oh come on," he playfully whined, "you're using my title and I don't even get a bite of your food?"

She took a moment to glance between him and the path in front of them. "One bite."

"Only one? We'll see."

Farren punched his arm lightly, that smile still on her face and laughter bubbled from her chest. He laughed with her as they traipsed past the residences of people they knew. They waved, they smiled and Farren ignored the questionable looks she received when she practically yelled in excitement when she smelt fried sugar, so she dragged him toward the market with the strength of a tiny horse.

Different foods, crystal vases and mechanical objects that made the mind wonder littered the stalls that outlined the village square. Vendors stoked fires and pulled cloaks around them to prepare for the long day in the cold. The sun did little to warm the square but that didn't stop the smiles that covered the sellers' faces. Brentham was in the perfect position for markets, a small through-way near the Capital and the market was a large source of the village income, especially in the dead of winter as it was that day. They were lucky the market graced them that year with how severe the snow had been.

At the far end of the square, stalls continued to be set up. It was near those stalls that the fire pit was formed. Every year there was a bonfire that lit up the whole village. That was something that even the Night Creatures would not deter the villagers from enjoying. The pit itself was nothing more than tall logs and a circle of stones when they reached it. It was also where the food stalls were to stand. It was in that direction Farren dragged Argen.

Once they reached their target Argen simply flashed the King's emblem which sat on his shoulder and a much larger crest was emblazoned on his back. The vendors were on him in seconds. Questions were thrown, queries were mentioned and there were some who simply wanted to shake his hand. Farren's lip twitched as she watched her friend –who blushed thoroughly at the attention- be bombarded with compliments.

Between the flurry of words Argen's attention fluttered between her and the vendors, "t-thank you but we-we are here to assist if we can."

"Please," one of the vendors started, "let us repay you somehow."

Farren bounced on her heels as she tried to look as innocent as possible but it was Argen who replied, "we will take any treats you would spare, but please let us help." The vendor chuckled, nodded and gestured to the pegs that kept his tarp in the mud.

Argen got to work, but Farren didn't speak, not as her attention was stolen from her red-faced companion to what sat across the bonfire pit. How had they missed such a colourful tent? Reds, yellows, blues, such vibrant colours were stark against the grey sky. It was larger than the stalls at the front and was fully erected. Runes covered the open flaps of the tent, held to the ground by ropes far stronger than the ones Argen tried to pin down. Something pulsed from inside the tent and then again until it was a throb in her vision.

"I'll be right back..." Farren excused herself and half-jogged around the pit to the tent.

Heat and mint met her at the threshold. A wooden step and red carpet sat before her; it beckoned her inwards. She placed one foot on the wooden step and peaked inside. There was a foyer and a small room covered by sparkling beads. A round table stood at the back, a pack of cards stood proudly in the middle. Scarves and trinkets hung from the ceiling, they covered the top-part of the tent. A wooden bar that mimicked one from a tavern held tonics and potions like an assortment of whiskeys. The labels were too small to read from where she stood but some sparkled in the watery light, others were dark and thick like molasses. She leaned her elbows on the bar and pushed herself forward to view the contents. Many of them had medicinal names, some with herbs and others were named... oddly. There was a hoot behind her and she pressed a hand to her chest. On a carved perch sat a tawny owl who watched her with eyes that were far more aware than an owl should be. Having been caught in her snooping she blew out a breath and made her way over to the bird with a smile.

She brushed a hand down its wings and cooed, "and who are you?"

"Her name is Elira," the voice was slightly accented and silvery.

The owl hooted again and she turned back to the bar only to find a red-haired, tanned skin man. Elira flew over to him as he offered the owl his arm. There was a small smile on his face as the owl nibbled on his ear. What he wore was not a dress nor a tunic but something in between. The white fabric hugged his waist and shoulders where it tapered into long-fitted sleeves. Emerald circlets wrapped around his wrists which contrasted with the rings that adorned each finger. He wore green boots that stopped at his ankle, his toned leg peaked from the slit in the fabric. Farren thought of the snow outside and how frostbite would hurt if it claimed an entire leg. The man before her did not so much as shiver.

Farren shook away the shock, "I'm sorry to just barge in but the tent was open, I mean the tent flaps were open and it seemed so pretty, not that that is a reason to trespass, I mean-"

He chuckled, walked over to where she stood and placed the owl back on its perch. With graceful steps he moved toward her, back around the bar where he picked up different tonics and even stooped toward small drawers she did not see earlier. Before she stepped away his voice stopped her, "it's alright you being here, though I don't think your village friends would agree."

"Why do you say that?"

With a quirked lip he gestured around the tent. She followed his arm, eyes ghosted over the wonders she saw earlier. A few interesting pieces stood out around the tent, but there was nothing more prominent than the man before her. Despite the intricate designs and beautiful items her eyes always made their way back to him. The longer she looked the sharper his features became, even his cute nose seemed longer. If the villagers were not weary of the tent beforehand, one look at the striking male who accompanied it and there were sure to be enquiries.

"If you think the village will judge you or worse, riot against you, why set up here?"

The man paused, his hands folded before him, "this village has something in it that I am quite invested in, and I wanted to see it for myself. Being a part of this market was the easiest way to do it."

Farren tilted her head, "what are you invested in?"

He tapped his finger against his leg absently, "I'm interested in the Veil. There is a small sliver of it nearby. I wanted to check on it."

Farren's eyes narrowed, "why now?" He stopped his tapping. "It's been here for as long as I can remember. Why turn up now?"

"Rumour has it," his fiddled with a couple of his rings, "it has moved, shrunk actually. It's thinner and I want to know why."

There was a moment where the world dropped away but Farren asked, "what does that mean for the village?"

"Hopefully nothing." That was not the answer she wanted. "But it is certainly interesting."

"Interesting or terrifying?"

The man turned to the side toward the table at the back, "shall we see? I can give you a reading if you like?"

Their earlier conversation hung in the air but Farren gulped, "what would that... entail?"

"The cards offer different paths: past, present, future and sometimes all at once. They are," he chuckled, "fickle but they are not usually wrong. Some people ask them questions for a specific reading."

"To know someone's future, that's a large burden for someone to carry isn't it?" Despite her question she followed him. The beads which hung between them and the table looked like the shimmering Veil, the scarves had runes etched into them and some of the liquids moved on their own. Magic thrummed inside the tent, it kept the two occupants warm from the outside chill and soon enough her coat made her too hot, the baby-hairs stuck to her neck. She pulled at the collar and his eyes remained on her, their piercing green stopped her thoughts dead. It took a big reserve of will power to remove her eyes from the mysterious man but as he sunk to the plush stool, she followed suit, eyes on the outside world.

His voice brought her back into the room, "magic is attracted to more magic." He shuffled the cards. "The stronger the pull, the more accurate the reading." His eyes bore into hers and she forgot how to breathe for a moment. "The future can often be unkind but for what it's worth, when people see a good card, the burden is worth it." Another shuffle of the cards and he placed them before her. "I'm sure they will be kind to you."

Farren couldn't help the snort that escaped her. The only kindness she had with magic was when the Night Creature did not rip her to shreds. She was sure Mrs Hillcrout would not think magic was so kind after her son overdosed on magical Opioids. She was sure a guard's widow would not agree after his being disintegrated by who-knows-what on his nightly patrol. Yet there she sat, surrounded by beautiful trinkets about to receive a tarot reading. "I'm not sure magic has been kind to this village."

The man's eyes flashed brightly for a second, so fast she barely caught it, "magic is much like humans, there are different strands, different elements

that can set it off. It is up to the K-those who use it to bend it to their will."
His smile was as beautiful as the rest of him. "It is rather accommodating if
you treat it with respect. The Night Creatures for example." Farren leaned
forward, eyes quickly on the tent opening. "When was the last time they
bothered the village?"

Farren let out a breathy chuckle, "a few nights ago." The man froze with
his hands over the cards. "One of them reached the Church with an injury," at
the sadness that flittered across his vision she quickly continued, "I healed it!"
She lowered her voice, very aware of the people outside the tent. "My medical
skills are basic but I think I stopped the bleeding. I just hope it made it home
okay."

His smile turned to one of awe, "you healed it? What did it look like?"
Farren recounted each detail down to the shade of its eyes. "That Night
Creature is a long way from home. It is odd that one of them would travel this
far South."

"What do you mean? Plenty of Night Creatures scour this area."

His head shook. "That was a Night Creature from the North, they thrive
in cold water and caves. They live in the Northern most region of the other
Realm, they barely travel past their borders. That one must have been lost, or
someone asked it to be here..."

"You certainly know a lot about them," she smirked.

"Yes, yes I suppose I do."

There was a lift to his lips, and his eyes drifted to the cards in his hold.
Farren marvelled at the artistic talent displayed on the back of the cards. Three
were placed from the deck between them; the soft cloth that covered the table
crinkled under the brush of his fingers. Those fingers gently reached across
the table and he held his palm out to her. Blue locked with green and she

gulped. Her gloves were removed and placed in her lap. With a shaky hand she placed her hand in his. The decorative rings were cool beneath her fingertips which were softer than any bedspread beneath her calloused hands. She nearly winced as she imagined how rough hers must have felt to him. The red-head did not acknowledge it; instead he lifted her hand above the cards and left it there to hover. Her eyes were on his the entire time.

"I'm going to say a few words and the cards are going to flip over. The first should be your past, then present, then future. They may all be your future. Do you have a question you particularly want answered?"

The muscles in her body tightened. There were so many questions, some selfish and some for her family. *Would Eydis ever recover? Would her father ever get out of debt? Would her uncle ever accept her help? Why did the Veil shrink? Would she become a King's Guard?* Farren made to open her mouth but there was a rustle of the breeze through the silken table cloth and the cards moved. They flipped, one after the other on a phantom wind. Her eyes were wide as they revealed beautiful pieces of art with numerical symbols at the bottom. The writing beneath the numbers were in a different language, an old language if the sharp lettering was any indication.

Farren whispered, "I didn't ask them anything?"

He blinked down at the cards then at her dumbfounded face, "not verbally."

"So," she swallowed once again, her hand still flexed above the cards, "what do they say?"

A shout of her name and the tense nature of her muscles tightened further. The cards were stagnant and the Magician's hand covered hers in warmth. Tingles erupted over her body and the moment it faded the source of the voice –Argen- stormed into the tent. He froze at the colour in the room, at the smell of mint, at Elira who stared at him from her perch. He stepped away from the bird with his hands slightly raised at his sides. Like a wet dog he shook his head and shot straight for Farren. She braced a hand between Argen and the magic-peddler but the guard's eyes burned as he surveyed the man sat opposite.

"Argen, are the stalls all set up outside?" Farren asked, almost sounding surprised he entered the tent.

His nostrils flared, "yes, when you didn't come back I had to see what kept your interest for so long," he surveyed the tent again, "now I see it was," he paused, "is this a Magician's tent?"

"It is; it's pretty isn't it?

Argen's gaze was glued to the hand that covered Farren's. The red-head watched as the cogs in his mind whirred. Farren shifted her own gaze between the two men, the atmosphere near-stifling. When Argen leaned forward she furrowed her brows at him, nothing but confusion in her gaze. "We need to leave, the fact you have been in here for so long will draw attention."

"Argen," she patted his arm with her free hand, "if you purse your lips, attention is drawn in this village. People are going to talk simply because the tent is here. There is nothing untoward going on, okay?"

Whether that was true or not she had yet to see, but so far the Magician had been nothing but kind, polite and a nice reprieve from the faces of her everyday life. Argen's jaw feathered and his hands curled into fists, but that was concession on his face. The look he gave her made her smile and he blew out a breath. The guard made to turn, his shoulders slightly slumped and a pout on his face.

His retreat was stopped by the Magician's voice, "is there a problem with my tent being here, guard?" Every joint in Argen's body locked and Farren's free hand pinched the bridge of her nose. The hand under the other man's hand flexed but his touch remained soft, calm, as did his voice.

However, Argen glared and the sound of ground teeth nearly filtered through when he replied, "you pedal magic, you purposefully made your tent vibrant and large, the scent of mint and sage has started to waft through the square and the unnatural heat that engulfs this place is... too much. I need you to pack up your things and leave."

Farren stared wide-eyed at her friend, "Argen-"

The Magician's smile bordered on feline, "and what authority do you have to order such a thing?"

Argen's chest puffed up, "I am Commander Argen Bray of the Brentham Guard. I am the highest ranking member of this village and I demand that you leave this market and this village."

Farren hissed his name but it was the other man who replied, "as true as that may be, I have authority from a much higher power to be here."

"Yes? Who?"

That once near-feline smile widened, "a King." Argen looked as though he would combust on the spot. His nostrils flared and there was a moment where Farren thought he would start to scream. Red engulfed his face from the strain. Authority from the King... she very much underestimated the man next to her. "I think you will find, Argen was it? That the peddling of medicines, jewellery, scarves and pretty tarot cards is not magic. I am breaking no laws."

The vein in her friend's neck throbbed, "the unnatural heat is magic," there was a waver in his voice as though he second-guessed himself the moment he spoke.

"I'm not peddling that."

Farren placed her hand on Argen's arm once again; her touch was firm through his jacket and he moved his eyes to her. The pinks of his cheeks glowed in the heat and the muscles in his forearms were tense beneath her fingers. She sent him what she hoped was a reassuring smile. "There is nothing more for you to do here Argen, give me a minute or so and I will follow you out." She pointedly stared at the tent opening.

"You-he-I-two minutes, then I'm coming back in here and dragging you out," Argen left the tent with a glare toward Elira who, if she were a human, would have stuck her tongue out.

The Magician's eyes were soft on Farren when she turned to face him, "why does he act like that?" It was an innocent question. There was no judgement behind it just sheer curiosity. Yet Farren couldn't help the mixture of a scoff and a chuckle that sounded from her chest.

"He was going to leave and you provoked him," her words were light and filled with the remnants of that chuckle

He inclined his head, "you are correct, I should not have goaded him like that, I am sorry."

She waved her free hand between them, the twinge of her heart at his saddened face strong enough that she said, "no, honestly, he," she sighed, "he means well, he was just uncomfortable, concerned even."

He replied, "that does not give him the right to give you time limits"

Farren playfully rolled her eyes, "he is Commander of the guard, he technically does have the right." There was a pause from both of them and he looked like he wished to say something else. Finally, she slipped her hand from beneath his. During the altercation with Argen their hands fell to the cards. Her eyes were drawn to them once again. Detailed faces and weapons stared up at her. "I don't think we have time for a full reading," Farren stated.

The sharpness of the Magician's features softened, he nodded and told her to wait right there. A glance to the tent opening and back and she nodded. There was an alcove, similar to a small broom closet that sat behind the table. Stacks of boxes were piled high against more shelves. The sun shone through the beads into that back room so she tilted her head and watched the light dance around the room until he returned with a small box in his hand. Velvet covered the outside but that was soon thrown behind him as he showed her the contents. A pendant dangled from his fingers. When it caught the sun it was like a living flame, the oranges and red matched his hair. It was no bigger than a walnut and hung from a thin golden chain.

"It's beautiful," she breathed.

"It's yours."

"Sir, I cannot afford such a beautiful necklace."

"It is a gift." The Magician gently grabbed her hand, unfurled her fingers and dropped the pendant into her palm. The jewel was heavier than it looked, like the weight of a piece of coal. It was a sharp contrast to her pale hand and no magic throbbed against her hand like she imagined it would. It looked like a vibrant, wild flame. She looked up at him as he closed her fist around it. "Please," he smiled, "think of it as a thank you for not running scared the moment you stepped foot in my tent."He released her hand. "It will keep you warm."

A sad smile sat on her lips because nearly everyone in the village would have, "thank you, it truly is very beautiful."

He inclined his head and no more words were spoken between them. As she made to leave he twitched, it was subtle but Farren felt the urge to stay, to speak more with the magic-peddler, but Argen called her name from outside and broke that train of thought. A short wave and she walked through the beads and past the owl whom she sent a blinding smile. The Magician chuckled as Elira hooted in response. Then Farren was gone, her skirts billowed out of sight and her hand shoved the pendant into her jacket pocket. Argen proceeded to huff and puff about magic as they walked back over to the food stalls.

Left alone in the tent, the Magician stared down at the upturned tarot cards. The longer his eyes stayed on the images the wider they became. He read the inscriptions over and over, the pictures doing little to ease his discomfort. Farren was nearly called back; he nearly demanded she know what the cards said but he spied her beyond the tent, a strip of jerky in hand and her brow raised. Instead, he sighed and left the cards on the table. As he went about his day the three cards remained silent, remained still against the table. That was, until the third card which depicted a beautiful golden crown, shook.

After the market was set up and Farren ate her fill of jerky, she visited her aunt, a small gift of candied almonds in tow. Eydis sat on the window seat overlooking her gardens with a faraway look in her eyes. A smile pulled on her chapped lips but her body looked so small, so frail, against the large window. Farren knocked, the sound soft so she wouldn't startle her but there was no sign Eydis registered the noise. The older woman did not move until Farren stood next to her, her gaze on the garden. The haze in Eydis' eyes remained but her smile was brighter. It was like the scent of Farren's perfume or the sound of her breathing eased her somehow. Farren sat next to her on the ledge, her skirts pushed behind her and her hands close enough that Eydis could grab them if she so wished.

"How are you feeling Aunt Eydis?" Eydis' raven hair fell forward as she nodded. Farren pushed it back over her shoulder and nodded too. "That's good, have you eaten?" If someone were to walk in they would see a picture of two upstanding women illuminated by the afternoon sun, the dead trees framed them from beyond the window.

"The flame, it has found you at last..." she trailed off, "or perhaps you have found it..." Farren's brows furrowed and she squeezed Eydis' hands lightly. She spoke her riddles with such confidence that it made Farren's chest hurt. She wished she knew what they meant or how to decipher them just like her Father's papers. Her aunt meant the world to her but there were days when she wished it was just *easier*.

By the time Farren formed her questions, it was too late: her aunt slipped back into her head. Farren pulled her hands from beneath hers and stood. Eydis returned her gaze to the garden, or rather *through* the garden to whatever world she resided in. A knock on the door pulled Farren away from her wistful aunt to turn to a solemn-faced Lyla. The cook's apron swished as she walked, her calloused hands pressed to either side of Farren's face. Tears threatened to fall at the soft nature of the hold. A sharp breath through Farren's nose lead to a shaking breath. The tears were never shed but instead they lined her lashes and made her eyes shine. The tightening in Farren's throat was not because of the decorative band around her neck. She swallowed as best as she could and removed Lyla's hands slowly.

"I want to get some shopping done before the bonfire, come with me?" Farren kept her hand in Lyla's when she nodded. The pendant that hung against her chest burned a metaphorical hole against her jacket as they left the large house, down the gravel path and toward the centre of the village. The entirety of Brentham crowded into the market square. Children ran around the bonfire pit where men prepared more wood, and in between stalls giving the owners a good level of anxiety. The woman who sold bracelets from the South snapped at one child who got too close to her goods. Lyla snorted into her shoulder as the child skulked away with an angry frown. They stopped to browse different stalls. Farren cringed as she saw the length of the queue in front of the fudge stall and Lyla clicked her tongue as she saw what stole her friend's attention. A sharp tug against her hand and Farren stumbled after the cook. She tugged back as they passed an older gentleman who looked to be selling nearly as many herbs as the Magician. Lyla found nearly all of her ingredients and busied herself talking to the seller about the recipes she planned to make with them. Ideas were swapped back and forth. It was so familiar: Lyla had a way of talking to people that left them in awe. She was a walking battleaxe so fierce it was a wonder she was not part of the King's Guard, but then she created intricate pastries, fondant flowers and sponge cakes that set people's –Farren's- taste buds alight. As the cook finished her conversation with a man who stood just a bit too close to her friend, Farren watched the villagers talk and play. That was when a flash of colour lit up the side of her face. A squeak escaped her and she pressed her hands to her face. Laughter jingled toward her so she removed her hands to find there was no blood nor was she blinded; she was not injured at all. Another flash of colour and Farren's eyes flew to the Magician's tent.

Colours burst from the short pole he held in his hand. With the dying light the colours looked brighter. Children giggled and ran around him in circles. In his empty hand a small orb shone: it hovered in the air like it was- Farren's mouth fell open a fraction. Magic held the ball aloft; magic kept the children entertained; magic lit up the dull market with colour. It was magic that turned the smiling villagers into frowning humans. The entire village was gathered for the bonfire so nearly every eye who lived there turned toward the flamboyant man. Farren made to step between the slowly forming mob and the Magician but one minute the illusion was there, the next second he showed the children and awe-eyed adults how it was done. A parlour trick he learned in the Capital. The colours were created the same way fireworks were and the orb, well that was just a perfectly placed glass pole and a trick of the light. Elira took that moment to join them, flying through a hoop that dangled from the entrance to the tent. She landed on his shoulder gracefully which earned a treat and a squeal of joy from the children. As the Magician knelt so the children could pet his friend his eyes raised to hers. It suddenly felt like the centre of his attention was a very interesting place to be. The villagers turned into blurs as she pursed her lips. Mirth swam behind his eyes and she fully grinned at him. When he straightened, the orb was thrown to the side and the pole was raised once more to produce light.

Lyla tapped her shoulder and held up a satchel filled with goods but her friend's eyes moved slowly from Farren to the man with the colourful rod, "that Magician is making a fool of himself."

Farren snorted, "you sound like Argen."

Lyla scrunched her nose and looped her arm through Farren's. They walked past the dancing Magician and further away from the crowd of people to survey the goods Lyla procured. However, Farren watched the red-head until he was blocked by one of the food vendors, "I think he's fantastic, a real performer!"

Lyla slapped her arm, "you and I both know that was magic –*real magic*- he was using back there. Don't be one of those fools who fall for its handsome wielders."

The Magician's toned legs, lithe arms and striking cheekbones came to mind. The silken strands of his hair came to life in the colourful sparks, and the clothes he wore only accentuated his toned body. Farren's answering grin was nothing short of feral. "You think he's handsome?"

Lyla's spine straightened as though she could stop the image of the Magician from reaching them by sheer force of will. She huffed and dragged Farren into a brisk walk. They breached one side of the square and lifted their faces to the dying sun. The golden hour would soon be past so the two women soaked up what rays of sun they could. The comfortable silence was broken by Lyla, "has Argen spoken to those idiots at the barracks yet?"

Farren slipped her eyes closed as the sun warmed her chilled cheeks, "he told me he was speaking to them tonight."

Lyla cracked open an eye, "you haven't checked?" Farren shuffled on her feet just for something to do. No, she had not checked if Argen kept his word. If he did then it meant her training would be over and she would be thrust at the men who'd been guarding their little village for years. They watched her grow up and she watched them train. *Loyal soldiers until the end.* Farren shivered. "You have a *lot* of faith in him." Lyla turned her head to the side, her eyes pierced into her. "He might be your friend but he's also loyal to the men that run this village, your uncle included."

A roll of her eyes and Farren finished sunbathing. "Theron will have no say in whether I do or do not become a King's Guard. Besides," she shrugged, "he has no idea I even want to become one; he just thinks I'm sleeping with one."

A throat cleared behind them and Farren prayed to Griselda that it was not Theron. The Goddess smiled upon her because as she and Lyla turned, a red-nosed, bashful Argen stood behind them. The sun bounced off his curls and haloed around him. He looked like one of the Church's stain-glass depictions. The sweet young man who would save the Humans from evil. His raven sat on his shoulder, its wings tucked in at its side. "That's not entirely true."

Farren stepped forward; he stepped back, "what do you mean 'that's not entirely true'? What part of it is not true?"

Lyla shifted her eyes away and stepped back. A smirk sat on her lips as she caught Argen's eye. His vulgar gesture did nothing to calm Farren's nerves. Farren nudged him with her boot and his eyes moved back to her. The expectancy and barely concealed frustration in her eyes only made him shift on his feet.

"Your uncle is a smart man Farren," Argen started and Lyla hid her snort of laughter behind her hand and something similar to 'great opening idiot' escaped. "When he saw us the other night he put two and two together."

Farren sucked in a breath, "he just thought we were sleeping together Argen, 'training' so to speak, how could he possibly know I'm going to take the trial?"

Argen swallowed and shrugged, "he must have figured it out, because he definitely knows. He stopped me on way from the barracks and asked me how your training was going, and I don't think he cares enough to ask about our... romantic relationship."

Nausea, a tight throat, and lead in her limbs settled. Theron knew the one thing she'd kept from her family for years... *Theron knew.* Farren took a deep breath and pushed her hand through her hair. Luckily for her, no matter what Theron said so long as the Commander of the Brentham Guard had her back there was nothing her spiteful uncle could do to stop her. Her eyes shot to Argen's, "did you speak to the guards?"

Argen pushed his hands in front of him, waved them as a barrier between their bodies, "of course I did Farren, I'm a man of my word."

"Then why are you shaking?" Lyla chimed in.

Argen looked ready to run. The laughter of the children behind him turned into dull background noise as he stared at Farren. She took another step forward and he audibly clicked his knuckles at his side. "Everything's fine, they are more than happy to let you take the Trial. I've seen what they have planned, it's nothing too difficult. I can't tell you, obviously."

A breath she didn't know she held was released. The noise from the market rushed back in; the glow in Argen's hair seemed too bright but the relief in his eyes nearly made her laugh. An agreement from the guards put her a step closer to the King and to the Capital. When she became a Captain her ceremony would be grand, she would make sure of it. The finest cheeses, sweet bread, cakes and pastries as far as the eye could see. Beautiful dresses and courtiers twirling around a polished dance-floor. She would shake the hand of the Country's Commander and bow before the King. Her grin was unstoppable. She flung her arms around Argen. The hug was so fast he stumbled back as he wrapped his arms around her. The raven flew above them with a squawk. Lyla rolled her eyes at the sight but a smile curved at the corner of her mouth. After a moment of joy Farren pulled back. Argen's roll of the eyes and smile was all she received. She twirled in the pale sun, hands in her hair and she yelled. She cheered and yelled at the top of her lungs because she –Farren Attarah- would become a King's guard.

Darkness filled the sky, the stars and moon bright against the black. Men and women whispered as the large logs that filled the fire pit were adjusted and covered in dry grass. The children who spent their evening playing and laughing were slumped against their parents exhausted. Some were asleep against their mother's skirts, curled up like kittens whilst others watched with baited breath as two guards lifted and shifted the logs. Farren stood to the side, the stalls closed down save for one or too hot wine vendors. She glanced around the large circle the people made, candles in their hand to aid the guards in their sight of where to throw their match. Argen was beside them, the match in his hand ready to be struck, and with a countdown from ten, it was. He struck it against the sleeve of his jacket and let it fall between the logs and onto the dry grass. Once the match caught, Argen and the other guards stepped back and watched as the fire pit became a beacon of light. He made his way over to where she stood, his hands folded into his armpits as he sought warmth from the winter chill. Soon enough the fire would radiate enough heat that it would be a pleasant evening.

"Why are you not with your parents?" Argen asked.

"My parents are enjoying themselves, and honestly I'm nervous for the Trial so I wanted to establish some sort of plan without them asking whether I was feeling alright," she chuckled lightly.

The same could be asked of his grandmother who seemed to be missing from the crowd much like her aunt. The old woman was strong, independent, someone who chose to live on the outskirts of the village so there was no shock on Farren's face when she noted the woman's absence.

She looked across from her to see her parent's smiling faces but a few inches to her Father's left stood Theron, his face as blank as ever. Eydis was nowhere to be seen, her body and mind too frail to be out at such hours.

Reds and yellows danced across Argen's face as he watched her shift on her feet. Her eyes moved from his soft features back to the fire. Ash curled into the sky and landed around them. There was something about the flame, the way it danced against the night sky, even the way it smelled that had Farren excited to be alive. That buzz passed through the villagers as they crowded around the spectacle.

"Are you sure you are not avoiding your uncle, Farren?" a loud voice sounded from across the square. Enrys, one of Argen's most trusted guards sidled over to them with a mug of wine in his fist. A large grin sat on his plump face and his ears stuck out like bicycle handle-bars. The shadows that were cast along his shoulders made him seem much larger, like a beast from a book and yet she smiled back. He clasped Argen in a large hug, grins on both their faces and he handed his friend a mug of his own. A short glance between Argen and her made his eyes narrow minutely.

"I'm avoiding him just like you are avoiding Roseanna. What did you do this time?" she teased.

His face changed in a flash and a large sip was taken from his wine, "she says that I'm too arrogant, can you believe that? Me? Arrogant?" Farren turned her head away, her face once again toward Argen and stifled her laugh. Snot nearly flew from her nose from the pressure of holding it in. The white-haired man paid her no mind as he took another gulp of alcohol. Argen's own mug warmed his hand as he slowly watched Farren. Steam rose and swirled between them as Enrys proceeded to ramble, "I care about her you know? I don't understand why she won't just accept that I'm the perfect fit for her and embrace me with open arms," he hiccupped, "look at how cute the two of you are!"

Both Argen and Farren froze, the heat from the fire no longer registered and they slowly, simultaneously, like clockwork, turned to him with wide eyes. Both their faces were crimson red, and Farren opened and closed her mouth like a fish. Enrys laughed a full-belly laugh as he watched them struggle to gather their thoughts.

It was Argen who broke the tense silence, "maybe if you just tell her that you love her then she will forgive you," his words were strained but he emphasised them with a tight smile.

Farren cleared her throat, "just don't talk about yourself when you apologise."

"But she thinks the issue is me," Enrys countered.

"*Is* the issue you?" she raised a brow with a smirk.

He took a final swig from his mug and slung his arm around her shoulders. They both stumbled but Argen's hand on her back and her own steady feet righted them. She smiled in thanks and he made sure to keep his hand there for a moment longer as Enrys leaned forward dramatically. He stared at the ground for a long moment, his lips formed a frown, his brows a straight line and his eyes hard. Then his head shot up as though he remembered something; his eyes locked with the side of her face and sighed. The smell of wine wafted over her and she crinkled her nose. Yet, Enrys remained sober, his eyes clear and stance steady with his arm a weight over her shoulders. It was familiar and yet there was something in his face that stopped her short.

However, he broke her from her thoughts, "Farren, you really have become grown haven't you?"

"We are the same age?"

"Yes but look at you, you can stand upright with me, *me* pressed against you! It'll help you for the Trial."

Farren glanced back at Argen whose lip quirked as he listened, "thank you, and in my defence, when we were children you were a lot more violent than I was."

Enrys nodded slowly as though she spouted the words of philosophical genius, "yes, but our dear Commander over here tells me you're prepared for the Trial and I have no doubt that it will be one to remember. In fact, I think I'm going to enjoy it." Farren raised a brow at Argen who shrugged. Enrys slumped further against her but the other man was around her side in seconds, looped his arms under Enrys, and removed him from her person. The full amount of air returned to her lungs and her back ached from the strain but she laughed none-the-less as Enrys hung off of Argen like a ragdoll. His laughter boomed as they walked away. Argen mouthed a quick 'see you' as they walked away. Enrys' voice boomed through the square, "see you tomorrow Farren," both he and Argen laughed.

With that, he walked off, his colleague's hulking form acted as a cloak. Her eyes roved the surrounding area to find that people still drank and laughed and chatted. The other guards stood around the pit, their eyes on everyone and everything lest a Night Creature burst through the square. Farren glanced at the trees that poked over the houses then returned to the fire before her. The heat hit her in the face full force so that the cold no longer threatened to claim her fingers and toes. She stepped toward it, her palms outstretched to fully enjoy its warmth. Ash landed in her hair like snowflakes and she closed her eyes. The light was bright even with them shut and she smiled.

"Where I'm from bonfires are a symbol of peace and hope." Farren spied the Magician over her shoulder as he walked toward her, the pole and orb retired for the night. Elira sat on her perch outside the tent which was tied shut with thick rope. "I thought bonfires were only used for burning the fallen?"

There was nothing but pure curiosity in his gaze so she replied, "they usually are, but because of the cold and spectacle of it all, Brentham has a bonfire every year when the market returns to celebrate the fact that we didn't die in the cold or from the Night Creatures," she paused for a moment, "and that we live to earn more money."

"It would be safer in the day if you fear them."

She leaned closer to where he stood, a smirk on her face, "then it wouldn't be as big of a spectacle, would it?" That smirk turned into a grin at his melodic, sweet laugh. Villagers turned to the beautiful sound so he covered his mouth and cleared his throat, though his smile remained. Farren narrowed her eyes at those nosy villagers.

"You know, there once was a King of Fire." Farren's eyes shot to his, her body automatically moved closer so he lowered his voice, "he was an arrogant man, he commanded powerful armies of which he stood on the front line and he was smitten with a woman he met only a handful of times. But he loved his people dearly, so much that he sacrificed his soul for them. They believe an ounce of his soul is in every flame, a signal that he will always be with them, protecting them until the end."

The fire sparked in acknowledgement to his words; a squeak left a woman's mouth who was extraordinarily close to the pit's edge, "do you believe it?"

The Magician chuckled, "no, it's only a story isn't it?" But his attention was only on the fire. The colour of his hair matched the flames perfectly, a mixture of the hues formed waves atop his head. The light brightened his eyes to a near glow and Farren took a moment to breathe. He was astonishingly beautiful. The bonfire roared above their companionable silence. There was no need to say anything else, they both stood side-by-side with their eyes on it and when Farren left for the comfort of her bed, the Magician remained, his eyes glazed as the logs turned to ash and there was nothing but embers against the ground.

The marketplace continued to thrive on day two and the villagers were in a much better mood after the bonfire. Farren past a few early risers on their walks as she made her way across the hills toward Theron's home. The door to his kitchen was held ajar by a maid's foot as she dumped dirty water into the street. The liquid barely avoided by Farren's boots so she took the door from the other woman's hold and they both walked inside, one more sheepish than the other. The smell of pork and rosemary filled the air and Farren dragged in a deep breath. The cooks and servants bid her a good afternoon whilst they prepared for the evening's dinner. Lyla stirred a large pot, hand on her hip as she watched Farren slump into her usual armchair. On queue Theron stormed down the stone stairs into the bustling kitchen. It was as if he sensed Farren's presence in his home. Nobody stopped their work which was the wrong thing to do because the second he spotted the wine glass on the shelf lined with oils he threw it against the wall. The glass flew over the heads of the staff where it smashed against the wall above the fireplace. Servants dashed away from the shards and one scurried to find a broom. Small pieces of glass skittered towards Farren and under the large workbench. She shot from her seat and Theron's eyes roved from the shivering servants to his niece. Burning rage made way for a cold mask. *Oops... did she just witness Theron exude an emotion? Without his permission?*

"What are you doing here?" He was a different person, older somehow than moments ago. It was the face of a nobleman that stared at her through thick lashes and not a hot-headed merchant's son. For that was what Theron was; he was no nobleman, he served them as much as Lyla served him.

"I thought I would arrive early before seeing Aunt Eydis," Farren paused and held her mouth open for a moment as her brows furrowed, "you are aware you just smashed a glass against the wall for no reason?" It came out like a question.

His feet were light against the floor, long legs aided him in manoeuvring around flour bags. She glared up at him, arms slightly in front of her body in case she needed to use them quickly. Theron leaned down so he was nose to nose with her. A sneer pulled at his features, his pointed nose bunched at the side. "You need to start minding your own business, Farren."

"You need to start acting like a decent human being, Theron."

The kitchen had never been so quiet. The glass shards remained on the floor as the kitchen maid stood with her mouth agape and broom in her outstretched hand. Lyla situated herself behind Farren with the stealth of a house cat. Theron straightened and the lapels of his jacket were fixed into their pristine position. There would never be a stitch out of place; appearance was everything in business. He removed his eyes from Farren's glare to snap his fingers at the maid. She shot to work on her hands and knees. Tears in her skirts and glass on her knees were no worry for Theron. He clicked his tongue at the mess on the floor but averted his eyes to the book that sat on her chair just like the morning before, so he walked around Farren, picked it up and flipped through the pages.

"This is how you occupy your time?"

"How I choose to occupy my time is none of your concern."

Despite the urge to tear his throat out with the meat cleaver perched on the end of the bench she allowed Theron to stare her down. He flung the book over his shoulder and rolled his eyes, "I don't care what you do so long as you do not do it in my house."

Lyla's hand pressed against Farren's arm which tensed beneath the sleeve of her sweater, "yes, you and your massive house with your numerous servants... how do you pay them Theron?"

A loud crash flew from upstairs. It was déjà vu. The servants shared glances and the missing link to the kitchen team —a young girl of fourteen- rushed down the stairs. Her eyes were wide and silver lined and her face was flushed. It was not because of the cold. "Sir, it's Eydis she-" The girl did not have time to finish her sentence before both Theron and Farren sprinted past her and up the stairs to the foyer. A vase was scattered across the wooden floor and there, convulsing amongst the fallen debris, eyes wide and lips parted was her aunt.

"They are so beautiful... The stars, the pretty stars... Look how they shine for you..."

Theron couldn't move with limbs of stone as he watched his wife stare hazy-eyed at the ceiling of their front foyer. Her leg twitched beneath her thick robe and her arms reached for the lanterns in the wall. Her skin was deathly pale, cheeks hollow and nails longer than was proper. The satchel of medication lay in the hall where it was dropped in the servant's haste to get to Eydis. Farren pushed past him and fell to her knees beside Eydis. The sound of her bones against the floor made him cringe but her hands were gentle as she pushed the hair from Eydis' face. "Aunt Eydis can you hear me?"

"Farren?" Theron's breath hitched at the sound of his wife's voice. "Farren! Oh Farren can you see the stars, can you see how pretty they are?"

Farren glanced back at Theron. Smoke from the bonfires and chimneys covered the skies and the trees covered the rest. The last time her aunt saw the stars was at the summer solstice but even then she was not fully present. Her eyes flung back to Eydis as she gripped Farren's collar so tightly it was a miracle her bones did not snap."They are waiting for you Farren, the stars, they wait for you."

"Alright Aunt Eydis, I will go and see the stars." Finally, Theron moved. He crouched on the other side of his wife and pulled her hand into his. His moves were slow, deliberate and his eyes were soft. Farren averted her eyes form her uncle. It was as though she was intruding on a private moment as Eydis stopped yelling about the stars but the glaze in her eyes remained. Her exclamations of Farren's name turned to mutters about finding the stars, being with the stars, loving the stars. Her hand released Farren as she curled into her husband's chest. Her body was lifted from the ground and into his arms, so Farren trailed behind, clammy hands and a sheen of sweat covered her body. Theron laid Eydis gently on the soft sheets of her bed. He demanded a separate room be made for her when the likelihood of her episodes increased. Farren hated him for it, called him a coward. She was twelve and all she saw was her aunt shipped to another room whilst her husband remained in the grand master bedroom. Wrong, she had been so terribly wrong about it. Theron was a lot of horrible, slimy things but he loved his wife. Farren had to believe that. "Do you want me to stay?"

He shook his head and without another word she excused herself from the room. The door clicked softly and she sucked in a breath. It had been a while since Eydis had such a frantic episode. *They are waiting for you Farren.* There was nothing more ominous than a delirious woman who sounded so confident. The stars were waiting for her? Would the bunny rabbits start talking? Would the sun shine on her command? Farren ran her hands through her hair and kept them there. A thread had come loose from the hallway rug and as she breathed she focused her mind on that thread. It was out of place in her uncle's perfect home but there it sat, defying the laws of the household after years of people walking up and down the long hall. Farren let loose another long breath and pushed her foot over the thread. As her eyes rose from the rug to the window across from her she gasped. Sat peacefully on the window ledge was Elira. She was busy preening her feathers just as Argen's raven did. Farren smiled at the bird and something lifted from her chest. With a lighter step she made her way back downstairs. The house was silent save for the pots and pans she heard clang from the kitchen below. One foot hit the top step of the kitchen and she was greeted by Lyla's raised eyebrow.

"How is she?"

Farren shrugged, "not good but Theron's with her."

A curt nod and a hand on Farren's arm was Lyla's response. She went to open her mouth but something behind Farren caught her eye. Amusement danced in the cook's eyes and she looked back at her friend. "Is your final training session today?"

"Yes, why?"

"At what time?"

"Ten o'clock."

Lyla swallowed back a laugh as she pointed at the grandfather clock behind Farren. She turned and widened her eyes. Three minutes! She bid Lyla goodbye and rushed out the front door, her friend's laughter followed her into the street. Her feet pounded against the icy paths and up her own pathway until she slammed through the front door. She blew a quick kiss at her father whose tea stopped halfway to his mouth when she sped up the stairs. The skirts she wore were ripped from her body and replaced with her training gear. With her sword strapped to her belt and her hair tied behind her she rushed back into the hall, down the stairs and past her still wide-eyed father. She promised to explain everything at another time, in a hurried yell.

It was her last session with Argen before the Trial later that night; it meant there was no issue in who saw them or what questions they asked. There was nothing that would lower her mood. She and Argen went through every manoeuvre they knew; they used swords, knives and hand-to-hand to ensure she was prepared. Her muscles ached in a way that made her feel fearless. She was ready and Argen knew it.

The glow of the setting sun shone behind the Church to cast an eerie glow on the surrounding woodlands. A group of birds flew overhead, more shadows against the purple-sky. The Night Creature's blood was covered with fresh snow so there was no stark reminder of the hideous wound or her shoddy medical skills. The stones were covered with more sludge than ice but fallen needles from the trees beyond made a path to the doors. The wind ripped through the branches and was filled with the bite of winter. No torches were lit inside or out so she stopped in front of the open door and narrowed her eyes. There was no sign of life, no warmth from the inside of the stone building. Argen's raven was nowhere to be seen and there were no tracks in the sludge beneath her. That being said she called out, "Argen?" silence answered so she tried again, "Argen? Hello?"

The wind flew through her hair but there was no human response to her calls. They had a break of two hours between her training and the Trial which had to be initiated by her commanding officer. Someone had to hear her cry across the empty plain. She stepped away from the Church and stared into the trees. The dying light cast shadows along the ground. Pine needles met the bottom of her boot as she walked to the tree line. She didn't breach the line but the sound of a snapped twig caught her ear. Just as that twig snapped blinding pain echoed across her skull. She fell to her knees, a hand braced against the back of her head. Enrys stood poised above her with the hilt of his sword pointed at her. Shadows made his face seem sharper than it was, and far more sinister. White hair sat flat to his head and curled beneath his ears. Farren never thought of him as handsome but as he stood there, frown on his face, she thought he was the ugliest man she'd seen.

Before she could question him a boot came down hard against her side. She coughed against the assault. She hadn't heard anyone approach. The twig snap had been a diversion to get her into the shadows. Curses covered her tongue because her poor judgment hung over her. As she curled in on her side four guards -all of whom lacked their usual armour - walked from the shadows. They each wore training gear similar to Argen's, it was gear that allowed them to blend into the night and become unidentifiable to villagers and guards alike. They were outfits that often helped her and Argen remain anonymous lest anyone break curfew for a night-time stroll. It was not an outfit she ever imagined the rest of the guard would wear. Their Commander was not among them but it seemed their leaders were Enrys and an older man –Ritrio- if their puffed chests and sneers were any indication. Ritrio was never one to sugar-coat things, and he advised the men the best he could; he was the man who trained Argen, his respect well earned. That was a fact that made Farren's cheeks blaze in fury. They were taller than her and pure muscle but Enrys was slow, he always had been which is why he made up for it in brute strength.

They each stepped forward, boots poised to attack and attack they did. The force of their kicks kept her on the ground whilst the jabs of their fists added to the ringing in her ears or was it her screams that made them throb? There was a moment, brief but useful, where she staggered to her feet. One of her ribs was broken and her arm ached like Hell. Blood filled her mouth which she spat at Enrys' feet. It forced his boots backward to avoid the projectile. The red mixed with the white and grey of the winter ground and she glared. Her look was so fierce that it hurt her injured cheeks to perform it. The sword that hung at her side was drawn in that brief moment and she staggered again, ready to take them all down.

"Look at this Lads, Argen's plaything thinks she can beat all of us," the men laughed as Ritrio spoke, "you can barely stand."

"What do you want?"

Laughter rang out between the trees and through the Church clearing but it was Enrys who replied, "what we want," he swiped his tongue along the inside of his cheek, "is for you to keel over."

Spit flew from her mouth again and she spread her feet as Argen taught her. Where was he? Was he too much of a coward to follow through with the ambush? Perhaps he was blissfully unaware of his friends' intentions. Thoughts for another time swirled and settled like muddied water. Her vision swam from the blow to the head but she lunged and felled one of the guards. They were too busy laughing to notice when another guard is slashed across the chest. Arrogance or stupidity or possibly both, but either way she would not be taunted by overgrown children... overgrown children she once admired... Blood gushed and mingled with her own at her feet. The laughter stopped immediately and their faces changed. One strike, two, three, four strikes to her blade and she dropped it to the snow. The moment she lost her grip was the moment she felt their hands on her. They pulled and tugged at her clothing and pushed her back to the ground. She struggled beneath them, kicking, screaming, slamming her knees in every direction just to hit something, anything. She screamed as another kick landed against her side. Another rib broken.

"You didn't honestly think we would let you take the real Trial did you? This is it Farren, take it or leave it," there was a pause as Ritrio held her foot to the ground with his own, "you're nothing but a spoiled brat who decided to defy her Uncle by joining up with the big boys. It would have been easier just to *fuck* one of us."

It was Enrys who received the sharp jab of her knee to his stomach so he doubled over with a gasp. "No wonder Roseanna kicked you out, you're a waste of space Enrys," she wheezed.

One of the other guards whose name she never learned slammed his hand against her own stomach in return. Bile covered the inside of her mouth as she curved upward. Enrys' groan turned to a growl as he stood. He towered over her with his feet on both her sides and gripped the front of her shirt. He swung a leg over her and proceeded to drag her through the snow. Frantic kicks disturbed the soil beneath as she tried to find an even footing. When her heel caught on a rock she yelped and her hands clawed at the hand on her chest. He dropped her torso to ground-level and a splash responded. He dumped her in the stream behind the Church. The water ran quick enough that the ice had not taken hold. It was big enough for most of her body to be pressed against it and deep enough that the water would cover her head if she weren't perched on her elbows. She spluttered against the splash and tried to take even breaths despite the scream of her ribs.

Enrys kicked her elbows from under her and just as quickly he pressed on her shoulders. She bucked as her face submerged beneath the rushing water. The cold bit against her skin, her lips turned blue and her joints locked. She pushed against his shoulders, nails digging into the fabric of his jacket. Several nails broke against the heavy fabric but she persisted. His voice was muffled by the water as he called for his men, "will one of you hold her the fuck down?!" The other guards removed her hands and pushed them against the ground. Her legs were pinned by Ritrio once again so all she could do was buck her hips to try to throw Enrys off balance. He laughed as she struggled beneath him. His knees were pressed to her sides and he increased the pressure on her shoulders. The ringing in her ears was overpowered the sound of rushing water and her vision blackened at the edges. Water rushed up her nose and across her tightly shut eyes, the cold water hurt nearly as much as her damaged ankle.

"Farren!"

Her lungs burned.

"Farren!"

Who was that?

"By Griselda! Get off of her!" Argen flung Enrys from her body and the guards followed. The first thing she noted was the lack of pressure which is when she rolled onto the bank of the stream and hacked up what was left of her lungs. The two broken ribs she received threatened to puncture her lung if she didn't calm her breathing. "What is the meaning of this?"

"Relax Argen, it was just some Trial training."

Farren fisted the mud and grass beneath her as she forced her breathing to return to normal.

"That's Commander, Enrys and this," he pointed to Farren's shivering body, "is not training. It's attempted murder."

Enrys stepped toward Argen who moved between him and Farren's hunched body. Enrys' head tilted to the side and a glare shone in his eyes, "it is proof she doesn't have what it takes. Take your charity case elsewhere *Commander*, we don't need her."

"You'll be court marshalled for this."

Ritrio snorted behind his younger counterpart, "nobody cares about a village girl, Commander, even you wanted to make sure you weren't pissing off anyone in the barracks by training her. You wanted our approval before you did anything." His smile was unpleasant. "You were too busy fawning that you weren't paying attention to your men and now two of them are dead."

Something similar to "good," choked out of Farren's mouth.

Argen ignored her comment and instead addressed the men before him, "this is not what we discussed Enrys, you were supposed to fight her in the Trial, instead you try and kill her."

Enrys scoffed, "that's what the Trial is supposed to be. If she can't beat us, she can't beat most of the men out there. We've done her a favour."

"Not even you would have survived seven men against you Enrys. You're all dismissed," Argen's voice was firm, loud, the voice of a Commander.

Enrys rolled his eyes, kicked a rock and said, "whatever, this stopped being fun minutes ago."

There was little satisfaction in watching the guards limp away. Some clutched their sides and Argen's gaze drifted to the men face-up in the snow. Blood still seeped from their wounds and they watched him with open, white eyes. The nausea that built in his stomach threatened to lurch up his throat but he gently closed their eyes as he knelt before them, his own closed in a thought to Griselda. He did this as Farren struggled to find her feet. The sound of her grunts made him turn and he splashed across the stream to place a hand on her back. She weakly shoved him away from her and he tried again. That time she shoved him harder. Finally her feet found a footing beneath her. Her ankle sprang to life and she grit her teeth against the pain. Water dripped from her hair and clothes, the blue which tinged her lips mixed with the pink of her neck and nose. Some of her blood mixed with the water running from her face. She looked as pathetic as she felt. With her hands out to balance her she stumbled across the stream toward her fallen sword. She sneered at the guards who bled on the ground and retrieved her weapon. Argen's steps sounded behind her and she turned, the tip of her sword stopped a hairsbreadth away from his chest.

"Farren you need to get to a healer. You-"

"Did you know?" she rasped.

Argen blinked and something akin to hurt flashed in his eyes but she was too cold and wet and in pain to care. He shook his head and held his palms upward. "Farren you have to believe me, I had no idea they would try something like this. I spoke to them yesterday and they were more than happy to let you take the Trial. Enrys offered to..." he trailed off. Realisation and horror flashed in his eyes. Whatever image formed in his head was enough to make his hands shake. His eyes travelled over her sopping clothes and hard face then down the length of her sword which remained pointed at his chest. The lump in his throat tightened almost painfully and he stepped back. "I didn't know," his voice was quiet. The answer he gave only brought more questions to mind. All of which had to wait until she could properly speak. With a blink she demanded he leave. Instead of doing as she asked he reached behind him to his bag which hung low on his back. A medical pack was offered to her. "Your wounds look bad, Farren, please let me help you."

When all he did was hold out the pack, her blade caressed the side of his neck. The step she took sent a shot of pain up her leg. Blood covered her slashed boot but she forced her weight onto it anyway. "Leave."

His throat brushed against her blade as he swallowed, "you need to have a Healer look at those wounds and you need to get dry before you freeze to death out here. At least use the bandages to cover the wound on your leg." Farren's chin rose and she repeated her order. Something in her eyes made him retreat from her blade and from the stream. His head shook but she did not move. Slowly, he placed the pack at his feet and stepped back. "I'll be waiting outside your father's house in the morning." Thus, he scurried away.

Once he was out of sight she dropped her sword and fell to her knees. A combination of blood and water was coughed up, some bile added to the puddle on the floor. The pain in her chest threatened to swallow her whole as she breathed through her wrenching. When her stomach finally gave up she clumsily grabbed the medical pack, found a roll of bandages that replaced those she used on the Night Creature, and nestled herself against the tree to assess her wounds: two broken ribs, her face covered in cuts and bruises with one eye swollen shut, an ankle that was likely sprained with a cut alongside it and abdominal bruising. Luckily, her jacket was thick enough that her arms remained stiff but uninjured. There would be bruises on her wrists in the morning from having the weight of two men on them but that was the least of her concern. The bandages were sloppily slapped against the wound after she rolled up her trouser leg, which in turn staunched the bleeding. The trouser was rolled back down over the bandage, nothing fully secure but it pressed against the wound. The longer she sat against the tree the more violently her body shook. Home was not an option, her uncle was busy with Eydis and anyone with a guard uniform was the last person she wanted to see. Argen was long gone, no-doubt to inform the families of the fallen guards that they were dead so there was no way she could or would call for him to help her, no matter how much she needed the help at that moment.

Before her eyes slipped shut a deep red glow eddied around her. She lifted her hand –where there was no longer a full glove- to find her skin encompassed in the light. The pink and purple of her chilled skin was warmed by the soft light. The shivering ceased and the chill that wracked her bones eased away to a comfortable heat. *Magic*. The sound of clicking bones sounded in the back of her head as she leaned further into the bark. A need to rest her eyes and sleep accompanied the glow on her skin. No- not on, the glow emanated from under her skin. Lyla would have kittens if she saw the reckless magic absorbed within her but she lifted her hand to the source of said magic a smiled. The pendant around her neck pulsed in response to her touch, warmed her chest and abdomen, so she closed her eyes and settled against the tree and as she did the Magician's words echoed in her mind:

It will keep you warm.

Farren faded in and out of consciousness, her eyes barely open enough to register the sky move above her. Strong arms pulled her body closer to their chest and the comfort pulled her back into the darkness. The first thing her fully conscious mind noticed was the smell of herbs: sage, mint and a mixture of other plants. Her eyes crinkled as she pressed her eyes closed against the light that shone over her. A pillow sank under her face when she turned away from it. It pressed against a cut on her cheek so she hissed and cracked open her good eye. The wall in front of her was a buttercup yellow with small mirror hung above her. She blinked at the oval frame and shifted her arms. She was tucked loosely beneath a bare comforter; her jacket and boots were folded at the side of the bed. Slowly, ever so slowly she lifted her arms in front of her face. A matching bruise sat on either wrist but there was no damage up the length of them. Less positive results were found after she lifted the sheets from her body. A thin shirt the colour of emeralds adorned her body and was bunched up just below her breasts which let her eyes roam the splotches of angry purple and black, some of them turned yellow at the edges. The pendant the Magician gifted her sat amongst the injuries; it sat docile as any other necklace as though the glow and warmth from the night prior was nothing more than her mind playing tricks on her.

"You're awake."

Farren's heart pounded against her chest as she turned her head. The Magician stood in the doorway, his hands folded before him. She noted the small room they were in: a travelling caravan decorated with trinkets and flowers. Between his fingers sat a roll of bandages that was to no-doubt set her ribs back into place. The salve that coated her wounds would act as a sealant and was the reason for the excessive smell. He took a short step forward as she sat up. The snarl of pain did nothing to shift the frown from his face.

"Where am I?" she groaned.

"It's where I sleep when I'm not working in the tent." She leaned forward and swore. "Careful, your wounds are too fresh for you to be moving around so carelessly." At her hiss he added, "please, I don't want to see you hurt yourself further let me-" A knock on the door brought his attention away from Farren. He looked through a small window and nodded to whoever was outside. Farren finally stilled, but she nearly lurched to her feet when hazel eyes found their way to hers. The already aching muscles in her legs tensed and she found herself with her palm pressed to her side. The groan that pulled at her lip was pushed back as Argen walked past the Magician who narrowed his eyes and moved further between them. "I found you soaked and asleep against a tree so I brought you here. I sent Elira to find him while you rested."

The Magician carried her across the village and into his wagon with their only accomplice being Argen. Farren had never been more grateful for the Night Creatures creating a curfew than right then. Her injuries must have been worse than she thought if she hadn't stirred until morning. With both hands pressed to her being she flicked her eyes to Argen. He shuffled on his feet, "I wanted to ta-take you to your uncle's the moment I saw you in this ma-man's bed, but," he turned from Farren's frown to the Magician, "he was willing to help you heal." At her widened eyes he flapped. "All natural, no magic. It's probably why you are still in such bad shape."

The Magician moved toward her, "your injuries are bad, my tonics can-"

"No," Argen cut him off, "no magic."

The muscles in the other man's shoulders bunched and the glare he sent him was so opposite to the kind, calm way he spoke to her. Instantly, that look was gone and the red-head knelt before her, his hand slowly removed hers from her side. At the sight of the awful bruises Argen turned away.

66

Farren kept her curses at bay as the Magician's soft fingers danced across her injuries. They soon found their way to her face where she winced. The cuts and bruises throbbed at the contact. Her eyes were screwed shut as he gently tilted her chin to the side to get a better look at her.

Argen's voice surrounded them, "I wrote to Captain Adrastos and explained what happened. I-"

"You did what?" she did not mean for it to sound so sharp but she could not find it in her to care.

The Magician turned her chin in the opposite direction and her eyes opened to glare at the man who spoke behind him. "Don't worry, I told him you fought valiantly, I also told him the extent of your injuries and that there were seven of them..." he trailed off at the storm that roiled behind her eyes.

Before she opened her mouth to scold him the kettle to her left rattled then let out a screech. The Magician's hands left her and he stood at his full height. He turned the stove off with a flick of his wrist and grabbed a small bowl from the cabinet above him. Scoops of leaves and herbs were placed into the bowl and topped with the hot water. Farren noted his distraction and pushed herself from the bed. In a second he was there, the bowl on the countertop and his hands against her shoulders. "Please Farren, you mustn't move too much."

She didn't respond, her own hands dug deep into his bare arms as she glared at Argen. "What do you think is going to happen now, Argen? Do you think they will read about how I got my ass kicked and think 'huh, maybe we should let her take the Trial anyway'?"

Argen blinked, "you-you still want to take the Trial?"

Exasperation flew across her face, "of course I do! Just because Enrys is a prick and you're," she shook her head, "I *will* take that Trial."

A fervent nod and he said, "I can make a recommendation, I can ask if you can take it in the Capital, I can ask Farren, don't worry."

All of the fight drained from her at once, her body slack in the Magician's arms and he lowered her slowly to the mattress. "I think you should leave now Argen, inform her parents that she will be under my care for a couple of days at least." He glanced at her and she did not hesitate when she nodded. Argen went to protest but at the dark circles formed under Farren's eyes and the way she clung to the Magician, it made him pause. In the stark light of day she looked worse than before, the light brought forward the truth of what his men did.

Farren's voice stopped him at the threshold, "please, don't tell them what happened."

"What do you want me to say?"

There was only one version that they would believe, so she replied with a flinch, "tell them it was a Night Creature attack." The Magician's hands paused their work and he stared holes into her face. They both hated the idea of blaming a creature that did nothing wrong but the alternative would have her locked away in her room for the rest of her days. That was a fate Eydis was confined to but at least she had her illusions and fantasies, Farren would simply sit there and resent her parents with every fibre of her being. It was the lesser of two evils but she still felt the nausea hit her like a wagon. "Tell them I provoked it," she continued, "tell them I was simply in the wrong place at the wrong time, I came upon it feeding and it attacked me out of self-defence."

It didn't matter, not really, because all her parents would hear is that a Night Creature attacked their daughter, but it was something she could offer that didn't add to the horrid feeling that settled in her gut. It sat alongside the need for Enrys' head and the faces of the guards she killed. The close of the caravan door behind Argen broke her from her thoughts.

"I am going to place a salve on your bruises and wrap your ribs if that's okay?"

She nodded, her hands moved to push the shirt fabric beneath her breasts once again. No chest wraps sat beneath her fingers and she flushed. The thought of a man as beautiful as the Magician seeing her in such a compromising state was too much for that time of day. She noted the fresh pair of trousers that adorned her legs. One of the trouser legs were tied higher than the other, the cut on her leg wrapped cleanly whilst she slept.

"Thank you," she mumbled before she clamped the shirt fabric between her teeth.

"You never need to thank me, but," he dipped his hand into a pot of salve sat next to the tea, "I hope you don't mind me asking." He gently smoothed his fingers over the bruises that littered her body "What really happened?"

The ache in her body seemed to throb at his question and she removed the shirt from her mouth for a second, "training gone wrong."

"Training? You mentioned something about a Trial, did you mean the King's Trial?" She nodded despite the stiffness that settled into her neck. "That's the trial that lets someone be a King's Guard," he said it more to himself than to her then shot his eyes to hers, "you want to be a Guard?"

Another nod from her and his mouth fell slightly open. She snorted at his reaction then winced as the sound pulled at her ribs. That disrupted his stare and he unrolled the bandages. With quick hands he pushed and pulled against her body and was gentle as he could be but they needed to be tight against her body. Apologies were said throughout, and she wasn't sure if it was the anguish in her body or the kindness he showed her but she cried. The water in her eyes that built up from the strain finally fell across her cheeks. The salty tears stung against the cuts but she used the edge of the shirt to dab at her face.

Wordlessly he handed her the bowl of hot water and motioned for her to drink. There was a pause before she did so, the narrow of her eyes suspicion enough. "I would not use magic on you without your consent," he answered her unspoken accusation.

A light sigh and she sipped the bitter liquid. The concoction was so similar to her father's medicines that she continued to drink. It was hot on her tongue but the action and taste forced her to focus on something other than the pain.

Following their previous conversation he asked, "will you have to take the Trial again?"

"Probably. I'm not sure what happened is considered an attempt at the Trial." She took another sip. "Those men never wanted me to take it in the first place and they certainly made themselves clear about that."

"How many?"

She didn't miss a beat, "seven."

The Magician nearly stormed out of the caravan there and then but her wide, watery eyes stopped him, "they should never have laid their hands on you like that, Trial or no Trial."*And feet*, she wanted to add but instead she rolled the shirt back over her bindings and pushed her hair away from her face. Her left side was practically useless as she tried to lift her arm higher than her hip. The Magician bustled around the small space, his eyes flittered between her and his constantly moving hands. Everything he did was graceful and purposeful, so out of place in Brentham where there was nothing but the chill and hard-worn people. "It is good that the Captain knows," he mentioned, "it means the King will know soon enough and then it cannot be ignored."

The Captain of the King's Guard: the second most respected man in the country after the King himself. He had been in many battles, stood face to face with nobles and commoners alike. Not a lot is known of his personal life but what is known is that he was a man you wanted on your side and not against it.

"And what do you suppose the King will do with the information? He won't let me join the Guard if he knows how badly I failed."

"You didn't fail."

She fixed him with a disbelieving look, "I nearly drowned."

Light flared to her left and she winced away from the brightness. As quick as it appeared it was gone but she blinked away the black spots that appeared in her vision. Her brows furrowed as she looked at the calm man's still figure. Red strands fell into his face as he leaned on the counter, his eyes slipped shut and his breaths were long and even to compose himself. Once he straightened he brushed the hair from his face and looked at her so kindly, so softly. He nodded at her to take another sip of her drink, "but you didn't drown."

"The only thing the King will likely offer is hush money. He won't want people thinking that his Guards will attack villagers on a whim."

"The King is a human of loyalty, he will not let such a crime go unpunished," it was reassurance that bordered on a promise but the way his eyes moved slowly away from her showed he didn't one hundred percent believe it either. She opened her mouth to ask what he meant by 'human' when a drowsiness overcame her. The room spun around her and she reached her arm out even though she was sat static in place. That once solid body swayed with the room and he was upon her instantly, where he guided her to lie down and she gripped onto his shirt with trembling hands.

"It is a pain reducing tea, medicinal according to the instructions. It is to help the user to sleep which heals a body quicker than if it were awake." Panic flashed in her eyes. "It will only be for a few hours, you will be safe here Farren, I will not leave your side."

Despite the thunder of her heart against her chest she felt the medicine kick in sharply, her eyelids too heavy for her to hold open. The grip on his shirt loosened but he only moved away from her when her breathing evened out. Not once did he leave her side. Any food or medicine he needed and did not possess –which was rare- Argen's three hourly visits allowed for their retrieval. Farren spent the next day and a half in and out of sleep. When she was conscious the Magician helped her hydrate and eat small bites of vegetable soup. The medicinal tea was a staple in her diet and when she succumbed to sleep it was a reprieve; it was just an endless ocean of darkness. It was on the morning of the second day that her parents showed up on the caravan doorstep. A stream of questions flew from their mouths, all of which her new healer answered. The ones that he himself did not know about Argen answered; between the two of them they spun a believable lie and one that would ease their worry for their daughter. Lyla visited, brought food, checked on her wounds and left with a warning look to the red-head.

Near the end of the fourth day Farren awoke refreshed. The bruises on her went from black to purple and also yellow, the cuts scabbed over and her ankle allowed her more fluid movement. She blinked against the dying light only to find the feathery face of Elira above her. She pressed a hand to her chest and smiled at the bird. Elira clicked her beak and the woman sat up slowly, her hand pressed to her ribs which remained painful. She took a long breath only to find that breathing deeply remained a chore but her hand reached well above her hip without assistance.

"Good evening," the Magician's voice floated over to her. She watched as he lit the lanterns around the room and stretched into the decorative candle holders to light them with long matches. The colours of his clothes glimmered in the light, a sharp pink and white to contrast with the dark blue outside.

"What time is it?" her throat scratched.

The water glass beside the bed she occupied was nearly finished but she sipped the remaining liquid before he spoke, "it is nearly five. Dinner is almost ready, I hope you can stomach some solid food."

It would be the first solid food she ate in days; she didn't know if she could look at a mushroom the same way again after those spoonfuls of soup. She smiled at his back then glanced around the room: the kettle was already on the stove to boil and the smell of rabbit filled the space. Her sock clad feet pressed against the wooden floors as she dared to stand up. At the sight of her body pushed from the bed he walked toward her, hands outstretched to catch her. However, she held her own hands up in a signal to wait. She wanted to try it on her own; she wanted some semblance of independence even if all she could do was hobble to the toilet unaided. Only one groan slipped past her lips as she grit her teeth and walked across the floor. She was aware that many people had received worse injuries, longer lasting injuries than her broken ribs and cut leg were to be, but that did not stop the curses of pain that emitted from her when she originally tried to walk after her first night in the Magician's caravan.

Once she finished her business he called out to her, "Farren, Argen's here."

At the thought of her friend she felt her chest tighten. The one man she trusted above all others whose name tasted sour on her tongue and made her fists clench. There was a knock on the door and Argen's head poked back through, "um, Farren you're going to want to come out here."

"Is he here?" the Magician asked.

Argen nodded but Farren just stared in confusion between the two men. She found herself sat back on the bed whilst the Magician helped her with her jacket which was slipped over one arm and draped over the shoulder of the other. A wince and her boots were next, the soft leather slipped over the thick bandage on her ankle. As she lifted her eyes from the laces of her boots, he helped her to her feet and she forced herself to walk just as she did moments before. Beneath the door, two steps lead her to the outside world. The smell of snow and the remnants of the market hit them once the door was opened wide. With a hand on the Magician's arm she pressed the other to the doorframe and swayed against the wood as she stared at the men in front of her.

Argen stood back so that she could perceive the full picture: a man dressed in the Guard's armour -far cleaner than Argen's ever was- smiled at her, his hands clasped behind his back. The dirty blond hair on his head was tied behind him and fell just shy of the middle of his back; his skin was tanned from hours outside and the short moustache on his face was full, well-combed. He cleared his throat before he spoke, "I'm sorry to disturb you Miss Attarah, my name is Adrastos Mallark." Farren's eyes widened and instantly her spine straightened and she gripped the doorframe tighter lest she fall face first into the snow. "It is important that I speak with you." Without hesitation she nodded and he proceeded to explain, "allow me to apologise, I received a letter from your Commander and what he described made me sick. Those men –those boys- will be dealt with, rest assured but that is only partially why I am here. I need a favour, Miss Attarah."

74

"What can I do for you?" Because when the Captain of the King's Guard stood before you with a request, you did not ignore it.

"I would like for you to accompany me to the White Castle. Commander Bray tells me that you still want to complete the Trial." Her eyes flicked to Argen whose own gaze never left her. "You can do so with my blessing, but the King wishes to speak to you about it himself."

"But why?" the question flew from her mouth before she could stop it.

"I will not lie to you, this does not come without stipulations which is what the King wishes to discuss personally, but it is a true offer. Commander Bray speaks highly of you and your skills and I have read in great detail of your training, an impressive resume indeed."

The heat rose to Farren's face at the compliment. All of those nights she snuck from her room and into the night, risking her life and Argen's if only to become one of them flooded her mind. She thought of her bruises and muscle-aches after every session, of the money the position would offer, the connections. A smile covered her lips but then she thought of her current injuries, her worried parents, and finally Eydis. As though he read her mind, Argen said, "Eydis will be fine without you Farren, she has help and she has Lyla and your Mother."

A reassuring hand landed on the small of her back and she turned her attention to the man at her side when he spoke, "is this what you want?"

Gradually, she nodded, "it is."

Adrastos chuckled, "you asked her that as if you yourself are not going to be at the castle, Soter."

The tips of the Magician's —Soter's- ears turned pink and he scratched his nose just for something to do. A magic-peddler at the White Castle, had she been asleep for so long that the laws on magic changed? The frown on Argen's face answered her.

"I will be there in an advisory capacity, nothing as exhausting as you, Captain," Soter smirked.

"True, but which one of us gets paid more?" Adrastos' attention was once again on her, "my troops and I will be here for two more days, take that time to think over the King's offer." Adrastos smiled as he left, waved at her and was followed by Argen through the square. She let out a breath and slumped against the door frame. Soter's hand remained on her back but his body turned so that he faced her fully. She lifted her eyes from where the guards disappeared, to his face. Amongst the racing thoughts of her future one stood out: she never asked the Magician his name, even after all the kind and selfless things he did for her.

"Soter huh?" she smiled.

He nodded with a smile of his own, "I might get to see some of this training of yours at the castle."

She limped back inside, "if you're lucky."

They both settled back into the caravan with a bout of chuckles. Dinner was lovely and they spoke of the Capital and what she imagined it was like, what she thought the King would say. Amongst the calm that filled the room she ate her meal and sipped her water and watched as the man before her enjoyed her company. With a light heart and a full stomach, she knew exactly what she would tell the Captain.

The hardest thing about leaving Brentham was when Farren said goodbye to Eydis. It was not the way her father told her to stay for the business, it was not the way her mother worriedly asked her if she was okay being travelling all that way with Argen -a question she had yet to know the answer to- and it was certainly not the condescending raised brow her uncle sent her when she turned up on his doorstep for a final visit to her aunt.

"The court will accept you my girl, you do not have to worry," it was the most coherent sentence her Aunt spoke to her in a while and the thought lined Farren's eyes with silver.

The young woman's hands tensed in Eydis' and she nearly ran to Adrastos to tell him 'no' but Eydis was clear, she was happy for her to go. That was why Farren smiled and nodded. "Only if you promise me that you will be fine without me."

Eydis blinked and leaned forward. The slight chap of her lips pressed against her cheek and she felt her throat tighten. Eydis pulled back only for her eyes to glaze over and Theron pulled her from the floor all while he stared at Farren with his usual frown.

Seven days passed since the guards of her small village attacked her and since then her ankle healed, she translated what she could of her father's notes and she accepted Captain Adrastos' offer. The White Castle was a three day ride from her village, two and a half if they never stopped. Lyla saw them –her and the guards- out of the village, something hard in her eyes but she brushed off Farren's concerns and double-checked the raven-haired woman's provisions. The strong build of her shoulders and the firm grip on Farren's arm ushered her into the carriage. That would be the strength the Brentham guards would witness; Lyla swore she would visit the barracks that night and Farren shivered. She nearly felt sorry for them. Adrastos said they would be punished for their crime but she felt there would not be much left of them when Lyla was finished.

"What are you thinking about?" They had been on the road for over a day and Farren had yet to acknowledge Argen's existence. Her injuries seemed to ache more in his presence, or maybe it was because every time she looked at him she saw Enrys and the grit of his teeth. Argen was her carriage companion whilst three more carriages formed a line on the road, like ants in an orderly queue. There was a small moment when she first met the rest of Captain Adrastos' troop but there was no introduction and they were quick to leave the small village.

The daytime skirts she often wore were replaced by loaned clothes: the shirt of emerald green she spent most of her days in –washed for her before her departure- and a pair of brown trousers Soter found at the bottom of one of his drawers, the dullest of his clothes and also the smallest. The boots were her own dark ones and they laced up to her knee, the matching jacket acted as her pillow at night. Her old training gear was left with Soter where they remained soaked in sweat and droplets of blood.

Most of the travel was spent in silence; she occupied herself with the books she packed from home: combat medicine, fairy tales, Altin history books, and there was one particular book she hid in between the binding of an old journal of her father's. It was a book Soter offered to her for the journey alongside the clothes. It was that book which held her attention, a chapter which described the migrating patterns of Night Creatures. It turned out they were not allergic to the light as the village believed but rather their eyes were better suited to the dark, of course there were exceptions which included the type of Night Creature Farren encountered. They were 'scaled-Night Creatures' and were similar to the lizards on the Continent. They loved anything shiny, they had bodies that were severely affected by the weather and they ate deer. Farren furrowed her brow; there was no mention of the consumption of humans.

Her thoughts were broken by a tap on her boot. As she raised her eyes from her book she quirked an eyebrow. Argen scratched the back of his neck and removed his foot from her vicinity. "Are you going to ignore me the entire trip?" With a hum she returned her eyes to the book. Perhaps if she wished for an apocalypse it would've kept him busy enough that his attention might leave her. "Farren, I already told you..." he trailed off and glanced out of the carriage window.

Adrastos' voice flew toward them. *Keep an eye out for bandits.* Farren made to open her mouth but Argen placed a finger against his lips and shushed her. She huffed but did as he said. The world outside was filled with thick evergreen trees and bumpy roads. It had not snowed while they were on the road but sludge lined the way. Her sword was packed in the back with her belongings, so she opted for a dagger for lighter travel and ease of access which was tucked into a strap on her thigh. It had been a few more hours of bandit watch and her eyes and limbs were strained. Her ribs creaked and an exhausted sigh escaped her. She did not wait for Argen to usher her to nap, she laid flat against the blanket covered bench and closed her eyes. Her hand lay on her stomach whilst her other hand wrapped over her chest like a shawl. Her legs were crossed at the ankle and soon enough her breaths were even- The carriage jolted and her peaceful sleep was over. She braced a hand on the wall behind her to stop her body from being jostled. With wide eyes her foot slammed to the floor with her hand. Argen let a laugh escape as she fumbled for her dagger. Once unsheathed, Argen's laughter filtered into nothing. The afternoon sunshine filled their carriage and the shadows it caused sharpened his soft, round features. His beard glowed in the light turning it near-rust. As she scanned his face the carriage jostled again and she knocked into the wall to her left. Her hand braced against it before her side crashed into it but the tremor rattled her brain in her skull. Everything throbbed and Argen shushed her for the second time that day which made her eyebrow twitch in irritation.

Incoherent shouting flew at them. Some were from their men, others from voices neither of them recognised. The sound of steel on steel followed, which forced Farren to tighten the grip on her blade. Argen cursed as he gripped the hilt of his own weapon. He chose to keep his sword with him, his skill greater with a blade than hand-to-hand combat.

"Do not leave this carriage," was all Argen said before he flung the door open.

Farren gaped at the space he left in front of her. The door swung back into place and she was left with the thundering of her heart in her ears. Curses, yells, the grunts of the wounded. Her foot tapped against the floor of the carriage and her hand flexed around her dagger's handle. Her body screamed at her to *go, move, help them* but she forced calm into her veins. She would be as useful as a wet towel is at drying people. There were no locks on the doors so she focused on the door to her right and stared as though she could weld it shut with her mind. *Do not leave this carriage.* Her hand twitched at a particularly pained groan. She had to think of her injuries, of how her ribs would take longer to heal if she started to swing a blade around-

"Farren!"

On the other hand- Farren shot forward, her palm nearly went through the wood of the door. Dust and stones flew away from her as she slammed onto the floor. Blood splatter covered the stone and dirt. She gripped her side but held her knife as a shield with the other. The guards fought against rag-clad bandits, three to each man. Either they were expected or it was sheer bad luck. Adrastos fought at the front, his sword clanged with his opponent's; the solid concentration on his face made Farren turn to his Second who was twice as large and knocked a bandit to the ground with just his fist. Argen fought

80

further to her left as he teamed up with the other member of Adrastos'
carriage. It was not the first time she saw Argen fight but the awe she felt at
his precision made her realise exactly why he was given the title
'Commander.' The horses whinnied and tried to break free from their reins so
she placed a gentle hand on the side of her carriage's horse. It kept all hooves
on the floor but neighed in her ear. The sound wracked her eardrums so she
stepped away and shook her head. Behind her a guard's sword chimed against
the side of the carriage. A man she never got the name of was pressed against
the vehicle, his back arched against the side door. Farren's feet moved before
her mind caught up and soon the tip of her dagger sunk into the bandit's back
then sliced across his throat. That was her third kill in under two weeks. She
did not allow herself to think about it, not as the Captain's knee thudded to the
ground after a slice to the thigh. The guard she saved nodded his thanks and
she rushed toward the fallen Captain, but a shield of muscle stopped her
midway. The bandit's movements were smooth as silk as he intercepted her
path. Farren raised her bloodied knife, the adrenaline steadied her hand and
she narrowed her eyes.

"I'm having a very weird week so if you would be so kind as to
move-" At the sight of the swing of his fist, she leant backwards, the air
brushed against her forehead. As she righted herself she blinked rapidly. He
did not make another move to attack but Farren took another step back in
case. With the size of his hands, one punch to her ribs and she would be down
for the count.

The hood he wore slipped from his head to reveal patchy tufts of hair
and a scarred face. His eyes lacked pupils; the solid white glowed in the
sunlight. No, that was not sunlight but an internal glow, just like the pendant
that hung beneath her shirt. As the glow brightened his mouth opened. Yellow
teeth and dark gums greeted her. The price of a human wielding too much
magic was not a pretty sight. The voice that sounded from him was gruff and

strained as though he had not drunk in weeks but it was the words that flew from his mouth that stopped Farren cold. Old magic, forbidden magic, phrases and words only the oldest books had written inside. His mouth moved with a speed she did not know possible and she was so focused on the chant that she failed to notice the growing magic around his body. It forced its way outward and as he finished his chant the force surged against her like a tidal wave. Her body skittered across the ground as she was thrown backward. She hissed as her ribs pressed against the floor and stones broke the flesh on her face.

Adrastos' voice rang across the road. *There are Magic Users in the field!* Everyone paused but seconds later the fighting continued, this time with more vigour. Farren groaned, her hands pressed to the ground in an attempt to sit upright. A piece of her hair that was once behind her fell into her face which she blew upward. The white-eyed man had his arms out to the side, palms skyward and head tilted down which allowed more bald spots to become visible. A hand pressed to her shoulder and helped her to her feet. The Captain's Second stood beside her but his eyes were on the bandit in front of her. Fresh blood covered his armour and she chanced a look at where he fought. Three bandits laid in their own blood, one of them struggled to breathe around the liquid. She swallowed and corded-arms pushed her behind him with little effort. With her eyes on the magic user she followed the Second's lead and peered around his side. Her dagger was back in her hand as the Magic User locked his eyes on them and chanted once again.

"When people start chanting the smartest thing to do is run," Farren commented. The look the guard gave her told her that was not an option. The chanting bandit convulsed and fell to his knees. The necklace that dangled from his hand –a long chain of purple beads- shook violently as his face tilted to the sky. The whites of his eyes were replaced by red-veined, blood-shot versions when they rolled to the back of his head. Blood seeped from the inner corners and his ears but the chants never ceased. The Second watched with a disgusted furrow of his brow, his sword pointed at the man but he did not move from her human shield.

Therefore, Farren huffed and surged forward. No-doubt the magic he tried to conjure had the capability to injure –or even kill- everyone on that road and she would not wait for it to kill its host first. With the adrenaline in her veins she dodged the guard's attempt to grab her, marched as close to the magical perimeter as she dared, and threw her dagger. It lodged between his eyes and as his body slumped to the floor, his back bent at an odd angle, the other bandits fell around them like ragdolls. There was no warning as they dropped their weapons and collapsed to the floor. Heavy breaths filled the road and everyone stared at the scattered men.

"Something must have connected them to that spell, or to the Magic User himself," Adrastos flicked the blood from his sword.

"Are they," Farren stared at the bandits not covered in their own blood, "are they dead?" He stooped over one of the bandits at his feet and pressed his fingers to his neck. The bandit looked so much like the guards she cut down nearly a week ago. The Captain nodded and removed his hand. When she killed the Magic User she killed the others. A few were already felled at the hands of the guards but those others, they were the ones who had not seen their death coming. They did not see their blood on a blade or hear their neck snap by someone's doing. One minute they lived then she flung her dagger into the wrong person's head and they were dead. She took a shaking breath in and coughed as she exhaled. Another groan as she gripped her broken ribs. The Captain's Second was at her side, a hand on the hem of her shirt. She did not stop him as he lifted the fabric to assess the wound. He pressed the tips of his fingers against her bindings and she bent away from him. Other than a strain on her previous injuries she left the fight unscathed, but she felt sick and filthy in her own her own skin.

Argen moved to her side in seconds and hastily pushed the other man away from her. To assess her injuries for his own peace of mind, his eyes moved a-mile-a-minute. He made to graze a hand over a bruise on her hip but she shuffled back and removed his hands from her person. His eyes continue to roam her body and snagged on the shallow cuts on her face. A hand reached to check them but she took another step back and faced the Captain. The wound in his leg bled freely but he ignored it as he stood above the body of a fallen guard whose hand was frozen reaching for his weapon. They may have won but the bandits got a good hit in before they followed. Farren squeezed her eyes shut as she saw the fallen village guards in his place. The fact she could only see them did not help the churning feeling in her stomach.

The rest of the group lived, a few minor injuries, blood splattered on their armour and adrenaline-soaked looks on their faces. It was why Adrastos' voice was strong as he said, "we will camp here for the night so we can say goodbye our fallen brother." Everyone's eyes were on the dead guard whilst she glanced between the body and Argen. It made her wonder if his own guards were given a funeral. The haunted look in Argen's eyes did not answer her so she walked over to the Magic User's body, stepped over the necklace and gripped her dagger. A gag hit the back of her throat at the crunch of his bone as she pulled the blade from his face. Blank eyes stared up at her and she stumbled back until she hit a solid wall. No, not a wall. The Captain's Second looked down at her as she turned.

"Sorry."

He nodded and gestured toward the woods to their right, "we need firewood."

Farren followed him, her dagger at her side and Argen's gaze glued to their backs. She trailed behind and took the chance to survey the Captain's Second: he was tall, his hair cropped close to his head with chocolate brown, wavy hair on top. It was not styled per-se but swept upward like the tail of a tropical bird. She pressed a hand to her mouth to prevent a laugh from escaping. People *died* yet a bubble of laughter stuck itself in her throat. She swallowed it down with a cough which her ribs did not thank her for.

"Thank you, for trying to help me." He glanced at her when she spoke and grunted. "I had no idea people so willingly used magic near the Capital, I thought I was going to be in serious trouble after that power slammed me to the floor." A nervous chuckle escaped her and he bent to pick up a group of twigs. She surveyed the ground around her then at her scraped hands. The dagger hung limply in her right hand. The blood had yet to dry so she wiped the blade against the bark of a tree and ground her teeth. It found its way back to its sheath on her thigh and she followed his lead. Smaller twigs and some logs bundled into her arms. She hissed against the strain in her muscles and followed him further into the woods.

"You should not be standing right now. Those injuries are something to be concerned about and yet you fought not one but two bandits, one of them who had magic. How did you manage it?"

Farren blinked, "it must be the shock."

He shook his head, "that's not it." She narrowed her eyes. "So how?"

"Sheer strength of will."

Another grunt greeted her ears. Once they gathered armfuls of firewood and kindling –no dry grass due to the previous snow- they made their way back to the carriages. The forest was silent save for the sludge of their footsteps. The rustling of leaves underfoot broke through the peace; Farren dropped the logs in her arms and pulled her dagger in front of her. The Captain's Second sighed behind her, "I thought you were supposed to have some training under your belt."

"Forgive me for being cautious after surviving a surprise attack." Whether she meant the one they just endured or the attack in the village she didn't know. He watched her as she swallowed back the adrenaline that never really ebbed away. Farren was the picture of a surviving soldier with her bruised face, pained side and startled look in her eyes. Another grunt and he focused on their way out. With her dagger placed back in its hold and the logs returned to her arms, they carried on. A colony of rabbits hopped through the bushes she previously pointed her dagger at and she sighed. The food in the carriages meant they would not need to hunt the furry creatures whilst they camped.

The others milled in and out of the carriages whilst Adrastos wrapped the fallen guard in a sheet. Blood soaked through most of it but he continued to tie it tightly around the body. The wound on his thigh was also wrapped tightly and he struggled to keep his weight off of it. The horses grazed near the other group of trees and anyone who needed to get to the castle would be stopped by a carriage blocking both ends. A pile of logs and sticks gathered by the others was made in the centre of the road. Farren and the man before her placed their logs on the pile and he proceeded to build a shelf for the body to lie upon. Burning was the usual method for soldiers to dispose of their dead. The First Great War –or perhaps it was the Second Great War- started the tradition. It allowed for efficient disposal on the battlefield so that they could burn many bodies at once. It then filtered to the Capital and the Continent as a sign of respect. If a soldier was buried it often meant they had been disgraced mainly because Magic Users found uses for the bodies in their craft; sometimes there were things worse than death.

Once the sky turned dark and the pyre was built with what they gathered, the men formed a half-circle around it. The soldiers carried the body and placed it gently on top. Adrastos remained at the forefront of the group, head bowed as his Second placed a burning tree branch against the kindling.

The flames took almost instantly and it burned through until it engulfed the bottom of the body. Farren stood at the back of the semi-circle, away from the grieving faces of the guards, away from the intimate nature of the burning. They each took turns in telling tales of their fallen brother and only she and Argen remained quiet. She glanced at the Commander who sent her a grim smile in response. The heat of the flames flickered on her skin but the warmth did not reach her bones.

The remainder of the journey was uneventful which was a welcomed change to Farren's previous week. Each guard grieved in their own way: some pretended it never happened, some spent their nights training rather than sleeping, others kept to themselves whilst the remaining made sure to talk through everything. Farren kept her distance but observed them. Argen had not broached a conversation with her since the burning ceremony but he watched and waited for her to speak first. Despite their lack of communication, he was like an overbearing mother hen as he fussed over her wounds. A headache formed and became constant the more he hovered. When they weren't in the carriages she found herself sat with the Captain's Second whose name she learned was Rorke. He introduced himself after she gave him a rambling speech about wanting to know her new friends, not that she considered them friends, though she'd only had two friends so maybe he was; she carried on like that for a solid two minutes before he stopped her with his name. Her answering grin made him grunt and they returned to the silence.

The travelling party soon breached the gates to the Capital. The city sat at the bottom of a valley. Most of the buildings were made from the white salt-stone found in the ground beneath them. The public buildings had domed roofs whilst the residential areas, those that surrounded the business-centred middle, had flat, black stone rooftops. The Capital was full of life and a busy population. A mixture of smells hit Farren at once: beer and sewage, smoke and dough. She gagged against her piece of bread but swallowed her mouthful. It was nothing like she imagined. She thought the Capital would look grungier like her village but instead it smelled a lot worse than it looked. There were winding roads and pathways for pedestrians but there was one that ran directly through the centre. It was the road which lead directly to the White Castle: a building covered in different shades of white and tall spires. Before the castle sat a long bridge high above the moat. The castle itself was perched upon an island of rock whilst watch towers sat at each compass point. On the opposite side of the moat were more residential houses, the houses of the lords and their staff. Farren always thought it was silly to have every important person live in the same place but Argen insisted it allowed for efficiency. *Yes, efficiency of multiple assassinations.*

There was no time to bathe or look in a mirror before the meeting with the King so she ignored the knotted hair that hung below her shoulders. The carriages clattered into the castle courtyard and the guards' boots hit the cobblestones. Farren shucked on her jacket over the shirt she tucked in moments ago and buckled it across her chest. She pushed her hair from her face and grabbed her sword from the back of the carriage which she strapped to her belt. Argen walked beside her, his eyes filled with amazement. The only sign of his nerves was the distinctive shake of his legs. The King and Queen of Altin lived in those walls and she –Farren Attarah- was about to step foot inside. The interior of the castle smelt far better than the city; the smell of rose encompassed the marble-floored hall. A grin plastered to her face as the nobles eyed her with distaste. Compared to them she looked like she crawled from a sewage drain with their pale dresses and sharp suits. Their gazes soon became the least annoying factor to their march as she felt Argen's eyes on her. Every few seconds he shifted his eyes from the back of Adrastos' head to the side of hers. She refrained from snapping at him then and there but her teeth ground together beneath her grin.

As the beautiful double-doors of black wood and silver-carved roses opened, everyone sucked in a breath. Two thrones sat atop a black and white marble dais. The larger throne —one fit for a King- was painted a deep black, with two white roses perched over the back whilst the smaller throne -one that proved the Queen was not his equal- was as white as the interior walls with two black roses to match the King's. Those thrones were the symbols of peace in the kingdom and the symbol of oppression. Farren focused so hard on the Queen's throne that she nearly missed the Captain's cleared throat. Her eyes widened as she found the guards around her bent at the waist because stood to the side of the dais was the King of Altin with an amused smile on his face. After that observation she quickly bowed which pushed her teeth together at the pain.

She hid her wince as she dipped her head, mercifully the King chuckled, "rise." They stood in unison, hands clasped behind their backs, feet shoulder-width apart, and chins forward. As she surveyed the room further she found the Queen stood at his side with a frown and her dark eyes set on her. Yet, Farren' gaze quickly shifted to the man on the other side of the King. Once, twice, and again she blinked. With his eyes aglow and focused on her, Soter smiled at her.

"Your Majesty, I would like to apologise for our tardiness, we encountered some trouble on the road."

The King waved off the Captain as though he swatted a fly but the amused look remained on his face. He was a kind looking man: white hair slicked behind his ears and a curly beard cropped a few inches below his chin. Crow's feet line his eyes and his hands were speckled from age. The King ruled Altin for fifty years, his sixty-sixth birthday soon approached. He stood before his throne and gestured for the Captain to continue. Farren listened as Adrastos explained the attack on the road. There was no shock on his face as the Captain spoke of the Magic Users, a common occurrence it would seem. As she listened her eyes were glued to Soter who smiled. He wore a similar outfit to the one at the market but instead of white, a dark grey, gold-lined number adorned his body. It made his hair look like a living flame.

The King's booming voice broke her from her staring match, "my condolences, I assume a burning ceremony took place?" The Captain nodded. "Good. Now," he clapped his hands together with a grin, "who have you brought me, Adrastos?"

Farren blinked as the Captain's first name fell so familiarly from his lips but she stepped forward with Argen at her side. The jitters that were originally in Argen's legs moved to her feet that shifted beneath her, but she kept her hands behind her back and chin high. Argen followed suit with a final glance at her. The King's smile faltered for a moment as he stared at her bruised and cut face. "This is Argen Bray, a Commander in the village of Brentham, he has been training this young woman to take the Trial." The Queen coughed behind a gloved hand whilst the King's brows rose into his hairline. "Her name is Farren Attarah, she's the woman I told you about."

90

"Ah, the woman who killed two of my guards." Farren bit back her sharp retort but Adrastos nodded. The King's pitiful eyes dragged over her body and all she wanted was for the ground to swallow her whole. Instead, she kept her shoulders straight and face forward, and ignored the sharp sting her nails caused against her palm. "What do you suggest we do, Adrastos?"

Adrastos kept his word and suggested the guards be punished under the King's Loyalty Declaration and Argen agreed to such a proposition. *Harsher, they deserved a harsher punishment*. She made to open her mouth but the subtle shake of the Captain's head stopped her.

"That's not good enough," Soter's voice rang across the room. The Magician had the courage to voice her thoughts aloud so, with baited breath, she waited for the King to speak, her eyes focused on his contemplative face. Nobody breathed as Soter's voice settled on the guards and royals.

It was Argen who responded, "you do not get a say in what happens to *my* men." Horror filled her chest at Argen's words and she hissed his name. They were his men, it was a fact she would never forget, but to defend them so wildly tightened her chest. He condemned them that night and he agreed to their punishment but to still defend them, to argue against a harsher punishment on the men that nearly killed her- she bit back the words she wanted to curse at him.

Soter raised a brow. "Your men should not have laid their hands on her the way they did," he stated it matter-of-factly.

The King replied, "thank you for your input, Soter, but it seems our meeting has been cut short by the return of my guards. Tell your Master that his terms are agreeable but I would like them in writing."

Master? In his tent he seemed like a travelling man who peddled magic to those who did not fear it and even to some who did. Yet there he stood, chin high whilst he spoke to the King of Altin with no indication of whether he was in the charge of another. A Magician and a political ally it would seem. When he mentioned he was there in an advisory capacity she assumed he meant regarding magic not on someone else's behalf. The confused tilt of her head was all she offered the conversation.

Soter inclined his head and stepped from the dais. The fabric of his clothes billowed around him when he walked and the scrolls in his arms bounced. She watched as he raised a brow and the men parted like curtains. As though he wanted to memorise every detail of their faces for later he looked over each and every one of them. Her eyes followed him until he reached her side, gave her a once over and pursed his lips. Something flashed in his eyes and for a second the green of his eyes swirled with a kaleidoscope of colour. It reminded her of the elegance and beauty of a weeping willow but as quickly as the light was there, it was gone. He lifted his hand to brush a knuckle against the bruise under her eye and she opened her mouth to ask him what that look meant but he carried on as though he hadn't stopped at all. Once the doors shut and Soter was out of sight it was the King's turn to walk toward her.

"I swear to you Farren." Not 'Miss Attarah.' "Those guards will be dealt with, they will not bother you again." The King appeased her questioning look, "they will be disbanded." He looked to Argen who stared at his feet. "With a full pension and the burning ceremony still in place for when the time comes." Farren's eye twitched. "They will be quarantined to Brentham with my order not to travel beyond its borders."

Every nerve in Farren's body wanted to scream. Money and a cosy life in a village they loved, what part of that was a punishment? Disbanding them did nothing to secure her safety, it did nothing to secure the safety of those in the village and it certainly did nothing to satisfy the pit in her stomach. She would let the King believe that he didn't just let the world's true monsters walk free.

"You all look tired from your travels and I see some of you are injured." *Yes, from the men you deem worthy enough to remain anonymous.* "So please, go and see the physicians on the lower floor. They will see to it that your injuries are tended to whilst you are here. I need you all fit and ready for the ball tonight." It was a dismissal and an order.

All Farren wanted was a hot bath. There was no need to tend to her injuries, she did not need someone else to tell her about her broken ribs and scratched face but the King would not allow such injuries to go unchecked because no matter the state they were in, they were to attend the ball. It was known around the country and beyond that the King loved his parties. He used any and all excuses to throw a party, from his first grey hair to the garden wall restoration; he once used the excuse that the oranges in the kitchens needed eating so they had a day-long 'orange festival.' What excuse he used for them was something Farren looked forward to.

They exited the throne room in the same two-man file they walked in but Adrastos remained behind. He ordered Rorke to take them to the physicians as the King suggested and with a curt nod that's what he did. Before they descended the set of white-stone stairs she glanced back at the throne room. How the pristine halls were not constantly caked in mud she did not know. Cleanliness aside, the men in front of her chatted and laughed, so carefree than the men she fought alongside on the road. Rorke on the other hand remained silent as they trekked down to the lower levels of the castle. The white stone faded to a soft grey and the marble flooring turned to cobblestones that matched the ones in the courtyard. Doors lined either side of the hall they found themselves in. Men and women who wore white robes and caps bustled in and out of those doors. Curses flew from the mouths of patients, and pestles against mortars echoed against the walls.

Rorke stopped one of the older Healers with a hand on her shoulder. Blonde hair was slicked neatly beneath her cap, robes pristine and a-line until they stopped at her white shoes. She stared at them individually and assigned each guard a room and a healer, but when her eyes fell on Farren a sickly green covered the old woman's face. Her mouth opened and closed like a fish without air and Rorke cleared his throat. Farren scratched at a scab on her face, eyes cast toward the door ajar to her left: a man sat with a plank of wood in his mouth as a middle-aged gentleman stitched closed a wound on his shoulder. A loud groan slipped past the wooden block and Farren removed her eyes from the trail of blood that curved around his bicep.

The Healer snapped into action: she called over a young boy –an apprentice- to take Farren to a room with a mention of another Healer. *Did she look that terrible?* Rorke followed her whilst Argen was escorted to another room. His eyes remained on her as she was guided toward the far end of the hall.

The room she walked into was designed around a platform-raised bed with white sheets and a thin pillow. Herbs and tonics lined the walls in every direction alongside rows upon rows of books. A Healer had her back to them as she stood over open texts: she was stout and curvaceous, the body of someone pulled from the paintings on the ceilings of holy places, like the ceiling of the mountain temples or the paintings hung in the houses of nobles. When the woman turned, that was where the painting resemblance ended. Her face was all sharp lines and angles and with her hair pulled behind her in a bun, the longer her face seemed. Her eyes were narrowed behind half-moon glasses as she scanned Farren's body. "Remove your jacket."

Farren did so and Rorke –who remained a shadow behind her- took the garment from her. He nodded for her to move from the door as he folded the fabric in his hands. Once Farren sat on the white sheets she crossed her ankles and rested on her palms. The sword on her hip was unbuckled and placed beside her. She looked at Rorke who followed the Healer's movements with hawk-like eyes. The muscles beneath his bloodied armour flexed and he cast a glance to her where she raised an eyebrow with a small smirk. In response, he rolled his eyes and returned his attention to the older woman. His back was pressed against the wall with his arms folded across his chest like a human barricade. The apprentice moved forward to check the hulking man for any harm done with a loud gulp; his voice shook as he asked Rorke to remove his armour.

"For Griselda's sake child, be more assertive. Do you see me dancing around this girl like a prima ballerina?" His boss scolded.

Farren choked on her laugh as the poor boy's eyes widened. He shook his head and made to repeat his request but Rorke removed the armour without argument. Firstly, he handed him Farren's jacket and the boy's shoulders sagged in relief. The jacket and sections of his armour were placed on a table in the corner. Each piece weighed nearly as much as the Apprentice did, maybe more so Farren made to comment on the boy's strength when the Healer stood before her. Farren sat up straight and folded her hands in her lap. Those hands were back to her sides and her shirt was lifted to just under her breasts. Her bindings were removed and they stuck to her skin with the salve Soter gave her. Farren held back a shiver as the Healer's eyes slowly trailed to her eyes. There was anger and frustration behind her lashes but there were no enquires, no questions asked. Her look spoke for itself. The Healer's hands were surprisingly gentle as she pressed her palm against the nasty bruise on her side. Farren curled away from the touch and she clicked her tongue. Rorke's eyes bore into Farren's bruises, a hard line to his brow and a flex of his arms. He kept his eyes on the dark purple and not on the dip of her waist, not on the way her hip curved into her trousers or the way the bottom of her breast poked from beneath her shirt's fabric. They were injuries he'd seen many times on his own men but somehow, amongst her freckles they looked vicious.

"Your ribs are definitely broken." The Healer walked over to the tonics where she removed a pale blue elixir. "If you put a drop in your drinks before bed every night then the healing will be less painful. Hopefully." The Healer raised her eyes to Rorke where she cleared her throat and with a pointed look he averted his eyes. A rosy dust covered his cheeks as he purposefully stared at the armour across the room.

Farren thanked her for the tonic and placed it beside her. There were no new bindings to be wrapped around her tired body, instead the Healer re-wrapped her bandages around her ribs with a tug against the fabric to keep it secure until she made it to her room, and it was a blessing because Farren was sure that if she applied new bandages, she would not be permitted to bathe. Before she hopped off the bed, the woman's hands cupped her face. She moved her neck side to side, slowly, as she rotated her field of vision. There was another click of her tongue as she surveyed the bruises and shallow cuts.

"You've been using a salve on your bruises?" A nod. "Good, keep doing so and drink that tonic as I said. You ribs should be healed in three weeks, your bruises even sooner. You are fit and healthy but you must not put too much strain on those ribs or they will take even longer, do you understand?"

Farren nodded once more and the Healer returned to the books on the desk. The Apprentice finished his assessment of Rorke: he asked the guard to squeeze his hand –which made tears spring to his eyes when Rorke complied- and he removed his shirt to check for injuries. Each vital point was checked by the Apprentice whilst Farren tried her hardest to note that there was not an ounce of fat on Rorke's body. He was hard muscle and scarred skin, flecks of white along his chest and arms, most likely on his legs as well. Despite the scars he looked smooth, as though his skin would feel like hot velvet beneath her fingers. The injuries he sustained in the road fight was nothing more than a small laceration on his arm which clotted over on the road. The cut was washed and bandaged, the two of them were sent on their way. Rorke grabbed her jacket from the table but left his armour for the Apprentice to deal with, as was protocol. Farren tossed a smiling thank you over her shoulder, her belt back around her waist. The Healer didn't acknowledge their departure.

As the door closed behind them they were greeted by Argen who stood against the opposite wall with his ankles crossed. With his shirt sleeves rolled up the tight wrapping around his wrist was revealed. "Is everyone fit and healthy?" His eyes were on her when he asked.

Rorke replied and guided them back up the stairs, "the Healer signed us off fit for duty."

"Oh really?"

Rorke grunted and they walked back the way they came until a sharp turn appeared at the top of the stairs and then another until they made their way down a corridor similar to that of the entrance hall: white walls and marbled floors.

"Is everything here monochromatic?" Farren asked.

"Yes," was Rorke's simple reply.

He pointed down to the middle of the hall where their rooms were situated. His was at the front alongside his squadron whilst theirs was further along, far away from Adrastos' quarters for the Captain's need for peace and quiet. Farren and Argen's doors sat adjacent to one another much to Farren's chagrin. Neither commented on it and before Argen grabbed her attention, she opened the door with her name on it, and stepped inside. Once the door was closed she breathed a sigh of relief. Avoiding a conversation with Argen would only work for so long, but she hoped the ball would be a big enough distraction that he did not try and speak with her. Her eyes slipped close: that was not likely. That's when her eyes flew back open. There would be a ball and all she had to wear were her travelling clothes, training gear and daily skirts. As far as good impressions went, her skirts were not under that category. The city was just on her doorstep so she could use what coins she had left to buy herself a dress or at least skirts that weren't the colour of wet soil.

"I should have listened to Theron when he suggested I expand my wardrobe." That conversation always made her head throb. Every now and then her uncle commented on her clothes and taunted her on how a Lady should dress. He then argued that if she wanted to be a partner of their business then she needed to look the part. Although, Farren didn't think her clothes were the reason Theron would not hire her. The skirts in questions were packed in the trunk that arrived before her. It sat at the bottom of a bed large enough for two covered in the King's colours: white and black. Two steps lead up to said bed but before that, on the right side of the room sat two rose-carved bookcases and a writing desk. A plush, white-silk covered stool sat before it. On the left was something Farren dreamt of for days: a claw-footed tub with an array of bath salts and hair tonics piled into a pyramid at the head. Two soft, white towels laid next to the bath products and there was even a slip-proof rug beneath the bath. The King thought of everything for his guests –for his guards.

With a flick of her wrist the door was locked and she padded to the inviting tub. She stripped as she walked, her jacket then her shirt then she carefully unwound her bindings. The sword was placed on top of her trunk, alongside her boots and trousers. When she reached the tub she was clad in only Soter's necklace. She often forgot it was there, the small jewel brushed against her skin lightly. It wasn't long after she turned the tap that hot water filled the tub. Steam floated through the room and Farren bent to look through the various salts and tonics. A pale purple liquid filled with the smell of lavender was added to the water. The once clear liquid turned milky.

First a toe and then her body submerged under the calming water. Her hair bobbed around her, entangled with the necklace. She found a thicker tonic than the bath milk and poured a generous amount of lemon verbena hair tonic into her palm. She scrubbed her fingers through the tangled tresses and made sure to pay close attention to the dried blood at her ends. She used more of the lavender tonic to scrub at the dirt beneath her nails and the mud on her neck. Days worth of travel washed away to reveal faded bruises and freckle covered skin. The throb of her muscles ebbed away in the water and she leaned back, gently so as not to jolt her ribs. Before she relaxed against the curve of the tub she grabbed the smaller towel and placed it behind her head. The ceiling above her was a dull white but it wasn't long before the lavender aroma and warm water made her eyelids flutter. Soon enough her arms relaxed at her sides and she was asleep.

She awoke to the sound of laughter and the clink of glasses down the hall. Her body sunk into a large double bed with the curtains drawn but a sliver of red light peeked through so she pushed herself from the soft comforter and padded toward the door to the left of the bed. A shiver shot itself up her legs as her warm feet hit the cold floor. The bedroom did not hold her attention for long because the door opened up to a corridor made of black rock and decorated with the exotic plants. She brushed her hand over the leaf of a small palm tree as she followed the voices. The smell of lemon and lavender fought with the smell of burnt sugar that hit her as she made it to the bottom of a flight of stairs. The stairs broke off on the corridor floor then continued down to another level. Darkness swirled down the stairs to her left, the descent not possible due to the thick smoke. The ascending steps were clear and soft music played above her. It was beautiful and familiar just like the black nightgown that floated around her knees. The climb was short and once she reached the top of the stairs, the music stopped. A viewing point sat before her. It was bigger than a balcony but was too small for an open observatory. The room was empty save for the sheer curtains that framed the archways. Solid bars prevented anyone from falling into the chasm below and the red light from beyond her room shone into the open space. It emanated from the large rock –no, not a rock- the volcano in front of her. Veins of molten brimstone shone red through the cracks in the rock. The further she walked into the room the brighter the light became. When she passed the centre of the circular room the light flared, a dark red throb against her eyes. Her arm raised to shield her eyes but the light returned to normal once she blinked.

A silhouette appeared before the volcano. It had no features to be distinguished but it moved slowly, raised its arm toward her and held out its hand. The veins of the volcano matched the veins of fire that crawled up the silhouette's arm. It trailed higher until it crawled up its neck and stopped. It hummed and sharp white teeth grinned at her as she stepped forward. She found herself taking one step after another until she was in touching distance of its hand. Her own hand raised and the shadow grinned wider with a nod, its hand reached further, the heat of its body warmed her cold hands-

Water splashed over the sides of the bath as her arm fell into the water. She blinked at her suddenly wet arm and raised it to her face. The water was cold and her toes and fingers turned to prunes. She blinked the droplets from her lashes and shook her head. "What was that?" she muttered.

The shadows at the corners of the room seemed to swirl at her words and she was frozen to the spot. Then the towel beneath her head fell into the water and she was pushed to action, she grabbed a larger one from the floor and wrapped it around her body. She winced against the brush against her bruises but stepped from the tub and over to the trunk. She didn't make it five steps from the water before there was a knock at the door. With a final glance at the shadows she shook her wet hair behind her and padded to the door. The towel was pulled tightly around her and she peaked around her door and into the hall. Nobody stood on the other side, but sat on the floor, tied in a silken gold ribbon was a large box. Writing was scrawled across the top with her name and an arrow to the ribbon. She pulled the box inside which allowed the weight of it to keep her towel in place, and kicked the door shut.

After she placed the box on the bed and hiked up her towel, she untied the ribbon to find a note sat beneath it. The same writing was scrawled on the card: *I hope this is to your taste –Soter.* The ribbon slipped through her fingers like liquid and the lid was removed with ease. Inside, folded with care was a gown made of dusky blue and crystal flowers. The fabric was layered and thick but remained simple until it reached the neckline where sewn in gems created a waterfall of flowers. She pulled it from the box to find long, chiffon sleeves cuffed at the wrists in an off-the-shoulder fashion where more sparkles covered her collar-bone above more transparent chiffon. The fabric glimmered in the light. A belt of sparkles synched in the waste and Farren smiled.

After she saw to her bindings, the fabric tied tightly so that any movement would not disturb her ribs, she donned the dress with care. Soter's necklace was tucked under the blue so that only the thin chain was visible but not the vibrant jewel. The dress fit her perfectly and complimented the dark tresses of her hair so as she turned slowly in front of the tall mirror and watched as the fabric swayed with her, she admired herself. It was a dress for a woman who wished to make a good first impression. Yes, it would do just nicely.

A soft knock broke Farren from her admiration. The clock atop the desk told her it was nearly seven in the evening. The rumble in her stomach confirmed it. She opened the door with her hand pressed to her stomach as though to quiet the sounds by force. Argen stood before her with a furrow to his brow as he held up a pair of blue suede shoes. They were the same colour as the dress and she took them with a short nod. The door was left open as she sat on the desk chair to slip them on. The angles in which she bent her foot and leg so as not to strain her ribs was something he'd never witnessed. Argen peered into the room but did not break the invisible line she made between them no matter how much he wished to stand by her side. When she stood she pushed her hair behind her. Any intricate up-do was not a possibility with the stretch it would cause to her body. Instead they were in soft curls down her back and were tucked behind her ear.

"You look be-beautiful," Argen broke the silence.

"Thank you, it was a gift." she forced her voice to remain monotone and she stood.

"From who?"

"Soter."

"You are kidding? Why would he give you a dress?"

She brushed down any wrinkles in the dress. "Because I needed one and he is a very kind man."

"Not a man," Argen muttered but she missed it. When she appeared in the doorway once again he held out his arm. The sleeves of his best shirt were closed with cufflinks engraved with the guard emblem and his jacket was finely pressed. His arm dropped as she walked past him whilst her hands fiddled with her hair. His shocked scoff sounded behind her which made her more determined to keep her eyes on the end of the corridor instead of his indignant face. "How long do you plan to stay mad?" They walked in silence. Farren sent the two guards at the end of the hall a quick smile before they turned down another. Nobles milled about talking and drinking. Despite being on time it looked as though she and Argen were late with the amount of guests in the castle. The eyes of those guests remained on their friends —or were they each other's enemies?- as they walked past. "I *am* sorry Farren, I had no idea what they were planning and if I had known I would have-"

She moved quickly: her feet stopped and she whirled on him. The fabric of her skirt shifted around her in a soft brush against the floor. He braced his hands in front of him lest she collided with him, and widened his eyes. With her hands clenched at her sides she moved toward him. Wisely, he backed up a few steps.

"I don't care if you're sorry, I don't care if you think it's not your fault, and I don't care what you would have done if you knew about their plan. It is your job to know about their plans, it's your job to keep them in line, it's your job to protect people, and I know it's your job to apologise to victims and their families but I do *not* want to hear it," she paused for a breath, "you fucked up, Argen and I just- I need some time."

Then, Argen's own hands clenched. "So that's it? You get to be angry for however long you want, forget the fact that we have been friends for years? And what, I'm supposed to sit around and wait for you to get over it?!" The moment those words flew from his mouth his eyes widened and he stepped forward. "Farren, no that's not what I-"

The restraint it took for her to not put him on his ass was great but as her hands shook with the effort, and she lifted her chin. Blame was an interesting thing. She knew that it was not Argen who pegged them against her but it was Argen who knew his men, who was in charge of them. *He* told her they wanted her on their side, *he* told her that they were intrigued to work with her, *he* was the one who spoke to them about her joining the Guard. It was his job to lead them away from dishonour yet her ribs were broken and her face was bruised. It was not his fault that every time she looked at him she felt the icy water of the stream and the look on his face when he saw those dead guards.

The laughter of nobles from the ballroom diverted her attention to the present. Two giggling women walked past them which forced a smile on Farren's face. They smiled back and continued toward the celebrations. She turned her back on Argen who looked lost in the middle of the hall. The muscles in her shoulders rolled; there was no need to get a cramp because of Argen Bray.

The ballroom was filled to the brim with people wearing pristine suits and dresses. Many of the women wore light colours whilst the men wore suits of varying degrees of black and grey. Her eyes cast over the many faces who twirled around the room to the string-music. Buffet tables lined the right side of the ballroom where cakes, steamed greens, smoked fish, fresh bread and colourful fruits made her stomach growl loudly but a glint of gold ripped her eyes from the mouth-watering food. She raised her head to find the King's goblet lifted in welcome. His smile —even from the large distance between her and the back of the ballroom- seemed strained. She bowed none-the-less as best as she could and moved from the open doors. She shuffled next to a large man who, when she did a double-take, was Rorke. He glanced down at her and performed his own double-take when he noticed the dress.

He cleared his throat, "you look nice."

She grinned. "Thank you." And took that moment to survey his suit; she noted the way it hugged his figure and made his shoulders look that much broader. "You look nice too." He nodded in thanks and they stood in comfortable silence until the music changed. "Do you maybe want to dance?" Suddenly, her voice was sheepish.

"Rorke doesn't dance." Farren's attention was stolen by Adrastos who held a half-finished glass of wine. He chuckled when his Second frowned and stood straighter.

"Does he not?" She teased as she glanced between the two men. "Well it's for the best considering I don't know how to waltz either."

"I know how to waltz," Rorke interjected, "I just *don't*."

Adrastos stopped his glass part-way to his mouth and gaped. He proceeded to hand his glass to Rorke and bowed, hand was outstretched toward her. "Allow me to be the first to dance with you then." Her hand landed in his and he whisked her to the dance floor.

The music encompassed them as they stayed on the edge of the dance floor and she definitely bumped into his side more than once. The training she received allowed for most of her footwork to flow seamlessly, although there was a moment when she made to step between his feet and she misjudged how narrowly he stepped. He grunted and the song morphed into a slower tempo which allowed him to be a solid weight as they swayed. The injury to his leg slowed him down somewhat but he remained standing. Her eyes strayed to where the bandage laid beneath his trousers but he tugged her closer which brought her eyes back to his.

"I must say you look stunning in that dress. It's a miracle I get to speak with you, I thought Rorke was going to demand he be the one to dance with you," he chuckled.

Farren's cheeks flared pink and for a moment her eyes moved to find Rorke in the crowd but he remained against the wall, a glass of wine in his hand as his eyes flickered every which way. "He will have fun tonight won't he?"

"He will probably leave after the King's speech and retire for the evening. Speaking of Rorke," he twirled her gently, "he told me that your injuries were a lot worse than Argen let on."

Farren shrugged, "he either over exaggerates or under exaggerates. There is no in-between with Argen."

"How are your injuries?"

She placed her foot beside his. "Two broken ribs that should heal in a couple of weeks, fading bruising and shallow lacerations. It's nothing I can't handle."

He scanned her as though he could see the injuries beneath her dress and nodded. "Will you be fit to train in the morning?"

There was no hesitation when she replied. "As long as I bind my ribs tightly enough it should be fine."

Adrastos raised a brow but nodded, then his name was called and he excused himself before he could reply. He turned on his heel for a second and told her where to meet him the next day. A haze covered her mind as she watched him leave. The words he spoke settled over her and it slowly dawned on her that she would have to wield her sword against the Captain of the Guard; she would have to *punch* the Captain of the Guard. Once the shock wore off she closed her mouth and spotted a man who carried trays of sparkling wine which she swiped before he moved past her. Wine and food were on her list of things to hunt down. The food was easy, she made her way to the buffet and sampled various cheeses, a skewer of roasted peppers and cured meat. The King's generosity was something she gladly accepted as she ate her fill of dishes she both recognised and did not. There was a slimy fish that she opted not to touch as well as a dreadful bowl of pickled cucumbers that she stayed far away from. Her mouth was filled with soft cheese when the Queen approached her with a stern look on her face. If Farren didn't know better she would say she was related to Lyla. The cheese was swallowed quickly and she folded her hands behind her with a shallow bow.

The Queen's eyes raked her body with the grace of nobility and the precision of a trained killer. The thought stuck in the back of her mind like a bad smell. The Queen wore a magnificent gown made of white and silver like the edge of a blade. Her short, brown hair was slicked behind her ears which allowed her jewellery to be appreciated in full: solid diamonds were held together by silver. Her deep umber skin was covered with shimmering powder so that it was not just the diamonds that sparkled in the light; she was starlight incarnate. Silence stretched between them as they stared at one another. The Queen's eyes scrutinised her whilst Farren kept her eyes firmly on the Queen's diamond earring.

"The King has made a lot of decisions in his life but this one... You must know you are not here simply because my husband felt sorry for you."

Farren curled her tongue and she slowly moved her eyes from the earring to the Queen's. "Whatever do you mean, Your Majesty?" *Play stupid.* The one thing that being a woman in a man's business taught her was that it was much easier to observe than to be locked out. She kept her face neutral, open but the Queen's own features hardened.

Her eyes were cold and unkind. "The Captain may have found you and brought you here, well," she scanned the crowd behind her as though she were already bored with the conversation, "not you specifically. He was ordered to find someone reckless and with little to lose." She moved her eyes back to Farren. "That's you dear."

The World blurred at the edges and the Queen's words embedded themselves in her chest like knives. "Why?" The King took that moment to sling his arm over his wife's shoulders with a smile. Something flared in the Queen's eyes but it was replaced by an icy calm.

Despite the bomb the Queen dropped on her, Farren bowed low for the King; his giggle responded to her. "I hope you are enjoying the food Farren, I can imagine that you are starved after your trip."

The young woman glanced at the array of delicacies and her stomach turned, "yes Your Majesty, the food is delicious, my compliments to your cook."

Before the King spoke again the Queen placed her hand on his chest. He looked at her the way Farren one day wished to be looked at. There was a shine to his eyes but the Queen only glanced at her husband before she focused fully on Farren. Every nerve in her body buzzed and her 'flight' instinct screamed to be listened to. The King followed his wife's eyes with a softness that only illuminated his kind features when his wife spoke, "I was informing Miss Attarah of her duty to the Crown."

Not 'Farren', no, the woman before her did not want a rapport like the King did. He scratched at his beard and his rings glinted in the light. As he stared at Farren through his lashes, he looked so long. A beautiful man aged by years of tough decisions.

"This is most unpleasant," he sighed, "I had hoped to talk to you after your session with Adrastos tomorrow." When Farren stayed silent he continued, his voice lowered. "My daughter has gone missing, whisked away in the night by those... those beasts in the other Realm." Farren swallowed. "There is a man who calls himself 'King' who has broken the peace treaty and the Accords. He took my daughter from me, so what I need from you -what I am asking of you- is that you bring my daughter back home."

There was a moment after he spoke where Farren's brain refused to work. Breathing became a chore and she blinked owlishly at the Royals stood before her. For a split second she thought he was joking, the laughter threatened to bubble from her chest, because the other Realm did not only house Night Creatures. The other Realm —more aptly named the Kayei Realm- was home to powerful, humanoid beings that were as strong as they were immortal. They used magic and tricks and honeyed words to make human lives Hell. A Kayei's life was far more luxurious, far easier than even the richest human could dream. They were arrogant and powerful; the Kayei were the reason the King's Guard was so vast, and why they were in every village and city in Altin. The First Great War was the first glimpse at what the Kayei were capable of and it was those beings that brought forth the birth of the Veil, or perhaps they strengthened the Veil, the texts were mixed on the facts, but that war was also the birth of a very thin, very vague peace treaty, one that had been tested many times over the few hundred years... and the King of Altin wanted her to test it once again.

"How-" she swallowed her suddenly dry throat, "how am I supposed to find her? How am I going to survive on my own without magic? It's practically a suicide mission!" As she remembered who exactly she spoke to she added. "Your Majesties."

The King shook his head, "heavens I would not send you there alone!" He looked at the Queen who bordered on furious. "I will send one of my Guards with you, one of the best of course."

He took a minute to survey her, but before he opened his mouth once more the Queen stepped forward which forced Farren to look her in the eye. "If you do not retrieve my daughter, well, just think of your poor family back in Brentham." Farren's fingers closed into a fist. "And how *disappointed* they would be to find out their daughter was a failure, that she was incapable of winning the King's favour." *Jokes on you, my parents don't even know why I am here.* "Think of what could happen to the business, to your father's income, if you should fail."

Farren kept her mouth clamped shut with the ever so slight tilt of her head. The Queen's eyes narrowed but the King moved between the two women with his palms raised. A beseeching look was sent to his wife who removed herself from Farren's vicinity and lowered her head; if Farren wasn't on high-alert she would have missed the subtle movement.

"My wife is eager to have our girl home. It is nothing personal Farren, we just need this done." An excuse for his Queen's behaviour but not a denial of what would happen should she refuse. Farren removed her eyes from the Queen and watched as the King searched her face. Whether it was for fear, anger, or a straight dismissal she did not know, but she unfurled her fists and slowly nodded with a dejected sigh. A grin returned to the King's face and he clapped his hands together. "Wonderful! My guard will be able to guide you through the Realm. We are sure of who took our daughter and he is not shy about where he resides. He broke our laws, Farren, he broke the treaty without triggering our guards. If you save our daughter we will discuss you joining our forces."

Her stomach turned once again, "when do I leave?"

If she managed to beat a soul-less, demonic creature who snuck in and out of the Human Realm without anyone noticing she would be permitted to join the King's Guard. The Kayei Realm was to be her Trial, and she wanted to argue against it. Something akin to sympathy shone in the King's kind eyes and he braced his hands on her shoulders. The informality alone made her eyes water.

"Two weeks, that should give you enough time to recover and train as best as you can." *Training.* Intensive training was required and not just in combat. She needed to know the different types of magic the Kayei might use to kill her, and how she might avoid it. She needed to know the terrain, the plant-life, and animals: both predator and prey. Then there were her ribs: if she were train them too harshly they would take longer to heal which meant performing her Trial severely handicapped. What she told Adrastos was not a lie because training with them bound tightly was possible, but that did not mean it was not also a detriment. Her mind spun but she nodded once again as she swallowed back the nausea. The Rulers dismissed her and returned to hosting.

Throughout the evening she pushed down the shock and smiled and made small talk, mainly with Adrastos. She watched as Argen drank glass after glass of wine; he drank so much his feet were unstable beneath him. The Commander was broken from his loud laughter after the King clapped his hands. The room went silent save for the occasional hiccup, and the band folded their instruments into their laps. Farren leaned against the far wall, narrowed eyes on the bejewelled King and Queen. Dutiful and fearless guards stood beside their Rulers.

"My wonderful guests, thank you all for being here." A light chatter followed the King's greeting. "It is time I finally told you why you are all here." Farren's breath halted, she was in no position to be introduced as the King's new saviour. "It has been brought to my attention that there are men in my Guard who think it funny to prey on those weaker than them. I do not care whether they are stationed in the Capital or if they are stationed on the Northern border, they represent this Kingdom. Each guard is to uphold their duty to me, to my Queen, and to my people. This duty is a simple one, I think you will all agree," he waited for a sea of nods, "loyalty, dignity and trust, it is not so fantastical that I ask this of my guards, but there are some –I shall not name names- who thought they knew better than their duty, who thought they were working for me and not against me..." He trailed off as he sighed dramatically. "Seven guards upon one civilian is not okay and that is why we are here, and celebrating."

Farren's brow quirked upward, a glass of wine half-way to her lips. Adrastos sipped his at her side, his attention not on the King like everybody else but on her. Rorke stood in the doorway with a deep frown and his arms folded across his chest. Neither men were particularly pleased with their King's speech but it was the unadulterated shock on her face that kept their eyes on her. She braced herself for whatever else His Majesty had to say, "because we have a fantastic Commander in our midst. No matter how well trained a Commander is, there are some who would betray him, some who would break the trust every guard should have with one another. Incidents such as these should be dealt with professionally and in this case, they were. It was dealt with by a man who not only reported his guard's breach of duty, but he saved a young woman's life doing it." Farren thought she would be sick. "She was battered and bruised, nearly killed but the Commander did the right thing and contacted Adrastos. We may have some coals in the mine but let us not forget about our diamonds. This particular diamond is none other than Argen Bray, and we are here tonight to celebrate his bravery and his selflessness. Thank you, Argen, for being a true, upstanding man."

Applause filled the room as the King raised his glass. Argen received pats on the back, chants of his name and praise. A smile filled his lips and the wine he drank earlier made it harder for him to thank them in a more succinct manner. There was not enough wine in the world that would allow Farren to forget the sheer frustration she felt at that moment. The laugh that escaped her was short and vicious, to think she thought the King of Altin would throw a ball in her honour. She had half a mind to ask him why he did not send Argen to fetch his daughter and not her. No, her teeth clenched, he would not lose a guard as 'brave and selfless' as Argen to the other Realm.

Blue fabric flew behind her as Farren rushed from the ballroom. There was no time for her to wait for Argen to stumble over to her; everything she ate and drank churned uncomfortably in her stomach. Nobles and servants parted from her speeding form. There was no time to apologise when she trampled over a Lady's foot. Her indignant yell followed her down a flight of stairs at the far end of a corridor. There was no map or muscle memory to guide her but she ran. If the dust which floated in the air was any indication, the stairwell had not been used in months, possibly years. It did not stop Farren from falling to her knees and returning the food she ate.

The cold followed Farren from her village to the Capital. Frost covered the grassy courtyard but she paid it no mind as her boots crushed the blades beneath her in an attempt not to be late. It took ten minutes to find her way around the maze-like corridors and multiple staircases –including the one she threw up in the night before- until she found the garden and then the Western courtyard. Multiple courtyards with no signs... the Captain would surely scold her for being late. When she spotted the figure stood with his arms folded and chin raised in the middle of the garden she pushed her legs to go faster. Visible puffs of air flew from her mouth when she stopped in front of him. A ragged apology followed but he made no comment. When the breath finally returned to a steady rhythm she stood tall and pushed a few flyaway hairs behind her.

"Remove your sword." She gripped the handle and pulled but before she unsheathed it fully he stopped her. "Remove the belt from your person. You won't need it today." The belt slipped through her fingers and onto the frosty ground. His own was removed and he threw it next to hers. Like water, his body moved fluidly; his feet slid into a comfortable stance and he raised his fists in front of his face. Both his hands were covered in black leather gloves whilst his hair was pulled high atop his head in a bun. That allowed her

113

to see the sun shine off of his cheekbones whilst his eyes darted over her form which had yet to move away from her fallen sword. "Hit me."

"Pardon?"

"The Commander taught you hand-to-hand combat, yes?" She nodded. "Then show me what he taught you." A smirk crept onto her face and she copied his stance. The bindings that covered her ribs were so tight she thought her lungs would burst from her mouth but it allowed her to move freely. The occasional twinge shot through her but the pain medication Soter and the Healer gifted her were true blessings. She lunged. One punch and he grabbed her wrist with a speed that made her mouth fall open. His own injury did not slow him down. "The Kayei will be quicker than that," he pushed her back to her starting position, "again."

They carried on like that for half an hour before she finally landed a punch. Adrastos and Argen were in two completely different categories. The Commander lacked speed and a sharp eye, whilst Adrastos moved before she thought of where to land her next kick. Two hours in and both she and Adrastos breathed heavily. Farren braced her palms against her knees and stared wide eyed at the grass beneath her. The Captain stared up at the brightened sky whilst his chest heaved. One of his hands were braced around his injured thigh. The sound of their breaths were broken by a string of giggles. Two Ladies on their way to who-knows-where descended the garden steps but paused at the sight of the worn out duo. Their giggles turned to whispers and Farren straightened with a wince. Their faces were blurred due to the distance but there was no longer a chipper giggle in their voices when they spied Farren. It was as her eyes settled on the women, hands on her hips instead of her knees, that they scurried down the steps and out of sight.

Adrastos chuckled and Farren turned her gaze to him, "is everyone going to treat me like a sideshow attraction?"

The Captain shrugged but the look in his eyes answered for her: everyone knew who she was, Argen's loud gob from the night before made sure of that. It would have been better if they knew she was under the King's orders instead of the frail woman who was saved by the great Argen Bray. The more she thought about the Royal's plan for her, the hotter her blood boiled. It was inhumane and cruel, it was near impossible and they knew that, but she *would* go and she *would* succeed. She would not fall to a group of overpowered men and women who wanted to play games with a human Princess. That said, the odds were not in her favour -her spine straightened and she clicked her neck- if they weren't in her favour then she would have to even them out. With that thought she smirked and shifted into a defensive position. Adrastos rolled his eyes but swung his fist and they continued their session.

After four hours Farren's lungs wanted to collapse. Her ribs screamed at her, the muscles in her arms shook and her feet were covered in blisters. Oh she would feel that session the next day. Despite the aches and pains, Farren smiled at Adrastos who was drenched in sweat. His hair was still tied high on his head but strands fell over his shoulder as he tried to breathe as deeply as possible. They both sat on the sodden grass whilst the sun tried to peak through the clouds so Farren closed her eyes.

"I'm surprised," Adrastos started, "that you haven't asked me which guard is taking you into the Kayei's Realm."Adrastos bent to sheath his sword into his belt and she cracked open an eye.

"I didn't think you knew."

He rolled his eyes with a smile and kicked her sword toward her. "If one of my guards is going to go traipsing into a dangerous Realm filled with magic, I'm going to know about it."

"Thanks for the reminder." She blew out a swirl of breath. "So... who is it?"

"It's up to his Majesty but it will either be myself or Rorke, you know, my Second in Command who adores long conversations?" That triggered a bout of laughter and her arms gave way when she flung her head back. The sound had a couple of blue tits flying away and Adrastos laughed with her. Her arms wobbled as they pressed against the grass and she was on her feet despite the slip of the frost. The tremor of her fingers did not stop the quick way she looped her belt back through her trousers and adjusted her sword against her hip. Adrastos watched her every move with calculating eyes. "That's enough for today, breakfast is calling and you look like you could use some." Just the thought of buttered breakfast pastries and bacon made her mouth water. Adrastos gestured toward the garden stairs and stepped to her side.

As they walked side by side she asked, "is this normal, what the King has asked?" He glanced at her as they passed through the Castle door. "What I'm asking is: has he asked his guards to go to the Night Creature Realm before –or the Kayei Realm, I mean?"

They passed more guards the deeper they walked into the castle. Some wore armour and others wore casual clothing similar to her own, but there was definitely no mistaking the guards from the nobles. At the end of the corridor Adrastos steered them down towards the door to the canteen. Forks against plates and low voices trickled toward their approaching forms and the smell of food brought Farren's tired body back to life.

He shook his head, "no, but I imagine that is why the King offered Rorke the job. He is one of the few guards that has been there and survived. I do not know if it is worth him going back, however."

Before Farren told him that was the least helpful thing he might have said, Argen's form appeared. It was too early for an argument so she nodded to Adrastos before she grabbed a plate from the table by the door. Food lined the middle of the long-stretch tables: porridge, toast, butters, jams, and meat-filled pastries. Bacon and sausage piled on dishes too, and she breathed deeply whilst her mouth salivated. Men were scattered along the benches, some held conversations whilst others looked so tired they would fall into their breakfasts. One man who sat alone, book in hand with a spoon of porridge halfway to his lips was Soter. He wore simple trousers and a shirt, the cufflinks matched those of his first outfit and his hair was wild. The green of his outfit was bright against the dull greys, blacks and whites of the guard uniforms. Farren's own outfit was a charcoal black, so, like a boat in the dark and Soter was her lighthouse, she walked over, plate in hand and sat beside him. Without tearing his eyes from his book he asked, "did your training go well?"

There was no point in telling him about the bruises that started to form from her relationship with the ground. "It did."

"What about your injuries? How are you feeling?"

She pushed her hair from her face. "Everything aches but my ankle is much better, thank you, and as you can see, my eyesight has been fully restored." She smiled.

His eyes flicked to her face, danced across her features and returned to his book. "That is good to hear. I was worried, the Captain does not pull his punches."

"No he most certainly does not."

After her smile moved from Soter to the food, she piled a large amount onto her plate. Once she was satisfied with her plateful she dug in. It was easy to ignore the glances from the guards a few seats away as she primly cut her bacon and chewed slowly. The urge to stuff her face like an animal starved rushed through her but there were too many eyes and she did not plan on making a fool of herself on her first day. The pastries she picked up with her hands, but she used a napkin to wipe off the powdered sugar rather than licking it off her fingers. Every movement was soft which was a stark contrast to her previous activities.

Soter watched as she stabbed another rasher of bacon and turned to him. "I've been meaning to talk to you."

"Oh?"

She nodded as she chewed. "I wanted to thank you for saving my life."

"How did I do that?" A smirk was hidden behind his book.

The pendant felt light against her chest but remained hidden beneath her clothes. There was no warmth or glowing light but the night she sagged against the Church tree flashed in her mind. Her hand drifted to the place on her chest where the pendant sat and she swallowed. "I forgot to mention it back in your caravan but the pendant you gave me, it was the reason I didn't freeze to death behind that Church." Her voice was no louder than a whisper and with the chatter around them nobody paid their conversation any mind. Pity sat in his eyes but it was gone as quickly as it arrived and she drained her glass of milk.

He lowered his book but a small smile remained. "That is a very dangerous accusation to make." He glanced at where her hand once sat. "That pendant is nothing more than that, a pendant." The glass slid back onto the table and she furrowed her brows because *no*, that pendant was not just a pendant. *It will keep you warm.* Why say that when he gave her the gift? 'Warm' is a very specific word, not 'happy' and not 'pretty'. Her eyes narrowed and he continued to eat his porridge.

"Well if you won't take my thanks for that, then I wanted to thank you again for healing my injuries, and for the clothes." She gestured down the green shirt that had been cleaned since her travel.

"I told you," he chuckled, "you never have to thank me." There was a sliver of silence where he watched her chew her breakfast. "I heard what happened at the ball last night." His eyes returned to his book when she stopped mid-chew.

"What about it?"

"I heard that the King made a speech dedicated to Argen, how is he?"

Farren ran her tongue across her teeth and stabbed at her food "Hung-over probably and giddy with the honour of the King's praise." She rolled her eyes.

"And the King? I saw him speak to you."

"You were there last night? I didn't see you," she slightly pouted.

With his book closed he replied, "I was in and out of meetings, but I saw you with the King," he trailed off as he awaited her reply.

"Honestly." Her laugh was near forced. "He asked a favour of me and there's not much I can do about it." She fully turned toward him, legs either side of the bench. "What meetings were you in?" There was a glint in her eye when she asked.

"Those on behalf of my court."

A Court... There was only one court in Altin –the King's- and two more on the Continent. The clothes he wore did not match the Continental attire nor did the Continent allow the peddling of magic. Her eyes shot to his- *not a Human court then*. Not only was he a Magic User but someone – something- powerful enough to cross through the Veil. The King mentioned something about Soter's 'Master' which meant it was likely he knew about Soter's magical abilities, about the Kayei that held his leash. A Magic User in the castle forced her to take a deep breath but she did not gawk, she did not shudder, she did nothing but stare with a tilt of her head like a puppy dog. How had she not noticed before: the sharper features, the slightly pointed canines that were hidden behind his kind smiles, eyes that were too old and too *other* to be human. The green of his irises leaked into the white of his eyes like ink on parchment. It was subtle, no-doubt a reason why he was able to walk around the Human lands unscathed but it was there and it was proof enough.

"A Kayei court?" She whispered.

Soter sat back and his smile faded. Their eyes bored into one another before the noise of laughter from the other side of the room broke through their stares. There were too many people with swords that could overhear his response, so Soter moved first, his eyes shifted from hers to the book face down on his lap. The table was far too sticky to put a book down. As he fell back into the words on the pages, Farren shifted so that both her legs sat beneath the table. Her final pastry became cold but she picked at it anyway, her stomach finally quiet and sated. Soter was kept in the corner of her vision as she ate but the silence that fell over them as they continued their respective activities was broken by the thud of two boots across from her. She nearly threw her pastry when she saw who it was. Soter went still as death beside her as Argen slid onto the bench and opened his mouth. The guard did not acknowledge the Magician's existence.

"Move," that voice did not belong to Argen.

Farren's eyes slid to the towering form behind her former friend. Said friend twisted and gaped at Rorke who held an empty plate in front of him. He wore a white tunic tucked into grey trousers; there was no sign of his armour much like many of the men in the canteen. The sleeved-tunic was pushed up to his elbows -a sign that he had yet to step outside- which revealed a smattering of scars. Argen swallowed, and like a man without a death wish, he scurried out of Rorke's way. He didn't so much as look back at her. Rorke plonked down in the empty space and she opened her mouth to thank him but the look he shot her as he reached for the bacon closed it again. *Not a morning person, good to know.* The thought made her snort against the rim of her second drink.

Farren kept herself busy by picking at the pastry crumbs on her plate. Her legs ached from her training session and she wanted nothing more than to crawl back into bed and sleep until the next one. Yet, as she picked up her drink, Rorke looked up from the bowl of porridge he procured and put his spoon down. Her eyes widened, she met his gaze, and she put down her glass. Her attention brought forth his voice, "the King wants to see us after breakfast."

The food in her stomach turned to lead. Despite the fact she wasn't sure whether or not she could face the King so soon after being 'offered' a mission, she nodded. Rorke took another mouthful of porridge as though he had not just unsettled her to the core. She removed her eyes from him and returned them to her nearly-cleared plate. Soter shifted next to her, and it was the first movement he made since Argen appeared. The page he had been on moments ago, the start of a new chapter, stared up at her. She flicked her eyes to the profile of the Magician. His lip quirked upward at the feel of her eyes on him and he purposefully lifted his hand slowly and turned the page. Observant but not entirely stealthy.

Rorke tapped the table with his spoon and her attention was stolen by the stern-faced Second who gestured toward the door. The lead in her stomach remained but she forced her sore limbs to move as she swung her leg over the bench and followed Rorke. The eyes in the back of her head could have been any of the guards but she peaked over her shoulder to find Soter's unwavering stare. The smile on her face was genuine as she gave him a small wave and continued to walk behind Rorke.

More people milled in the halls as the morning stretched on and Farren pulled her spine straight, hands folded behind her back. She was the picture of an obedient trainee whilst Rorke looked like a honed warrior. Whispers followed them down corridors as people spied the third most powerful man in the castle. His eyes stared straight ahead; he never strayed from the path in front of him. There were no glances to the pretty ladies, no nods of acknowledgement to the gentlemen, he just continued to walk toward the throne room. Farren swallowed but she was so focused on the gossip around her that she nearly collided with Rorke's back.

The first thing she saw was blood, lots of blood. A pool of it trickled toward their boots but upon closer inspection she realised it wasn't *only* blood in that pool. Dark whirls and swirls curled in between the red. The light shied away from the liquid and the smell made Farren recoil. As her eyes trailed upward she felt her heart stutter. A man stood before them with a blood covered, freshly sharpened knife and a deranged smile on his face. He was completely naked and the dark liquid –blood with oil or something else entirely- covered his entire being because those were bodies at his feet, three of them. Each of their throats were slashed and two no longer had their arms. The other was slit crotch to collarbone and his eyes were wide open, but those eyes were yellow, slit through with black. That was when she spotted the slightly pointed canines and graceful features mixed with something that was so innately human. Half-breed Kayei. Oh how she wished she never ate breakfast. Her eyes continued to drift over the bodies and then to the once white wall behind them. More inky-blood covered it in deliberate slopes, letters and runes, a mixture of languages and the ramblings of a mad man. She read what she could but the blood dripped and dried in odd places which made the letters hard to read.

"You!"

The bloody knife was pointed at her. Rorke's arm sat between them. She glanced at the warrior angled in front of her and forced a smile on her face as she looked back at the man covered in blood. He was 100% human and shook like a leaf. "Yes?"

The man blinked and his tremors paused for a moment as though her voice broke through whatever attack he experienced, then they returned as though ice itself had gripped onto his bones. "Bring me the Princess!"

Farren scoffed, "no."

"She is a danger to this Realm! Such an abomination cannot walk these halls! She must be sacrificed to Goddess Griselda!" Farren's eardrums rang with the level of his voice.

Sacrifices to Griselda? Those were stories parents told their children to keep them in line around the holidays. When Griselda fell in the First Great War, humans sacrificed their young and beautiful to keep her happy, to keep her protection. A load of nonsense thought up by the Churches but there were some who believed Griselda needed to be sated. They often ended up as mad as the man before her. It was why many Churches around the country were abandoned.

Rorke decidedly had enough of the conversation, glared and stepped forward. The man curved his knife upward and- he was disarmed in a second and the knife scattered across the hall. The crazy man rushed forward and Farren shifted her weight to grab him but Rorke pinned him beneath his knees with a scowl and curse on his lips. She barely saw him move before the man spluttered beneath him. Rorke called for more guards who rushed down the corridor, their armour shuffled up and down their chest as they ran. Two guards hauled the man from the floor whilst Rorke stood next to her to watch as the man —who continued to splutter- was dragged toward the dungeon.

Rorke rubbed his temple whilst she uttered, "that was far too much excitement for a morning."

The further down the corridor the crazy man found himself, the louder he screamed. Farren winced but stepped around Rorke toward the jumbled, unreadable message. Her brows furrowed as she stooped to her haunches, her boots an inch from the dark liquid. It was warm beneath her fingers and thicker than blood. Against her pale skin which she dipped in the liquid, it looked near black. The metallic smell in the air intensified as she rubbed it between her fingers.

"What is it? The liquid I mean. It's not just blood and last time I checked the Kayei-" Rorke shushed her so she lowered her voice. "Their blood is red, not black. Right?"

Rorke shook his head. "It was likely added after the murders."

"But why? And why kill half-breeds?"

Rorke's hand wrapped around her upheld wrist with a face as hard as stone. His eyes followed a thick globule that trailed down her hand; once it touched his skin he pulled her to her feet. She steadied herself as he forced their hands above their heads for a second. The liquid flew from her hand with a flick of her arm but she grimaced at the stain it left behind. Rorke sighed and handed her a sweat rag from his pocket. She wiped the blood from her hand and handed it back to him with a 'thank you.' When he pocketed the rag and they started to walk, he said, "these puritans are crazy. They want to impress a dead woman so badly that they would kill whoever they want."

They climbed a flight of stairs and found themselves in the long stretch of hall before the throne room, but there was something else that snagged at her mind. "How did nobody see him do it?" With a hand on her elbow, Rorke stopped. His brows were furrowed as he looked at her. The nobles they passed before the scene had not been fazed from their usual milling and gossiping nor had she heard a scream from the canteen. There was no disruption around the castle; the guards only looked confused when they were called to action. The metallic smell of blood did not hit her until it trickled toward her as though- she shot her eyes to Rorke's. "Is there any way to check for a barrier, some sort of," she made a blocking motion between them, "a shield?"

"What makes you say that?"

"There was a tent at my village's market, it used something to keep the inside warm but it did not seep out into the square. It was only in that small space so I thought that maybe it could be the same for sight and smell... what? Why do you look like that?" Something flashed in his eyes and he marched them toward the throne room without a word.

Sat on his throne was the King of Altin. He wore a ring on each finger and a pale grey robe atop a suit of white. His golden crown was perfectly straight as was his spine. A scroll curled against the back of his hand as he read its contents with a finger against his lips. The Queen was nowhere to be seen and the other guards were silent statues against the walls.

The King glanced at them, took one look at Rorke's face and leaned forward. "What happened?"

Rorke bowed and she did the same, her hand braced against her side and eyes on his white slippers. Three heartbeats later and Rorke walked until his boots touched the dais but she remained rooted to the spot as he whispered something to the King with lowered eyes. Farren shuffled on her feet as she watched their hushed conversation. Once the one minute –or maybe it was two minutes- conversation ended Rorke walked back over to her and mimicked her stance: hands clasped behind his back and chin raised. He didn't look at her as he faced the King but his jaw was tense, his fingers curled tightly around each other. It made the King lower the scroll to his lap and lean back, hands on the arms of the throne.

"Your Majesty, with your permission we would like to perform a few tests of a," Rorke trailed off as he searched for the right word, "a few tests of a magical nature."

Farren risked a wide-eyed glance at Rorke but kept her mouth shut. Magical tests were not exactly the norm in Altin. It was a surprise he could even utter the word 'magical' in the throne room. She wondered what his people would say if they heard the King was condoning magic to be performed in the White Castle. Soter's tent came to mind and the way Argen restrained himself from demolishing it, she swallowed; there would be a riot in the Capital if word got out, so she braced for the King to demand Rorke watch his words, but instead a sigh escaped the old ruler. The King scratched his beard and nodded. There was a shadow across his face; the look of a man who had to resort to unpleasant methods covered him. Rorke proceeded to turn to the guards who flanked the doors and ordered them to retrieve Soter from the canteen. If he was not there then they were to find him by whatever means. Supposedly, Soter was the only magic user in the building.

"And we are sure he wasn't a part of the attack in the first place?" the King asked.

Farren spoke before Rorke, "he was in the canteen with me since half past nine this morning. The corpses were fresh, the writing on the walls only just written, and there was a manic man holding a bloodied weapon above them. All these facts point-"

Rorke's voice cut through hers, "His Majesty understands." She clamped her mouth shut with speed and narrowed her eyes at Rorke. "The barrier was the only magical element, and it is possible that someone like him could have performed it from afar." There was no mention of mysterious liquid in the blood. The King remained silent, hand in his beard. Soter was always a suspect to them. There was no-doubt in Farren's mind that any

127

murder, magical or otherwise, he would have made the list. The frustration the two men felt at asking help from Soter was immense but she ignored it and curled her hands behind her back. Soter was nothing but kind, warm. To suggest he had any connection with the naked maniac sat uncomfortably with her. The roll of her eyes was forced forward. "We don't want any tests to be performed so close to the thrones." Rorke glanced at Farren. "We can use your room," at the indignant horror on her face he added, "can't we, Farren?"

She had half a mind to kick him in the gut and storm out but she knew that was the only accessible option: she was nobody, she was new and she had no position to ruin so she nodded and kept her tongue firmly behind her teeth.

"I shall ask that you act as a tether as well, Farren." The King informed her and she tilted her head slightly with a furrowed brow. "It is someone who Soter will link to. This will stop him performing any unsavoury tricks and it will mean that you can test each barrier without any adverse affects." The King smiled gently.

So she said, "of course, who knows, it might be fun."

The more Farren stared at Rorke the more he reminded her of stone. They stood outside the throne room doors, backs against the wall and arms folded across their chests but nothing on his face changed, his eyes were a solid weight on the corridor. "Why are you staring at me so intently?" Farren jumped at the sound of his voice.

"No reason, sorry."

He shrugged, "it's fine, I just assumed you wanted to ask me something."

Farren tapped her boot against the floor. "I do have one question: what do you plan to do with the insane man?"

Rorke snorted, "he's been taken to the dungeon and I plan to speak to him later today."

"Why do you think he did it? And what does the Princess have to do with it? Do you think he knows she's missing?" she whispered.

Rorke flicked his eyes to hers where incredulity shone. "You can ask him whatever you want later."

With her shoulder pressed to the wall she grinned. "Really?"

"I have never seen someone look so happy to visit the dungeons before."

Rorke's attention was stolen from her and he nudged her foot with his. Farren lifted her eyes from the guard's boot to the figure down the hall. The red-head raised his hand with a small smile. Soter held a book in his other hand and once she waved back she and Rorke pushed off from the wall. They walked in sync until they reached Soter. The muscles in her shoulders relaxed and she unclenched her hands as a sense of calm rolled over her.

Rorke stepped forward and spoke first "there was an attack in the centre of the castle," Soter's head pushed back. "Three half-breeds are dead and there was some indecipherable symbols or letters written on the walls."

"What state were the bodies in?" Soter asked.

"Necks sliced open, one split naval to throat, two had their arms missing." Rorke rattled off like it was a shopping list and they started to walk down the corridors toward her room. Rorke flanked the rear whilst she walked alongside Soter.

She craned her neck to face the guard behind her. "Let's not forget the fact that he thought he could take you on."

"And you," Rorke chuckled.

"I should have pointed my sword at him, see how he likes it," Farren muttered.

"He threatened you?" Soter's voice was soft and that was worry in his eyes so she shrugged.

"Rorke handled it before I could put him on his a-"

Rorke cleared his throat and she hummed but Soter added, "that does not sound like simple ritual killings. The Books of Griselda do not mention the removal of arms, unless of course this is a new form of ritual sacrifice."

"I'm sorry." Farren paused her movements and held her hand up. "'the Books of Griselda?' What are those?"

Rorke rolled his eyes and answered before Soter could, "they are history books about Griselda and what her life was like, how she died and why she created humans."

"Some say there are hidden messages in the pages but mostly it is used by humans to justify killing people."

Rorke stared blankly at the back of Soter's head. "Unless those books talk about murdering half-breeds then they are useless to us." They reached her door and Soter stepped aside to let her place the key in the lock. The men behind her stared at each other. They were a painting of light and dark, two worlds collided, of elegance and brute force. She entered the room first and they followed, then the three of them stood in the open space before her bed. "We believe that the man was using a barrier to hide from everyone."

Farren nodded and continued his thought, "it wasn't until Rorke and I walked closer to the scene that the blood and," she screwed up her nose, "and the bodies were visible."

Soter nodded slowly and opened the book in his hand. Runes were displayed on the front and he read the words quickly. As soon as he was finished he looked at Rorke and his immaculate eyebrow raised. "Am I to do this without a tether?"

Rorke answered, "no," then nodded to Farren, "she'll be helping you."

Soter could not help but ask, "is that because she was there or because your King does not value her as much as he values his guards?"

Rorke stepped forward, arms uncrossed and face blank once again, but a red-faced Farren moved between them. "Shall we test these barriers?"

Soter curled his wrist delicately and outstretched his arm toward her. When her hand entwined with his the blood rushed to her head and the room brightened slightly. It was like a firework went off behind her eyes until it settled back to normal. The hairs on the back of her neck rose and she flicked her eyes to those entwined hands. Light flared around them and the world rippled. The first barrier reminded her of the Veil, it was translucent but swelled with colours as it arched over them to form a dome and continued higher until it reached the ceiling. A barrier that high would have been able to hide the scribbles on the wall and the bodies on the floor but-

"I can see the colours," Rorke commented.

The barrier changed into a thicker, shorter one. Rorke shook his head and it changed again so she removed her hand from Soter's and stood back. Neither she nor Rorke could see the barrier but there was the ripple of Soter's figure beyond it. He opened the book in his hand and read a few lines and the barrier solidified further.

"Walk toward it," Soter called out.

It held as she walked forward, a pressure on her chest and forehead, "we couldn't hear anything at the time either, but I honestly don't understand: the killer is a Puritan, they aren't known for being pro-magic."

"That's where the Books of Griselda become hazy. A passage within states that a person should 'do what they must' to ensure Griselda is satisfied. Then there is a later passage about how she hated killing innocent people."

"Surely if Griselda was so against magic, they would not use it?"

"Griselda was against her people being slaughtered," Rorke said. She looked between him and Soter but nothing else was argued as Soter produced another barrier. Her hand fell back into his and they continued to form walls. One after another they held against Rorke, but finally with deep concentration on his face, Soter produced a barrier that shimmered then settled around him. It was wide enough to protect three dead bodies and a maniac, tall enough that the stains on the walls would have been covered and when she released Soter to walk toward it, the shimmer faded to reveal Rorke stood there with a raised brow.

"That was a reactive barrier. It was tailored to only allow certain people to be able to break it. I touched you so I was able to tailor it around you, but most Magic Users would require something of yours, namely hair or recently worn clothing."

Farren's nose crinkled at the thought of her dirty laundry in the hands of a maniac. "I didn't recognise him and my room was locked." There was no time for her to mingle with anyone at the castle or to speak to anyone that wasn't in the King's Guard. She had been with Adrastos, then Soter, then Rorke that morning, and the night before she was preoccupied. Her eyes drifted to Rorke. "Did you recognise him?"

"No, nor did he seem to recognise either of us."

"Soter," Farren started, "is there any way for someone to use that barrier without an item or piece of the person?"

The red-head tapped his leg in thought. "Not unless he had a deep well of power himself. Let me attempt something else." He gently grabbed her hand and lifted his free one in front of him which is when he recounted some words from his book. The same shimmer of the previous barrier soared above them and quickly turned solid. It settled at Farren's back so she stepped closer to Soter's side to allow him to continue his incantation. His hand tightened on hers and the green of his eyes glowed brightly when he completed the spell. The air itself tingled with magic, so much so that she thought she felt it on her tongue, but her main focus was on the swirl of colour and light in his gaze, pure mesmerisation on her face.

Rorke spoke, "nothing is happening," his voice was muffled.

"That is the point," Soter said but the sound bounced back toward him. Two seconds after he spoke, the barrier fizzled away and both she and Soter were visible again. Rorke blinked and stepped forward, his hand outstretched to meet only air.

"I couldn't see the two of you," he informed them.

"Or hear us apparently," Farren added.

Soter loosened his hold on her hand but did not let go when he spoke, "that was a timed barrier. It is more complex but can be done. It does mean that the man wanted to be found eventually."

"Or he didn't even know that there was a barrier. He could have an accomplice," Rorke said pointedly.

Soter smirked and stepped forward. "Are you insinuating something, Rorke?"

Farren tugged the Magician back to her side gently. "No he is not. There could have been an accomplice but there is more than one Magic User in this Capital, and no-doubt in the castle itself." Rorke raised an eyebrow and opened his mouth to disagree but she continued. "The only way we can figure out what the motive was and if the Princess really was the target is by talking to the maniac, Soter," she turned to him, "do you have anything that we can scan him with, like a magic tracer or something?"

Rorke snorted into his hand and Soter looked ready to burst into laughter. "The only thing that can see magic is a Kayei." Soter let a chuckle escape. "I'm sorry."

'So, you?' She wanted to ask but like he read her mind he subtly shook his head and flicked his eyes to Rorke. The King might know what he was, but that did not extend to the rest of the guard unit. As far as they were concerned –just like Argen was- Soter was simply a Magic User.

During their mini mental conversation, Rorke continued to compose himself with his fist raised to his lips. She shrugged and let go of Soter's hand. What she failed to notice was the way his fingers twitched back toward her as she moved toward the door. That was when a knock sounded against it. She pressed a hand to her chest but opened it to reveal Argen. The immediate frustration on her face nearly broke Rorke's efforts to remain calm.

"His Majesty asked me to retrieve-" Argen stopped mid-sentence as he spied the two men in her room. His eyes drifted from Rorke to Soter and then slowly made their way back to Farren, who stood with her hand around the door handle. The frown on her face and slightly narrowed eyes greeted him. Soter opened his book and started to read, a hand on his hip nonchalantly.

However, Rorke moved around Farren and braced a hand on the doorframe. "Is the King looking for us?"

Argen nodded. "You and Farren, yes."

Rorke returned the nod and gestured out of the room. Argen had yet to move but the clearing of Rorke's throat did the trick as he let them past. Soter followed, eyes on the pages of his book and not on the flabbergasted look on Argen's face.

"What were the three of you doing in Farren's room?" he asked as she locked the door.

"Talking," Rorke replied bluntly. That was when he, Farren and Soter started to walk. Argen followed behind, his eyes still slightly wide at the thought of the two men in Farren's room. She made sure that she kept her eyes forward and hands at her sides whilst Soter read his book and Rorke marched them toward the throne room.

The King waited for the doors to the throne room to click shut, his guards on the other side alongside Soter who bid Farren and Rorke goodbye. Argen was ordered on another errand, one that was usually beneath a Commander but he accepted it with a quick bow. That left Farren stood beside Rorke in front of the King once again. If the lines on his face and the tense state of his shoulders were anything to go by, it was a conversation she didn't want to have.

"Farren," the King spoke, "I appreciate that you and Rorke may have been in the middle of something but I thought it best that I brief you on what happened." He smiled softly. "Before I send you to retrieve my daughter."

'I don't want to know, it's bad enough I have to go into the Kayei Realm with one person as my backup, do I really need to know how or why they kidnapped the Princess? Will it change your decision to send us?'

"She was in the garden on her usual walk, the guards say that a shadow simply washed over her and she was gone." Rorke's jaw feathered whilst the King relayed the information. "There is no doubt in my mind that it was a Kayei who took her. There is a long list of those who would want revenge against my crown, against my Kingdom, but there are few who can get through the Veil without being detected."

"You mentioned there was a King who broke the Accords, Your Majesty?" she asked.

He forced a chuckle, "this is not the first time he has done so, but he has always evaded justice. This time he has crossed a line." The King clenched a hand in his beard. "My daughter is not a toy to be played with." When she stared at him expectantly he sighed, "his name is Nero, we once thought he was an ally, our strongest connection to the other Realm, but then he goes and does something like this," he trailed off with narrowed eyes.

Rorke visibly shivered next to her. Whatever he went through across the Veil... She imagined claws and wings, and darkness, and magic that tore flesh from bone but then her mind rested on the beautiful cards and scarves in Soter's tent, the way it drew her in and made her curiosity peak. There was the warmth that kept her alive in the woods, the grateful eyes of the Night Creature she healed: the pearlescent scales, the large paws and its snout as it crouched in the snow. Such beautiful things surrounded by so much dangerous stigma. The smart thing was to be scared, and she supposed she *was* but the thought of the beauty and mystery that awaited her made her heart leap and something akin to excitement filled her chest. The mixture of emotions must have been on her face because Rorke stepped closer to her and whispered, "don't try to make sense of it; you'll spend your entire life doing it."

The King spoke again, "the worst thing you can do is trust them, because if they get a whiff that you are of my stead then they will do anything to eat, sell or sleep with you. If in doubt, listen to Rorke." That unsettled the excitement.

The guard nodded. "My job is to make sure that you get the Princess home safely which means keeping you alive and stable."

Her pride deflated. She was capable of fighting, capable enough to stay stable in the face of danger, capable enough to fell two men in one go without thinking about it, but she kept her mouth shut and her fingers flexed. Rorke's eyes flicked to those fingers then her face. His pointed stare was ignored as the King looked at her with nothing but pity. Both Farren and

Rorke bowed, straightened, and walked toward the doors. As though they sensed her, the doors opened with the neutral-faced guards holding the handles. They did not look at her or Rorke as they breached the threshold into the hallway.

Once they were a safe distance from the throne room she asked, "should we not take a cloaking spell or trinket with us? We are going to need some extra protection, not that I doubt your abilities, I just do not fancy dyi-"

Rorke moved quickly. His arms quickly caged her against the wall. In her shock, her side barked in pain and her head collided with the stone. With her hands pressed against his chest, she blinked away the pain. Rorke's eyes darted up and down the corridor and then landed on her. Her own eyes widened and she forced her body to go slack lest the strain to her muscles worsened. As he roamed her face his gaze softened at the look of discomfort. The tips of his fingers brushed against her hair and he found the heat of her palms to be a comfort. With a deep breath, his palm spread across the stone and his head lowered. A headache formed at the base of her skull and the glare she focused on him whilst she rubbed her head was smouldering.

"You need to be careful what you say around the castle," he ground out, "if the wrong person heard you talking about *magic* you'd be dead before they could read you your rights."

Her voice was a whisper when she replied, "we just spent the day analysing magic and then spoke to the King about it, forgive me Rorke but it seems like it isn't as taboo as people want us to believe."

That was the wrong thing to say because his gaze turned to a glare, "it was necessary and His Majesty made sure that only a handful of people knew about today's activities. If anyone other than that handful heard your questions, not even the King could save you from the gallows."

"Doesn't he control who does and does not go to the gallows?" She raised a brow.

"He would be challenged and a revolution would occur if he didn't allow them to hang you."

"You think that a revolution would occur if the King decided not to hang a woman who asked a *question* about magic?" A deep sigh pushed his hand harder into the wall. His breath brushed her face as his large form deflated. The dark circles beneath his eyes were visible at that distance and he looked pale, like he hadn't slept properly in weeks. She herself sighed and ran her tongue along her teeth. "So, that's a 'no' on the protection charms?" She made sure to whisper the word 'charms.'

He removed himself from her person with a stiff nod and a feathered jaw. "Neither of us can use them, unless you want to end up like the man you plunged your dagger into the other day." There was a pause as he surveyed her form. "You need to make sure you can counter men bigger than you." She blinked rapidly at him. "You were slow to put your feet into the correct position and your hands were limp when they pressed against my chest." Everything he said was true and she felt her cheeks flare in embarrassment, especially when he grabbed one of those hands and flexed it against his pectoral. He tapped the back of her hand and she flexed it to push him away just like he wanted. When her fingers tensed he released her. "We will have a talk with the killer after dinner and I can let Captain Adrastos know that you need to work on your speed."

A nod and she turned and pushed stray strands from her face. With a short nod and another once over, he gave her a small wave and walked away. Where he trudged off to she didn't know so she stormed through the corridors. She smiled at those who watched her walk but kept her feet forward. She let her gut guide her down a similar corridor to the one her room was in but there were much less doors. The conversation she had with Rorke swirled in her mind as she followed the tug in her stomach until it dug into what felt like her soul. A sensation of calm encompassed her as she stood before a simple wooden door. It was painted black, standard for the King's guests. With no time to waste, she pounded against the wood. Luckily for her there were no prying eyes at that end of the castle so it wasn't until she heard the lock on the other side click open that she stopped her incessant knocking. Surprise filled Soter's eyes as he beheld her tense form.

"I have a favour to ask."

He said nothing but he opened his door wider. A large double bed and simple wooden bookcases filled the room. It was much smaller than her own; the King favoured his guards more than foreign correspondents then... or perhaps it was because Soter was from a Kayei court. Her nails dug into her palm but her grip loosened as she spied Elira sat on her perch by the window. A hoot sounded upon her arrival and the bird put a smile on Farren's face as she stepped into his room with another long breath.

Three words Farren used to describe the White Castle dungeons: dry, dingy, dark. It smelled of dust and perfume that attempted to hide the excrement. There was nothing pleasant that filled her senses as she followed Rorke down the stairs. The torch in his hand allowed them to watch their boots on the worn stone stairs whilst she kept a hand against the wall. The tips of his hair brushed the ceiling when he walked and the stairs may have been dark but they were not long. Once they reached the bottom, darkness stretched before them: an open chasm of torture. It opened as Rorke placed his torch into a bowl which lit up instantly. The flames caught against the line of oil along the top of the cells and soon illuminated the large room. It was a circular chamber and the ring of fire around it which allowed Farren to see the table and chairs sat in the middle, both old and worn metal. There was a loop around the table legs that were designed for shackles. Cells were piled upon cells and a set of stairs at the back of the chamber reached onto the higher levels. Luckily for her training-tired legs, the prisoner they were there to see was on the bottom level.

"How many people are here?" she asked.

"Not all of the cells are full."

"I'm not sure whether that is a comfort or not."

He grunted and they moved to the other side of the table and into the shadowed curve of the chamber. Whispers filtered from the cells above them, some in a language she didn't understand but the cell in front of her remained silent. Rorke walked up to the bars and tapped his fist against it once, twice. A shaking breath responded. The torchlight was bright enough that both their faces were visible to the prisoner as were the weapons at their sides. The sound of scrabbling reached her ears before the man from earlier that day flung himself forward. The chains around his ankles and wrists prevented him from reaching the bars but the whites of his eyes were visible, they practically glowed.

Rorke started the interrogation, "who are you? How did you get into the castle?"

The man tilted his head at an awkward angle, enough that it clicked. "Emmett," he paused, "this castle is not unsusceptible to bribery, you know?"

The Second scribbled down his answer on a short roll of parchment. "Why did you kill those people?"

"Not people," Emmett hissed, "abominations."

Farren's teeth clenched and she wrapped her hand around a bar. The insane grin was gone in an instant. He rushed forward again. Pieces of raw flesh poked from his wrists and legs as the chains dug into his skin. Without hesitation he pulled against its tether in the wall. He was granted clothes but they were filthy from the ground beneath him. The smell of unclean teeth and metal washed over her so she stepped back with a wince, her hand between her and the bar as though she could physically push away the smell and sight of him whilst he desperately tried to reach her. "Why sacrifice them to Griselda if they are abominations?"

"Better Kayei sacrifices than the lives of my own." That was pride on his face, insanity and pride.

"And what does the Princess have to do with these sacrifices?" Farren asked.

Emmett's lip lifted. "She is dangerous, an abomination. I was promised her, I was promised, she was to be mine to kill!"

She blinked, "did you just threaten to kill a Royal?"

"She'll murder you all, you would thank me, the whole world would thank me if I did it. She is not fit to breathe the air of this kingdom, and I just want to cleanse this place that is covered in *Kayei*." He pulled against his chains and one of his shoulders popped with the effort. Both Farren and Rorke braced a fist against their mouths at the sight. Yet, he kept pulling.

"You used magic when you sacrificed them." Rorke looked between the two of them. "Isn't that against your code?" *As much of a code as puritans could have.* Emmett smiled once more, or rather he bared his teeth and looked at her. Shadows danced across his face which made him seem more demon than human, a fact he would surely bury her for thinking. His head tilted to

142

the opposite shoulder, another click but there was no sign of pain on his face. "Opioids," Rorke answered her unspoken question.

Emmett went still and blinked. "It was necessary when dealing with sacrifices." He could either mean the Opioids or the magic. "I was under specific orders to make sure you don't interfere with her plans, but then I saw those Kayei and I," he chuckled darkly, "I let Griselda guide me."

Farren's brows furrowed. "And she guided you to kill people who are half of her species?"

"Watch your mouth," he growled.

Rorke braced a hand between her and the bars. "Who gave you those orders?"

"More importantly why order you to keep us away?" Farren added.

Emmett raised his finger to his nose and tapped it twice before he retreated back to his shadowy wall. "She's a vessel for Griselda's voice who has big plans for this castle."

"Is it your cult's agenda to kill the Princess?" Rorke nearly yelled through the bars.

"She is no Princess of ours."

Bone cracked, then the squelch of wet muscle and through the shadows they watched as Emmett slammed his head against the wall again, and again, and again, and again. Rorke scrabbled for the keys that hung at his side. Another crack sounded and Farren cursed. She pulled on the bars as though her sheer will and thin arms would tear them open. The shirt on her arms fell back against her bicep as she strained as hard as she could against the metal. Her subconscious screamed at her to stop being moronic but the need to stop Emmett's death coursed through her veins, namely her hands.

Rorke found the correct key, plunged it into the lock and twisted. That was blood which cascaded down the stone toward their boots. Emmett's skull was caved in, fragments of bone and matted hair hung from his corpse. It was an image that would be seared into her mind for a long time.

Farren broke the tense silence, "shall we take that as a confirmation?"

A grunt from Rorke. "We need to round up the Puritans a-"

"And hope they all don't find us boring enough to cave their skulls in."

Farren's pack weighed heavy on her shoulder as she carried it toward her horse with the items she borrowed from Soter buried beneath her spare clothes. The King supplied both her and Rorke with castle horses, both of them black and pure muscle. The gloss of their hair and neatly braided manes allowed the sunlight to bounce off the creatures. Farren pushed her own braid behind her and ran a hand down her mare. Despite the less-than-intimidating name, Petal was *the fastest horse in the Capital.* By the muscle that filled her leg Farren did not doubt it. She giggled into her sleeve every time she or Rorke called its name. When she did so for the umpteenth time Rorke shot her a glare which she pointedly ignored and climbed onto the saddle. Rorke's own horse stood tethered next to him but he had a name that could strike fear into the hearts of their enemies: Tygre. They were twin warriors as they sat atop their horses, armed to the teeth with knives, swords and there was a bow strapped across Rorke's saddle. What wasn't visible were the two bottles of poison they were to hide in their jackets that the Captain gifted them that morning. *If you get caught.* Farren refrained from throwing the small bottle against a wall. Rorke decided he would hold onto them until they reached the Kayei's Realm. She did not object.

The horses trotted out of the stables and into the cold breeze. The riding leathers the King gifted them hugged her body. There were no emblems or designs that traced them back to the White Castle but the King's colours were dotted across them. White lined the navy, near black leather. The trousers sat high on her hips with a button clasp and a lighter grey panel detailing. The jacket matched perfectly and was buckled across her chest. Her white shirt was tucked snugly against her body. A navy cloak sat across her back and over her satchels. Rorke's own cloak hung to the side of his body as he steered her and their horses over to the small group of people stood at the bridge's entrance. Farren's back straightened subconsciously as she beheld the

King and Queen next to Argen. The latter fidgeted on his feet and kept his eyes trained on her face. Adrastos had other duties to attend to but he wished them luck that morning at breakfast; his hand grasped hers as though she were indeed one of his Guards so the grin she sent him was blinding.

"Your Majesties," Rorke greeted them.

Farren lowered her head. When she raised her eyes to the two her heart stopped in her chest. The King spoke to Rorke with a smile on his face but the Queen- Farren swallowed and fingered the reins. The Queen's dark eyes bore into hers with a frown. The intensity in her gaze nearly had her falling from her horse. It felt like ice seeped into her veins the longer she stared. She felt the chill under her clothes and it crept up the back of her neck. Argen broke her from the cold. He fussed with her pack and with narrowed eyes, placed a hesitant hand on her leg which she glared down at but the worry in his eyes -the fear- made her swallow. His hand tightened, "you have worked too hard for this opportunity; do not let the Kayei take that away from you."

There was nothing she could say so she nodded and patted the back of his hand. Rorke clicked his tongue, bowed his head and they continued on their way. Before Petal's hoof hit the bridge the King called her name so she twisted on her saddle and waited. "We await your return with bated breath."

She smiled, bowed her head once more and followed Rorke onto the bridge. As she twisted back she marvelled for the fourth time that day at the lack of pain in her ribs. The Healer must have been mistaken about the healing time. As they made their way across the bridge she pressed a hand where her broken ribs healed one week after she saw the Healer. *Farren turned over to face the ceiling where streams of winter light danced. She rubbed her eyes and paused. There was no pain, no pull against her skin, no pressure that hitched her breath. She slowly pulled the sheets from her body*

and lifted her shirt. The bindings sat snug against her ribs. She crossed her
legs beneath her and unravelled the material. They fell away to reveal bare
skin, not a bruise or welt in sight. She blinked and walked over to the mirror,
her night shirt held up by her teeth. The mirror revealed the same: pale,
injury-less skin. Her free hand drifted across the area where pain struck her
during training and pressed down. Nothing. She pressed harder but still her
ribs remained intact and her skin was springy. Healed, just like the cuts and
bruises to her face and leg. It was like nothing happened, like a new woman.
Her teeth released the night shirt and she grinned.

Rorke's voice broke through her thoughts as he ushered her to quicken her pace. Farren rolled her eyes and they made it to the end of the bridge where a familiar figure stood. Unease filled Soter as they trotted by. His eyes followed Farren with a deep frown and his hands were folded in front of him so hard that his knuckles were white from the pressure. Rorke's eyes narrowed until the Kayei stepped back so that they could push their horses into a gallop.

Run down houses lined the outskirts of the city, some flew the King's banner whilst others were covered in wooden boards. People milled about; many shivered in the winter chill. Farren pulled her own cloak tighter around her. After the edge of the city was travelled, they slowed their horses back into a trot they rode in companionable silence. Questions swirled in her mind but she wasn't sure which one to ask first, which would be the most important and which would cause Rorke to scowl. She opened her mouth, unsure of what would come out, but he spoke first. "There is a piece of the Veil a few miles away which is guarded by a woman," he shook his head, "by something that will play games with you." Farren pressed her tongue to the roof of her mouth, took a deep breath and asked him to elaborate. "This thing is charged with ferrying souls in between the Realms. Although she does favour the humans more than the Kayei. When someone wants to travel through, it tests them and if you pass then she lets you through."

"And if you don't pass?"

"Your soul will be lost in the Veil," he glanced at her and swallowed, "that's what we've been told." *In* the Veil did not sound pleasant. Farren felt a headache form at her temples and she pressed against them tightly. In the space of a minute, Rorke informed her that she had another test, on top of the relatively large one she was ordered to do by the King, one that would determine whether or not she could actually perform her test. There was no curse foul enough for the frustration which bubbled in her chest.

Yet, there was one saving grace. "you've been through here before right? What was the test? Maybe we can strategise before we reach the Veil." She sounded hopeful.

His solemn look broke that hope into pieces. "Each person is given a different test. You and I will not be facing them together."

A shiver ran down her spine. With the way he spoke, there was no doubt in her mind that the tests were both horrible and taxing. Rorke's grip was tight on the reins, his shoulders solid like a barricade against what awaited them. They continued on for a few more minutes and the trees parted to a small clearing. The smell of the city dissolved into wet soil and leaves. She forced her heart to calm its racing and inhaled deeply. There was no way to possibly prepare for a test neither of them could imagine.

"There might be a way to reason with her, a way to travel across the Veil without being tested on who-knows-what," Farren put forward.

Rorke scoffed, "she is a creature that is used as a vessel for a large amount of magic. There is *nothing* to reason with, no soul and no humanity, Farren."

That would not stop her from trying.

When they slowed their horses through a dense patch of trees she asked, "if you've already travelled through, why do you have to go through the test again? Surely she can't test you on the same thing?"

Rorke's eyes flicked to her. "There was no test when I travelled to and from Realms."

"Why?"

"There were too many people." Five, twenty, one hundred, possibly more. Rorke did not specify the number or the circumstance in which 'too many' people wished to travel through the Veil. Something similar to a dark cloud hung over the two of them as that information settled in the air.

Her eyes searched the sky. "Is there any chance she would see two people as 'too many'?"

"No."

Soon after, they trotted into another clearing that shimmered at the edges. The Veil was brighter, more colourful than she remembered. Colours flicked against the floor and at the leaves where it met the tree line and grass. There was a lake between them, but sat on their side of the body of water was a hut. It was well kept and small charms dangled from the rafters but they did not sway in the wind. The grass around the hut was dead. It's like time stood still around the hut as the grass grew lush and green everywhere else. Additionally, the water that covered the ground was still as death. Ripples from the wind carried across the rest of the water until it reached the bank.

They dismount and tethered the horses to a thick-trunked tree. "We'll leave the horses here," Rorke said as he tied Tygre's reins into a knot.

"I have to ask: if you never went through with the test before, how do you know so much about it?"

His body froze, hands mid-tie and jaw clenched. "It's information I was given a long time ago."

"So it might not be correct?"

His eyes bore into hers. "It is correct."

"But how can you be-"

"Farren," he blew a breath from his nose and stepped toward her, "if you want us to survive, I need you trust me, starting now." A pregnant pause stretched between them, and when Rorke was certain her questions were finished for that moment, he pet Tygre on the snout and turned toward the hut. Their feet moved in synchronisation as they stepped across to the dead grass. The closer they found themselves to the hut, the thicker the air became. Farren sucked in a deep breath whilst Rorke pressed a hand to his chest as though he could will the air into his lungs faster. The air remained thick and Farren forced her focus on her breaths and the knife at her side. The muscles in her back tensed as the door to the hut opened on a phantom wind, but Rorke's hand was on her shoulder before she moved. "Remember, none of it is real." The world turned and blurred around them then Rorke was gone.

As the world shifted around her a woman's voice that was both old and young circled her, "such a pretty aura.... so strong.... so bright.... nothing like the soldier boy.... he hasn't got a chance."

Farren tried to steady her vision and kept her feet rooted to the floor. The breakfast she partook in earlier swirled but she forced it down. When the world finally came into focus she stumbled. The voice disappeared as the sky stretched before her with brightly shining stars and endless darkness. Warm wind whipped through her clothes and hair which she found to be unbound.

Loose black trousers and a long-sleeved top that felt like it belonged to someone with a lot of money adorned her body in place of the riding leathers. A cliff stood before her which dropped into a river of water. The smell of bonfires and orange trees floated on the wind. Laughter rose up to meet her: it was melodic and full of joy but there were no people down below or on the Cliffside next to her so she turned to find the cliff sloped toward a town littered with lights and pale buildings.

Something in her chest ached at the sight of the town. Her body felt lighter, her eyes brighter. She moved to join the bustling townspeople then the world warped. "Not yet," the voice hissed and Farren was plunged underwater. Bubbles rose around her as she plunged deeper and deeper until the voice deemed it necessary to stop. Farren kept her lips pressed together. It was dark, murky water, nothing like the Cobalt Sea she'd seen paintings of. The sunlight above her cracked through the surface of murk like a golden eye looking out for her, but the water moved. It surged around her and she sucked in a breath on instinct. More bubbles floated around her as they pushed from her mouth. *Enrys kicked her elbows from under her and just as quickly, he pressed on her shoulders. She bucked as her face submerged beneath the rushing water. The cold bit against her skin, her lips turned blue and her joints locked.* Farren started to flail. Her limbs pushed against the water and she willed her eyes to stay open against the torrent. Her arms and legs strained as they swam toward the sunlight. Quicker than she expected the light blinded her when she emerged. She slicked her hair from her face and stared at the now-blue, still ocean. There was no sign of land, of people and thankfully no deadly creatures. Water filled every direction.

She spluttered up the water she swallowed and sucked in deep breaths. Drowning must be her destiny but to kill her is not to test her... she stared at the endless blue and found her riding leathers returned which stuck uncomfortably to her skin. The sun shone directly overhead which meant it was no later than noon. Did time even matter wherever she was? It meant that there was no way to discern East from West, not that it would necessarily help. There was one weapon in her arsenal that might work so she sucked in another deep breath, closed her eyes and tilted her face toward the sun. "Hello? Mystical voice, are you there?" Silence reigned. "Can we talk about this?" There was a thick pause and Farren cursed Rorke for being right. "If not, can you at least give me an idea what my test is because for Griselda's sake this is just water!"

Water trickled through her upheld glove for emphasis but her hand splashed into the water as the voice replied, "just water?"

Farren swallowed, she tried to keep her- it- the Veil Guardian's attention. "I am willing to follow your rules and complete this test but I think I need a bit more than being perched on a cliff then plunged into an ocean. I mean, is drowning honestly my test? Actually, please don't answer that I just- I'm new at this magic thing and I have no idea what you want from me, or what you want me to do in an ocean."

A grating sound filled her ears and- the voice chuckled, "maybe I should have started with a smaller body of water."

Everything shifted on its axis and the water around her shrunk. Farren stood knee-deep in a stream which travelled past her. The water was so clear she could see her boots on the smooth stones. Meadows of flowers surrounded her and it looked like the stream cut through the flora like a whip. Despite the many flowers the smell was faint. She wrung her hair through her fingers and found the sun shone less harshly in that scene. "Do you want me to follow it?"

She received no reply, but carefully, she moved her feet over the uneven ground and followed the flow of water. Just like the ocean, the meadows and stream were endless, however, her feet continued to move and her eyes canvassed the area. There was no way for her to gauge how long she walked through the water but once it became shallower -the clear-liquid at her mid-shin- she stopped. There was no change in her environment, the cloudless sky hung overhead so she crouched and formed a cup with her hands and brought it to her face. The water glistened in the sun and droplets fell down her sleeves. She tentatively sniffed then brought her hands to her lips. The cool water ran past her lips and down her throat. It did nothing more than quench a thirst. The next cup-full of water was splashed onto her face.

With a sigh, she raised her eyes and faced the edge of the stream. It took her brain a moment to process what she saw, but when it did, she blinked owlishly: the injured Night Creature leant against a rock on the other side of the stream. Blood seeped from its wound and stained the grassy-bank; it made its way into the clear water, the red an angry contrast to the tranquil aura around her. It whined and stared up at her, and begged her to help with just one look. Without a thought she ran toward the creature. Her movements slowed as though the world around her had been placed under sludge. The sole of her boot took seconds to meet the rocks beneath her and her thigh movement was slow, as though a force pushed against it. The Night Creature faded into the bank and the world turned. The foot she poised to hit the water thudded against ash and dirt and she stumbled ungracefully.

"Please, stop doing that," Farren spat as she righted herself.

A yellow stone castle stood proud against the fallen ash. Columns lined the front door covered in twinkling white lights. A balcony ran around the red, pointed roof and orange flowers hung from the railings. The fountain at the front of the house was the centre of attention with the stone carvings of lovers entwined. The water that once filled the fountain was gone but the beauty of the stone remained. That beauty was overpowered by the smoke that filtered from the castle's open windows and doors. Flames flew from a third floor window accompanied by screams. The smell of the smoke seemed too real, the heat from the fire flushed Farren's face. She covered her nose and

153

mouth with the sleeve of her jacket whilst her eyes darted across the building. There were people behind her yelling and coughing, two people rushed from the door and fell to the ground as they coughed up the smoke in their lungs. Darkness stretched at her back and a single bucket of water sat next to her. Her eyes snagged on the item and she kept her eyes on the water despite the faceless people being ushered out of the building. The people weren't important but the bucket of water was in sharp focus.

"What do you want to do?" The Voice asked with an excited lilt to its tone.

Flames flared bright as another window shattered under the pressure. Farren covered her head as shards rained down. When another person –the same person she saw when she arrived- stumbled from the flame, the scene before her seemed to blur in and out of focus, like her eyes tried to comprehend exactly what she was witnessing. As the man coughed, she moved her attention to the sky where plumes of smoke blotted out the stars. "The fire, I need to put out the fire."

The voice answered, "then put it out."

The man and flames were brought back to clear focus and Farren's lungs pushed out a breath. The leather of her gloves served as mufflers when she pressed her hands to her ears at the same time that the screams intensified. The dull buzz in her ears was from the Voice, to help her concentrate or throw her off balance, but there was no point dwelling on it, not when she was sure someone called her name amongst the screams. Finally, she moved and forcefully planted her hands on the coughing man's shoulders. "How many people are in there?"

The coughs that started off as tickles wracked his entire body so she let him stumble away with a curse. More accurately he shoved her toward the castle. When she surveyed the scene for the final time, her eyes snagged once again on the bucket. The limited amount of water made her nose scrunch but she rushed toward it. When she removed it from the ground, the hairs on the back of her neck stood on end like lightning touched her fingertips. The water sloshed around the bucket so she steadied it with both hands and watched as the liquid surged like the Dark Sea. The moment that the water swirled of its own accord, she dropped it to the ground with a yelp. A groan flew from her lips as the liquid seep into the ash covered grass. There was only one option left: Farren dodged the fallen glass and stormed into the burning castle.

In a blink of an eye the fire and smoke were gone. What it left behind was the bite of the cold and the whip of the wind in her hair. The smell of smoke lingered but there was not a char mark to be seen. The screams disappeared, replaced by curses and a demand to 'hold her down'. The voices grew until she found herself in front of the Brentham Church stream; five men struggled in front of her. What they fought against was a young woman who flailed in their arms, her hands clawed at the leader and Farren's stomach dropped. She stepped back as she watched as a past version of herself tried to scream. From where she stood the men looked so much bigger than her, hulking forms rather than simple villagers. Enrys was the largest of them all, his shoulders twice as large and his face twice as ugly. Whilst she focused on the men, Ritrio's own hand wrapped around her wrist but –she looked down- it was a phantom feeling, one that carried from the woman on the ground. Farren moved again. It was a simple shift of her feet but it brought everyone's attention to her. Where their eyes used to be were empty sockets, holes of black that burned into her. Black ink oozed from those sockets and mouths as they opened them in a supernatural groan. Another step back and Ritrio growled, inhuman and vicious.

The Voice broke through the trees, "this is interesting... These men had such hatred in their souls but you..." It trailed off as Past Farren's body was dropped from Enrys' hand. "You were furious, and scared, and stubborn. You fought them because you would not die easily, quietly. It's.... interesting."

Farren shot her head upwards. "Interesting?!"

Enrys cleared his throat, "you're nothing but a spoiled brat who decided to defy her uncle by joining up with the big boys." They were words he spoke to her on that awful night. They were words that rang through her chest but The Voice chuckled as though her trauma was dinner theatre. Farren didn't know whether to glare at Enrys or at the sky where she assumed the invisible-entity resided.

"'The big boys' he says," the Voice chuckled again, "he has no idea what you are capable of, what you could do to him. That little human wouldn't last a day in the Kayei's Realm."

Farren muttered, "he doesn't have to." With Argen in the Capital there had to be an interim Commander, which was a position that automatically fell to Enrys. No Commander travelled near the Realm let alone through it; Enrys, in his cowardly glory never had to do what she was tasked with. Whether he was disbanded or not. Farren rolled her eyes. The King said the guards would be punished but there was no doubt in Farren's mind that Enrys still acted as head of the Brentham guard whilst Argen did the King's bidding, whilst she endured psychological games. His punishment would not start until Argen returned or a new Commander was named because Griselda forbid the village of Brentham be without a Commander.

"The King cares so much about his guards that he would see a boy like... Enrys... in charge of a village?" the Voice asked.

"The King likes order and loyalty, Enrys will be punished but only when it is convenient for the country."

"Show me, what would you do differently?" The scene seemed to move backwards, one second her past self was on the ground then Enrys pulled her to her feet and pushed her toward Present Farren. They stopped a few inches away from her, the chill from their clothes radiated toward her. There was a sword in Past Farren's hand, one that pointed at Ritrio who looked down his nose at her. Both Farrens grit their teeth. She should have run him through first, then Enrys, the rest of the guards would have fled the moment they saw them fall. It was a nice thought, but the two guards who died rushed at Past Farren. They swung their swords and metal clanged. Battle strategies and training moves filled her mind but none would have made a difference against seven men. *What would she have done differently?*

"I should have been faster, more aware. I probably could have focused on Enrys if those two guards weren't such a surprise to me. I was dizzy, I think, from the blow to the head." Present Farren lifted her hand to where the blow landed. "It was a blur, the beginning fight I mean, I don't know if I could have done any differently. One minute I was looking for Argen and the next-"

The scene moved along: Enrys grabbed the front of Past Farren's shirt once again and dragged her toward the stream behind them. Just as before he plunged her under, the water was around her face, hair, up her nose. The ice bit at her skin and Enrys called for backup. All five held her down whilst Past Farren struggled and writhed beneath their hold. Farren watched it happen, her fists clenched and her eyes ablaze. The cold transferred to her face, the feeling of water cascaded across her numb cheeks and across her lashes.

"So much emotion in one moment," the Voice mused, "but you do not use any magic."

Farren sniffed. "I don't have any magic to use."

"And if you did?"

Farren paused. Humans used magic like a drug, one taste and they wanted more. If she had magic in that moment more than two men would have died. If she had magic, her lungs would not have burned, she would not have endured the pain on her face and in her ribs, she would not have struggled through her first days of training with Adrastos, she would not have been so weak. If she had magic there was a possibility she would not hold Argen in such contempt. Magic meant that Enrys and Ritrio and all seven of

158

them were brought to justice, maybe she would have seen fear in their eyes. It was a notion that sharpened her eyes but the truth was- "I would be dead if I had magic. Self-defence or not, I would have been executed for using it."

The Voice countered, "if the King could not touch you..?"

There was no need to speak because the scene continued to move, but instead of Argen's grand entrance, the trees around her morphed and grew in size. Once they were distinctly larger, the tentacle-like branches shot forward. Farren called out but it was too late, the branches wrapped around the limbs of the guards, one of them wound around Enrys' throat and lifted him from Past Farren's body. The woman spluttered and coughed, the pain in her ribs still present but she didn't nearly die, her lungs did not burn. Enrys squirmed in the tree's hold and soon enough the branches squeezed and he stopped moving. Then the scene reverted back to Past Farren's face beneath the water and the trees returned to normal. One minute Enrys sneered down at her, the next he gasped for breath; he removed his hands from her body and clutched at his throat. The other men did the same. They were being choked, because there was not enough air for them to take in, yet Past Farren sat in the water unaffected. Once again the scene rewound. Everything moved slower than before, the rush of the water was sluggish, Enrys' voice was deeper and the words were elongated, Past Farren's bucks were more like slow thrusts. It gave Farren the opportunity to see the water around her other self rise and curl. It danced like a living flame, and morphed into a wall behind her. With the water elsewhere Past Farren was able to breathe, the deep breaths she took in enough to steal Enrys' attention from the water to her face. Farren didn't know whether to look at her past self or at the water that surged forward, the guards covered in the icy liquid. It rushed down their mouths, up their nose and even into their eyes. Past Farren's eyes glowed a vibrant blue as she glared at Enrys who no longer pressed his hands to her shoulders but struggled against the current next to her.

159

The Voice spoke, "you could have used Earth Magic to bind them, Wind Magic to suffocate them, Water Magic to make them feel as you did, what do you humans say... a taste of their own medicine."

"You think I should have killed them." It was a statement, not a question.

"Only if it was necessary."

"Was it necessary?"

The Voice let the question echo around the scene. "If your friend... the Commander... had not appeared... it would have been." If Argen had not appeared it would be her corpse on the ground alongside those two guards. Enrys would not have been killed, Ritrio would be fine and the other three would continue to live their lives. The Voice offered her an option that was impossible. There was no scenario where she would have survived on her own and there was no plausible scenario where the men who attacked her would have died. After her eyes drifted over the guards, they fell on her past, crouched form.

"Why do I look like that?" Past Farren's eyes turned to where she stood. It wasn't a simple light blue haze that resonated from her gaze, it was a swirl of grey and navy blue like a roiling storm. Her hair rose and fell behind her like it bobbed on invisible waves, and when she opened her mouth to breathe, sharp teeth filled her mouth.

"When magic is used... a person sometimes changes... that is what you look like using it."

Farren moved around the still bodies of the guards for a closer look at her past self. The water acted like a living being and curved around Past Farren toward her. It swirled in a miniature tornado then around her arm to pull her closer to the scene. She stumbled forward until she was nose to nose with her other self. Past Farren's lips curled up into a smirk and she tilted her head just like she often did. On the Voice's perception of her it looked creepy, animalistic almost. Farren moved her hand to touch the vision and Past Farren did the same until their fingertips were a hairsbreadth away. "Is the change permanent?"

"The eyes maybe..."

"Maybe?"

The wind soared through the trees and her hair in answer. Past Farren blinked until the same eyes she saw in the mirror every morning stared back at her. Both Farrens lowered their hands and hung them at their sides, heads tilted to the opposite side of the other. She –Past Farren- was like a museum artefact, curiously odd, like she was a completely different universe, a different era.

"Tell me, what magic would you have used?" The Voice asked after Farren was allowed to survey her clone.

"Why does that matter?" She moved from her position and walked to where she originally stood. It gave her some time to contemplate the question. "They were all affective and all of them -hypothetically- saved my life. I think-" Farren replayed all the attacks in her head, each time Enrys suffered but there was one that replayed over and over that brought some sense of victory to her. Then she looked at the water that remained a wall behind Past Farren. "Water Magic. It was quick but it did to them what they were doing to me. It let them feel the cold and the panic... It was justice."

As she spoke the guards moved; they no longer stood over Past Farren but instead turned their attention on her and Ritrio spoke, "come on Farren, how about round two?" The sneers on their faces crinkled their cheeks beneath the black holes of their eyes. Farren swallowed. Their swords were unsheathed and pointed at her making her very aware that she had no weapon on her person.

Everything stopped and the Voice pondered, "no, not these men... maybe..."

The guards vanished along with Past Farren. Every muscle in her body relaxed. She took the time to marvel in the fact that the forest around her was a perfect replica. If she closed her eyes she could nearly smell the chimney smoke in the village, but as she basked in the cool air and familiarity of it all someone else joined the scene. The person walked on silent feet, until it reached her still form. They tapped her on the shoulder which flung her eyes open with a hand pressed to her chest, so she whirled. Argen stood behind her, his hand still outstretched as though he was unsure of whether to touch her again. Something in her stuttered because he looked so normal: his hazel eyes remained in his head, his curls sat haphazardly atop his head and his beard was trimmed.

"What are you doing here?" It was a question for him and for the Voice.

Argen shrugged and retracted his hand. He wore his training gear, something that suited him far better than the guard uniform ever did. There was a sword on his hip, but it did nothing but swing in the wind. There was a weight at her side and true enough her own sword was returned to its rightful place. Slowly, Farren lifted her eyes from her weapon to Argen. Just as slowly, he released his weapon from its hold and brandished it toward her. She followed suit, the sword a comfortable weight in her hand.

"Do you remember your footwork?" he asked. Each of his steps were mirrored, their movements synced. Firstly, he slid one foot behind the other and used his back foot as leverage to widen his stance. Then he held his sword higher. It was a challenge and a warning. "You've improved."

Farren grit her teeth, "are we really going to do this?"

She waited for the Voice to intervene, a hope that the world would change once again. Argen raised a brow and his sword higher. A fight was what the Argen before her wanted and she had no qualms about partaking in it, so she lunged and he parried. Clang after clang sounded in the forest as their blades met. Hand-to-hand or sword-play, he taught her it all.

"Please Argen! I really want to learn," Farren whined.

Young Argen —no older than twelve- laughed. The girl hung off of his arm as he held onto the hilt of his new sword. It was a gift from his grandmother, a promise for the future and a sign of his hopes and dreams. His eyes sparkled as she stomped her feet in the dirt, her skirts short enough to show the dust that covered her boots. She stared back, her cheeks puffed in a pout. Argen scratched the back of his neck with his free hand, his face a nice shade of strawberry pink.

"Your Uncle would kill me," he mumbled.

Farren countered, "then we just don't tell him!"

Argen searched her eyes, the sureness in them made him nervous. If he didn't offer to teach her, no-doubt she would have found someone else or possibly even taught herself. That would require more explanation than if he simply showed her his sword. Their eyes locked once again and the girl snuggled closer to his arm, so he caved. "Okay." She gasped when he spoke. "One lesson."

All of her teeth came into view as she beamed. His finger was held up between them, a gesture of finality. Yet, it never was just 'one lesson', it started off as the occasional occurrence but once Farren started to succeed in slicing through the air, that training turned to hand-to-hand, then tactical lessons and soon enough they saw each other nearly every night. Some nights

—when they snuck ale from her father's pantry or even from her Theron's wine cabinet when they truly wanted to celebrate- they sat in the Church and talked. After training it was never about battle plans or fighting styles, it was about Lyla and Farren's dogs and whether or not they thought the butcher would tell his attractive customer that he fancied her.

It then became a habit of Argen's to carry booze around with him, for any occasion he might need it. Farren never warned him off the stuff, she simply watched as he gulped down ale whilst she hydrated on well-water. It wasn't her place to scold him, but that did not stop her eyes from remaining on him, from watching his movements after he swigged on his skein or spent the night at the pub with the guards. Despite his habit, he always trained her, she even thought he looked forward to it, and not once had he been late until-

"What were you doing, that night at the stream, why were you late?" It was a question that haunted her even in sleep. Her best friend was a man so vigilant in his work but he was late to her Trial. Tears lined her eyes but Argen's face did not change. The air was still, the stream silent. It was like the Voice searched for the correct response. Whether what exited test-Argen's mouth would be the truth, was something she had to ask him when she returned.

"There is no excuse that you will believe."

Farren blew out an exasperated breath, "I don't want an excuse, Argen, I want the truth."

Their swords remained pressed to one another when he replied, "one of the guards were worried that the Veil had moved. They asked me to investigate it," he gulped, "I told them I had prior engagements, believe me I did, but they were so panicked I-"

"You had to at least look at the Veil," Farren finished for him.

It explained the horrified look in his eyes when he figured out how his own guards slipped past him. It was a set up, a cruel, calculated set up. Magic was not to be trifled with, especially not by a common villager. It was Argen's duty to investigate the claim, she knew that but it did not stop the ache in her chest or the tears that threatened to fall. Frustration replaced her previous anger.

They both moved again, metal upon metal, feet firm against ground, the ice not a hindrance to either of them. Their fight continued for what felt like hours. The tears she held back ran freely down her cheeks as she fought Argen but both ignored it. There was no interference from the Voice or the guards. Her muscles started to ache and her breathing became ragged. With another lunge on her part he grabbed her wrist and pulled her close. There was no emotion in his eyes, proof that he wasn't real, but they were the same colour down to the dark ring around his iris. It struck her to the core that there was no kindness, no shy, bashful look when a woman smiled at him. With her focus solely on his eyes and not on his feet, he caught her off guard. One swipe at her feet from beneath her and she fell backward. The crunch her body made against the ground was the only sound. Argen disappeared and the guards returned, frozen in place. That allowed Farren a moment to breathe.

The Voice sounded, "that boy, he's all over your soul... bits and pieces... like he was sewn into it..."

"Yeah well," she gulped in a breath, "we aren't exactly friends anymore."

"Why?"

"Surely you know the answer to that?"

"... He failed you." Farren nodded, hands on her knees for stability. "That does not mean that he does not care for you."

165

Farren glared, "maybe if he was better at his job we would not be having this conversation."

The Voice chuckled, "are you only friends with him because he is Commander of the Guard?" Farren didn't respond. "No... you were friends before that... and you will remain friends after."

"He called me crazy because I was angry at him, at the guards, that's not very friendly."

"He's a human man... they say stupid things when frustrated... he is important to you... he has apologised..."

Farren bit her cheek and mumbled, "it's not enough."

The Voice hummed and the world started again. Farren's eyes shot to her guards in front of her, the second she did, they lunged and she sprang into action. The tips of their swords grazed her jacket as she jumped back. She twisted her body and ran full pelt through the trees. They were on her heels, no sign of Argen anywhere, and as she ran through the trees where a pathway was supposed to be, the world blurred at the edges. Her feet kept moving until she skidded around an evergreen and through an opening. She thundered through and watched as the snow covered ground morphed into dead grass and her boots met solid earth not slush. Behind her there were no guards or curses but an open lake and the shimmer of the Veil. The sunlight temporarily blinded her so she squinted and shadowed her face with her hand. The world no longer turned, there was no blurred vision and swirled colours. That was solid, real ground beneath Farren's boots. There was no Argen, no guards, no burning buildings or snow.

Her knees hit the ground at the same moment she spotted the hut. Rorke had yet to appear and the faces from her test rattled in her mind. Her heart thundered from the exertion. The Voice's words rang through her head.

Forgiveness was earned and all Argen did was apologise... and told the Captain of the attack... and made sure she got to the Capital safely... and ensured Soter helped her. Farren groaned and scrubbed her hands down her face. When she lifted her eyes fully toward the hut she caught sight of the small bucket of water which sat half-full with the clear liquid. A mockery of what occurred before what felt like her 'true' test began. With a glare at the inanimate object she pushed herself from the dead grass and stormed toward the structure.

The way Rorke spoke about the tests made it seem like she had to decide whether or not to kill someone she cared about and not... whatever her test was. She shook her head as she continued toward the hut, her eyes fixed to the door. Once she was a few metres away, said door flung open to reveal a dishevelled Rorke. A breath of relief escaped her and she stopped her march. Rorke's chest rose and fell in rapid breaths as he rushed toward her. Once he reached her he gripped her arms tightly, his breath warm and sharp against her face. Sweat covered his brows and neck which was a stark contrast to the shivers that rippled through his body. She steadied his rattled form as he leaned on her. All that remained from her own test were the tear tracks down her face and the uncomfortable feel of her heart in her chest.

"Farren, are you okay?"

She nodded. "Are you?" No visible injuries covered him, only the shadow across his eyes told her of what he possibly endured. His hands flexed against her arms. The strips of tendons could be seen beneath his gloves and she lifted her own hand to squeeze his shoulder. "Did you pass?"

His brow furrowed and he blinked down at her. "If we failed we would not be standing here right now."

A shiver ran down her spine at the thought. The Veil stood tall behind her, its colours prominent against the grey sky. Without speaking, Rorke pointed toward the large field behind her. She blinked rapidly and stepped back so that she stood at his side. That field was not there when she found herself on solid ground. The Veil shimmered on the other side of the field instead of where the lake stood. Neither adventurer took their eyes off the grassy field as they walked to the horses. The steeds happily grazed on healthy grass, no sign of any harm done to them whilst they were gone. Farren looked around, how long *were* they gone? Rorke's hand released her shoulder as he untied the horses and mounted his. Farren purposefully swung her foot against the bucket of water which rolled across the grass and she watched as it rolled and came to a stop, but then something moved out of the corner of her eye. The blood in her veins nearly stopped at the sight of a woman who grinned freely. The Voice's too straight teeth gleamed in the light of the Veil but her eyes –pure black orbs- sucked in the pale sunlight. She looked no older than fifty. Glossy hair sat atop her head that was a mixture of pure silver and gold like the Goddess' weaved it from molten metal. Long blood-red robes fell off her shoulders like the Eastern paintings Farren had seen on her Uncle's ships. Gold hung from her neck and ears: a woman of refinery yet she lived in a hut by a lake no bigger than a hunting shack.

The ethereal woman waved as Farren started her horse into a trot toward the Veil. Farren's mouth remained slightly agape even as Rorke guided them finally through the barrier between Realms. The warmer air tore her eyes from the woman. The feeling of light-headedness fell over her and she braced a hand on Petal's neck. Trees stretched before her, brighter than the dull forest sat behind them. There was no mistaking the shimmer of magic over everything. It was like they stepped from the dead of Winter to the middle of autumn. The leaves were a mixture of oranges, reds and yellows which glimmered in the light of a low hanging sun. The air remained cold despite the mild autumn that was depicted. "It's so vibrant," Farren commented.

Rorke grunted. "The ruler of this land likes to keep to his aesthetic all year 'round." Farren nodded absently in reply whilst she stared at the beauty around them.

A path wound before them and into the heart of the forest. The magic around them brightened the leaves above them and sharpened the brown of their horses' eyes. The weight of her weapons comforted her as they started down the mud-covered path and they each kept a hand near the knives on their legs, but companionable silence encompassed them as they travelled through the colour-rich forest. There were no words to be exchanged about the test or their surroundings. Rorke's breathing slowed to its normal rate but his hollow scowl was a permanent fixture on his face whilst Farren's own heart thudded in her chest.

A few minutes ticked by before Farren asked, "where exactly are we going?"

His scowl wavered when he glanced at her. "There's a territory further inland called Kavan but to get there we have to travel through Aureum."

The leaves around them flew in the wind and he gestured toward the trees. There was no sign of Night Creatures or the Kayei as they made their way through the territory. There was no warning system, no watch towers, and no guards when they crossed over. The ethereal Veil-Guardian was obviously deemed strong enough not to warrant any. Though that did not stop Farren from wondering why the Ruler of Aureum let her dictate who came into their territory. *A friend to Humans perhaps?*

"Is there a possibility of talking to the ruler of Aureum? What I mean is, can't we ask them for help? Maybe explain our situation and explain that it is against the-" Rorke stared pointedly at her and she slowly closed her mouth but her eye twitched as they continued on in silence. "How are two humans supposed to travel through an entire territory –kingdom- whatever you want to call it, without getting noticed?"

He shrugged, "I know a short cut."

"You know a..." She blinked; *of course he knew a shortcut.* "What's the shortcut?"

A deep sigh passed his lips but the shadows under his eyes told her it wasn't frustration. "Can you please stop asking me so many questions?"

Yet, she rolled her eyes. "Excuse me for trying to see the whole picture whilst I *risk* my *life*. I admit that I should have asked these questions before we left, but I'm asking them now."

There truly was no sign of anyone but them in the forest which was why she didn't mind the loud nature of her voice. Despite the volume of her voice, Rorke kept his voice low, "you signed up for this mission, Farren."

He wasn't serious?

"My family was threatened, my livelihood!"

"How noble," he muttered.

A growl reverberated in her throat which forced Rorke to do a double take. Questions swam in his eyes which stuttered as they scanned her face. On Rorke's less-than-reassuring stare she scanned their surroundings with a precision Argen would be proud of. She coughed away the thought of her old friend and focused on the trot of Petal's hooves. The forest around them darkened as they travelled beneath a denser canopy of leaves. The sun was little more than a few flecks on their hair. The breeze lessened and the still forest stood around them like pillars. Before she gave him a piece of her mind, her mind swimming with insults and explanations, the ground beneath them shook. The questions in Rorke's eyes faded and he whipped back around to face the path. The horses were steadied with soft hands on their necks and a sharp tug on their reins. Farren followed every move Rorke made. Their tension-filled moment was forgotten as he pushed his horse into a gallop and the colours of the trees rushed past them. She levelled her horse with his but the rumbling of the earth continued. Hooves pounded against the ground which morphed into rich, green grass. The further they travelled the less the ground shook and both Farren and Petal appreciated that fact. Farren begged her limbs and teeth to stop chattering from the vibrations whilst Rorke shook his arms as though he were shaking off a spider; not that Rorke was likely bothered by spiders but the image of him trying to fling one from his body made Farren snort.

Trees circled the area of grass but the canopy continued to shade the ground. The horses were pulled to a stop and Farren furrowed her brow. Stood in the middle of the clearing were two gnarled creatures. They spoke in hushed tones and animated arms. The sunshine lit small specks on their robes like dusty books in a library; they ducked away from what little light shone above them. The whispers stopped and they shot their heads up like deer. Their faces were made of swirled gold flesh similar to nasty burn scars and even their bare arms were comprised of swirled and overlapped skin. Considering the temperature in the forest she imagined they could not feel the cold; the tunics were cut at the shoulders or rather the sleeves were torn from the body. Their eyes were goat-like with the black rectangular slit in the centre although the colour of their iris' were not white nor yellow but a dark purple. One of the creatures stepped toward where they stood in the shadow of the trees and sniffed. The foliage around them hid the main bodies of the horses but one breath and the creature would likely spot them. Once it lowered its head and locked its eyes on the shadows a growl filled the air. It raised the hairs on Farren's arms and every part of her body froze.

"Back away slowly," Rorke whispered with his eyes locked on the creatures. Farren shifted her weight and gently pulled the reins but as quietly as they approached the louder they revealed themselves: Petal whinnied as loud as she possibly could and pushed back on her hind legs. Her front hooves kicked at the air and Farren was flung backwards. With the wind knocked from her she had no time to grab the reins to calm her horse before it galloped in the opposite direction. After she watched her horse run away, Farren turned to find Rorke on the floor with her, a single bag between them. Castle Horses were more scared of the creatures than they had been of the Veil.

Rorke pushed himself into a crouched position and looked her over. Satisfied with what he found he stood and offered her a hand and she allowed him to pull her to her feet. No-doubt they were both bruised but nothing was broken or sprained. Yet, the look on Rorke's face was sour enough to curdle milk.

"Is there a chance we can out-run them?" Farren asked.

"No."

"Have you ever tried?" The second creature walked to its friend's side which cut off Rorke's reply. He and Farren pulled their weapons from their sheaths. Whilst a single sword sat comfortably in Rorke's palm, a knife and sword sat in hers. She braced them before her like a shield and a cackle sounded from the creature on the right. The shadows were useless against their keen smell because shiny black teeth grinned at the two humans.

Both pairs moved in tandem. "It was a mistake for you to come back *soldier*." The creature on the left stopped and sniffed the air again. "But it was smart of you to bring *them* a gift." The creature on the right shot its eyes to where Farren stood. She gripped her weapons tighter and glared. Rorke didn't acknowledge that anyone spoke but Farren was sure he had yet to blink. The breaths that passed his lips were calculated. The muscles in his back tensed and he shifted his weight toward the trees behind them. Her eyes widened fractionally; surely they weren't going to run through the trees like bandits? That conversation was had and shot down, by Rorke no less, so if he planned on running, she wanted a warning.

Suddenly, the creatures moved. Too quickly they were upon them. One of the gnarled faces hovered in front of her before she could blink. It swiped the blades from her hands and she watched as they flew further into the shadows. Everything moved too quickly. Another knife sat in her boot but as the creature stepped toward her she used that foot to kick it backwards. Leaves and grass entered her vision as she forced her boot from the ground. The creature ran back to its companion before her boot swiped the air before her. Loud cackles taunted her.

"And you," it grinned, "you smell different." It turned toward its friend. "Doesn't she sister?" The other creature nodded. "She smells like lilies and something," they both sniffed and curled their hands, "off." Farren tilted her head to subtly sniff her shoulder: nothing but leather.

Rorke coughed sharply. "We are in the middle of the Harvest so we will be on our way."

The creatures' giggles stopped; those clawed hands held Farren's attention when they stepped forward. Once again they were outmatched by speed and the creatures were before them in a second. Without her weapons, all Farren had to shield herself with were her forearms so she braced for impact as she stumbled backward. Rorke swung his sword in front of him as the creature's sister lunged. The blade hit its mark as black blood sprayed across the grass. Twin screams made the birds in the trees –which Farren had not noticed until then- flock elsewhere. There was not a spare moment to reach for the knife in her boot: sharp swipes of their claws had Farren retreating step after step until one of them forced her on her back, pinned to the earth. A sound of a popped bone and it opened its mouth. Its skin stretched harshly across its cheeks and forehead as the dark chasm stared at her. The smell of rotted flesh filled Farren's nose so she resisted the urge to throw up her breakfast. In the corner of her eyes she saw that Rorke kept swinging but the sister evaded each attack despite the black blood that seeped through its cloak.

"Two humans participating in the Golden Harvest is a foolish move."

Farren turned her face from its open mouth. "Consider us fools then."

"Farren," Rorke grunted, "stop taunting it."

"You started this conversation," she groaned out.

The creature on top of her whipped its head to Rorke and growled. The sound shook her bones, rattled her teeth and made her glare. Its tunic covered most of its body but its legs were visible beneath the flowing material as they squeezed her hips. Despite looking stick thin the muscle that threatened to bruise was by no-means weak. She kept her eyes on those legs as she trailed her fingers toward her boot. Over the hem of its cloak she spied the hilt of her knife, if she only stretched just a little further- A scream ripped through her as the creature's claws dug into her shoulder. Spots appeared in her vision as blinding pain shot through her body. She hadn't seen its hands move. Every nerve in her body sparked and her travel-weary-muscles barked at her. When she returned her gaze to the creature's face, its eyes weren't on her but remained on Rorke whose wide eyes darted from Farren to its sister. Its other hand was around her wrist that was *so close* to her hidden dagger. It squeezed and Farren forced herself to breathe through it. Blood seeped from the wound in her shoulder where its claws remained and her bones creaked as it moved her hand away from her boot. The drool from its open mouth dripped onto her neck and jacket to mix with the red that coated her arm and chest.

More drool flew as it shook its head. "You're not here for the Harvest, you are looking for someone."

She panted through the pain. "Oh yeah, who?"

It was the sister, with a feral grin, who answered, "you want the Human Princess. Why else would-" Distracted, the creature did not finish her

175

sentence before Rorke's sword sliced clean through her neck. More black blood coated the ground and her head rolled into the sun-spots. An echoing yell erupted from the creature above Farren that made her ears ring. It used her already damaged shoulder as a solid surface to launch from. A groan flew from her lips and the trees blurred around her. It sped at Rorke who sliced his blade through the air, the blade which was covered in its sister's blood. It evaded the weapon and skidded across the clearing. The growl it emitted was low and reverberated around them. After a groan and roll on the ground, Farren scrambled to her feet and rushed to her fallen weapons. The heat of the creature's gaze followed her, so with those blades in hand she whirled and pointed them at the growling creature. It stood from its hunched position, blinked, but made no move to strike either of them.

"They'll definitely be interested in *you*, Malumrem."

"Malum-excuse me?" Offence dripped off of Farren's tongue.

The way its mouth twisted, black teeth on show, eyes wide, it was as though it smirked at her. Its eyes flicked to Rorke but before it moved his sword was through its neck. Both humans panted on the edge of a sun-shy clearing. Their eyes were wide and their muscles ached as they held their weapons at their sides. Farren's shoulder continued to bleed whilst Rorke's eyes were trained on the dying –dead- creature at his feet. He plunged his sword through its neck once more, the tendons and flesh severed from bone until the head was no longer attached. Its eyes remained open as it stared at the golden leaves.

"What the *fuck* were those?" Farren swallowed down her racing heart. Her chest heaved as she lifted her eyes to her companion. She hadn't meant for the curse to slip free but as she stared at Rorke's back she didn't care. His attention remained on the severed head. Black blood flew from his blade when he flicked his sword then wiped it on a clean patch of grass.

176

"They're called Kuroguine. They call this part of the Realm their home." He walked over to her with his eyes on her wound. "They would have eaten us slowly while making sure we stayed alive while they did."

She lifted her lip in a sneer as she stared at the fallen heads. "How did they know about us, the mission?"

He peeled back the shredded fabric of her jacket and she winced. Blood seeped from the disturbed wound, over Rorke's fingers and down the inside of her arm. The claw tore through leather and cloth then skin; the injury was not a pretty sight. Thank Griselda it wasn't her sword-wielding arm.

"Why else would I be back here?" *You want the Human Princess. Why else would-* They read Rorke like a book, better than she had in the three weeks she'd known him. It was Farren who was there for the Princess, Rorke was only her guide, her... protector. He was in the Kayei Realm to protect her from the Kuroguine and who-knew what else. The tightness in her throat was swallowed down as her eyes flicked back to the fallen creatures. They narrowed when they landed on Rorke who sheathed his sword. Afterward he picked up the fallen bag and feathered his jaw. There were two directions to choose from: through the clearing or back into the forest. Rorke stared at both with equal displeasure but when he watched her press her hand to her wound - which stung like a thousand bee stings- his jaw softened. "There's a water source nearby. We can clean and dress your wound there and continue moving on foot."

The last two words were grunted but she nodded and offered her hand for the bag. He shook his head and moved back into the trees but this time not on the path they arrived on. The blood from the fallen bodies mixed with one another and soaked into the grass. The puddle formed behind them and neither guard looked back. There was no need, as black blood covered Rorke's chest and face like demonic war paint. It was thick and stuck to his face like jam.

177

What she couldn't tear her mind away from was how dark it was. "Wait! The Kuroguine's blood, could that be what was mixed with the half-breed's blood?"

Rorke took the chance to look over his shoulder. "It has a similar thickness to the black liquid, but it's a strange substance to add to blood."

"Even if it was something from this Realm, would the Healers be able to detect it?"

Rorke sighed, "probably not."

"Then what is-"

"The point is that if it is something human then we can detect it."

Farren pulled at the damp fabric of her shirt. "And if it is not?"

"Then we ask Soter."

She raised a brow. "For someone who hates the Kayei you have a lot of trust in their word."

"Soter is different." Before she opened her mouth to ask more he raised a hand. "Do not ask me 'how', he just is. The King keeps him in the court for his own reasons and we must respect that." Farren hummed and with a click of her strained neck the two humans walked away from the carnage, deeper into the Aureum forest.

ALLIES

When Rorke said there was a water source nearby Farren did not think he meant only a mile away. As dense as the forest was, there was no warning before they broke through the tree line and out into the open. A river sat before them, across which sat a golden bridge. The reflection of the afternoon sun allowed the gold to glimmer on the water, the ground beneath her soft and malleable as she knelt on the bank. Fish swam with the current and the water was clear enough that Farren did not mind drinking from it. *Not like she had a choice,* so she drank deeply as Rorke dug through the bag. Most of the advanced medical equipment fled with the horses but they saved a roll of bandage –one roll was stashed in every bag- and a needle and thread. Her wince was poorly hidden behind another drink of water and she slowly, *slowly* pulled her jacket from her body.

When he knelt beside her she asked, "have you encountered the Kuro..." She scrunched her brows, *the Kuroguine.* "Right, have you encountered them before?" As he poured a handful of water onto her wound he nodded. "Are there any other creatures you know about that I should?"

He stopped his movements. "I didn't withhold the Kuroguine from you on purpose."

"Then why didn't you tell me?" She pushed her braid behind her.

"I thought they would be too occupied with the Harvest," he locked his eyes with hers, "I never expected to fight them while we were here. The shortcut was also a way for us to avoid any locals."

She raised a brow. "Are there any other locals that you don't anticipate fighting?"

"We do not have enough time for me to list them all, and I don't know every one." Rorke's words did not comfort her but she knew he was

179

right: the longer they were idle, the more likely they were to be spotted by the dangerous beings. That was why she was not surprised when Rorke hurriedly removed his gloves and dipped his hands in the river. The sweat was washed away with the water and he turned to face her once again. Stern eyes scrutinised the damage done to her shoulder and the way in which the breeze ruffled the pieces of fabric not stuck to her shoulder in blood. The plasma soaked through the shirt, down her chest and arms and dripped into her glove. She removed it slowly and dropped it to her side. The only sound was that of the river as Rorke gently peeled her shirt from her skin, ripped open the fabric and proceeded to sew the wound closed. With every drag of the thread she swore and flinched. Without the horses and their packs there was no alcohol to sterilise the wound or to numb the pain. She whimpered as he tugged the thread through another piece of broken flesh. Cries accompanied her curses as he reached the deepest part of her injury. What she needed was steady hands and sharp eyes, two things he offered her, not pretty words. The pain only got worse, however.

"That was a hell of a fall, how are your ribs?" Farren blinked. With everything that happened she hadn't told anyone about them being healed, so she shrugged and claimed they were fine. The look in his eyes told her he didn't believe her. Just like in the forest when they gathered firewood, he didn't believe a word. His lashes fluttered as he ran his eyes over her torso. Once he bandaged her shoulder he made to lift what remained of her shirt. In response she leant away from him with narrowed eyes. "There is no way that after that thing tackled you that your ribs are 'fine.'"

"Well they are. Do you hear any wheezing? See me shifting weirdly? Have you seen me check my bandages once since the first week of training?"

His hands remained mid-air as though her shirt was still between his fingers. "If your ribs are still injured you could be a liability."

Her eye-roll was deep. "Then maybe the King should have thought about that before only granting me two weeks before sending me on this mission." She stood with a slight stumble, his tall form soon followed. "My ribs are healed, don't worry Rorke, if we get into any trouble it won't be because of a couple of broken ribs."

He grabbed her arm and pulled her toward him but remained aware of the injury to her shoulder; his face was like thunder. "Do you think the King is so incompetent that he only relied on one plan? He does not have the magic of foresight, nobody knew you were coming so of course there were other options."

"Such as?"

Rorke kissed his teeth. "He wanted to send private hire assassins but they were too scared to cross the Veil. There was one man who offered but he was found dead the next morning. His Majesty finally gave in to the thought of sending one of his own men. It was just going to be me," he ground out.

"But I was told the King had not decided that you were going to accompany me until after I got there."

His eyes were glued to a spot of blood on her shoulder. "Adrastos offered to take you; he thought it would be easier for him to protect a civilian." Farren bit her tongue. "His Majesty made it clear that Adrastos was needed there."

"Then why am I here, Rorke, if you already agreed to this mission?"

The bridge behind him became a point of interest as he sucked in a sharp breath. "You wanted a Trial and this was the easiest way to grant it." At the disbelieving way she raised her brow he continued. "Two is better than one, you had something to lose if you didn't agree and you have the relevant training." There was a darkness in his eyes when he spoke.

"When you say 'two is better than one', you mean that *one* can find and save the Princess whilst the other one of us," she gestures vaguely to herself, "is bait for the Kayei, right?"

"No."

She nods but just as he didn't believe her, she didn't believe him, so green eyes slipped shut and he released her arm. She took the opportunity to step back but then her gaze stopped on something across the river. Her mouth fell ajar and she started forward. Laughter bubbled up in her chest, the noise near strangled as she tried to stop the sound. The guard cleared his throat and stared at the cloudless sky above them, his mind a whir as he tried to think of what to say, but her sudden hand on his chest made his attention shoot to her. The atmosphere suddenly changed as her fingers tapped against his jacket rapidly. "Rorke, you are not going to believe this."

Finally, he looked across the river and he nearly choked on the air he breathed. With their snouts in the water, hair rustled by the breeze, stood their horses. They both looked unharmed and unbothered by their surroundings. Rorke's bow sat undisturbed and the rest of their packs remained tied to the saddles. A chuckle flittered from the guard's mouth and Farren couldn't help but let her laughter free. The horses had yet to lift their heads in acknowledgement. It was Rorke's whistle which caught their attention. For Castle Horses they weren't very aware, a fact that Farren commented on. Rorke was inclined to agree.

They allowed themselves a few moments to check their bags and have their fill of water before they climbed onto their horses whom were happy enough to let them. As Farren checked their supplies her hand paused on a small note tucked into the strap of one of the bags. Written on it were runes and swirled penmanship. The writing was delicate and the scent of men's cologne drifted from the parchment. It read: 'A word of advice for the two of you, keep your horses away from the wildlife.' Farren gaped and handed the note to Rorke. He read the note, crumpled it in his fist and shoved it into the bag. There was no discussion, Rorke back to his usual silence. He guided them over the golden bridge and paused on the other side as he stared up at the sky. Once he was satisfied he turned so they faced the setting sun and started off in a trot. The land before them was vast but clear of trees. With their cover no longer available the wide skies and fields left them able to see for miles. "There is a palace to the East of these fields that we can take refuge in."

She blinked and forced him to a stop with a tug on his reins. "Is the palace inhabited?"

"Yes."

"So when I asked if there was a chance that we could speak to the Ruler of this territory and you refused to answer, that was because...?"

There was a slight tinge to Rorke's cheeks when he replied. "I was still disorientated from the Veil, and I wasn't fully listening to what you were asking me."

"Excuse me!?" She blinked. "Why in Griselda's name would a Royal Kayei grant us refuge?" His face was neutral but there was a subtle twitch to his brow that made her say, "you know them?" He shrugged and continued to ride in front of her. "I wouldn't have to ask so many questions if you stopped leaving things out." Tygre slowed so when he came to a stop she was forced to yank on the reins.

"You'll know everything you need to when it becomes necessary. We're going to visit the Aureum palace before moving on to Kavan where the Princess is likely being held. We will have to avoid interacting with anything else when we travel because this Realm is full of dangerous creatures that want to eat you. What more would you like to know?" The question was rhetorical.

Son of a-

On the horizon sat a glinting building as though made of pure gold. A beacon in the field of colours. Their previous conversation forced a silence over them, save for the horse's hooves and the occasional caw of a bird. To past the time Farren went over everything she could remember from the books from her home, whilst Rorke remained a brooding force at the front. The animals they had not seen earlier followed their movements like miniature spies. The majority of the wildlife were the same as back home like the bunnies and the rare deer with curled antlers. Farren was so focused on her memory and the creatures around her that she hadn't noticed the light started to dim. The sunlight no longer shone in the grass or the manes of the horses. They'd been riding for hours and yet it felt like mere minutes, she supposed keeping the mind occupied would do that.

Rorke spoke "we need to hurry up if we are going to take refuge under a roof and not the stars."

"A roof please, but I imagine the stars are quite beautiful." She tilted her face toward the sky. "There are so many different constellations compared to the Human Realm."

Tygre slowed to match Petal's speed whilst Rorke stared at Farren as she watched the sky above them. A few stars started to wink into existence and she smiled. They were significantly brighter without the smoke-filled skies in their Realm. "How do you know that?"

She turned her smile to him. "It's obvious. It makes sense for different Realms to have differing star formations."

"But?"

A chuckle escaped her, "but," she elongated the word, "I also read about it at the White Castle."

The sip from his skein he was midway through caused him to choke. "Where did you find reading material like that?"

She stared at him for a moment. "Huh, look who's asking the questions now." He averted his gaze from her face to his horse's head. The smirk on her face was too much for his shocked scowl to handle. The action made her falter, her fingers twitched against her thigh. "It was practically useless anyway; most of the books are about pendants and trivial tonics. There is hardly anything on the Realm itself."

"Are you completely insane?"

A click of her tongue and she pushed her horse forward. "I needed information and you certainly aren't inclined to give me any."

He pushed forward as though he would ram straight through her. "You could have been found out-"

"I know bu-"

"-and if that happened you would have been arrested and-"

"I know that too, but-"

"-then you would have been killed for dabbling in magic."

A threat he promised back at the castle "All I did was read a couple of books."

"You aren't that naive, Farren, you know that one book could have your neck snapped in the gallows." The Captain's Second shook his head and galloped ahead.

They bickered until they reached the gates to the palace Rorke spoke of. Stood before them was a gate of iron. Two gargoyles guarded the entrance to what looked to be grand gardens. Dark red leaves peaked over the edge of one of the gargoyles' head. The wings on the one on the left were flared whilst the other kept them hidden behind a vicious snarl. Intricately carved fur adorned each gargoyle; it was akin to staring at a pair of winged Baltars. Farren wondered whether they were based upon real creatures or were there for decoration. The stone creatures cast long shadows over them as the sun lowered behind the golden palace, its crest peaked over the three spires and allowed for the rust-coloured leaves to glow as they fluttered across the staircase beyond the gate.

"So, how do you know the owner of this palace?" At his sideways glare she rephrased, "how formal do I have to be?"

"I don't care, neither does he."

Charming. They dismounted their horses but Rorke took the initiative to try the gate. She sighed as he pushed against it and it shook but remained locked. The gargoyles flared with remnant light. It was like the wind blew life into the stone as they crawled to the edge of their posts. Their eyes followed Rorke's every move which caused the guard to glare up at the now-animated creatures. Farren shushed the horses which allowed the furry creatures to turn toward her. She paused with her lips pursed, a hand on Petal's neck, eyes on the gargoyle. The glint in its eyes mimicked a human wink. She squared her shoulders, winced as the stitches pulled and stared it down. Cooler air thrummed with magic when she locked her eyes with the other statue. A tilt of its head and it sank back to its haunches. The other gargoyle did the same. Their eyes flashed and the lock wrapped around the iron bars fell to the floor. Rorke pushed again and the iron gate swung open. Farren tugged at her horse's reins and guided her through the gate. Rorke followed suit, his own eyes on her.

Breath-taking. That was the only way to describe the gardens around them. Gleaming statues sat next to golden-leaved trees, some so detailed that they made Farren blush. The grass was trimmed neatly against the cobblestone pathway. The palace itself was not just gold but cream as well. Tall windows and yellow vine-covered towers greeted them but it was the man –the Kayei- that stood at the foot of the steps that caught her attention. His clothes were slim fitted and embroidered with maple leaves. The main fabric was cream-coloured which allowed the leaves that lined his slim shoulders and trailed down his arms to contrast. He was the epitome of regal.

"Rorke Alliard." The Kayei clasped the guard's arm in way only comrades did.

Rorke visibly flinched and pulled his arm back to his side. The guard rolled his eyes and gestured to the well-dressed man. "This is Janus," he then gestured to Farren, "this is Farren Attarah."

A person's name was like gold to the Kayei, worth more than money to some. The fact that Rorke spoke hers so willingly told her everything she needed to know about the man before her. The Kayei –Janus- bowed at the waist and grabbed her free hand. He raised that hand to his soft lips and smiled. It was nothing short of mischievous and promised both trouble and pleasure; it was one she found herself returning. However, his smile faltered and his nostrils flared, eyes on hers. It was as though someone paused his entire being: he froze his lips against her skin as though he remembered something important. The flash in his white eyes was gone as quickly as it came.

When he released her hand he straightened and travelled his attention back to Rorke. "I received your letter a couple of days ago which means my home isn't completely prepared for visitors." He glanced over his shoulder at his grand palace. "I hope that won't be a problem." A shake of both their heads and he waved widely. "Your horses can rest in the stables while the two of you eat something. I can't imagine the Oracle was kind to you," 'The Oracle,' just another name for the Veil's guardian. "The first time I travelled through I threw up everything I ate that morning. It was not a pretty sight for my travelling companions. Before my 'test' I told her I was no threat so such a thing was unnecessary." Farren giggled. "But instead of granting me access she made my test much longer than my companions because of my 'blinding arrogance."

Farren was glad she strayed from that idea. "My test was definitely interesting," she chuckled

Janus hummed, "she picks and chooses her favourites," he glanced at Rorke, "no-doubt she was not kind to you."

Rorke's eyes were like stone when he locked them with the backward walking Kayei. "No."

Farren watched closely as Rorke's hands balled into fists behind him. "So you're not one of her favourites?"

Janus smirked at her, "no, I'm certainly not, not everybody can be Nero."

The name rang through her like a bell. "Nero?"

Rorke's fingers gripped the back of her jacket tightly but he addressed Janus, "with the amount he abuses the Veil it is a mystery why she has not cut him off."

Janus raised a perfectly plucked eyebrow. "Nero has not travelled through the Veil in years, Rorke, and if he had, your Realm would know about it." He turned to Farren whose face was a ghostly white. "Trust me lass,

Nero is not someone you want to be associated with, not in this Realm, not anymore."

Rorke's voice seemed lower when he said, "Nero travelled through the Veil weeks ago, so you're right, our Realm would know about it."

"Not possible." Janus paused all movements. "He has been busying himself with this Realm. You humans hold no interest to Kayei like him." Janus watched as the two shared a look and the grip on her jacket tightened ever-so-slightly. Both she and Rorke's mouths were dry but they continued up the stairs once Janus gestured to the doors above them. His eyes scrutinised their movements but he soon returned to his cheeky self with the shuff of his clothing. "The two of you can tell me all about your mission over dinner and I want every. Last. Detail."

"Good luck with that," Farren muttered just as her stomach grumbled.

The Kayei chuckled and proceeded to list meal after meal that they could possibly have at the palace in front of them: roast duck with plums, chicken with steamed greens, mashed potatoes and steaks. Saliva finally filled her mouth as she thought about the rich food. "Trust me, my cooks are the best in the Realm. You'll be spoiled in that regard."

Farren felt her spirits lift as they ascended the steps toward the open door but half-way up she faltered. The rapid blink of her eyes nearly made her dizzy, because sat before the door with its feet tucked beneath its large body was the Night Creature she helped all those weeks ago, and it looked directly at her. The sun set behind the palace but the glow on the Night Creature's scales was beautiful. They glimmered in shades of white, blue and grey, so at odds with the golden features that surrounded it. Its tail thudded against the top step as the trio approached. He really was a large, scaled, puppy. Janus laughed as it bounded toward them. Rorke's hand was on the hilt of his sword but Farren walked forward to meet it where it stopped a step above her and nuzzled its face into her outstretched hands. The scales were cool against her touch and it was much gentler than that day outside the Church. She laughed as it nearly nudged her down another step. With gentle fondness her hands grazed its scales. Both she and the Night Creature purposefully ignored Rorke's incredulous look. A scar protruded from its side, the main feature which originally caught her eye. Mini scales started to grow back around the wound, but there was pale blue skin that was visible because of them.

Farren smiled. "I'm glad you're feeling better."

"The poor creature came back with mortal bandages wrapped around him, and your scent soaked into his body. What you did saved his life."

Farren swallowed but continued to stroke the creature and her mouth opened to explain. It snapped shut when Janus raised a hand. The knowing look in his eyes straightened her spine but Rorke inched past her and the Night Creature, his eyes filled with disbelief and a flicker of fear. She sent him what she hoped was a reassuring smile and followed him. The Night Creature padded behind them with a soft huff.

"You healed a Night Creature?" Rorke quickly asked. Farren shrugged and wiped her boots, an action Rorke did not reciprocate before they entered the extravagant hallway. The entire palace was decorated specifically to Janus' tastes. Although she'd known him for a few minutes, what she saw before her was like the leakage of his soul. It was covered in gold and cream. Paintings of foreign cities, naked women and men, and gardens created with watercolours hung on the walls along with decorative masquerade masks.

"Why masks?" Farren whispered to Rorke.

Janus was the one to answer, "don't you like them?" He smirked at her slightly open mouth. "They remind me of a less tense time."

"What do you mean?" She asked.

Janus stopped at the entrance to the dining room. "The last time I held a masquerade ball was before the Veil was erected. People from both Realms enjoyed a good dance and nobody wondered if the person standing next to them was going to kill them with magic or otherwise." He brushed a hand over a white, porcelain mask on a stick. "They were wonderful events, but balls like that are too dangerous now, who knows what can happen when ones' identity is concealed." His eyes drifted to Rorke who cleared his throat gently.

Janus removed his hand from the mask and led them into the large dining room built to entertain many more guests than the two of them. A long table carved of dark wood was the centrepiece of the room. Cream-cushioned chairs surrounded it and the table had been set for four, a habit or an instinct on Janus' part. No surprise but the cutlery was gold plated. Two chandeliers hung from the ceiling along with more masks, one of which was as large as the chandeliers. A fireplace covered in golden swirls and curves framed most of the back wall, it held mere embers yet the room remained warm. It was in front of that fireplace that the Night Creature curled in front of.

Their host gestured for them to sit and made his way over to a shelf full of wine where he proceeded to pour three glasses. The action jolted Farren as she stared at the large room they were in. She heard no servants - human or otherwise- nor had she seen a glimpse of life except for Janus and his Night Creature, but the fire was lit and the place was clean. Rorke beat her to it by asking, "where are your staff?"

Janus shrugged and turned, wine glasses in hand. "They wanted time off for the Golden Harvest so I let them," he chuckled as they sat, "I couldn't get rid of my cooks though, they are just too good." A comfortable silence fell over them as they each sipped their wine. Rorke settled into his chair and rested an elbow on the table whilst Janus practically lounged across two chairs opposite them. The silence and warmth allowed for Farren's muscles to relax and for a yawn to escape. She stifled it behind her hand and settled into her seat beside Rorke. A few beats after her yawn, Janus spoke, "all your letter said was that you were on a mission and might need a place to stay now and then. Not that I'm complaining, I'm more than happy to house Altin's third strongest man." The smile that appeared on his face was sensual and he winked at Rorke's flushed face.

The Guard stared pointedly at Farren who blinked. "thank you for allowing us to stay, it truly is a beautiful home."

With a grin, Janus nodded his head in thanks but she gazed at the sparkling chandeliers so she could pretend not to notice the way Janus intermittently sniffed at her. If Rorke planned to play coy then so did she; one too many things *sniffed* her in the Kayei Realm and she had yet to know whether that was a positive thing or not. However, she did not miss the way Janus' nose crinkled and he shook his head like a dog. Her eye twitched but

192

the irritation she started to feel faded when the smell of fresh greens and cheese hit her. The first course was carried in by short, pointed-eared creatures with upturned eyes and thin hair, but they were dressed in golden garbs. They didn't so much as glance at her and Rorke.

It was Rorke who spoke as the plates were delivered, "Farren is under the King's orders to rescue his daughter." She forced herself to chew. The way he spoke was like Theron in many ways yet the tense nature of his jaw and the furrowed brows were entirely Rorke. What was not like him was the willingness to part with information.

Farren drifted her eyes between the two men. There was a history between them that Rorke either pretended wasn't there or he pushed so far behind him that he forgot about it. The animosity he showed toward their host was overshadowed by the way he kept eye-contact and spoke about their professional affairs as though he spoke of the fabric of their clothes. After she swallowed a mouthful of green beans covered in cheese sauce she joined the conversation, "the King believes that one of the Rulers of this Realm kidnapped his daughter three weeks ago."

"Or she came willingly," Rorke added which narrowed Farren's eyes.

When did that become an option?

"He didn't want to cause tension by coming himself, so he sent us, his new favourites."

Janus chuckled, "lass, not only will it cause tension but it's against the Accords for a King or his army from the Mortal Realm to set foot in this one." The glare she sent Rorke was deadly but he simply dug into his plate of food. *That was certainly something the King failed to mention.* Noting the look, Janus let out a low whistle before he took a sip of his wine. "Who does your King think stole the Princess?"

Farren circled her wine glass with her finger and turned her attention to Rorke who sighed, "Nero."

Janus slowed his sip. "Your King's information is wrong." At Rorke's furrowed brow he continued, "Nero hasn't been in court for months and you're telling me that your Princess has only been missing for what, three weeks?" A lump formed in Farren's throat. "Nero might be demon spawn but he's not stupid enough to kidnap your Princess with no court to fall back on. Like I said, he has been busying himself with old friends."

Farren leaned forward. "Is there anyone who *would* be stupid enough?"

A deep laugh sounded from Janus and he nodded. "Schylus is probably at the top of that list but he doesn't have the power reserves to cross Realms."

Rorke shook his head and kissed his teeth. It didn't matter what Janus said, they had orders to travel to Kavan even if the Princess wasn't there. They had to check, for the King's sake and their own. At least -she watched Rorke out of the corner of her eye- at least that was what Rorke implied. The Kayei Realm was huge, if the Princess wasn't in Kavan- Farren gulped on her wine.

The next course was carried out after the same creatures cleared their plates. It was a dish filled with roasted lamb, creamed potatoes and more green vegetables. They ate in silence, both she and Janus shared the occasional glance as Rorke remained stone faced. As he proceeded to ignore their stares she asked, "where is Schylus likely to be?"

Before Janus opened his mouth Rorke slammed his hand to the table. It rattled the tableware and half-drunk wine bottle. His glare slowly drifted from Janus to Farren who held it with her own. "Leave it alone."

Despite the authority in his tone she replied, "no."

The hand he slammed against the table curled into a fist. The Night Creature shot to its feet and growled. Its tail raised and claws elongated but Janus lifted an elegant hand and it settled back into a ball with a grumble. The humans held each other's stares as he poured more wine into each of their glasses. Once the Kayei sat back down Rorke rolled his shoulders and turned back to his meal. Farren clicked her tongue and she too returned to eating. If they were anywhere else she would have screamed at him. Instead, the rest of the dinner was eaten in silence. Farren's own fingers were tight around her cutlery as she took her last bite of lamb. The meat melted in her mouth with the creamed potatoes and she felt she would never have a meal as luxurious again. Those thoughts were only solidified when she took a mouthful of the moist lemon cake Janus presented her. It was the best thing she ever tasted; she told him as much. "Thank you, my cooks are well trained in cakes and pastries more than savoury dishes."

"Those were delicious as well."

Janus smiled and turned to Rorke. "She's a lot nicer than the rabble you used to hang around with." Farren's chest puffed with pride at his words and polished off her dessert. A smirk tilted her lips as she watched at Rorke out of the corner of her eye. He rolled his shoulders and pushed his half-eaten slice toward her. The light in her eyes brightened and she dug into the offered slice. Janus chuckles, "when do the two of you leave; I hope your horses weren't too spooked by our creatures?"

The note, the playful warning, they were gifts from Janus. Despite not yet knowing why they were there or if they had any ill will toward his people, he found their horses. A sign of peace to an old friend or a trust for humans... Farren was willing to put her money on the former. She had no idea what their plan was had they not found the horses at the river. She hoped that the

Kuroguine were to be avoided for the rest of the trip, lest Petal and Tygre choose a Kayei's stable to hide in and never return.

The final bite of her cake was swallowed and she wiped the corner of her mouth and finally, Rorke removed his gaze from her. "Tomorrow morning. If what you say is true and Nero hasn't been at court then it's the perfect opportunity to infiltrate his palace and find out if the Princess is there or not." Janus did not voice it, but the look he sent the two of them over the rim of his glass told them exactly what he thought of their plan. Farren was nearly inclined to agree but she kept her thoughts locked away, especially as Rorke scoffed and leaned back in his chair with folded arms. "You've never been one to hold back an opinion before, Janus."

The Kayei raised his arms to his sides. "I think it's a suicide mission."

Farren winced. They were words she thought of not so long before they arrived, so the wine in her glass did not remain there as her travel companion stared at Janus with a clenched jaw. She leaned forward and braced her elbows on the table, both slices of cake devoured and the plates were piled beside her empty wine glass. That aspect of the glass was soon rectified by Janus after he gasped. A good host before anything else.

Farren's head tilted, then she spoke, "just a thought, but if we are going to infiltrate a palace unguarded by its Ruler then it is likely there will be magical barriers, guards of some kind, possibly even traps. Let's be honest they won't be guarding for humans but instead highly skilled, powerful Kayei."

Janus pointed at her and grinned. "She's good."

Rorke rolled his eyes despite the slight lift to his lips. "We'll need to get a rough idea of the layout both inside and out before we infiltrate." He trailed off and quirked a brow at Janus.

"Absolutely not."

Rorke stared. His body shifted so his arms were braced on the chair rests, wrists loose and his head leaned back. He looked like he was posing for a professional portrait. Farren scanned his relaxed posture and the heat in her cheeks blazed at the outline of muscle she spied beneath his shirt. Everything about the man beside her was solid muscle. He unbuckled his jacket when they sat for dinner whilst she removed hers entirely in the warm room. Janus did not comment on her blood soaked shirt or the bandage on show, nor did he scowl at the sight of the filth in his pristine home. Rorke's shoulders twitched as he felt two pairs of eyes on him and he refrained from looking at Farren who couldn't tear her eyes from his chest. Janus' eyes trailed the soldier with hooded lids and once he was satisfied he blew out a breath. That broke Farren from her ogling which coloured her cheeks further.

"I don't remember a lot, any time I was there –which wasn't a lot- I was roaring drunk." Janus proceeded to tell them what he knew of the palace and its layout: the dark corners he knew about, others that he guessed were hidden and where. It was limited but by the light in Rorke's eyes it was enough. The Kayei agreed to fulfil Rorke's request to draw a map and he waved them off saying it would find its way into their bags in the morning. The bottle of wine -and a second one after Janus' insistence- was finished before the night was over and his description of Nero's palace was mixed in with stories from the parties held there. That was how they spent the rest of their evening until Farren yawned for the hundredth time. Both Janus and Rorke shooed her from her seat. The Night Creature whined its goodnight as she exited the room. *Up the stairs to the left, second door on the right.* Rorke made no move to follow her. She managed to drag her feet to the stairs but only made it up the first two when Janus sighed, "she's too nice to be working for your King."

Rorke did not miss a beat, "it's her job. If she doesn't complete this mission there are people back home who will suffer for it."

Janus hummed, tapped his fingers against the table. "That makes more sense than her willingly being a part of the Guard."

Farren's hand clenched around the banister and she lowered her head when Rorke replied, "that's what the King has promised her. It's *her* mission."

"The poor lass was covered in blood and you've been here what, a day?" There was a pause. "So you're going to tell me *you're* here because your King had a momentary glimpse into his humanity and realised she might actually need help?"

"My job is to keep her alive."

More wine was poured and Farren continued up the stairs. She followed Janus' directions and found her bags sat atop a double bed. The sight made her tilt her head. For Janus having no servants everything was neat and tidy. A double bed sat against the right wall and across from the door were tall windows with cream curtains that were kept closed to prevent any moonlight from shining through, or perhaps to prevent any spying. A washbasin sat in the far corner with an ornate mirror hung above it. Both were decorated with painted autumn leaves and vines and sat beneath them was a chair similar to those in the dining room. Gold sconces sat in the walls and they each lit up in golden light when she walked into the room. It was like the light –not fire but golden light- sensed her presence. She locked the door behind her and stripped from her riding leathers. She moved her bags to the floor and tossed her half-torn jacket on top of them, not worried about the condition of the leather. The fabric stuck to her skin as she tugged at her blood covered shirt. The dried blood hardened the fabric and she was glad to hang it over the basin which she filled with water from the tap. A wash cloth sat on a shelf beside the mirror which she used to scrub at her face and body. Pink water swirled down the drain. Clean bandages were found in her bags so she removed the blood stained one around her shoulder and gently, she cleaned the stitches. A long shirt was pulled over her head and she checked the windows and door. A habit that made her long for home. Leaving Brentham was something Farren dreamed of for years but as her shoulder throbbed and her eyes drooped she wished for her own bath and bed, one with different pillows and worn bedding. It wasn't long before sleep took her.

A scream ripped through her as the creature's claws dug into her shoulder. She hadn't seen its hands move. Spots appeared in her vision as blinding pain shot through her body. That time the Kuroguine's eyes weren't on Rorke but it stared at her like she was Janus' lemon cake. Immobility covered her body as it lowered its other hand into her leg and used its teeth to tear open her stomach. Its voice rattled inside her head but it was so jumbled that Farren couldn't take a minute to decipher the words from her own screams, but then it lifted its blood-soaked mouth from her abdomen and grinned wickedly. "Your blood is delicious." It licked its leathery lips. "Your father would be just as tasty, his large body enough to feed me and my sister for a week or more. Perhaps I will devour your mother, she will taste as sweet as her pastries or." It took a bite out of her hip. "I have always wondered what a crazy person tastes like, how about I eat Aunt Eydis and find out?"

Farren turned her face from the evil grin to find its sister had its teeth sunk into Rorke's neck. Tendons hung from the open wound; his head was nearly severed from his body. Blood, there was so much blood. His green eyes glazed over and an empty shell stared at her across the clearing.

Farren's eyes burst open to be greeted with silk curtains. Cupping her head in her hands, she pushed herself into an upright position. Her throat was dry and her limbs ached. The headache that should have arrived hours ago hit her like a cart and she groaned. With her feet planted on the floor she padded over to the basin and braced her hands on its sides. Heavy breaths shuddered through her lungs which pulled tightly against her shoulder. The cold water she splashed on her face cooled her flushed features and travelled down her shirt which she removed from her person. She didn't bother donning another one. There was no way of knowing what time it was but the sky remained dark outside so she hoped for a few more hours of sleep.

When she looked at the mirror a pale, haunted face stared back at her. All colour fell from her skin which left her grey and beads of sweat covered her neck and hairline; the bags under her eyes were a dark purple. *Their eyes were goat-like in design with the black rectangular slit in the centre although the colour of their iris' were not white nor yellow but a dark purple.* Her entire body shivered and she felt her dinner churn violently in her stomach. Moments later she deposited it in the vase by the window which was luckily devoid of any plant life. Once she washed her mouth out with water she risked one more look in the mirror and held back her scream: her greyish skin was aglow, her features more prominent as though they were outlined by an invisible quill, and her eyes- They were no longer storm blue but a bright ocean blue with ripples of grey and navy as though a roiling sea sat beneath her iris. Her canines were longer, sharper. Hallucinations were not uncommon for those with poor sleeping patterns or those with severe stress so she nodded, because that had to be all it was. Her fingers pressed against her face for good measure and sighed when nothing felt different. With a shake of her head she risked another glance in the mirror. Normal, she looked normal. *And human*, a voice whispered in the back of her mind. Before she climbed into bed a scratch and whine broke through the room's silence. She unlocked her door to find the Night Creature sat on the threshold of her door with large, hopeful eyes. The doorway was big enough for the creature to stoop under and the room tall enough that it could sit comfortably but she still stared at the creature with a raised eyebrow. There was no way Janus allowed the beast on the furniture but after their short staring match she sighed and locked the door behind it as it skipped over to the side of her bed where a plush rug sat.

"You better not snore."

As the Night Creature curled into the plush material, Farren climbed back into bed and settled under the soft sheets. She ran her hand over her new friend's head which made it rumble beneath her fingers. With a smile she snuggled deeper into her pillow and fell asleep with hand against the scales of the Night Creature and her face buried in the bedding.

Once Farren slipped back to sleep there were no more dreams, good or bad so she felt surprisingly rested. Rorke looked no different than any day as he sat across from her at breakfast. After she went to bed Rorke and Janus stayed up for a few more hours to map out Nero's palace together and with the amount of wine they drank Farren was shocked Rorke wasn't a groaning mess. Instead, he ate his fill, eyes on his food. The cooks created an assortment of delicious pastries and fruit for them to enjoy along with so much coffee. After Farren took her first sip she felt every vein in her body buzz. Coffee beans were hard to acquire in the Human Realm –or perhaps its true title was the 'Mortal Realm' like Janus said- so she'd never tried any. Rorke had not bothered to warn her against the drink so she filled her cup and drank her fill. Her companion stuck with water whilst their host was nowhere to be seen.

As soon as they finished breakfast they grabbed their bags and started to tow them to the horses. "Did you get enough sleep last night?" Rorke asked when he handed her one of the bags filled with clothes and bandages. Farren shrugged and looped it through the handle of another bag. Then she paused, her eye on a different bag as she checked its contents. The two vials of poison sat atop one of Rorke's shirts, casually, as though they did not contain life threatening liquid. She frowned down at them but simply slapped the leather flap shut. That in turn caused Rorke to pause his movements. "I heard you turn on the faucet from the other room."

She muttered, "I'm sorry for keeping you awake." He pulled on the sleeve of her jacket which still had a hole in the shoulder. Earlier that morning she scrubbed the blood from the leather so that navy shone in the golden sun. The cool of the wind broke through her shirt but it was welcome in the autumn sun.

"You didn't," he swallowed but continued, "I'm not sure I'll sleep well for a while after what that bit- the Oracle put me through."

There was a beat of silence. So that her palm rested on his elbow, she twisted her arm in his grip. Her eyes softened as he stared at his hand on her sleeve. The Oracle tested him and Griselda knows what she forced him to do. Farren imagined her test was child's play in comparison, hers was more confusing than haunting but he looked like a man ravaged by war and she wondered just what he had to endure to travel to a Realm that he hated. It was no wonder she heard Janus' footsteps outside his door last night, or the low mutters of a conversation then the sound of his door shut behind them. Farren refrained from asking whether Janus remained in his bed or what the Kayei did to comfort him, instead she asked, "do you want to talk about it?"

She gave him her undivided attention as he stared down at her. "Not right now. Maybe when this all over we can." He ruffled his hair. "Maybe we can talk about our tests."

The unspoken agreement settled over them and they mounted their horses. Before they started breakfast Farren snuck into the kitchen to thank the cooks for the delicious food and to offer Janus a farewell message. They were so shocked by her presence Rorke found her on the kitchen stairs wide eyed, with arms filled with food. He relieved her of half the burden and they tucked the food into any space they could find in the bags. Farren's bloodied shirt was used to wrap any medical items away from the food. With everything packed and the map Rorke and Janus created –with too many blank spaces for Farren's liking- they started their path North.

Behind the palace sat fewer meadows and more forests. They kept their horses from travelling into what trees there were as they stayed in the open. During the Golden Harvest it was safer than the forests, Rorke told her. Whatever the Golden Harvest was Farren did not have the energy that morning to ask. By avoiding the forests they also avoided any interaction with creatures that would eat them alive. That was a fact she was thankful for. The horses trotted along happily, their snouts buried in the occasional tuft of grass. Where the beginning of another forest sat to their right, a stream sat a few miles North and a small group of houses sat further to their left. With their skeins half-finished, Farren dipped them in the clear water that was full of colourful fish and smooth rocks. They completed their business, used the trees as a toilet and made sure their horses drank from the stream.

Whilst Rorke took his turn against the tree, there was a brief discussion about where to make camp: there were a few small clearings in the meadows or they could stay at the edge of the forest where they weren't in the open. That discussion continued as they travelled along empty roads.

"Anyone participating in the Golden Harvest won't travel this far North or to the edge of the forest. They won't risk being vulnerable to air-born Night Creatures." When Rorke told her that little snippet she felt her head shrink into her shoulders as though she herself could shield from those creatures.

The edge of the forest they camped upon was sat on a hill high above a settlement of houses. They would not risk any locals spotting them or informing Nero that they were so close to his territory. The weather turned frigid before they ascended the hill and the clouds that rolled over head were carried on a chill wind. Farren set up their bedrolls whilst Rorke offered to collect firewood. Despite the need for discretion, a lack of fire would have them both sleepless and frozen by morning. She grazed a hand over the pendant that still hung around her neck; it would not be enough warmth for two and she doubted Rorke would even accept her offer of using magic. Therefore, she focused on pulling bread and cheese from their bags. She snuck an extra bite of cheese with a smirk but that triumph faltered as she closed the satchel: the crack of twigs behind her and the sharp rustle of leaves met her ears. When the sound reached her she subtly tilted her head and glanced quickly over her shoulder. She dared not call Rorke's name but her hand was on the hilt of her sword. The horses in front of her did not stir as the sound of- those were tinkling bells that sounded from the bush. Slowly, so as not to disturb whatever stood before her, she knelt one knee on the ground and reached her hand toward her boot. Without another second to spare she pulled out the knife and threw it toward the sound. Both the tinkling bells and rustling stopped. Moments later Rorke appeared with an arm full of wood. He paused before the knife and stared down at it with a questioning frown.

"I thought I heard something," she explained, her hand outstretched in its throwing motion. A nod and he began to build the fire. Due to his hands being full Rorke was unable to hand her knife back so she moved around him and stood over the weapon. Small, silver bells sat trapped beneath the knife which was lodged into the soil. If she weren't so confused by the bells she would have been proud at the accuracy. The knife was pulled from the ground and slipped back into her boot. The silver bells were next as she raised them in front of her and shook her wrist. No sound came. She blinked and placed them back beneath the bush. Somebody —or something- might have missed them.

Rorke kept his eyes on the fire as Farren pressed her hands close to the flames. Comfortable silence fell over them as they warmed themselves and ate the bread and cheese Farren unwrapped, but once they both finished their respective meals he stood and unsheathed his sword. Then he motioned toward the throwing knives in the bags, a weapon Adrastos trained her in for a week. It was why she had so many knife straps on her body. They were at easy access points on her body: two on her thigh and one against each calf, tucked in her boots, one of which was always filled with a blade. The sword was always a last resort for them, and she tried to adapt accordingly. If she were permitted —she shook her head- if she had thought the fight with the

Kuroguine through, the knives would have been her greatest ally yet she panicked and grabbed her sword on instinct. However, she dusted off her trousers and raised her arms just as she had done against the Kuroguine, that time with the throwing knives in her hands. Rorke's sword tapped against her thigh. Once she slipped her feet into the correct position he lunged. Steel clanged against steel as she protected her side with one of the knives. The tendons in her wrist pulled and she pushed back. That was how their training continued for minutes on end.

A training session kept them spry, prepared, and busy in the unfamiliar forest. What didn't help was that her left shoulder was nearly out of commission but the pull of her damaged skin did not deter her. Suddenly, Rorke swung his blade upward, her legs jumped backward and the tip of his blade grazed her shirt. She returned to her defensive position with a roll of her neck. Swing after swing Rorke forced on her yet she defended herself against each one. As she thought to say as much a sharp lunge from Rorke and she was against a tree. The knives were knocked from her grasp and he plunged his sword into the space above her. Shards of bark fell into her hair and she flinched.

"You are constantly on the defensive; you need to be on the offense once in a while. Surely the Captain taught you that?"

She gulped down air. "I only had two weeks."

"An excuse. You trained with Argen for more than that, so what's wrong?" Flashes of sneering faces, boots on her ribs, freezing water played before her. She swallowed around her tightened throat and averted her eyes to the fallen knives. The action was not lost on Rorke; he nudged her hand softly which forced her to look up at him. Whatever he saw in her face: anger, sadness, fear, made him sway slightly on his feet. Farren huffed and folded her arms across her chest in a bid to push the images far, far away from her conscious. Her chest rose dramatically before she exhaled slowly. Rorke didn't rush her, he didn't ask for any details, he stood before her with his hands at his side and his face open. The faces never left her vision, they swirled in her mind like a fog, made her fingers clench around her jacket and forced her to take another shuddering breath.

"There were seven of them and they nearly... I was overpowered- I couldn't..."

Realisation fell onto his face. "The guards."

A tear slid down her cheek as she nodded, then another, then another. It was the first time she truly stopped and thought about the damage that night had done. The Oracle forced those men into her test, she had them try to drown her past-self over and over yet she thought little of it. It was just something she went through, something she survived and healed from, nothing more, but the sheer effect that night had on her was more than she wanted to consider, more than she wanted to acknowledge. Rorke moved closer to her, his movements slow. The pad of his thumb brushed away stray tears whilst sniffles escaped her. Dark lashes brushed against his hand as her eyes fluttered closed. The calluses were rough against her face but it reminded her where she was, it kept the feel of icy water from her skin. It made her focus solely on *him*.

"You won, Farren."

She shrugged one shoulder. "I killed two of them but the only reason the others stopped was because- because of Argen. I would have drowned if he hadn't shown up."

A shiver wracked through her at the thought but Rorke said, "killing two men is not easy." His spare hand clenched at his side. The other hovered by her face as though he was unsure whether or not to touch her again. They

207

both knew 'sorry' wasn't enough but after a few more moments of silence, she forced a smile and rubbed the back of her hand over her face. Rorke moved ever closer to her, the hand that was by her face eventually moved to cup her cheek. Soft brushes of his thumb made her breathing shudder. Her own hands came to rest on the lapels of his jacket where she splayed her fingers across the fabric. The tears stopped flowing and her breath mixed with his. There was a slight tilt to his head, his eyes on her and her alone whilst the bark pressed into her back. With her chin tilted at that angle she could nearly lean upward and-

Rorke licked his lips and leaned back. His eyes were hooded and he swallowed deeply. Farren blinked slowly and straightened her back. The knives were then in her hands and once Rorke was clear from her personal space she turned and wiggled his sword from the tree. Once the weapon was in his hands she resumed her stance away from the tree. Hesitation filled his body as he watched the raven haired woman stare him down. Her eyes were rimmed-red and her lashes remained wet. A sniff and her fingers flexed around the handle of her knives. "Attack me again." He glanced at the sword in his palm. "Trust me."

After a nod he did as she asked. She twirled and pressed her blade above the inside of his elbow: a demonstration that she could in fact slice open his arteries if she so wished. His eyes widened fractionally and he dropped the sword in defeat. "You recover quickly." The smile on her face was genuine. One of his own tugged at his lips. The moment they shared hung between them so they continued to spar until the sun went down. She won some, he won some, either way they were panting, sweat-soaked messes when they finished. While Farren retied her hair behind her, Rorke offered to take first watch.

"You really don't like sleeping do you?" She joked.

He rolled his eyes as she snuggled deep into her bedroll. The night was much colder than when they first arrived in the Realm, it was as though the 'autumn' wind turned into the Mortal Realm's winter chill. Before he moved to the edge of where their camp sat, he gazed down at her with a soft smile. Something throbbed in his chest when he crouched down beside her. For the first time in a long time Rorke worried about whether or not what he was doing was the right thing, because what his King asked he did, but the woman before him had different standards: she acted for herself and for her loved ones not simply because the King asked. She wanted a future, she wanted her family to succeed in life, and she made sure she asked for it. His jaw clenched, it was a mindset she would lose in the Guard, something he hoped to protect alongside her life. When her eyes rolled in her sleep he stood to his full height and moved to his watch position, the lingering thoughts of Farren kept him company.

With the warmth from the fire and her thick bedroll Farren slept soundly, but just before she succumbed to the deepest sleep, the sound of tinkling bells reached the far recesses of her mind- Then she was jolted awake by Rorke's hand on her shoulder as he violently shook her. She lurched from his touch and pushed herself from her bedroll. Instantly one of her knives was in her hand whilst Rorke's bow and arrow was held at his side. Their swords hung from their saddles.

He knocked an arrow toward the darkness of the trees. "The Golden Harvest has reached the edge of the forest."

Her whisper was sharp, "I thought you said they wouldn't travel this far North, no, no, somebody –like you for example- needs to explain to me what the hell this Harvest thing is and why you are so jumpy about it!"

For a better vantage point of what seemed to be pure darkness, he circled behind her. The faint lights from the houses below were no longer visible and the fire remained blazing, but there was something unnatural about the dark in front of them. It was as though it stared back at them just as they stared at it.

"When we get out of this damn forest I will tell you all about it." Like Rorke's stern voice summoned them, in every direction torches were lit one-by-one. Farren –who opened her mouth to rebut Rorke's statement- stopped. The tinkling bells returned and she refrained from swatting at her ear like the bells were flies. Giggles and growls flew from the darkness. Farren's heart thundered in her chest and in her skull; ten, maybe twenty torches surrounded them. More creatures stood beyond. If they untied the horses and made a break for it there was no way to know which direction was the safest or if any direction was safe. Farren steeled her nerves and grit her teeth. It was possibly the only option.

"Rorke," she didn't know what to ask, what to suggest. All she wanted was to escape the Aureum forest alive. Then she never wanted to stay the night again. Negotiation, politics, maybe the creatures before them weren't as bloodthirsty as the Kuroguine... Maybe some of them *were* Kuroguine. The thought shook Farren's hands. The stitches in her shoulder mocked her as she lifted her other arm higher toward the darkness. Her voice did not waiver when she asked, "what do you want?"

Rorke's neck nearly snapped with the speed at which he looked at her. Without averting her eyes from the darkness she offered a one-shouldered shrug but turned so that she faced the opposite direction he did. Their arms brushed and he removed his eyes from her profile. Mutters sounded from the dark but nobody answered. At least, not verbally: an arrow flew toward them and Farren turned just as it careened between them. She stared wide eyed in the direction it flew from. That set everything in motion. More arrows rained down on them and Rorke did his best to aim at the torches. Farren sliced through the arrows that flew too close for comfort. They were destroyed at a speed that allowed her to dive for her other knife. From her position on the floor, knee bent and shoulders back she threw the second knife. It glimmered in the torchlight as it sliced through the air. The sound of tearing bone and flesh reached her ears so she blindly followed the sound, and the torch in front of her fell to the ground.

Movement caught the edge of her vision and she barely made out boot-clad feet when they stumbled away. The knife was yanked from their fallen comrade's chest with her eyes on the darkness. Farren didn't pause to look at the human-like face that stared blankly at the canopy. There was a split second where she was granted the time to grab the torch from the floor. That too, she plunged forward where it caught the cloak of a creature. It screeched and flailed its arms as the flames set its body alight. In its panic it stumbled into more of the creatures who also caught alight. Three more screeched and writhed whilst others moved as quickly away from the flames as possible.

Farren then flung the torch in the opposite direction where it caught on a set of bushes. She followed the line of fire and when she turned to the darkness in front of her, she twisted the knife in her palm and plunged it into the face of the brave soul that rushed toward her. Each movement was like water as she glided her feet beneath her to land blow after blow. Screeches and curses in two languages swirled around her and she was deafened by a particular yell that she failed to notice the arrow that shot past her. By a hairsbreadth she dodged so that the weapon did not lodge into her skull. Instead, it grazed the side of her face where blood seeped from the scratch. She licked the front of her teeth and moved positions again. With both knives bloodied she ran back to the fire, leapt around it and focused on the horses. They remained untouched but skittish so she proceeded to untie them.

"Rorke!" He glanced at her over his shoulder as another one of his arrows hit its mark. "Back up towards me!"

At her words the arrows stopped firing down upon them. A growl sounded behind her and one of the creatures –a dark-skinned, sharp toothed man- ran from the darkness behind her. It seemed he had not learned who they were dealing with. With hope of getting the message across, she spun on her heel and sliced through his throat. Blood as red as any human sprayed the tree next to them. Her clothes and face were impacted but she ignored them as the creature clutched at his throat in desperation. Loathing shone in his eyes- and fear. *Fear of death*. The smell of his blood and sulphur encompassed her as he fell to the ground. There was a collective breath and then a growl from the darkness.

Farren wasted no time in extending her hand toward Rorke who swiped a torch from the floor and they clambered onto their horses to push through a very narrow gap. Farren felt the blood stick to her body and the metallic taste of it coated her mouth. That did not stop the harsh gallop she pushed Petal into. Rorke was at her side with Tygre but she had no time to check any injuries or to even glance at him. They simply rode forward. Along the dense forest path –the only path they were able to take- ropes and hanging metal objects hung in the way so they both laid as flat to their horses as physically possible and hoped the booby-traps did not hit them. The horses were trained well enough to dodge the bear traps that littered the sides of the path and the ropes that were intended as trip wires. Everything in that forest was set up to kill whoever dared ventured into it and Farren narrowed her eyes as the horses ran like the wind, the adrenaline was the only thing keeping her awake and atop her horse until morning.

The Aureum territory branched away from forests to rolling hills and large mountains in the distance. It was similar to the lands which surrounded the Altin Capital but with the layer of magic it was more serene, more peaceful. There was no barrier, no guards, no gateway to pass through. The lands simply morphed together at the border, a swirl of green on the ground beneath them. They rode around the outskirts so as not to gain more attention from royals or otherwise. It would be a good life if she never had to fight another magical creature again. She mentally laughed; the likelihood of that wish coming true was slim. Soon after they crossed territories they found a merchant's path. The blood that covered Farren was hidden by the night sky but as the sun rose above the homes of locals she realised they were more of a display than they planned. At the mention of her attire Rorke cursed. There was no water source for miles. With that knowledge Farren tried to wipe the blood from her face with the sleeve of her riding jacket. It was successful in smudging the liquid but not removing it fully. She hissed as it dragged against the cut on her face and it painted her nose and cheeks rouge. The sight forced Rorke to stifle a snort into his shoulder as he spotted her red stained face.

She crinkled her nose. "Now that we are out of the woods- heh get it?" He rolled his eyes. "Can you please explain to me what this Golden Harvest thing is, because I plan on avoiding it for the rest of my life."

He nodded. "The Golden Harvest is a competition held every year in Aureum. The winner is given a position in the army and high position in society. Who claims them is decided between the Rulers." That was disgust in his voice. "It is entertainment for them."

A thought dawned on her which caught her breath in her throat. "Does that mean the Rulers of this Realm know we are here?"

"Probably."

She slammed her face against the reins. "How are we supposed to *infiltrate* a palace now?"

"With more stealth than we anticipated. I don't think that will be a problem for you, you can just slice Nero's neck open within seconds and we can go home." It was the first joke he made since they entered the Realm... it was the first joke she ever heard him make. The laugh that flew from her was a full, chest shaking laugh that had her head thrown back. It was so joy-filled that he would never have thought she'd been in a life-threatening fight mere hours before. The column of her throat was pale in the morning sunlight and stole Rorke's attention from her blood-covered torso and torn jacket, a distraction from what awaited them.

After a few more miles, they trotted into an orchard of fruit trees, both the humans and the horses were tired from their ride. Farren slipped from her horse and slumped to the floor despite the damp grass. There was no hesitation or discussion as she made herself comfortable. Her body fell under the shade of a large apple tree, and she slipped her legs from under her and laid flat on her back, arms and legs spread like a starfish. Sleep took her quickly when she slipped her eyes closed. Rorke chuckled and tied the horses to the tree she slept under. He poured them each a small dish of water which they drank heartily from. Then, he sat beside her head with his back against the trunk and closed his eyes; soon enough his chest rose and fell into slumber.

As per the laws of the universe the sun moved across the sky and so the shade moved with it, meaning the bright light broke Farren from her dreamless sleep. The lids of her eyes wrinkled as she squeezed them until she blinked against the light and pushed into a sitting position. Rogue strands of hair fell in front of her face which she shoved back with a huff. Her once tight braid was haphazardly strewn around her back and atop her head. There was a grunt beside her and she watched as Rorke's chest lifted steadily. It was in that moment she truly admired her travel companion: strong jaw, hair that was usually pushed from his face now fell over his forehead, broad shoulders, soft, tanned cheekbones, eyelashes that she would kill to possess. The riding leathers the King gifted them did nothing to disguise the strength of his arms or the shape of his legs which were sculpted for fighting. Flecks of white covered his neck and face, a battle worn solider, which were accompanied by new, minimal injuries from the Golden Harvest attack, but as he slept he was calm, smooth, peaceful. For a man with such a harsh temperament he was beautiful. A chuckle sounded from her when she trailed her eyes down his chest toward the hand that was clasped around his sword.

"Shouldn't you still be sleeping?"

Farren yelped and pressed a hand to her chest. It would be blamed on the scare that her heart skipped a beat and not on the smirk he sent her. A scoff and she kicked his boot gently before she stood and pulled two apples from a low hanging branch. They were ruby red with golden stems but with Rorke's stiff nod they each took a bite. She nearly moaned at how sweet it was compared to the apples she found in the Mortal Realm. Every piece of the fruit was devoured by grumbling stomachs. After they polished off the apples and offered two to the horses they continued on their way.

The orchard they slept in was on the cusp of Aureum and another territory which gave them time to cover the plan once more. The thought made Farren groan. They had been over the plan countless times: pretend to be servants so they could find the Princess' whereabouts, confront said Princess and explain who they are, then sneak out the servants' entrance to grab the horses which will be hidden far enough away that they would not be detectable inside the palace. The escape route was mapped out accordingly but Farren's heart continued to thud uncomfortably against her chest. Their only source of protection would be a knife in each of their boots but for a moment she cast her mind back to Soter's items stashed at the bottom of her pack and snuck a glance at Rorke. The picture of him throwing them into the river before they reached the palace crossed her mind which was why she kept her mouth shut.

They passed by small villages, hoods over their heads and pace slow. Many didn't acknowledge them as they kept their horses steady and their faces forward. Those that did acknowledge them simply watched as they moved across the country. They allowed for few stops and there was little interaction with any locals, including the small Faeries that lined the rivers and streams. They were small beings with soft wide wings at their back and fur covered torsos. Their short tails flicked at them when they passed by. It was at those streams that Rorke helped Farren wash the cut on her cheek and remove the blood from her features. They both also scrubbed at their scalps and hair so that the dried blood was removed thoroughly. It was not until they reached another village after an hour or two of riding that Rorke tightened his hands on the reins and pulled his horse to a stop. Petal slowed and stopped shortly after, her body parallel with Tygre's.

"Rorke, where are we?"

His gaze was on the horizon when he answered, "it's called Foras, we're close to Kavan City, but it's too far for us to ride to today."

"I thought Kavan was a territory?"

Finally he turned to her. "It is... sort of. It's technically a city but the it has its own King. This village is on the outskirts of Nero's power."

"So, his palace is in the middle of the city?"

"Unless it has moved back to his original territory."

Rorke started to move into the village but Farren called his name. "Wait, you cannot simply say something like that and not explain. Palaces do not simply *move*, Rorke."

He sighed. "Kavan is not Nero's original territory, but he likes to invade other King's lands and takes the comfort of his own home with him. If his palace isn't there then we have to go and search for it."

"Being a King and Kayei has its perks then?" She joked.

His face remained neutral and after her small reprieve of a chuckle his words finally sunk in. 'Search for it'... They had an entire Realm before them and Rorke wanted to go on an egg hunt for a palace that was likely no bigger than Janus'. Whatever his plan was didn't involve magic, just them and their horses. Farren herself had never seen a map of the Kayei Realm but she knew it was bigger than theirs which meant finding a palace on their own was -she tried to think of the correct phrasing- not her idea of a good mission. With those thoughts, she followed him into the village and the sight was worse than any scene in Brentham. The smell of rotted wood and manure filled her nose and she nearly gagged on the mixture. Rags were worn by the locals, dust covered roads contrasted with the lush green hills and orchards that they previously rode through. Dark, soot-covered houses, carts that were splintered and rundown, horses that were oh so skinny. The water troughs were either barren or full of murky water. The villagers' faces replicated their surroundings: dull, dirt-covered and severely pissed off. Farren leaned toward Rorke on her horse. "Why are we choosing this village to ride through?"

Rorke's brows furrowed. "We're in the Dead-Zone, it's where the Altin soldiers camped 10 years ago." He lifted his eyes to the villagers. "Nobody asks questions here, it's the perfect rest spot until we move into Kavan."

Farren swallowed. "They look like they are going to kill us for even being here."

"Are you still atop your horse?"

"Yes."

"Then stop complaining, keep your hood up and follow me."

Any villagers in the road parted with frowns. Some spat at the floor they rode on whilst others glared. They were soon off of the centre path and on a back road which wound toward a moderately sized stable attached to an inn. The horses already tied outside munched on short stacks of hay whilst the stable-boys brushed them down. An abnormally tall man stood in the open doorway of the tavern whose frown matched Rorke's usual sour expression. The King's Guard dismounted his horse and once Farren was on the floor, he walked their horses toward the miserable man. He watched as they grabbed their bags and handed the horses to a stable-boy. His hand shook as he took the reins from Farren who kept her head lowered but thanked him none-the-less. The owner –the abnormally tall man whom Farren assumed was the owner- watched as they walked close together, a glance spared at his large form and they entered the establishment. It smelt like ale and something that was inherently masculine and the scene before her could have been pulled from any human village if not for the vibrant clothing on some and the sheen of magic that covered everything in that Realm.

"Rorke," Farren started, "how do you suppose we pay for a room?" Before he responded she added, "and don't you dare tell me that you have money stashed in the bags that I don't know about."

Rorke pulled her cloak so that she stumbled closer to him, his lips near her ear, "I'm sure one of these Kayei has a purse on them." She whirled to face him fully. His hand was still wrapped in her cloak and his face was still tilted towards her. Their noses brushed as she stared at him dumbfounded. Neither of them moved as they stood inside the inn.

"You want me to *steal* from someone?"

"Yes."

"And why me and not you?"

Something in his eyes softened. "You're less intimidating than I am."

She sucked on her tongue and continued to glare. The fabric of her cloak was released from his grasp so she could step away from him, her eyes now on the crowd in front of her. The Kayei stumbled and yelled, their drunken stupor enough of a cover that she and Rorke were nothing more than weary travellers. Her companion moved away from her, his body much larger than most of the men in there but he never looked back to where she stood against an empty table, hands braced on the wood. The idea of taking someone else's money left an acidic taste in her mouth. There was no telling whether it was that person's last penny or if they planned to use that money to buy their sick relative a gift. Farren swallowed the lump that started to form in her throat and mentally shook herself. She had to focus on the people in the room, not those back home in Brentham. The owner remained outside, the barkeep moved back and forth between patrons who demanded refills, and those who sat at the bar guffawed loudly.

Coats hung off the patrons and the back of chairs but there was no way for her to gauge what was in those pockets so her eyes continued to rove across the bar until she spied purposeful movement. A man pulled a purse from his coat pocket, paid the barkeep and tucked the string beneath his belt. Of all the Kayei she saw he was the most 'normal' of them all: his teeth were pointed, yes, and his features were sharp but his ears were rounded, his jaw less prominent and his limbs were not supernaturally long. A human in- her thoughts stopped in their tracks as she spied his eyes from across the crowded room. They glowed a lime green that illuminated his face. Those eyes moved closer to where she stood near the path to the exit. Farren sucked in a breath, narrowed her eyes and counted his steps. Then she stumbled, her foot caught on the back of her ankle. She fought every instinct she had to twist her body, instead she clumsily flung her hands out only to collide with him. He let out a grumble as her body hit his and they both fell to the floor. Nobody turned their way despite the noise from each of them.

"I'm so sorry, I lost my footing, I am so sorry," she chanted out.

He dismissed her with a wave of his hand. "It's alright, truly, no harm was done."

"I am so sorry you were on your way out and I just slammed into you, that's not what you want is it?" A nervous chuckle escaped her. As she spoke her hands ran across his field of vision frantically. She patted his chest, his arms, the floor beneath them. He was so flustered beneath her that when her palm touched velvet and she pulled, he had no idea that he was just robbed. With the speed of her hands and her constant apologising she was able to tuck the purse beneath her waistband. A plan perfectly executed. "Again I am so sorry."

She helped him to stand, he brushed himself off, and stared at her for a moment. "It's fine."

With a nod of her head he blinked and left the inn. It wasn't until the doors swung closed that she straightened her cloak and pressed her hand against the uncomfortable bulge that sat against her abdomen. The guilt started to creep its way up her back but the press of the outline of the coins kept her steady. Rorke sat at a table near the bar, his face shrouded in shadows but a pretty, voluptuous Kayei leaned across his table with her chest on full view beneath her corset. Rorke's eyes were not visible but with the way the woman giggled there was no doubt in Farren's mind that a blush covered his cheeks. His head lifted when he felt Farren's presence walk over to them. The Kayei's red-tinted lips curled sensually whilst she brushed her slender fingers down Rorke's face, across his lips and followed his gaze to where Farren stood with a bemused smile. The woman looked between the two humans, asked Rorke another question to which he sheepishly nodded, and sauntered over to Farren where she paused before her. She moved like a cat and made sure to brush her lips against Farren's ear when she whispered, "he's all yours darling."

Farren's eyes widened and a blush climbed up her neck. The Kayei blew her and Rorke a kiss then set her sights on another patron who was a lot more accommodating than Rorke. "Have fun?" Farren smirked as she shook off the shock.

He stood and she spied his face, to find her hunch to be correct, his cheeks were a cute rosy-pink. "Did you get the money?" She tapped her fingers on the purse with a raise of her brows.

The barkeep no longer flittered between orders but instead cleaned used glasses, his eyes on the crowd just as Farren's had been. When he locked on them he straightened. They must have been a sight, two hooded strangers, stood snugly together, their eyes solely on him for that moment. Rorke kept a hand on the small of her back as he guided her through the throng of people.

"Are you sure this is a good idea?" Farren asked before they reached the bar.

"This is the only option." Once they reached the barkeep, his hand left her body. The solid weight of him against her vanished and she nearly swayed. To compensate she braced her hands on the wooden bar, hands splayed in a sign of innocence. Rorke's hands slipped beneath her cloak, his fingers brushed against her shirt and pulled the purse from her waistband. She

221

smiled sweetly at the man who watched Rorke's every move like a hawk and whose eyes brightened when the purse jingled.

The man behind the bar stared between the two of them then the purse, nodded and held out his palm. "Fifteen silvers for a room for two."

Farren nearly asked Rorke to throw the coins at the man instead of the calm way he placed them in his hand. A key was exchanged. Luckily, the Kayei she robbed was wealthy or the two of them would barely have enough for food also. With a curt nod the bartender pointed to the stairs and Rorke moved toward the rickety wood. She trailed behind him, hands close to the weapons at her side and her eyes on the tavern below. Nobody watched them go. Once they reached the top of the stairs drunken men and women milled about, some passed out on the floor, vomit on their clothes; some women convinced men to take them to bed, their hushed, sultry tones enough to bring any man to his knees.

"Rorke," Farren started teasingly, "did you find us a room in a brothel?"

"Most inns act as brothels in the Dead Zone." That was a 'yes' then and she could not help the smirk that fixed itself on her face, not as Rorke kept his eyes fixed firmly on the corridor. It was all very mundane; the Kayei themselves were speckled in different colours and hues, their features different and yet not. There was one woman whose skin was a bright pink, her eyes yellow and her hair the colour of strawberries, who helped a man to his feet.

Rorke followed her eye-line and automatically his brow rose in question. A quick glance between them, at her curious stare and minutely tilted head, and he offered up a sprinkling of information that she did not have to ask for, "she's a Kayei too." Farren jumped and turned her attention to him. "Most of the creatures in this Realm are Kayei, and magic changes the features drastically of some. Faeries, Night Creatures, and Kuroguine are sub-Kayei which is why they are more demon-" He flicked his eyes away from hers when she ran her tongue over her teeth. "They look very different to both humans and Kayei."

They dodged the unconscious and slurring Kayei as they moved down the corridor. Doors lined either side; some were decorated with 'do not disturb' signs and loud moans sounded from behind the pieces of wood. Farren pressed her fist to her mouth to prevent a chuckle from escaping and only released her knuckles when Rorke slipped the key to their room into its lock. She supposed it was karma for stealing from the Kayei.

The two of them slipped into the small room and breathed a sigh. The stench of alcohol was less prominent but lingered on their clothes as they stood in silence. There was a double bed pressed to the left wall covered in frayed blankets; the door faced a very small and narrow window –one so small that nobody could throw themselves from it- and a desk where a bowl of water sat on its own. On the right wall sat an open nook where a makeshift toilet made its home. It was simplistic.

"Fifteen silver pieces, is he joking?" Farren asked mainly to herself.

Rorke sunk to the bed, his hands brushed against the blankets and he lifted his eyes to survey the room. "It's convenient."

"And small." She brushed her hand through her hair. "Should we order food before we get settled in for the night?"

"I'll go, stay here and don't open the door unless it is me."

With a cheeky smile she asked, "and how will I know it is you without answering the door? Voices can be very deceiving you know."

He rolled his eyes but a small smile played on his lips. "I will knock *abnormally*."

Her cheeky smile remained when she nodded but despite the playful conversation he kept the key with him and clicked the door shut, so that she was left with only her thoughts. There wasn't a lot to snoop around in the room so she flopped on the bed, her back happy for the relaxing mattress beneath her. The cloak she wore was untied so that it acted as another layer between her and the bed, and she spread her arms out wide. The stitches in her shoulder stretched but the pain was nothing compared to the pleasure she felt at her muscles loosening. The plain ceiling stared down at her, the wooden boards of the floor matched the beams above her. There was no paint on any of the wood so the different shades of brown made a kaleidoscope around her. It was as she focused on a particular dark spot on the beam above her, that her eyes drooped. Her eyelids became heavier and she lost the battle between consciousness and sleep. That was how Rorke found her: passed out on the bed, boots barely brushed the floor and her arms were stretched out like an angel. He quickly placed the food he ordered on the desk next to the bowl and crossed his arms. For a moment he watched as her chest rose and fell in a breath, her face was smooth and peaceful, the last time in a long while that it would be so. Her lips were parted slightly and glistened from where her tongue grazed the skin. He wet his own lips and fought back the memory of their near-kiss, how her breath was warm against his face, how her hands pressed against his chest in an attempt to steady herself. The longer he watched her sleep, the darker his thoughts became and his chest ached at the thought of Farren face-to-face with Nero. He pictured her lifeless body at his feet, bloodied and bruised. The tightness in his throat was swallowed and he pushed away from the desk. That caused the bowl of water to rattle so Farren shot up from her sleeping position.

"Sorry." Rorke cleared his throat. "I didn't mean to wake you."

Farren wiped the drool at the corner of her mouth with her cloak. "No harm done," she sniffed, "is that beef?" Rorke moved from the bowl to reveal two plates of steaming food. Beef stew and mashed potatoes sat proudly on the wood. She clambered off the bed to his side where he handed her one of the plates with a fork. The moment she took a mouthful she moaned. Despite enjoying Janus' food previously, it felt like weeks since she tasted hot food. The meat was chewy but the buttery potato and sauce made up for it. At the contentment on her face, Rorke lifted his fork-full of beef to his mouth and chewed slowly. The two of them migrated to the bed; each of them claimed a side and sat facing the other whilst they ate. Farren's leg was tucked beneath her and she leaned slightly forward to eat her food. Rorke lifted the plate to his lips and practically shovelled the meal into his mouth. "How does this taste so good?" She asked around a mouthful of potato.

"We have been eating rations and bread, this is fresh food."

She nearly gasped, "did you just compliment a Kayei chef?" Rorke's glare forced her to take another bite and they finished their meals in silence. It was not uncomfortable or stagnant, it was simply restful, a recharge of their bodies. Farren placed the empty plates back on the desk with a twist of her body. By the time they finished eating, their cloaks were thrown on the floor with their bags and jackets, their boots were on their respective sides and Rorke's shirt was unbuttoned down to his pectorals. Once the plates were safely put to the side they started to swap stories. Farren spoke of her time in Brentham and Damera and Baltar whilst Rorke shared stories of his days as a beginner guard, one with such glee and ambition. They made each other laugh and Farren nearly fell off of the edge of the bed one too many times for Rorke to consider her sober. At the mention of alcohol Farren said, "when we get back to the White Castle, I'm going to teach you a drinking game Argen taught me. It gets complicated toward the end but if you win, your opponent gets so drunk it's too funny to pass up."

His deep laugh echoed through the room. "It won't be easy to get me drunk, Farren."

"Oh I take that as a challenge." Mischief glinted in her eyes.

More idle chatter was exchanged until the sun fully set and the sliver of light the window once let in no longer existed. The two of them made themselves comfortable under the blankets. The bed was big enough for both of them to lie comfortably but Rorke's stature was much larger than Farren's so when he took a deep breath his arm brushed against hers. There was something fragile about the atmosphere yet thick enough that Farren had to force long breaths into her lungs. For the first time since she met him, she felt awkward around Rorke, as though she was uncertain what to say or how to say it. What wasn't obvious to her was that Rorke's mind continued to swirl dangerously about the woman at his side. It had his muscles coiled tightly and his heart in his mouth. Her name was on the tip of his tongue but a soft sigh fluttered from her and he clamped down on what he was about to say.

"Goodnight, Rorke," Farren said despite the urge to say anything but. She wanted to talk to him, to have a proper conversation with him about the mission, about life. They may have bantered and told anecdotes of their lives, but there was nothing deep, nothing that made her feel like she knew the Second in Command any better. The grit of her teeth was practically audible as she fought against her restraint to ask him something more personal, but his light breaths told her she was too late. The Guard was asleep and she was left to stew.

PART 2: THE LION'S DEN

"I'M COMING FOR

EVERYTHING THEY SAID I

COULDN'T HAVE."

Her First

The two of them were covered in darkness, the companionable atmosphere shifted to one of stifling, non-spoken words. There was something about the darkness that dredged up memories and unwanted thoughts. Her hands clenched beneath the covers and she took in a breath, then she turned on her side so that she faced his stern profile. The faintest outline of his strong jaw and fight-scarred nose was visible. Yet, the way his lips parted were soft, just as her breaths were against his face.

"You're still awake," he commented.

"I know. How are you?"

Rorke turned to face her. "How am I?"

"Yes." Farren nodded even though it was unlikely he saw it. "We spoke for so long but I never asked you how you were, after Janus', after the Golden Harvest, about tomorrow," she bit her lip, "I know you were uneasy after the Veil ..." she trailed off, unsure of how to continue.

The sound of him swallowing followed. "I'm fine."

"If you wanted to talk to me about your test I'm willing to listen, intently might I add." She tried to lighten what exactly she offered him.

There was a pause before he replied, "okay." The bed shifted and his body fully faced her, his arm tucked beneath his head. "It was horrible."

"Great start," she awkwardly chuckled then apologised, "sorry, continue."

His own sheepish chuckle sounded. "I originally landed in the White Castle halls but nobody was there. My heartbeat was in my ears but I walked toward the throne room. It is the largest room in the castle so I thought it would be the safest. It was dusk so the torches weren't lit but there was enough light to see by. Captain Adrastos and our men filled the throne room. He offered me a sword which didn't belong to me but he insisted I take it." He shuffled on the bed. "His Majesty wasn't there nor was any noble I've seen in the castle. Then the scene changed and all of us were stood in this field. People were screaming and swords clanged; the smell of blood was so strong, like I was stood in a slaughter house. After the smell hit me, the dead bodies appeared. I barely knew them but they were some people I recognised from the castle, or maybe the Capital, they were familiar but not enough that I could mourn them. Then the world went dark and a shadow fell over the field. The men from the throne room were lined up in front of me with their weapons drawn. Some stared at the ground but the ones who looked me in the eyes were-" He turned to face the ceiling and she moved imperceptibly closer. "They were men I served with, men I work with now. That was when a voice echoed in my mind; it told me that I got a free pass last time and that I had to prove myself. I never responded to it, I just looked at the men. And then the sword was in my hand and pointed at one of them. I don't remember grabbing a weapon but they all moved at once to attack. I fought back: my blade sliced through every one of them. I can still feel their flesh as my sword ripped through them." His voice wobbled and Farren gently placed her hand on his shoulder. "I was covered in their blood only for Captain Adrastos to appear. He called me a traitor, wanted me dead, but I knew to win the test I had to kill him because that is what Kayei do, they take our worst thoughts and fears and entertain themselves with it." A bitter tone and het hand tightened on his shoulder. "Our fight was the longest, it dragged on for what felt like hours but finally I sliced open his neck." Tears lined his eyes. "And the next thing I knew the world blurred and you were stood in front of me."

The bed shook as his body shivered against the mattress. Farren scrambled closer to him, her hands were hesitant before she placed her other hand on his arm. Once her skin made contact with his he grabbed her hand.

Rorke was not a man who often sought comfort but the shine of Farren's eyes from what little light there was and the feel of her cool skin against his clammy body made him cling to her. The muscles beneath her hand tensed then relaxed under her hold. She kneeled above him as she rubbed soothing circles into his arm but he abruptly sat up, his forehead nearly collided with hers. So she could try and see his face she leaned back. They were close enough that they shared breaths and the feel of his heat radiated across her face. His grip tightened on her hand and he pulled her ever-so-slightly-closer. Their noses brushed and Farren's lips parted whilst they sat in the darkness.

"Farren," Rorke's voice was barely louder than a whisper, "we should get some sleep.

She nodded. "Yes, yes we should."

The hand around hers snaked around her back and gripped the fabric of her shirt. In one fluid motion he flipped them onto the bed so that they both lay on their sides. In turn her body was pushed closer to his. Her own hands cupped his face and scratched against the side of his temples. They both looked at each other through the darkness, breaths mingled and legs entwined. No words were spoken, only a peaceful silence and the warmth of their bodies filled the room. The tear tracks on Rorke's face dried but she brushed her thumb under his eyes for good measure, a comfort he offered her in the forest. Each movement was soft and gentle like the two of them were made of porcelain. That was how the two of them fell asleep, with their noses near-touching and the arms draped over the other's body. Neither wanted to break from the cocoon they created.

The sun barely peaked through the small window when Farren stirred. A heavy weight sat over her waist and kept her anchored to the bed. Her nose was pressed against something warm and solid, so close that she felt Rorke's

230

pulse through his skin. She shuffled in his arms, closer to the warmth and she rested her lips against his collar. One of her arms was pinned between their bodies but the other was free to trace the scars that littered his chest which was visible through his open shirt. Soft fingers drew patterns and connected each scar like connect-the-dots until the arms that wrapped around her squeezed ever so slightly then loosened as the man next to her stirred. She removed her face from the crook of his neck to watch as his face scrunched before they blinked against the pale light. "Good morning."

Immediately, his eyes shot to hers. "'Morning," his voice was gruff and gravelly. After he darted his eyes between hers, he scanned down her body to find her nearly flush against him. The sight brought a blush to his face and he cleared his throat. Her hand remained on his chest and cheeky smile threatened to take over her face.

Instead of teasing him she asked, "how do you feel? How did you sleep?"

"I can't remember the last time I slept that soundly. Thank you, Farren, for last night."

The smile finally made its way on to her face. "What are partners for if not to listen to each other's trauma?"

The mood was much lighter that morning. It was something about the sunrise or their impending danger that made the two of them grin at each other. During their exchange, Rorke's arms remained solid around her. However, when she shifted in his arms he loosened his hold so she could stretch her muscles. They slept in the same position all night so her body protested against the large movement. When she turned onto her back and lifted her arms above her head, the shirt she wore rode up to reveal the sliver of skin above her trousers. Rorke's attention was instantly stolen by the pale flesh. Subconsciously his hand drifted over her stomach, lightly, gently and goose-pimples rose on her skin. With her arms mid-air she turned her face to his with a raised brow. He looked from her face to where his hand splayed on her abdomen. "Is this okay?" She nodded and he massage across her skin to her side where he used it as leverage to pull her back into his body. "Is *this* okay?"

"Hell yes," she whispered then realised how eager she sounded and cleared her throat. "I mean, y-yes this is good-fine, I mean I'm not complaining, I mean-" Rorke's chuckle stopped her mid-sentence. With her lips parted she stared as the man who she fought alongside, who protected her from the Kuroguine, who travelled into a Realm he hated so that her inexperienced-ass didn't die, laughed at her flustered expression. There was something about Adrastos' Second that seized her chest and softened her touch, something that made her gaze linger longer than was socially polite, something that drew her to him no matter the situation.

When she continued to stare at him, no words spoken, his chuckle stopped and he raised a brow. "What?"

That shook her from her thoughts and it was her turn to blush. "Nothing." She looked over her shoulder toward the window and sighed. "Do you think we have some more time to rest?"

He too looked out the window. "I think we can risk another hour." He smirked. Farren nodded, and without hesitation, shoved her nose back into the crook of his neck and inhaled deeply. His arms returned to their position around her but they were not still: one hand rubbed circles into her clothed back whilst the other snuck under her shirt and danced up and down her side. His hand was much larger than her waist and he squeezed the flesh lightly between his fingers until he brushed against her ribs. The white cloth that adorned her body rode up with his ministrations so that the expanse of her skin was visible like before.

"You weren't lying," he muttered.

She shivered against him and pressed closer. "About what?"

"Your ribs really are healed."

A hum and a smile. "I told you." She slipped her own hand into the open lapel of shirt to stroke against his large pectorals and played with his chest hair.

After a few seconds each of them stopped and Farren lifted her head to face him properly. His eyes were already on her, nothing but sincerity in his gaze. Hesitantly, Rorke leaned forward, and as his breath hit her face, their lips met. Both their eyes fell closed and the hand on her back snaked around the join his other hand on her waist. She arched into his touch and glided her hand from his chest to his neck where she used him to drag herself closer. The press of their lips was soft, slow, like they had more than hour before they had to leave, but that serenity and softness did not last long because Rorke's grip increased in pressure and he cradled her against him. He was all consuming as his tongue brushed against her lips and slipped inside of her mouth. She gasped against his mouth so he slowed his movements, his tongue a mere brush against hers before he focused on their entwined lips. Not wanting Rorke to have all the fun, Farren's tongue followed his so that they met before he left her mouth a bruised mess. Their tongues played with each other whilst their bodies moved of their own accord. The grind of her hips against his brought a moan from her mouth. His own grunt vibrated through his chest.

Their lips pulled apart, a string of saliva held them together. "Are you okay with this?" Rorke kissed her lightly after his pause. "I *want* you, your nails in my back whilst I press between your thighs, but." He searched her hooded eyes. "If you aren't comfortable with that we should stop now."

Farren took a breath to scan his features but she smiled, kissed him softly and nodded. "I want that too, please," she nearly moaned.

"Fuck, normally I would claim you hard and fast but I need you to be able to walk," he chuckled.

At the deep nature of his voice and the way his eyes scanned her body, she felt her skin set aflame and her breath hitched. There was no more talking, no more questions as Rorke leaned over her, trapped her body between his arms and slammed his lips to hers. She tried to keep up with his speed; her lips left his to leave open mouthed kisses on his neck whilst her hands lightly scraped down his shirt. With that movement he pulled back, ripped his shirt from his body impatiently and worked on hers. It was a miracle the buttons didn't rip. Both their shirts were thrown to the ground and Rorke nearly cursed at the sight of her chest bindings which he also tore from her body and flung to the floor.

Farren gently raked her nails across and down his chest until he moaned out curses. Whilst she admired his muscular physique above her, he removed what was left of their clothes. Naked and flushed, Farren stared up at her companion, her partner, her *friend*. Where their first kiss was soft and gentle, the harsh kisses he pressed to the top of her breasts were anything but. She arched into his touch as she rolled her naked hips beneath him. The heavy weight of him brushed between her thighs and she sucked in a breath. She opened her eyes and watched as his abdominal muscles contracted with each contact. He was thicker than she imagined and for a moment she felt her body tense, a fear that it would hurt crossed her mind. That thought was exorcised by the swipe of his tongue along the column of her throat.

With eyes blown with lust he shook his head, grabbed her wandering hand, and entwined her fingers with his only to press them to the sheets beside her head. The world blurred around them as she locked eyes with him. He

234

kissed away the tense lines of her face when he thrust forward, until she softened beneath him. The sound of heart beat in her ears at the strong, sweat-covered sight above her: Rorke's hair was plastered to his forehead and his shoulders were coiled with tension. The pace he set was by no means slow and the bed rattled beneath them with each roll of his body. Every inch of him pushed and pulled against her. The moan that escaped her was no-doubt heard from the adjacent room. His name was a prayer from her lips, her own name a breath on his. The closer the two of them were, the harder he moved. The feeling in her stomach coiled tighter and just before she reached the edge, she wound her free hand into his hair and brought his lips against hers, only to trail that hand across his back and dug her nails into his skin. He moaned lowly, kissed her back and brought her to release. He followed shortly after, the muscles in his thighs tense and lips bruised.

There was a moment of silence where Rorke kept his body above hers. Slowly, she rubbed her tensed legs up his side whilst they caught their breaths. She removed her hand from his back, ran it across his cheek, and down the coiled muscles of his biceps. A blinding smile was gifted to him. A large grin shone back at her whilst he brushed strands of hair from her face. Then, he slowly leaned down to kiss her. There was a brief press of their lips together before it became merely breathing into each other's open mouths. With another quick kiss the large man rolled to her side, a hand braced against his abdomen and the other was tucked underneath his head. Farren curled onto her side, a slight ache between her legs but the smile remained.

"Not bad for my first time, right?" She exaggerated her wink despite the nervous shine to her eyes.

Rorke paused with his mouth agape. There was a moment where the information had yet to register, but soon after the whites of his eyes became more prominent and he cupped her cheek with his palm. This forced her eyes to look into his, not that she wanted to look away from the handsome man before her. "I was your first?" The nerves that threatened to shake her entire body were more obvious to her in that moment. She had no idea if he was happy or angry, sad or disappointed, so she swallowed and nodded. Her smaller hand cupped the one against her face and she hooked her fingers above his thumb. If she could savour his warmth before he pulled away, that was all she wanted in that moment. "Did I hurt you? Do you need anything?"

The nerves immediately vanished and her grip tightened around his hand. "No, you didn't hurt me. I just- can we stay here for a little longer? Then we can-" Her eyes flicked to the window. "Go and complete this mission." Her entire body melted at the worried look in his eyes that soon ebbed away to something much happier.

"Yes," he breathed. Their lips met in a languid kiss. The hand on her cheek corded into hair and kept her body held to his. The wild beat of their hearts thudded between them. They were wrapped around each other so that it was just the two of them: there was no threat of magic, Kuroguine, Kayei; there was no Princess to worry about, or a King to obey. It was just Farren and Rorke. They existed in a place that would not be reached by reality or time because in that instant they were consumed by the other. There was nothing and nobody that would tear the two apart. They were human, yes, but no force dared touch them.

The riding gear Farren became so accustomed to was replaced by common, servant clothes. What that meant was that she had to say goodbye to fitted trousers and shirts. The main fabric of her attire was a white, off-the-shoulder, waterfall-sleeved dress. It flared where it stopped at her ankle, but was loose enough that she could move around more easily. The second part of her attire was her long waistcoat: thick straps travelled into a corset then followed the seam of the dress until it reached her black boots.

Rorke's fingers deftly strung her corset together and tied it around her front. The action made her inhale sharply. He smoothed down the material of her dress, pulled her in for a kiss, and adjusted the strap of her corset so that it did not press against her injured shoulder. He ran his thumb gently over the bandage, but then it was his turn to get dressed. The muscles of his chest rippled with each movement and the sunshine did nothing to hide the planes of his chest. A worn grey shirt was pulled over his head and he reached for the trousers. The shirt covered most of his scars and scooped high on his chest as though any sight of chest hair would cause a lady to faint. Farren's eyes were transfixed as he pulled on the dark fabric and proceeded to tie the strings of his trousers. Purposefully, he slowed his movements and she raised a brow, her face was the colour of fresh strawberries. A bow sat at the junction of his hips which she tentatively reached out for. He caught her hand before she reached the tie, and kissed the back of it. Her playful pout nearly had him releasing her. The sound of rustled fabric and his breath close to her ear made her skin tingle, then the heavy weight of her hair was pulled behind her and draped across her damaged shoulder; it was the easiest way to hide her injury from prying eyes. She wondered why a dress with open shoulders was necessary, but it was a minor issue compared to the *acting* they had to perform.

It was well known in Altin that there were humans past and present who were under the rule of the Kayei, who were forced to work so that they were not slaughtered, to work for no money. Yet, those humans were supposed to be grateful for the opportunity. The women had to be grateful that male Kayei looked at them, touched them, spoke to them whilst they did their 'jobs'. The human men had to be grateful that they were strong enough for labour, that they were allowed in Kayei homes. That was what she and Rorke had to be: *grateful*. The entire situation made her skin crawl.

Rorke replied to her small shiver, "remember, we are here for the Princess, nothing else."

The thought of helping any lost souls crossed Farren's mind for a millisecond there was no denying it, but she knew that if they wanted to live – more importantly live with the Princess- then she would have to swallow her own feelings and continue with their mission. She looked up at him through her lashes and with a small smirk said, "do you think because I am a woman that I will turn into a 'bleeding heart'?"

"No." He sighed as he packed their bags. "I needed to say it because I want you to survive this, Farren, you will survive this."

"So will you, Rorke, trust me."

The sight of her confident smile filled Rorke's heart with light and he felt his chest warm. He moved a few strands of her hair just for something to do with his hands whilst her own remained on his chest which she used to straighten his shirt. The greens of his iris seemed more vibrant in the Kayei Realm, or perhaps that was because he stood so close to her she never realised just how green they were. As he had before, she lifted one of his hands to her lips. The rough skin of it contrasted with the warm softness of her lips and he licked his in response. Her lips barely grazed his skin before she removed herself from his vicinity. The moment was so out-of-the-ordinary for the castle guard; it was soft, it was gentle and it was what he wanted before they were to travel into Kavan, so his eyes followed her as she straightened out her skirts –an action she hadn't had to do in a while- and made her way to the door, her bag in hand. Rorke took the moment she pulled on her cloak to truly study her: the light in her hair and her delicate yet deadly hand on the handle of the door. Her silhouette was burned into his mind's eye and with her soft gaze he grabbed the bag at his feet, hoisted it over his shoulder and followed her from the small room which would forever be engrained with the two humans who bared their souls and left to save a Princess.

Kavan was a city unlike any Farren had ever seen. It was circular but the structures were each built upon roads which climbed into the clouds as though they made a makeshift hill. At the peak of that hill was a small castle, the spires of which soared into the sky. The sharp, black building was circled by birds with loud caws whilst the sun beat down on the city. The bustle of people drowned out the sound along with the wheels of the carts that thundered along cobbled streets. Farren craned her neck skyward as they entered the city gates. Only two guards stood watch at the large opening but the weapons they carried were enough to scare any sane person from trying anything. One look at the swords at their sides made the light weight of the dagger she slipped into her boot much more prominent.

"This is where Nero resides? It's so vibrant," she commented.

Rorke nodded. "No matter the Kayei, they like their audiences." He rolled his eyes. Janus lived in the middle of forests and meadows and his castle remained his own but Nero –Farren glanced up at the castle once again- he was in the centre of *everything*.

Their cloaks were pulled up to shadow their faces whilst the horses walked beside them. There were so many things to see and experience that it was difficult to keep their eyes directly forward and it allowed them to notice that the trek toward the castle differed the higher they climbed. At first, restaurants and shops were filled with patrons and life but soon that fell away to quiet back streets and empty houses. It was like a ghost town until they reached black, thick, high walls that surrounded the castle gardens.

Something heavy pressed against her chest, hard enough that she was forced to push her own hand against her sternum to try to ease the discomfort. She found that Rorke was in the same position. The pressure threatened to crack all her ribs, a feeling she never wanted to experience again. The air that was filled with the smell of smoke did little to allow her to breathe deeply. She cursed as she fell to her knees, hand braced against the ground. Rorke reached for her, a strong grip on her undamaged shoulder. He opened his mouth to speak but the two of them doubled over on their knees. No sound came from beyond the gate and the horses at their side remained upright with no sign of any magic having an effect on them. Spots appeared in Farren's vision as she tried to crawl away from the pain, but as quickly as it happened, it was gone. The two of them gulped in the air that returned to their lungs.

"Are you okay?" Rorke asked. His hand guided her back onto her feet and she nodded. A harsh blink followed in an attempt to clear the spots from her eyes. Her hand remained on her chest with the residual feeling of the pressure.

"That was unpleasant."

"Nero has something to hide. That was warding magic or something similar."

Farren's brows furrowed. "Then why not use a barrier like Emmett or Soter did?"

Rorke glared at the castle. "This way is more effective."

Her gaze followed his until it snagged on the bars nestled between the walls. The gardens sat behind the gate and just like the city below, the grounds were circular in shape but there was no sign of Kayei or human life. The walls curved around the estate like a fortress of stone and hid anyone from view.

"Do the walls go all the way around?" she asked. Rorke swiftly looked at the map he and Janus created, then back at the structure before them. There were rough scribbles about what was where alongside a wiggly line that depicted the garden wall. True enough, the wall curved around the back of the castle.

There was one entrance into the gardens, then two castle doors. Nero was smart enough to only allow one focal entry point, a fact that made Rorke's mouth curl downward. "We should still split up and survey the area; Janus may have missed something vital from the map."

Farren nodded but something on the map caught her eye and she stopped him from returning the map to his saddle bag. "Wait." She unfurled the parchment. "There is no mention of a dungeon or prison quarters. Isn't that unusual for castles of this size?"

Rorke's eyes followed where her fingers trailed over the drawn trellises and moved down to the bottom of the drawing. "This is what I mean, there has to be a cellar," he muttered mainly to himself then looked up at her. "As soon as possible we need to find those cells."

"What if there aren't any?"

"There are. Nero is not someone who would keep his prisoners in a plush room or allow them to roam the castle. There are cells in that castle, we just need to find them."

There was a moment where doubt clouded her mind but the hard lines of his shoulders brought the trust and belief forward once again. That was why, with a squeeze of her hand in his, the two of them went their separate ways. The horses were tethered to an abandoned fence which belonged to the residential house behind them. As she walked around the East side of the wall she noted the cracks and holes that formed in the stone. None of them were bigger than a rat's nook but it allowed her a sneak peek into the foliage beyond. Careful foot placements were important lest she disturb a creature hidden in the weeds or walls. There was the dim light to guide her, the sun behind thick cloud cover. Her attention flickered between the structure beneath her outstretched palm and the castle behind it. The spires looked as deadly as a knife and there were some open windows where red curtains billowed in the light breeze.

"You!" Farren whipped her head toward the voice. Three Kayei guards stood with their brows furrowed and scowls on their faces. They were decorated in reds and blacks, an emblem of intricate swirls were emblazoned on their chests whilst rapiers hung at their sides. Farren didn't know whether to verbally respond or run like she never saw them in the first place. That decision was quickly made when the guard in the middle raised his hand and his skin glowed like a hot poker. She quickly turned on her heel and fled. The ground pounded beneath her boots and the skirts she wore flew behind her. A shock of heat coursed past her face and hit the path next to her. She jumped out of the way before small debris hit her. She pumped her arms to go faster until she spied Tygre and Petal. She forced her legs to move faster until she untied Petal, swung her leg over the saddle and forced the horse to move. There was a whinny before they raced down the hill, away from the three Kayei and the ominous castle. Shouts from the men found her but she ignored each one; her only goal was to find an alcove and remain there until she was certain the men were no longer an immediate threat.

Locals moved from her speeding form. The narrow streets were difficult to navigate on her horse but Petal managed to dodge food carts and low hanging washing lines as she galloped through the streets. Sooner than she thought, Farren slowed petal to a trot and guided her into an alley wedged between two dingy, bordered up buildings. They were high enough that they remained in what was deemed the ghostly part of Kavan. Similar to the trek up to the castle, the buildings looked abandoned and unloved; gardens were overgrown and there was limited life to be seen in the area. What locals remained in that area only moved South. It was what made it the perfect hiding spot, and it was deep and dark so that any passerby might not have noticed the horse and woman who stood in the shadows.

Farren stared up at the sky, dismounted her horse, and gulped down a breath, placed her hand gently on Petal's neck and pulled her cloak back over her head. After she was certain her face we not visible to the alley's mouth, she opened one of the saddlebags. An apple from the Aureum orchard sat in her hand which she took a large bites from, then offered the rest to Petal who ate it greedily. Farren glanced back up at the sky and bit the inside of her cheek: Rorke did not know where she had gone or why. Kavan was a small city in comparison to most but it was big enough that he would not likely find her. They had no contingency plan for if the two of them were separated outside the castle, which in hindsight Farren cursed herself for. It was a matter of waiting until nightfall and hoping that Rorke remained near to Nero's abode.

"This was not what I had in mind," Farren huffed out to herself.

"Well I thought it was quite the show."

The hairs on the back of Farren's neck stood on end but she turned slowly, arms outstretched at her side. Ash sprinkled along her senses, the taste of it minor but present, so she coughed loudly. The hood of her cloak remained over her head but the full scene came into view clearly: leant against the corner of the opening, with his ankle crossed over the other was a man. His hair was the colour of golden straw; the strands hung either side of his face with a shallow undercut at the back of his neck. The clothes he wore were expensive, that much was for certain. His black trousers fit against his long legs and were covered by knee-length boots; a red shirt rolled up to his elbows revealed golden veins that snaked over his skin, but the vest he wore was where the money was. The black fabric looked soft and was lined with red and gold thread. Both the vest and the shirt were undone well past his collarbone which revealed sun kissed skin and more of those golden veins. Her eyes flicked from his attire back to his face where a smirk rested as though it were created for his lips but she didn't ignore the sharp teeth she glimpsed beyond them. Yet, it was those hooded eyes that caused her breathing to stop for a moment. Gold irises that glowed through the darkness put Janus' decor to shame. A Nobleman Kayei.

As graceful as a cat he moved toward her. For every step he took, she took one back, her hands lowered. The stranger, however, placed both of his in his trouser pockets. Her muscles tightened and her finger twitched toward the sword that protruded from the other bag. Petal did not move, the sound of her snorts light compared the thud of Farren's heart against her chest.

"You look scared," his voice was deep and velvety: a snake charmer incarnate.

She swallowed and flexed her fingers away from her sword, eyes on the opening behind him. "A stranger appears from nowhere, it's only natural I am wary."

He chuckled and leaned his shoulder against the wall of the building to her left. "Fair enough."

There was a silence that stretched between them. Petal stood beside Farren with very little movement but the woman kept her eyes on the blond man. The shadows seemed to swirl around him as though it both wanted to be near him but also cowered at his presence. She supposed that was how she was able to see him so clearly. Another glance behind the man and she felt her lip lift slightly. His eyes bore into hers, the glow of the gold like embers in the dark. The only relief she got from his fierce gaze was when he blinked. She too blinked. Those damn eyes seemed so familiar... like something she lost.

"So, what are you doing in this alley?" She asked.

"I saw a woman guide a rather large horse into an alleyway, so it got me curious. Why are *you* in this alleyway? Are you here for the festivities?" A hesitant nod answered him with a squint to her eyes. "Do you always hide in dark alleyways?"

Without hesitation she answered, "do you always approach strangers in alleyways?"

"You're not that strange." His chuckle was accompanied by a lazy shrug. "Why are you not at the castle?"

"I'm waiting for a friend."

The smirk never left his face as he picked a piece of invisible lint from his shoulder. "In a dark alleyway?"

She stayed as still as possible. "If you want honesty," she swallowed, "then I must tell you that we planned to meet here beforehand to... you know?"

That was when the smirk fell from his face. "You are working in the castle, for a guest I presume, but you broke away to have sex with your boyfriend?"

The offended look on her face was not well hidden. "Excuse me?"

"If the Ruler of that castle found you hiding here he might have an example made out of you." He gazed up at the sky. "You should get going."

"To rush to my inevitable fate?" She scoffed humourlessly.

Suddenly, he was in front of her; he moved at a speed greater than the Kuroguine. Farren barely had a moment to blink before his body was a few inches from her. With a hand around her forearm he steadied her stumble. Unnatural warmth radiated from his skin and he moved it from her arm to grab her chin. The grip was gentle but purposeful. His free hand pushed her hood back and he froze. The muscle of his jaw feathered and the upturn of his lips seemed forced. The gaze he skittered across her face was shaky and she wasn't sure he was breathing. The cut in her face was probably a sight but it was nothing compared to the scar that ran from the corner of his right eye and across his nose where it stopped at his cheek.

When she removed her eyes from their lock with his he let out a shuddered breath. As though awoken from a trance he brought his eyes to her chest and she almost slapped him for the blatant disrespect. However, he tapped the stone beneath her dress. "I see you have no problem with Flame Magic."

"I have a problem with men touching me without my permission," she snapped.

He leaned closer with a sly smirk. "That necklace you're wearing has a piece of my magic inside of it."

Her mouth went dry. "It is just a pendant," she mirrored what Soter told her. Whether it heated her bones or not, whether it was imbued with Flame Magic or not, since that night in Brentham it was just. A. Pendant.

"Whatever you say."

The man shrugged, stared at where the pendant hung for a minute longer than was necessary and then pulled a small, blue and white flower from his pocket. He brandished it like a scabbard and held it out to her. Farren's brow raised at the sight then there was a flash of an image in her mind; it was so quick that she nearly thought nothing of it, but it was a page from a book where a sketched picture of that exact flower sat above the words 'toxic' and 'dangerous.' Then Soter's long finger as he pointed out the colours of the petals. Once again, the Magician protected her. "As pretty as that flower is, I don't fancy handling a poisonous plant today."

The man's eyes narrowed. "How do you know this flower is poisonous?"

"A friend of mine is well versed in plant life so he leant me a book and that right there." She pointed to the delicate flower that hung in the air between them. "Should not be anywhere near either of us."

"That friend knows what he is talking about. This might have killed you," he said with a vicious smirk, "us Kayei like to hide them in each other's homes to drain our life-source." *Morbid creatures,* he paused with a contemplative head tilt. "Will your friend be joining us? Maybe he can teach me more about *flowers*."

"No, but I will let him know that there was an attempt on my life; death by flower will certainly make him laugh."

The entire plant was flung over his shoulder only to be replaced by a smaller, yellow flora. It was delicate but the entire bulb of it engulfed the palm of her hand. She glanced between it and the man who held it. Without any more words he tucked the stem behind her ear where the strands of her hair held it in place. As he used his other hand to keep her head still, he fussed with the flower and she glared. The smell of a bonfire engulfed her as he stepped into her personal space. Up close, the gold of his eyes were a myriad of shades: a dark yellow stone rimmed the outside of his iris and it seeped inward to meet a gold brighter than any coin or any light she encountered. His face was all angles: pointed chin, sharp jaw and a small curved nose. His elegantly curved eyebrows were dark blonde to coincide with the short hair at his nape. There was no woman –or man- who would kick him out of bed. Yet every nerve ending in her body screamed at her to remove his hands from her hair. The hands that remained at her sides moved slowly as though they would do just that with her fingers braced to push against his shoulders. However, his next statement stopped her cold, "I suggest you leave before someone inside that castle." He inclined his head in the general direction of the Kavan castle. "Finds out who you really are and kills you for it."

"Who am I?"

The once smirk-filled face turned hard, his lips were downturned and his eyes flashed in the dark, "You are no servant. That race through the streets made that painfully clear."

The whites of her eyes were more visible as she stared at him. "I have no idea what you are talking about."

"Do not," he growled, "act like you are stupid." The fear that filled her eyes loosened his grip. There was a moment where he searched her figure, then leant against the wall, legs crossed languidly as he stared at his nails. Strands of his hair shadowed his eyes as he picked at his cuticles. She was no longer the centre of his attention. That was her opportunity to manoeuvre Petal and run, so despite her sweaty palms and vibrating limbs, she moved her feet. The horse snorted in the Kayei's general direction and Farren hurried her along. "Give the human soldier my best!" His voice was light but his eyes remained on his nails.

Farren ran her tongue along her teeth and pulled Petal into the streets. In the saddle once more, she pushed her into a canter and pulled the cloak over her head. Her heart beat to the sound of Petal's hooves as she created more distance between her and the golden Kayei. There were the faint murmurs of life as she rode but her vision zeroed on the man who called out to her. Rorke's figure came into view as he stood against another bordered up building, hands clasped behind his back and head tilted toward her. She dismounted quickly, pet Petal's neck as a 'well done' and ran toward him. His hands were on her before she barrelled into him. His eyes were all over her.

No injuries, no tear of clothing, hardly any dirt in her skirts but then his eyes travelled to the flower behind her ear and he yanked it from her hair. She yelped as a few strands were pulled with it but the flora was on the ground and beneath his boot in seconds.

With eyes the size of dinner plates he asked, "where in the hell did you find that flower?"

So she explained. She told him about how she nearly finished her excursion when a trio of Kayei chased her from the walls, how she hid in an alley where another Kayei found her, only to warn her about Nero and placed the flower in her hair. He listened intently and his eyes never left hers as she spoke with a furrowed brow. She finished her tale with, "the man- I mean, the Kayei, he seemed to know you."

It was Rorke's turn to furrow his brow. "Did you tell him anything? What did he say?"

Farren fussed with one of her sleeves but the unimpressed glare she sent him was not unnoticed. "He asked if I was here for the festivities."

"That could mean anything. The Golden Harvest doesn't end for three more days but it's not usually celebrated in Kavan until the final day."

Farren's gut clenched. "I mentioned that I had a partner I was waiting for."

"Why would you do that, Farren?" His eyes snapped to hers.

"Because I was hiding in an alleyway with a horse looking very suspicious."

Rorke sighed. "You managed to get away and that is all that matters at the moment. If there is a party at the castle we can slip in easier."

She agreed, "the more guests, the more servants that are required. That Kayei just gave us our alibi. It will still be difficult though; the Princess will be harder to find in throngs of people whilst we also look like we are doing our jobs." Rorke's slightly agape mouth was closed when she continued, "I should probably avoid those three guards from earlier too."

They stood in silence as Rorke gathered his thoughts. "There is a servant's entrance at the back of the castle."

She inhaled deeply. "Alright, how do we get through the gate?"

The answering tilt of his chin and ghost of a smile came before he spoke, "we will do what you do best and talk our way inside." *And if they couldn't?* The question hung between them but they turned to the bag that hung from Tygre's saddle. It was where the map of Nero's castle sat comfortably. They studied the map until the sun sank behind the city and they had to use candlelight to see. Their plan was prepared and Farren felt better about what they were supposed to do. Rorke only spoke about the map and the plan, they no longer exchanged pleasantries; it was time for each of them to get serious, and she never felt her nerves steel so tightly.

THE BACK DOOR

'Talk our way inside' seemed like a simple task yet both Farren and Rorke did not account for the sheer amount of people they spied beyond the iron bars. Unlike their first encounter with the walls, there was no pressure that threatened to incapacitate them, only the flicker of the torchlight that flanked the gate. Guards that were not stationed there earlier, stood at attention as nobles walked up to the entrance, flashed sly smiles, and made their way through the gardens. Just like fauns, Farren and Rorke hesitantly walked up to those guards. At first, they paid the humans no attention, an un-subtle sniff and they raked their eyes over them. They took in Farren's thin form next to Rorke's hulking back with scrutinising eyes. There was a flicker in the guards' eyes –both an unusual colour- as they sized up the human man, but Rorke kept his chin down and eyes on her.

"Excuse me," she started with a placid extension of her fingers, "could you tell us how to get to the servant's entrance please?"

The Kayei who once had their attention on her companion, moved so that their bodies faced her. The one on the right –a woman with long blonde hair and dark red iris'- scanned her body like she was reading a book and turned to the other guard. She whispered something inaudible in his ear which narrowed his eyes. There was a question in his gaze when he moved it across Farren and Rorke, then to his partner. The blonde nodded slowly and gestured toward the castle behind them. "Proceed around the back," the male guard commanded, "and try not to disturb the guests while you do."

A slow, confused nod answered his words, from both Farren and Rorke. The female hurried them along and turned her attention to the nobles in the line outside the walls. There was no discussion on why or how they were let through, the guests did not deign to look in their direction, and Farren had a sinking feeling that Nero knew they were on his land. It was just *too*

252

easy. The thought coiled in the back of her mind and her hand reached for Rorke's. His larger one entwined with hers as they carefully walked around the edge of the gardens. With every steady voice she heard, the vertebrae in her spine straightened and the hand in his started to sweat. Regardless of the nerves that threatened to consume her, they made it around the side of the castle with no issues. They kept to the hedges and slipped around a Kayei couple who used the shadows to conceal their lip-lock.

Once the single, weather-beaten door came into view Rorke tugged against her hand. "Are you ready?"

"I am, are you?" She asked when she turned to face him. It was a wonder she kept herself from breaking down at the sorrowful look in his eyes. They were about to enter the enemy stronghold with no idea whether the Princess resided inside. A sad smile lifted her cheeks, but when she took a step to follow the line of servants through the door he pulled her back toward him. The kiss he gave her was soft, a promise of what he was capable of offering her. She smiled through the kiss and too soon his lips released hers. Her mouth remained parted as she blinked. There was nothing but Rorke's small smile between them as they walked across the gravel courtyard –where carriages sat in a row against the North wall- and joined the line of servants who walked through the door. All smiles were lost the moment they were across the threshold: humans of all ages, dressed similarly to her and Rorke, rushed around a large kitchen. Some carried food, others sewed jackets and dresses, plates filled with glasses were balanced in the palms of others. There was little speech shared and everyone kept their eyes on to the floor. It was hard to survey the room with the sheer amount of people that ran around it but there was a woodstove to her right and benches covered in flour flanked it. That was all Farren was able to discern before an elderly woman shoved two plain black masks in their hands. "Take those trays upstairs," the woman barked, yet they hesitated with the masks in hand. "Now!"

Argen would have laughed as Farren scrambled to tie the mask around her face. With her hands around the fabric she paused: *Why did she think of Argen in that moment?* She physically shook him from her mind and finished the knot at the back of her head. Her shoulder stung with the quick movement but she followed Rorke and grabbed a tray filled with bubbly drinks. It reminded her of the meeting with the King and Queen of Altin that had her in that position. The knuckles wrapped around the tray turned white as she glared at the Rulers across Realms.

Once they walked up narrow stairs, the castle opened up to a long room painted maroon whilst the floors were dark wood, the colour near black. Random potted plants sat against the walls with the leaves a sure sign of dehydration. Chandeliers lined the centre of the corridor and guided them to two sets of double doors. The large doors were thrown wide open which allowed music and chatter to sound toward the group of servants.

An inaudible, "wow," flew from Farren as she stepped into the grand room. Nobles dressed in bright colours practically glowed under the golden light and held beautiful drinks and fans. The room itself was the same dark walls and floors but it was comprised of high ceilings and paintings. At first glance, the artworks were intricate, skilful depictions of a king and his people, and were full of colour and soft strokes. Upon closer inspection those were Kayei with their whips, hands, and mouths all over humans. Blood ran from human bodies as the Kayei beat them senseless; it was starkly contrasted with the faces of pleasure on those who were bedded by the Kayei. Humans were used, and killed by the Kayei.

It was weird, what she thought of in that moment, how her mind cast back to a conversation she had with Rorke when they studied the Kavan castle map. It was a real life depiction of human and Kayei relationships:

"You knew Nero, didn't you, Rorke?" Farren asked.

Rorke slowly lifted his head from the map between them and blinked. "Yes, when I was sixteen." With a tilt of her head he continued, "when His Majesty sent human troupes across Realms to help with a Kayei war, Nero was a commander of a legion of 'rebels.' They were supposed to be the Kayei who were on the right side but he proved us all wrong."

Farren noted the bitter twinge to his words. "What happened?"

Rorke shook his head. "The men and I were having dinner before the siege in the morning. Back then we thought it was easier to mingle the Kayei soldiers with the humans." The grit of his teeth told her what he thought about that plan. "So we all shared ale and food. It wasn't until we were all very drunk that Nero stormed through the crowd of men and grabbed my Captain by the throat. He lifted him into the air with one hand and we were all drunk, so we were slow to pull our weapons out. The Kayei were quicker and pointed their swords at us." Farren's brows lifted into her hairline. "Luckily Nero didn't kill the Captain but he left him a shaking shell on the floor. I didn't hear what Nero said to him, but I remember the glow of his eyes and the snap of his teeth when he demanded we leave."

"But what about the war?"

Rorke scoffed. "The Realm doesn't look to be ravished by battles so whatever he did when we left worked."

There was another question on her mind: "why did Nero attack your Captain?"

"Because he is crazy," Rorke answered without hesitation. "He was having a bad day, so he determined the Captain was the person to take it out on."

"Sounds charming."

Farren forced her eyes away from the disturbing pictures and focused on Rorke at her side. He shook with the will not to rip them from the walls but with her soft hand on his wrist he glanced down at her. With a final glance spared between them, they got to work.

There was no sign of Nero but that didn't stop every muscle in Rorke's body from being tightly strung. The Kayei sneered as he offered them a drink and for a moment he thought that if he wanted to he could slit a few throats before he left the Griselda-forsaken Realm. With every glance at his body, he felt his skin crawl. That discomfort honed into something sharper as he watched a Kayei snarl at Farren. He pictured throwing one of the sweet-smelling drinks at the offender but he side-stepped another server to avoid a collision and the urge dissipated. After he dodged the other human he returned his attention to Farren: she was tall and nimble, and there was something about her that forced his eyes to follow her every movement when she weaved around the enemy. He was *transfixed*: the sway of her hips, the way her gaze moved across every face around them, the dance of her feet against the wooden floor. He convinced himself that with his eyes on her it meant that she would return home alive, but there was a voice in the back of his head -the voice that moaned in approval when she kissed him- who told him that wasn't the only reason he watched her so closely. The heat in his face and the fury that ran through his veins at the brush of Kayei clothing against his shirt, did not hide the marvel he felt at the fact they made it. A King's Guard and a merchant's daughter made it across Realms, and survived an encounter with the Kuroguine; that daughter cut down creatures in the forest with the skill of a fully trained soldier, with the precision and grace that he would be proud to have at his side on the battlefield. She was nothing compared to the women in the Capital, nothing like the women he took to bed, a thought which made his lips tingle. That was when Janus' words filled his head like a slap to the face and he moved to the back of the room.

Janus waited for Farren to click her door shut before he returned his attention to the haggard guard before him. Rorke finished another glass of wine and settled deeper into his seat, arms crossed. His eyes slipped shut for the briefest moment as he let the silence encompass him, but the feeling of Janus' eyes as they bore into his skin made him shift and glare. "What?" He snapped.

"You need to keep an eye on that one." Rorke rolled his eyes, just as Farren had done to him many times. "I'm serious. There is something not right about her." At Rorke's raised brow he lifted his own. "Did you never wonder why the King chose her?"

"He ran out of options. It's not pretty but it's true."

Janus leaned back in his own seat. "And that's it? No reason other than 'she was convenient?'"

Rorke's glare sharpened. "You obviously want me to say something specific. What?" The Kayei in front of him swallowed and averted his eyes. The blunt words stung and Rorke knew it, but the way the white-eyed man looked at him set his teeth on edge. It was like something crawled beneath his skin and begged to join the conversation.

Janus cleared his throat. "You humans have a terrible sense of smell so it's no wonder you can't tell. She's-" He paused and stared at his wine glass, in search of the correct word. "She's Malumrem, Rorke."

"What the hell does that mean?"

"Like I said, there's something not right about her. The King of Altin-" Rorke shot him a warning look. *"Either got really lucky, or he knows something about her that you don't."*

There was silence before Rorke's palm rattled the table for the second time that night. *"Are you trying to piss me off? Farren is more than capable of being a part of this mission, and she was the easiest option for everyone in Altin."*

"Do you not see how bad that is?" Janus' voice was soft.

"I trust her and she is skilled, but there you sit in your plush chair, with your golden chandeliers, and masks," he spat the word, "trying to get me to leave her behind, send her back home, kill her?!"

The atmosphere shifted: the hairs on Rorke's arms raised and the crackle of electricity sounded in the air. Everything was outlined in lilac, a threat of what might be brought to life if Janus so wished. Moments later – when their eyes locked- the crackle in the air and the glow receded. "I am sure it would amuse me greatly to have my statues attack you, but I would like to keep blood off of my rug." He sighed around his glass. "I do not want you to abandon her, I just want you to know that anyone with supernatural senses will be drawn to her, or repelled if you are lucky. Regardless of what you think, I quite like the lass, but you will always do what you want won't you, dear?"

Rorke ignored the last comment. "Are we in more danger?"

"More? No. You are in the same amount of danger as when you crossed through the Veil."

"If they sense her, will they go straight for her?"

Janus drained his glass. "They will probably seek her out, if only to try and gain answers. If you are asking if they will attack her on sight, probably not."

Rorke shook his head. Janus' words were an attempt at him being comforting but he kept his eyes glued to Farren. She was nothing more than a woman who bad things happened to and was offered a chance, even if his King didn't give her a choice. A sour taste was left in his mouth and Janus was shoved to the back of his mind and deeper until the only Kayei he glared at were the ones around him. At the thought of his king the muscles in his shoulders locked. He never wanted to return to the Kayei Realm, he never wanted to see another Kayei again and yet that damned magician showed up at court talking to the Queen like they were old friends. The wicked grins Rorke received from that creature set his teeth on edge. The King knew what Soter was, he knew that Rorke hated him with every fibre of his being yet at court he -it- remained and in the other Realm Rorke stood.

Another drink was taken from his tray and he nearly snapped. His eyes found Farren once more and the taste of ash filled his mouth.

Farren thought the Kayei nobles were exactly like any other noble, only covered in the sheen of magic. The sparkle and glimmer from the magic and the clothing were harsh on the eyes but it did not stop them from being beautiful. They were nothing compared to the Oracle, the ethereal magic not as strong, but they were exceedingly more graceful than the people in Altin. The churn of her stomach when she stepped into the ballroom disappeared but it was quickly replaced by the taste of ash in her mouth. What was it, with the damned essence of ash that started to stalk her since she entered Kavan? She spent her time with her eyes on the uncovered faces of the Kayei hoping, willing herself to find the Princess amongst them. At first there were servants who milled around the room alongside her and Rorke but the longer Farren stared, she soon realised there was no sign of other humans with her. Those who bustled up and down the stairs exchanged their full trays with either of them and the cycle continued, so she offered those with empty glasses drinks with a meek dip to her chin which worked in contrast to her steel spine. Not one Kayei thanked her.

With her tray emptied once more she walked to the double doors. A young girl waited for her with a new tray but before she handed it to Farren her eyes widened and she ran away and back down the stairs. Farren made to call after her but a hush fell over the room and everyone lowered their heads. With a sharp tug against her collar, Rorke pulled at her and pushed her toward the servant stairs. There was no spare moment for her to question his actions because the silence around the castle was dense; nobody even sipped a drink in the ballroom. The only sound was that of shoes on the low, wooden platform at the front of the large room. From her position next to Rorke - lodged in the middle of his body and the wall- the only thing she saw was a line of Kayei nobles. Their eyes were front-and-centre but they did not move, blink, breathe. Yet, they did not kneel for whoever entered the room, only a simple lowering of their heads were the sign of their respect. Farren glanced at Rorke whose eyes were already on her. A subtle shake of his head: they would not move until everyone else did. With her spine straight and mouth filled with ash she pushed out a shaky breath.

"Continue!" At the sound of the nasal-affected voice movement returned to everyone's limbs. Many moved toward the front to greet whoever spoke but Rorke held her at his side, his sweaty hand was a solid weight against her. He was a sickly shade of green, the look on his face made her throat bob, but they weaved their way through the servants who returned to their jobs. Farren handed her tray to an unsuspecting boy who had no choice but to take it from her hands.

The end of the corridor they rushed to was narrow and away from the noise of the ballroom and they were slightly hidden in the shadows which was a brief blessing because Rorke looked like he might pass out. The further from the large room they travelled, the taste of ash faded.

When they stopped she faced him fully. "Rorke, hey, are you alright?"

An absent nod. "That voice wasn't Nero's."

"Do you know who-?" A loud laugh bellowed from the party and into the corridor. "We need to start searching."

Rorke nodded, the sickly look on his face had yet to disappear. "Our best chance is by splitting up, but if you get caught." Rorke's eyes were hard when he dug into his pocket. "You need to drink this."

A small vile of blue liquid sat between his fingers and she nearly took the bottle before realisation overcame her face and she staggered back, mouth open and fists clenched. "You have got to be joking." At his solemn face she said, "no, Rorke, no!" He shushed her. "I am not taking a vial of *poison*. I thought we were beyond that plan?"

"This was always a possible outcome." There was a knot in his throat. "Please Farren, if you get caught this is the better way to go."

"How about I just don't die?"

Rorke forced her fist open and pushed the vial into her hand. "Then don't get caught."

She breathed deeply through her nose and steadied the angry shaking that covered her body. The glass was cool against her flushed skin but she did not look down at it, she simply tucked it into her bodice and tried not to frown at Rorke.

With a soft hand on her shoulder and her curt nod, they went their separate ways. Room after room on the lower floor was either occupied by Kayei who couldn't keep their hands off of each other or were void of anything. The first room she encountered like that made her pause. Dust covered the floors and floated in the air before her. The layer of dust had been undisturbed for months, possibly years if the spider family in the corner was any indication. It seemed the Ruler of Kavan hadn't ordered their servants to clean, or find use for the rooms. She closed the door gently and continued on her way. The lower floor had been covered, and the only reason Farren knew that was because she found herself outside the first set of ballroom doors. The castle was filled with doors and corridors so she supposed it was a miracle she found her way back. Roaming aimlessly took too much time, there had to be an easier way to find the Princess. Answers, that was what she needed, namely where the dungeons were. That was when she spotted a mousy girl stood by those open doors. The plan that started to hatch in Farren's mind was laughable but it was the only thing she thought of in that moment, so she approached the girl who practically had a heart attack when Farren placed a hand on her arm.

"Sorry, I didn't mean to startle you." The girl tucked a strand of hair behind her ear so Farren continued with an internal scoff at what she was about to say. "Can you tell me where the prisoner is, I've been asked to bring her water but I'm a tad lost?" Without a word the girl shook her head and ran downstairs. The curse Farren had yet to speak aloud finally sounded, accompanied by a laugh of disbelief. With no more information than an hour before, she started toward the stairs behind her.

"You are going the wrong way." Farren spun on her heel where a woman no older than she stood. "The dungeons are at the far end of the castle." She pointed toward the curve in the hall at the other end of the corridor. Farren's brows furrowed. That curve was shallow and lead into a wall, it was nothing more than a small alcove. Yet, the woman before her was so sure of herself that she offered a series of nods. Farren's skirts billowed behind her as she rushed down the servant stairs back into the kitchen. A bucket half-filled with water, and a ladle sat beneath a flour covered bench which she snatched and rushed out the door.

WORK FOR IT

The curve that Farren believed was an alcove- that Janus believed was an alcove- was guarded by an old, paint-stained door. It was dishevelled and un-threatening. Faded runes were revealed where the paint chipped away but many were too faint to make out. They looked so similar to the bloody marks painted in the White Castle. Emmett's crushed skull flashed in her mind and she twisted the metal handle. Cold air hit her in the face as she was greeted with a section no longer than a carriage. The cold was welcomed against her cheeks but the shadowed space before her was not, but stood like a beacon at the end of said darkness was a metal door. It was not ornate or polished but a simple sheet of metal. The grime that covered the door gave the White Castle dungeons a run for its money, so with her nose screwed up she wrapped her hand around the solid handle and pulled –nothing- and pushed –nothing- and pulled again, then slammed her hand against the door. She squeezed her eyes shut and took a breath but she did not feel any less frustration. A key, or gunpowder was what was needed... she chuckled to herself, a key was quieter. The bucket in her grasp was dropped next to her boot and she watched as the water sloshed at the bottom. There was only enough liquid in it for two ladles and it looked so much like the bucket the Oracle- *surely not?* Farren glanced around the small hallway then back at the bucket. She crouched so that she was level with it and brought it closer to her. With a deep swallow she focused on the water in the bucket with the same intensity as she did before the burning manor. Her palms were braced either side of the bucket and her face was nearly inside of it, but the water stopped sloshing. That was when she finally blinked. The water moved a millisecond later.

A cough sounded behind her and the water surged into a loud splash. In the process of turning around she bumped her head on the metal handle and clattered the bucket to the ground. Her glare did nothing to soothe the ache but it did offer some comfort as she spied the golden-eyed Kayei against the wooden door with a smirk in place.

"It needs a key," he stated, his hands in his pockets.

She pushed her hair from her face. "I don't suppose you have it on you?"

"If I do, what do I get in return?" The flash of his canines was sinful and Farren's face burned. There was something in the way he held himself that made her stomach whirl; she was unsure whether it was with arousal or fear, but as he stood before her, she wondered just what those teeth would feel like pressed against her- She grabbed the bucket from her feet and stormed toward him. If she needed a key then a key she would find. Only, she was stopped by the length of his arm. She stared at the offending article and trailed her eyes to meet his.

"You just said I need a key, so please move."

His smirk fell as he kept his eyes on hers because that was irritation in his gaze. "I thought I told you to leave."

"You made a suggestion. I could not abandon my duty." The double entendre was not lost on her.

The blond rolled his eyes. "Your duty is more important than your life, is it?"

"So it would seem," she forced out.

The look in his eyes vanished into boredom. Two servants exited the door to their right and paused. Their mouths hung open mid-conversation and their gazes danced between the two of them. They didn't stray on Farren long, but rather glued themselves to the Kayei. The fear that radiated from them was so thick she thought she tasted it. It was certainly visible on their faces. Without looking at the servants, his voice boomed through the corridor, "leave." He brought his eyes back to hers, "you too, love."

The arm in her path fell and Farren took that as her queue to duck away from him. She walked away just as the servants did and shuffled toward the kitchen. Rorke stood at the bottom of the kitchen stairs, his eyes on Farren's body immediately. She placed the bucket under the original bench and pulled him toward the back of the room where there were less servants and also a lower chance that they would be in one of the cook's way. Lyla hated when she had to manoeuvre around people when she worked and Farren did not fancy starting a fight with the chefs. While they stood there, she explained the metal door. There was a second where she thought to mention the Kayei she ran into but her deceit was intact and the longer she spoke, the colder Rorke's face became, so she thought better of it. "The lock was huge so I imagine the key would be larger than most," she concluded.

"The Head carries a ring of keys around with her."

Farren glanced behind her. There were so many people and none of which seemed to be the woman that set them to work. However, as she watched people sew the sleeve of a dress, shine the scuff mark from a shoe and place the finishing touches on a pie she spotted two maids giggle. Her brow furrowed slightly and she watched as the two women pressed their hands to their flushed faces and trailed their eyes across the King's Guard. It was like she wasn't stood next to him, all they saw was the broad-shouldered man at her side and by the smiles on their faces, they liked what they saw.

The Devil would have been proud of what she said next. "Rorke," she started with a slow smile, "do you remember how you asked me to steal the money for the room because I was the less intimidating one?" His brow rose with his nod and she averted her eyes from the longing looks thrown his way.

"Well, I think it is your turn to use your skill set to retrieve the key from the Head. Those women over there seem to find you extremely attractive." She pointed not-so-subtly to the squeaky women. "I mean, they have *eyes* so obviously they do."

"What are you trying to say, Farren?"

She swallowed the laugh that threatened to escape. "You need to seduce one of those women to try and get the key away from the Head. I would offer," she added, "but I do not think I fit the criteria."

A growled 'no' sat on the tip of his tongue but the hope in her eyes, the triumphant smile on her lips- He clenched his jaw. He didn't want to seduce the Head, he didn't want to seduce anyone, not when she stood at his side with such *life*. So he said, "seducing one of them will not get you that key. I will have to go straight to the Head."

"No, woah woah, no. You need to convince one of those gir-women to use the key themselves. The Head will believe that one of them needs it more than you."

"You can simply ask the Head yourself then."

Farren bit the inside of her cheek. "That's where the seduction – persuasion if you will- comes into it. I cannot simply walk up to a woman I have never worked with and ask for a very important key. She would suspect something was wrong because my face is too new, I am too inexperienced; not one sane Head would trust someone like that with a castle key. Those women over there." She pointed to the young servants again. "Are trained servers, you can tell by their hands and the way they walk around this place. They can be trusted with the key. Honestly, Rorke, have you never seen kitchen politics in action?"

"Obviously not."

She slipped her hand into his and gave it a squeeze before she grabbed a tray full of small pastry parcels. "Good luck!"

Just as she balanced the tray in her hands, the Head walked into the room. An expensive overcoat hung in her arms and she sent Farren a curt nod of approval. The grin she gave the older woman was genuine and she raised her eyebrows at Rorke. She slowly walked up the stairs and back into the large ballroom. The sneers and disgusted looks the Kayei sent her made her want to try and seduce the woman herself and force Rorke to deal with the nobles.

"Woman, when is the kitchen serving the sweet stuff?"

She forced her voice into submission when she replied, "I'll be sure to ask the kitchen."

Long fingers wrapped around her elbow. "Ask them now."

Her eye twitched. Oh how she wanted to slap the sneer from his face. "Sir I have to finish passing these around." The tray was removed from her grasp. It went against every instinct she had to keep her fingers loose and not curl them into fists, but the grip on her elbow tightened painfully. The frown on her face was pointed at the floor. She recognised him from her previous rounds but the words she wished would fly from her mouth were locked behind her lips. Silence was her friend in that castle; if only she didn't hate the quiet.

"Go. And ask them. Now." The man's voice was sickly sweet.

"Come now Jaeger, this young woman is obviously new." A tall woman with hair down to her backside grinned down at Farren. "We have to treat them like a new toy, gently, delicately, until we have them fully in our grasp." The new addition to the conversation yanked her into her chest and caged her in. "Then we can play with them as roughly as we want." With every tug against the woman, the tighter those coils of steel made flesh, bound her. The brush of her breath against Farren's neck made her shiver, but in the position she was in her hands were useless and there was no way to swing her body forward. The woman curved her body over hers and nearly bent her at a ninety degree angle. SO that her calf muscles didn't pull Farren was forced to bend her legs slightly.

"I must retrieve those sweets before they all get eaten by your friends, I wouldn't want Jaeger to miss out," Farren stated awkwardly.

The white-clad man smirked and roughly squeezed her cheeks. "Don't worry about those sweets now, these pretty lips of yours could be put to good use instead. Don't you agree Amelie?"

Farren felt the woman's chest vibrate in her agreement. "I think I'd like her dainty hands on my body." The Kayei placed her lips against her ear. "You'd like that wouldn't you pet? Or maybe you would rather my fingers in-"

"Oh trust me, you don't want me servicing either of you," Farren chuckled nervously, "I have very little experience in such things. You'll find my bedroom skills boring." All smirks and smiles fell. Instead, growls and scowls greeted her so Farren shifted uncomfortably in Amelie's arms. The stitches in her shoulder pulled her skin which brought a hiss to the surface of her lips. In the position she was forced into, her view was limited: the legs of Kayei filled her vision and each gap only granted her a view of the person in front of them. Not one of them moved, nor did they speak of what occurred only a few feet from them. The pictures hung on the walls were obviously more than simple artworks, rather they were depictions of what happened at Kayei parties. Her gust twisted because to them, the position she found herself in was normal. More laughter sounded through the room and the nasally voice from before shot toward her. For a moment Farren was able to crane her neck higher which meant she could find the man the voice belonged to. He was surrounded by throngs of people but what gave him away was the crown of brimstone and rubies that circled his long, chocolate hair and held the curve of a braid in place. The muscles in the back of her neck pinged so she dropped her head back down.

"See Jaeger, it's all a waiting game with humans. They tire themselves out eventually," she emphasised her point with a squeeze of Farren's torso.

The human took in what air she could but dug her nails into the sleeves of Amelie's dress. She didn't flinch at the action nor loosen her grip. There was no weapon within reach and Rorke was downstairs attempting to get *her* the key to the dungeon so she could find the Princess. The blond Kayei was also nowhere in sight, but Farren had yet to discern whether he was an enemy or ally so she squeezed her eyes shut and dug her nails in deeper. Once she controlled her breathing and opened her eyes it was like something possessed her: she slammed her boot onto the open-toed shoe of the woman behind her. The yelp was loud by her ear but she slammed her foot down again on the opposite foot which caused Amelie to release her hold. Farren quickly twirled so that she faced both Jaeger and her captor and held her hands out as a shield. The people around them stopped their conversations and honed in on the drama that began to unfold. Farren's eyes darted around the sharp faces in the crowd; she wondered what powers each of them held and how quickly she would be killed if they grabbed her again. As she swallowed down that thought and slowly cast her eyes to the dagger under her skirts, a loud crash echoed from the front of the room. Simultaneously the faces around her whipped in that direction.

"Goddess above Nero!"

"Are you okay Your Majesty?"

"Did you get any on your clothes?"

"Do you need my assistance, Nero?"

Farren's eyes widened and she took that moment to rush out of the room. In their moment of distraction, Amelie and Jaeger cursed but made no move to follow her. Nobody stopped her as she rushed down the stairs and pressed her back against the far wall. The adrenaline that coursed through her was swallowed down as she dug her palm into the stone. The scrape grounded her. A glare was sent up the stairs and she turned to grab another tray with the grit of her teeth and a sore torso. When she turned, her eyes snagged on Rorke's smile. It was small but genuine as the servant giggled in front of him. A strand of her hair was twirled around her finger as she looked up at the King's Guard. She raised a brow when the servant blew him a kiss and went back to work. Farren followed her movement until she left the room with her friend, each with large smiles on their faces. Rorke folded his hands over his chest and cast his eyes over the room. Farren raised her hand in greeting which made him swerve around the cooks and find his way to her side.

"So," she started, "you know how you mentioned that the man in the ballroom wasn't Nero?" She kept her voice low and he nodded. "Well, he's here. I was in the ballroom and the guests were fussing over him."

Rorke pinched the bridge of his nose. "If he's here then he would not be letting someone speak in his stead."

"Maybe he just couldn't be bothered. The nobles are beneath him right?"

Rorke stifled his laugh. "In his eyes they are."

Farren nodded but glanced away from him and up the stairs with a sheepish smile. "Another thing."

271

"What?"

"I may have broken a Kayei woman's foot, I mean it may not actually be broken but I did stomp on it really hard. I didn't do it for the sake of it, I want you to know that. She had me trapped and bent over and it was either that or her and her friend had some fun of their own so I had to do something and-"

"Farren," Rorke cut her off, "it's all entertainment for them, they likely forgot about the incident already."

"I pissed them off," she hissed.

"True. I will deliver the drinks and food; I need you to focus on finding *her*."

"Where is the key?" The arms that were folded across his chest were stuffed into his trouser pockets. His finger nails tapped against the large metal key and she grinned. That grin formed an 'o' when Rorke lifted a hand to her face and brought her hair further over her damaged shoulder. He brushed the back of his fingers along her cheek and bobbed his head. They broke away from each other and as Farren slipped by his side he placed the key in her hand. With the front of her body away from the bustling people, she slipped the large key under her corset and continued up the stairs with an empty tray in her hand. The curve was visible the moment her boots hit the corridor so she speed-walked past the open double doors and followed her previous path.

The paint-faded door remained open so she didn't stop, not as she pulled the key from her corset and inserted it into the old lock. The metal door groaned when she forced it open. The key was then tucked against her chest. Regardless of the fear that threatened to buckle her knees, she pushed forward. There was no time to waste and she would not allow the blond Kayei to catch her unawares for a third time that day. There was no bucket in her hand, nor ladle, only an empty tray and a dagger in her boot so she swallowed, glanced behind her and descended into the darkness.

Stone steps descended into the inky blackness and with the limited torches on the wall she kept a close eye on her boots. There was no sound save for her breaths against the cool air and the scrape of her hand along the stone wall. The air was filled with damp and smelt like nobody had bothered with the dungeons in years. Farren's shoulders slumped at the thought. The dungeons weren't too deep underground so she soon found the bottom of the stairs, a puddle of who-knows-what beneath her boots. The smell of piss and smoke and mould filled her nose which made her gag. The sleeve of her dress was pressed to her nose instantly; with her other hand she grabbed a torch from the wall and pointed it toward the darkness. Unlike the huge, multi-tiered, White Castle dungeons, the room before her was the same size as her bedroom and lined with cells. Rust found its home on the empty ones. There was no way to light the rest of the room so she kept the torch raised in front of her. The stone floor was soaked but there seemed to be no leak in the ceiling. The smell of urine hit her again and she forced her food to remain in her stomach. The second gag that flew from her throat echoed through the eerily silent room.

"Hello?" Her voice bounced off the walls. "Princess Cyrille?" She continued down the aisle between cells. In each cell sat a bed and a wooden stoop that was used as a makeshift toilet. Each one was dilapidated and dust-covered. It was at the final cell that she found a huddled form on the bed. The cell was decorated with tattered but plush blankets and pillows, pink and white, a stark contrast to the gloom around them. It was a slice of luxury for someone trapped underground. The person's clothes were no different: the prisoner wore a dirtied dress but one coveted from fine thread and fabrics. In the torchlight it looked to be a pale yellow and covered in flowers. "Princess?" The huddled figure raised its head at the sound of her voice.

273

A torch flickered behind the prisoner which cast shadows on the woman's face so Farren pressed her own torch forward. The figure flinched back into the dim light of her cell. It was difficult to make out her features and Farren had only seen portraits of the Princess but the fearful prisoner in front of her matched both the portraits and Rorke's description. She was the spitting image of her mother if a little more worn down. Where the Queen's black hair sat, dirty dark tendrils matted against the girl's forehead. Near-black eyes peered up at the woman as the Princess squinted against the light.

"Who are you?" She croaked out.

Farren looked behind her and grabbed the cell lock. "I'm here to rescue you, Rorke Alliard is upstairs so we need to hurry and get you out of this cell."

Cyrille pulled her knees up to her chest. "Why are you doing this?"

Farren paused. "Your father asked me to." The girl's eyes lit up at the mention of the King but it faded into a blank stare, one that Farren was all too familiar with.

There was no time to console the Princess so she pulled on the lock of the cell. No surprise, it was locked. One key was suspicious enough, if Farren asked Rorke to obtain another one they would surely fail, additionally, she would not leave the Princess to find him. When she tugged on the handle of the cell door Cyrille scrambled to her feet, her hands wrapped around the bars. She swayed on her feet so Farren huffed when the door simply jangled. The sharp breath fluttered the flame beside her which in turn cause triumph to shine on her face as she cast her eyes between the torch and the lock. The metal lock glowed when she pressed the torch against it. The red, orange and yellow that formed around the handle allowed a grin to find its way onto Farren's face. She flicked her eyes from the scorching metal to the Princess who watched the lock heat up. Suddenly, Cyrille's mouth opened and Farren

274

was happy for her input until she screamed as loud as humanly possible. The torch was removed from the lock as Farren used her free hand to cover the ear closest to the Princess. "Guard! Guard! Someone is trying to break into my cell!"

Farren's own eyes widened. "Shh, shh, please, Princess, shh, shut up." She tried her best to calm the Royal down but those were footsteps on the stairs. How they heard the Princess she had no- she left the doors open. *Fantastic*. With a final glare at the Princess Farren rushed into the aisle of the dungeon. A hiding spot, an exit, she needed *something* but the only way in or out of the dungeon was the way she entered. Frantically, she threw the torch to the floor and stomped on it before she rushed toward the open cell doors. The skirts of her dress made 'rushing' difficult so she picked them up and shot toward a cell in the middle and scurried under the narrow cot. The bed was covered in dark rags which allowed Farren to be fully concealed. She tucked her white dress beneath her, the floor left disgustingly murky marks on the fabric. The breaths that flew from her moved the rags so she pressed a hand hard against her mouth.

Three sets of boots marched past the cell. Over the sound of the rush of her blood Farren heard the Princess describe her to the guards with scary accuracy. She only saw her face in torchlight; Farren was mildly impressed. The sound of the Princess as she whined about her father's 'minions' and how she never wanted to go home assaulted her ears. The throbbing in her head resumed and her hand tightened around her mouth. Farren debated facing the consequences in the Mortal Realm if she left the ungrateful girl with Nero. She and Rorke travelled across Realms, faced a manner of nasty creatures, snuck into the enemy's stronghold and the Princess did not want to leave. Something inky inside of her roiled and the merchant's daughter dug her nails into the stone.

"Where did she go?"

The Princess sobbed, "she disappeared into the dark." The dark-eyed woman was hysterical as she begged to go upstairs and see someone called Schylus. *Wait-* Farren nearly groaned into her hand. *"Schylus is probably at the top of that list."* Janus practically handed them the information on a plate but Rorke refused to take it, and she refused to push further. Her jaw clicked as she ground her teeth. Two of the most revered Kayei were in the Kavan castle with her, and she had no idea what either of them looked like.

Amidst Farren's twitching eye she heard the guards calm the Princess down as they promised to bring her to Schylus, she just had to wear the 'metal bracelets'. Farren had an idea just what those bracelets were. The rattle of chains sounded along with Cyrille's sniffles, then the footsteps marched from the Princess' cell and toward where she laid against floor. Two sets of feet walked past her and up the stairs so she waited, her breath trapped in her throat. Once she heard the door creak shut she shuffled on her forearms from under the cot. Fortunately, the lock was left alone which reminded her of the key against her chest. Skin scraped against sharp cobbles as she brushed off her dress and stood with a wince. The liquid beneath her rippled, the air around her changed and she slowly looked up. From the darkness two pairs of eyes stared back at her. One of them cleared their throat whilst the other raised his hand to reveal light radiated from his skin.

All Farren offered were raised hands and a nervous chuckle.

Rorke glanced up at the stairs whilst he waited for more drinks to be poured. His arms were folded across his chest and a permanent crease was embedded between his eyes. His attention was torn between the kitchen door and the bubbles that frothed in the glasses. "What is wrong with you?" Rorke turned from the glasses to face the Head. The grey and brown of her hair was pulled behind her in a braid, the tresses only just long enough to be tied back. Her mouth was downturned and her skin was pale and free of blemishes; a few wrinkles prevailed beneath her eyes, eyes which flickered between brown and plum in the light. Rorke's breath jolted: she was a servant who was not entirely human. "Well," she urged him. "What is wrong with you? Can you not keep your head on your shoulders long enough to carry drinks up there without getting distracted?"

"Yes ma'am," was quick to fly from his mouth. "But I am worried for my friend, she has not been to gatherings like these before."

The Head folded her hands in front of her apron. "Your friend, she is a new servant, correct?" He nodded. "She is young?" He shrugged with another nod. "Listen boy, if she is up there she is doing fine, most servants no matter how new, are strong enough to work amongst them so stop your dithering and focus on your own work, just as I am sure she is doing." *It is not her that he should be worried about.* The Head narrowed her eyes, glanced between him and the door then wildly shooed him toward the stairs. Rorke moved as she asked, the tray heavy in his hands. There was no sign of Farren in or around the ballroom which allowed him a sigh of relief. Everyone mingled, laughed, talked, which meant they did not bother the other servants who meekly offered canapés and drinks. With each second that ticked by, Rorke felt his muscles bunch tighter and tighter. That was how his night progressed. It was when his tray of crab puffs was emptied that he leant against the wall beyond the ballroom. He took in a deep breath and rubbed a hand over his chin and beneath his mask.

A glass of water is shoved in front of his face. "Drink," the Head ordered and like the well-trained soldier he was, he took the glass from her hand and sipped at its contents. "Good. I need you hydrated so you can deliver another set of trays."

"Thank you." There is a bout of silence. "How long have you worked for Nero?"

She manoeuvred away from a rushing boy. "Nero? That man is nothing more than a shiny chess piece." Rorke nearly choked on the water. "I have worked for Schylus for fifty years."

Schylus let out a full-belly laugh at a joke Nero told whilst Janus handed him another glass of wine. Rorke sipped his own ale as he watched the tall Kayei fall onto his ass, Nero's shirt sleeve in his grasp. He snorted at the sight and leaned back against the dirt.

"Come on, that was hilarious! I cannot believe she asked you to jump out the window, four stories up, just to avoid her mother seeing you," Schylus declared through his laughter.

"She's obviously embarrassed to be seen with him," Rorke commented. Nero raised a brow at his forwardness and drank from his own cup. His hair was tussled wildly and his eyes were hooded, but they remained sharp when he dragged them across his men who sat amongst the humans, peace hovered around them. Janus linked his arm with Rorke's and nudged him. The sensual smile Rorke was granted set his cheeks aflame and he swallowed deeply.

"Here we are talking about Nero's failed escapades," Schylus yelled whilst Nero rolled his eyes. "When we should instead be gaining insight into Rorkey-boy's sex life."

The young man darted his eyes between Janus and Schylus, the heat near-unbearable on his face. "I... is that really necessary?"

"Why not, we're all friends here, right?" Schylus slurred with a smirk.

"Shouldn't we-" Rorke swallowed when Janus shuffled closer into his side. "Talk about our strategy for the morning?"

Nero chuckled and leant on his palms. The lines of gold on his chest and neck caught the firelight as he stared at him. Schylus shook his head with an indignant scoff. The truth was that was all they did that evening: they talked about escape routes and formations and squad leaders. Rorke's own brain started to pound from the talking they did but if it meant he didn't have to tell them- that he didn't have to tell Janus what ran through his mind when he saw him, then he would continue to talk about strategies.

"Leave him alone, Schylus," Janus scolded, then he leaned into Rorke's ear. "Relax soldier, you're too young for anyone here to consider taking you to bed." That hurt him more than anything else he might have said. Before Rorke replied that he was in fact man enough to take Janus back to his tent, Schylus launched from his seat and pulled him out of Janus' arms. Rorke was by no means a slight boy but Schylus' towering form and Kayei strength made it difficult for him to catch his feet. Schylus dropped Rorke's wrist the moment he stood and moved over to Nero's side.

"I'm going to try something." At Schylus' declaration Nero groaned. "And I would appreciate silence from the cheap seats, thank you." With a flourish he pushed back the sleeves of his jacket and stood shoulder-width apart. Rorke's eyes widened and he too held his hands out like a rugby player ready to defend. The light from his tent spilled into the circle of people and acted as Schylus' spotlight as he took another step back. "Tell me Rorkey-boy." Rorke grit his teeth and braced himself for whatever was about to fall from his lips. "How much of you is muscle?"

"What?"

"You can see he has a fair bit of muscle-mass, Schylus. Hurry up and do whatever it is you want to do," Nero snapped.

Janus nodded in agreement. "The poor lad looks like he is about sprint from this fire pit."

Rorke looked down at his muscular frame then back up at Schylus who grinned maniacally at him. The long-haired man rubbed his hands together and pranced on the spot. He lifted his eyebrows in question, but before Rorke got a word in Schylus ran toward him. One second he was in front of Rorke, then he felt a gust of wind and Schylus was stood behind the guard. The human blinked and pat at his body.

"Only three, I'm disappointed in you Rorkey."

Nero scoffed in his seat but made no comment. Janus looked between his friend and Schylus, his hands on his hips and a brow raised. The sound of his heart pounded in Rorke's ears. "Three what?" He breathed out.

"Three weapons."

"How did you know?"

Janus pulled Rorke to sit down beside him. "Schylus likes to show off just how fast he can be. He ran around you, then searched you."

"Show off," Nero chuckled and Schylus mockingly bowed. The laugh that followed at Rorke's bewildered face had him on his ass once more. Janus pat the human on his back and chuckled. Nero's eyes strayed over to where Rorke continued to gape. His eyes left him when a rustle was heard in the bushes behind them. Each man turned to the sound, only to find Rorke's Captain. The short, stocky man nodded toward the Kayei before he motioned Rorke over. Without hesitation he shot to his feet and clambered over to his commanding officer.

"Having fun, soldier?" It was rhetorical. "Say your goodnights, I need all my troops to get a long rest before the morning. I suggest you tell them the same." He nodded to the trio who pretended not to eavesdrop on the conversation.

"Yes, sir," Rorke spoke as he turned. Nero raised a brow and smirked at the Captain, Janus sipped on his glass, and Schylus —who remained on the ground- waved childishly at both of them. Rorke sighed, looked back at his Captain and moved toward the Kayei.

Rorke stared at the Head like she'd grown two heads alongside her usual one. Schylus did not know respect, boundaries, or discipline. Nor had he seen a sober day in his life; neither had Janus but Rorke cast that from his mind in that moment. Nero was Schylus' Commander, the man who helped lead the Kayei rebels, but Schylus treated him like any other fool who sat in his presence. It made Rorke wonder just what happened when the humans retreated from the war.

The Head broke him from his thoughts, "how long have you worked for your master?"

Rorke tightened the hold on his arms. "Since I was sixteen." His eyes searched hers. "Are you happy working here?"

"Happiness has nothing to do with it. The Master takes care of my family when he doesn't have to." Rorke closed his eyes for a brief moment and mentally sighed. He wanted to ask what happened in the years he was gone; he wanted to ask what happened to Nero's reputation; he wanted to ask Schylus how he became so revered. Instead, Rorke opted for a tight smile. That was when the Head tightened the hold on her fingers. "Who is it that you belong to?"

"Is that important?" Rorke asked whilst his eyes drifted around the corridor.

"Yes, I think it is. You say that you have served your lord since you were sixteen, yet you do not hold yourself like a servant. You have been in servitude, but not in a household; I think you have served as a-" She stopped abruptly and Rorke straightened. "I should have recognised a soldier when I saw one."

"I work as my Master's," he nearly choked on the title, "guard."

"Then why are you in the kitchens and not in that ballroom?"

Rorke looked toward the double-doors. "He did not want my services this evening, but just in case, he wanted me in the kitchens," he lied.

For a beat he thought she believed him, but then there was a scream that flew around the curve of the corridor and reached the ballroom. Guards from the other side of said room rushed out toward the sound. Muscles Rorke didn't know he had tensed and he watched three, toned, stone-faced Kayei run past him. The servants on the stairs beside him muttered and speculated but the Head simply stared. The poison in his pocket weighed heavy as he felt the older woman's eyes on the side of his face. He kept any emotion away from his features and he relaxed what tension he could. No weapons sat on the woman's body; there was nothing hidden under her skirt but he had no problem imagining that she would swipe for him with her more-than-human strength.

"Whoever that was, disturbed Schylus' party, they will likely pay for that with a limb or two," the Head said, "silly girl should have kept her mouth shut."

Rorke's heartbeat stuttered but he did not acknowledge her. His attention was focused on the direction of the scream. There was an ache in his chest as he watched a guard drag a dishevelled girl from the dungeon. Her feet stuttered beneath her and the chains rattled loudly. The dress she wore was covered in dirt and stains and her hair was unkempt but it wasn't Farren, not with the way she simpered and sniffled, face to the floor. The nobles rolled their eyes or laughed at the girl who was forced toward them, but they did move from the guard's path. It was the sharp coils at the crown of her head and the smooth, caramel skin that caught his interest. That was when the flicker of emotion travelled across his face. He had to remember how to stand. Princess Cyrille cried in the arms of the frustrated guard, who pushed her into the ballroom with little grace. She fell to the floor in a dramatic pile of skirts and tears, her hands pressed to her face as she continued to sob.

Rorke lifted his eyes from the Princess on the floor and slowly scanned the nobles in front of him. The Head had yet to remove her gaze from his face but she was quiet, eerily so. More guards jogged from the ballroom and stationed themselves against the corner of the corridor, so Rorke took a deep breath and prepared for who else was about to be dragged from the dungeons.

The guards cuffed Farren the minute she raised her hands. They were roughly pulled behind her back and clasped in iron chains. The guard with the inner light lead the way up the stairs whilst the other had his hand wrapped around the chain that connected her wrists. More guards greeted them at the top of the stairs. One... Two... three... for Griselda's sake there were ten guards before her. She cursed the Goddess, she cursed the King, she cursed Nero –Schylus– whoever the enemy was and she cursed the Princess. The royal's screams made her ears ring even as she was pushed through the dungeon door. Her knees barked under her weight; her shoulder pulled uncomfortably. All the people before her looked pleased to cause her any and all discomfort but she glared at them from her spot on the floor regardless. *Bastards.* She blew her hair from her face and pushed her feet beneath her. Once she stood, a female guard with leather gear turned her roughly and pushed her forward. Bruises already began to form from the manhandling but she kept her footing. Farren imagined the blood splatter and crunch of the guard's bone as she slammed the heel of her palm against her nose. It was wishful thinking as she strode forward. The twitch of her lip at the thought of beating each Kayei guard in a fight was very much real.

There was no sign of the party: no laughter, no music, no clink of glasses that she diligently passed around the Kayei, but then she lifted her eyes from the floor and found out why. A gaggle of nobles stood in front of the ballroom doors and she trailed along them until her gaze reached the Head and Rorke, stood side-by-side, eyes on her. Farren quickly shot her eyes to her right. In the brief second she saw him, Rorke looked unharmed and she noted the lack of chains around his wrists. The floor-length mirror that was her new focal point nearly made her laugh. The clothes she wore were covered in dirt and grime and a mysterious liquid. Her cheeks were flushed, eyes wide and she was jostled by the guards behind her. The mask still sat against her cheekbones but some of the liquid on her dress found its way onto the fabric. Her hair was a tangled mess over her shoulder, the wound beneath still hidden from view but the throb in her shoulder was something she was very aware of. A light cough held in her laugh. How far she was from the Brentham Church with Argen on her ass about the proper posture. She straightened her shoulders for good measure.

Farren was marched forward like a war criminal. A guard flanked either side of her and many of them walked at her back. She purposefully forced her eyes away from Rorke and in doing so she looked at the nobles. The Princess' sniffles reached her and she grit her teeth but continued forward with the guard's hand around her chains.

Rorke felt helpless as they guided Farren into the ballroom. Her back was straight, her face forward, and her eyes refused to meet his. He truly thought his heart stopped when she was shoved to the floor. The sheer amount of guards that surrounded her was enough to twist his stomach into knots. It was not his first capture, it was not the first time he saw one of his men captured, but each time he failed them. *He failed Farren.* What made his mind spin the most was that he knew, deep down, that the King would want him to leave Farren, to let the Kayei do as they wanted so long as Princess Cyrille was in his care. The twist of his gut bordered on painful, because Rorke was not entirely certain he was capable of leaving Farren, no matter his King's orders.

"Rorke."

The King's guard blinked the unfocused nature of his eyes back to reality and stared at the man in front of him. The gold of the Kayei's eyes flared when he locked them with his green ones. A sinister smirk caressed his face and he tilted his head back. The back of the Kayei's head thudded against the doorframe whilst his hands were placed in his pockets. For a man with such an evil past his hair was as golden as the sun and it fell behind his ears as he dared the human to step toward him. "Nero."

"You look good, what have you been up to?" The blond Kayei's smirk widened as he spoke, but Rorke did not answer. "Is that a friend of yours? She's feisty." He leaned forward. "But you already know that."

"Shut up," Rorke countered.

The smirk fell and Nero nodded for the Head to move away from the man beside her. Without hesitation she did as he commanded and Rorke finally looked at her. Daggers were thrown his way as she glared. Nero stepped forward. "Are you going to stand there and let that woman take all the blame?"

"I am not guilty of anything." As an afterthought he added, "neither is she."

Nero advanced until his hand slammed against the wall beside Rorke's head. Pieces of stone crumbled to the floor by their boots. The servants who previously watched in the stairwell scurried back to the kitchen with gasps. The nobles chuckled but with a glare over his shoulder, Nero had them scurrying too. "Get your ass in that room," he ordered Rorke. The deep nature of his voice vibrated through Rorke, just as the sheer dominance made him lift his chin and push past him.

Once he was on the threshold of the room, Nero was behind him, a hand on his spine. The slightest push and Rorke stumbled inside to where Farren and Princess Cyrille stood. Finally, Farren looked at him and feathered her jaw. Her concentration was soon stolen by the blond man at his side. Widened blue could be seen from where he stood but Nero did not bother to say anything else, not as he walked away from the entrance and over to the other Kayei in the room. Once he was situated at his side, the gold in his eyes stuttered like the flicker of a flame despite the bored expression on his face.

Stood next to him at the front of the room, with a bemused smile on his face was the long-haired Kayei Farren spied earlier that evening. The same chocolate tresses cascaded down his back and shoulders and the rubies in his headpiece glimmered in the light. He wore a matching red suit that was tailored perfectly to his lithe body. "Well, well, well, what do we have here?" The man with the crown asked. "Two humans not where they are supposed to be." His smile remained in place.

Farren didn't know whether to raise her head or lower it so she simply stared at him. Rorke was plastered to the right wall, his eyes on both Kayei. The doors beside him were closed so that it was only the four of them plus the Princess and her guard. Farren purposefully ignored the girl to her left lest she said something that was not becoming of her.

"She was in the dungeon, Sir, she made the Princess cry," the dungeon guard explained.

As if on cue, the Princess started to blubber loudly into her hands but the Kayei replied, "that is no difficult feat."

Farren ran her tongue over her teeth. The crown-bearer took long strides until he stood in front of her. Like a shark he circled her and she watched his every move. Her shoulders were pushed back and her chin was lifted slightly, certainly higher than any servant dared hold it. He never blinked as he surveyed her with such a unique mixture of animosity and curiosity. The racing of her heart was ignored but the way her skin prickled beneath his gaze made her wrists shift in their confines. The guard that previously held her in place walked out the door the minute the blond made an appearance so Farren was left with the entire back part of the ballroom to run to. Although, she was not sure her feet would move even if she wished it.

Everyone held their breaths until the Kayei found something that made him scoff. "What does a Malumrem like you want with the Princess?"

287

Farren had never felt so offended in her entire life. "A *what*?"

"Farren." Rorke stepped forward but the crown-wearer held out his hand to stop him.

"Ah, ah Rorkey-boy, we will get to you in a moment." He moved closer to her and sniffed. "How did you slip into my castle without a single guard sensing you?" The question was forced through bared teeth.

Farren looked him directly in the eye. "I didn't need to 'slip in', I was invited inside. I asked where the servant's entrance was and they gave me directions."

He looked between her, Rorke, the blond and the guard behind Cyrille with fire in his eyes, but he changed the subject quickly. "And it was just you, you say?" Farren quickly nodded. "You did not arrive with this soldier over here?" He pointed to Rorke who took another step forward.

"You know him don't you?" Farren bravely asked. "Is he not one of your servants?"

"Farren stop," Rorke pleaded which made the crown-wearer smile wider but her expression was not as kind as she looked between them.

The man in front of her whistled. "Trouble in paradise it seems, but I want to know why he brought you." He leaned down so that they were eye-to-eye.

"Who's to say I didn't bring *him*?"

"If that's the case then you must be a member of the King of Altin's army. Is that correct?"

"She's not part of his army Schylus, leave her alone, please," Rorke begged. The long-haired Kayei –Schylus- lost his smile and turned to Rorke with a dramatic sigh. Farren barely registered that he moved away from her. Schylus was the one in charge, he was the one who kidnapped the Princess, he was the one who forced the humans to work as slaves, he was the reason she was there. He was also the reason why Rorke screamed.

"I told you to wait your turn, Rorkey," Schylus taunted. One of his hands was wrapped around Rorke's wrist. That wrist was brought to eye-level and pinned to the wall where Schylus' other hand was curled into a fist. With his eyes focused on Rorke's he brought his fist down on that hand which successfully shattered all the bones. When he released the Second-in-Command his hand was twisted in places where the bones tried to protrude and he hissed through his teeth to alleviate the pain.

Farren swallowed the bile in her throat and pulled against her confines but it was Cyrille who called out his name, who tried to crawl forward on her knees toward him. On the other hand, Farren moved her attention to Schylus who strode back over to her. She did not balk under his gaze nor did she avert her eyes. She made sure he saw every ounce of anger and disgust she felt, and he laughed.

"Kneel." A quick glance at Rorke found him huddled against the wall with a groan, so she did as he asked. With her knees beneath her she lowered her head. Schylus used her vulnerable position to bring his polished shoe to the back of her head. He applied pressure and the more he did, the closer the floor became. Rorke groaned out expletives and demands whilst Farren tried to fight against the ache in her skull. Suddenly the pressure ceased but his foot remained on her head. "Who are you?"

"I am not a member of the King of Altin's army," Farren re-iterated, "I am just a woman who managed to get a job in your castle and-"

"And tried to break me from my cell," the Princess said through sobs.

Farren could not believe it and if she were not bent over for the second time that night she would have glared at her, instead she opted for: "are you honestly going to take the word of a mad teenager?"

"Farren," Schylus drawled as though testing the name on his tongue. "You haven't answered my question." He pressed hard against her head which made her neck throb.

"What more do you want to know, you have my name, you know I am not a soldier, what else?" She tried to keep the venom from her voice.

"How about your last name?" He suggested.

"I am not stupid," she fired back, "the Kayei value names and you have half of mine. What else?"

He chuckled. "Do you know why we value names? Because we can use them to spread rumours, to build a person up or bring them down, we can even whisper them to the Goddess in the hopes she will strike them down. You humans do the same. The only reason you fear giving it to us is because you think magic will be cursed upon you." He rolled his eyes dramatically.

"So why would I give you mine?"

He removed his foot from her skull. Immediately she shot upright on her knees but Schylus' attention was back on the blond. She too dragged her eyes over the silent man and blue clashed with gold because his eyes were already on her. Nothing but boredom radiated from him; his hands were slow and relaxed as he pushed them into his pockets. Schylus grinned fiendishly at him and the two Kayei swapped places. The blond was soon in front of her and when he was, he crouched onto his haunches.

"Leave her alone," Rorke said. She watched him struggle against the pain, the sharp breaths that escaped him. She moved to stand but the blond grabbed the front of her dress and pulled her back down to his level. She wobbled on her knees as she tried to stay upright. At Schylus' order to 'remove her mask', golden eyes scanned her face and he reached behind her to untie the knot. He was meticulous and slow, his eyes on hers as he pulled the fabric free.

The black material was flung to the floor to reveal pale skin, freckles and narrowed eyes. "My, my Rorkey, you found yourself a pretty one."

Farren's attention was split between Schylus and the Kayei in front of her who hovered his hand near her face. Once she focused on him that hand moved strands of her hair from her eyes then returned to his side. Schylus shuffled behind him and stared between Rorke and Farren like a child at Yule which made the other Kayei look up at his partner. The Princess had been ignored and the guard who held her chains looked extremely uncomfortable but Schylus did not care, not as he grinned at the three of them.

"Nero, take our mutual friend back to the dungeon with the Princess, I want to continue my talk with Farren.

Schylus was not how Farren imagined him at all. She pictured a blundering idiot, a stuttering fool, if Janus' description was to be believed, but the man who loomed over her was anything but an idiot. The way he held himself reminded her so much of Theron that she almost felt like she was at home, scouring her father's papers, but then a hand came down across her face and that feeling vanished. Schylus' version of talking was asking her a question they both knew she could not answer and then landing a slap against her face. The first time he laid his hand on her she froze. The sheer force of his swing made her worry if her spine would remain intact. There was no time for her to digest the fact that Nero and the golden Kayei were one-in-the-same.

After the fourth slap, she asked her own question, "why did you send Rorke to the dungeon but keep me here?"

"I find that humans tend to lie in front of their friends," Schylus explained whilst he grabbed a few strands of her hair and pulled her forward. "They often want to look more noble than they actually are, so tell me, what do *you* want with the Princess?" Wine infiltrated her senses as his breath fanned across her face and his hand tightened before he released her with a wicked smile.

She blew out a breath. "You want to know the truth?" He nodded. "I want absolutely nothing to do with her." The smile on his face fell and he raised his hand to slap her. "She is spoilt and she is whiny, and she obviously has no loyalties to human beings."

His hand lowered. "How does Rorkey-boy feel about this?"

"You would have to ask him, but it does leave me wondering what *you* want with the Princess?" Her voice remained steady and strong despite the sting of her flesh.

His reply was nothing more than a kick in the teeth. "I just wanted to have some fun."

"Then play kickball or bake a cake." The previously raised hand landed against her cheek and she coughed against the blood that filled her mouth. She swirled the blood and thought better of spitting it at his feet. That left her with no other option but to swallow the metallic liquid. The loud clang of metal on metal sounded from beyond the ballroom doors and Farren's eyes widened. She went to stand but Schylus promptly pushed her shoulder down. Griselda must have looked down upon her in that moment because his hand landed on her good shoulder and squeezed.

"How do you think you're going to help him, huh? Unless you have a sword in that bodice of yours," he paused and scanned her chest with a chuckle, "unlikely, then you're useless to him."

"If I'm so useless." She panted against the painful squeeze of her muscle. "Then how did you only just find me?"

She gasped when he released her with a flourish. "Yes, well, someone will pay for that oversight." He turned to look at the door with pursed lips. "I also need to think about what to do with you. Maybe I should give you to Nero, he is well versed in the art of *women*, or maybe I should lock you in the dungeon with the Princess you so hate. Oo, that would certainly be an interesting scene."

Farren bit her swollen lip. "Do I get to choose?"

"No." His gaze was no longer on her, sheer dismissal laced his tone. With a click of his fingers her previous captor marched inside. "Escort Farren upstairs, I think I know what to do with our intruders." The guard nodded and grabbed her chains. The last thing she saw was Schylus' wild smile before the world ebbed to black.

The cell Rorke was shoved into smelled like piss and rust. It was two doors away from the Princess who snivelled into her sleeve. He listened as she moaned about Schylus, about how he never had time for her, how he never paid her any attention. It made his stomach turn as she proceeded to cry about how much she missed him. Rorke sincerely doubted that Schylus felt the same, but it widened the question as to why he stole her in the first place; which of course lead to the question of Nero's involvement.

Rorke's good hand gripped the bars whilst the other was cradled against his chest. The pain faded to a throb, so long as he didn't try to use it, or think about it. He'd endured broken bones before but the sound of every finger cracking made him flinch. Nero stood beyond the cell with a torch raised and the flame flared as though he fuelled the fire that lit the space. In a way he did. It flickered off the strands of his hair as he stared down his nose at Rorke, but the latter simply glared.

"I'm shocked. You brought a civilian woman into a fight you know you could never win."

He swallowed. "What makes you think she's a civilian?"

Nero laughed. "She doesn't disgust every fibre of my being like you human guards do. Plus, she was too cocky, her undiluted confidence did not match the smell of caution and fear from you."

"You don't want to underestimate her."

Nero whistled. "Big words from a man behind bars, she wasn't so terrifying when Schylus pinned her head to the ground, or when he smashed your hand to pieces. I wonder how many fingers she will have in place when he's finished interrogating her." He was taunting him, calling him a failure so he kept his glare in place and said nothing. They both knew he was right. The two men stood with their gazes on each other before Nero deemed his company dull and the torch shifted as he turned to leave.

"Nero." The blond stopped with his head tilted backward. "Schylus he..." Rorke trailed off, there wasn't anything to say that wasn't obvious. "He turned into a prick."

Nero stared at the ceiling. "He's always been a prick."

"A prick you now take orders from." A question yet not. *How far the mighty Nero had fallen.* Nero once ordered the decimation of enemy armies and won, he gained respect from the other Rulers, all while Schylus sat on his ass with a bottle of booze in his paw. The worst legion commander he'd ever seen but there he was with Nero's crown atop his head and the power to kidnap a human Princess from her bed. Or had Nero done that for him? Bored with the conversation, Nero stalked away. Rorke called out once more, "what are you going to do to her?" The fading sound of footsteps answered him. Then he and the Princess were shrouded in silence. Her crying stopped when Nero spoke and now only her soft breaths puffed into the darkness. It was so quiet he thought she might have fallen asleep.

But then there was the soft call of his name and he'd never been happier to hear it. "Are you alright?"

He cradled his arm closer to his chest which turned dry with each inhalation of dust. "I'm fine, Princess."

"I am so sorry, Rorke." He let her speak. "My father should never have asked you to come here."

"I couldn't let you rot in a cell."

She slammed against her bars. "It's not rotting! This is where I belong!"

Rorke paused. "Is that why you're locked in a cell?" He sat on the cot which bowed against his weight.

"He distrusts people, so he is keeping me here temporarily and I do not blame him! If I were a proper Kayei prisoner I would have been tortured or worse! Just look at that woman who tried to free me. When he is certain I am no threat I will stand by his side as his equal." Despite the crown on Schylus' head he was not fit to rule nor was he in line to do so. He was a military runt, no more fit to be King than Rorke was. Taking Cyrille did not change his capabilities, nor did it bring him closer to being King. Her threat level was just as high, if not higher, from that cell.

None of those thoughts left his mouth because the desperation in her voice forced his mouth shut on the matter so he opted for his own conviction. "That woman was doing her job."

Cyrille laughed. "My father would never, ever, hire a woman."

"You're wrong." *That woman was captured because you screamed.* "Princess, what have they fed you?"

"What do you mean?" She sniffled.

"Have they fed you anything weird? Have they handed you any odd objects? Has he spoken to you in the Old Language?" Rorke finally realised why Farren insisted on her numerous questions.

Cyrille nearly didn't answer but her voice was small "He didn't use any Kayei tricks on me, Rorke. I care about him."

"Not possible. Princess, I must ask, how did you get here because last month you had no knowledge of Schylus, did you?"

Cyrille slammed against the bars once more. "You ask too many questions! He cares about me too, and any enemy of his, is an enemy of mine, I will no longer be answering your questions!" She slowed her breathing, "I am sorry."

The sound of rustled fabric and the creak of her cot reached his ears. He followed suit and laid back against the lumpy mattress. His head hurt like hell, and his heart thudded uncomfortably in his chest. He cursed at the dark ceiling. Farren's horror-stricken face flashed in his mind, the way she glared at Schylus like it was her life's mission to end his. His eyes slipped shut because any hope of their rescue lied in the perseverance and stamina of a merchant's daughter trained by a village guard against one of the most powerful creatures in the known world.

Farren was on her knees, head bowed, with her eyes glaring a hole into the decorative rug. The shackles remained tight behind her back and her face stung from the assaults. Purple stood bright against her skin which was swollen so that part of her vision was blocked. The cool air tried to lessen the discomfort of her injuries but Farren barely felt it against her skin. She found herself in a smaller room, one that was covered in ornate decor. *More privacy*, Schylus crooned when he walked in. A desk decorated with black vines stood before her and behind that a plush chair covered in blackened silver. She kept her head bowed so she missed the gruesome paintings similar to those in the ballroom and the nicked wooden board used for darts or throwing knives.

"You break into my home and try to steal what is mine. You can't expect me to let that go unpunished can you?" Schylus sat behind the desk with hands steepled in front of him.

Farren's heart hammered in her chest and sweat formed in her palms yet she lifted her eyes to his. There were no markings on his hands from where he slapped her, nor was his suit out of place. He looked like the perfect businessman about to close a deal. But she wanted that look to crack. "Like I said, I didn't break in, I was invited." She ignored the fact he called the Princess 'his.'

The chair thudded against the wall as he stood and he took his time to walk around the desk to crouch in front of her. "Don't get cute. You," he giggled, "you are not in a very powerful position."

"I just," she sighed and sat back on her ankles, "didn't want you to waste your time punishing me for the wrong thing." The expanse of her life flashed before her eyes as his hand gripped around her throat. The odds of her surviving were slim to none and she thought of the vial of poison in her bodice. One vial into Schylus' drink and he'd be a corpse at her feet. One drop on her tongue and she'd be dead at his.

"If you didn't smell so wrong I would have given you to Nero and been done with it."

"That's just rude."

Never had she been so happy to have an odour but she felt, even with the lack of bathing, she did not smell as bad as some men she encountered. The odour from the dungeon clung to her, but she was sure that wasn't what he meant, so she glared and pushed her shoulders back. The click of the study door sounded and Nero took that moment to walk in.

Schylus released her neck and stood. The lapels on his jacket were straightened. "Learn to knock! What if we were in the middle of something.... more interesting."

She coughed and the images around the room caught her attention as Nero said, "you would never risk your life just to bed a Malumrem." After a moment's pause he changed his mind. "Actually, you just might."

298

If one more person called her that she swore to Griselda- Nero's steps made their way to her side. Pure disgust shone from his features as he stared down at her beaten form. She wanted to ask him where the flirty Kayei went, where the man who warned her to leave was, but her mouth remained shut and her glare only deepened. Schylus shuffled the crown atop his head and sneered at his comrade. Whilst the crown glinted in the light, Nero stared at it with the same disgust he graced her with. Schylus either didn't notice or didn't care. "What became of the soldier?"

A one-shouldered shrug. "I left him to starve in one of the cells."

"Excellent." His wicked smile returned.

She jolted toward him with an animalistic snarl. Both Nero and Schylus slowly looked down at her, at the bared teeth and damaged face. Like a wild animal she pulled against her restraints. Schylus blinked at her and opened his mouth but Nero rolled his eyes and turned his back on her like she was the least threatening prisoner he'd encountered. Her surge of confidence simmered into a headache that threatened to force her into unconsciousness. They proceeded to talk like she wasn't there so she kept her eyes on the room around her: a single door guarded by two, maybe three guards, one window that was big enough for her to climb through but unless she was able to see out of the window beforehand there was no way of knowing how high they were. No weapons hung on the walls or in the cabinets which were reserved for scrolls and books. They didn't need them, she supposed, they were weapons in their own right. What she concluded was that there was no escaping from the study unless she killed two Kayei, one of them a King or three guards with her hands tied and a knife in her boot. *Not likely.* She shifted the weight of that leg and pushed back the laugh of disbelief. The knife remained strapped snugly into her boot. They didn't fear the weapon, or more accurately –she continued to glare- they didn't fear her. Arrogant bastards.

The Kayei were not immune to stab wounds, a biological fact she wanted to put to the test.

"I wish to inform my guests of the newest event of their stay." Schylus gazed at her like she was his next dinner. From what she knew of the Kayei she likely was.

He left her with Nero who stood with his eyes cast toward her chains. In the light of the study she was allowed to see the scar on his nose that seemed longer than the first two times she saw him and how sharp his features really were. His forearms were bare as he folded them across his chest and leaned against the edge of the desk, ankles crossed and eyes hooded as though he would fall asleep at any moment.

"I suppose I should apologise, I made it too easy for you get in. I can't promise the same for when you escape."

The words made a sob -or was that a laugh- wrack her body. She would escape and go back home where it was safe and free of magic. She would sit with Lyla whilst she cooked where her biggest concern would be getting Theron to listen to her. Her head dipped. She would be hunted for the rest of her life by the King, his guards and Rorke if he were to escape after her. The floppy-haired, green-eyed man's face flashed in her mind and something in her pulled tight. She would not abandon him to the likes of Schylus, not when he obviously endured so much at the hands of the Kayei. So she shuffled on her knees. "What do you mean you made it too easy?"

Nero's jaw feathered. "I gave those guards your description. I told them you might have a burly companion with you and that they should let you in."

"Why?"

A mischievous smirk crawled onto his face. "Because I could."

"Okay, but why help me inside, our first meeting wasn't exactly inconspicuous?"

"You're right, you were terrible at hiding and if I were any other person you would have been dragged to the castle. I wanted to know what your motives were; now I do." He raised a brow.

Silence fell over the room and she blinked owlishly and took the time to truly study him. The lean figure, the toned muscles of his arms, the way his hair framed his face and those golden eyes. The collar of his shirt remained opened to reveal his strong neck which was covered in golden veins like sun-strokes across his skin. He was attractive and she thought she would have tried her luck with him if he were human, or perhaps if he was simply on her side of the battle. Then, Janus' voice reminded her: "I thought you were supposed to be a fearsome ruler yet here you are doing the bidding of someone who apparently used to be a buffoon."

He let a chuckle fill the room. With his eyes lifted to hers she realised why he might be able to decimate cities. The citizens alone would crumble at that small smirk. *Snake charmer indeed.* "Who told you that?"

"Does it matter?"

The chains rattled as she made to stand but she paused: smoke trailed over body and feet like rope. It curved around her biceps and the chains already around her wrists until it crossed over her chest and remained. Heat emanated from the smoke to let her know it could burn her alive if Nero so willed it. So, she sat back on her heels and lifted her head where the smoke curled under her chin and rested there.

His own eyes travelled the smoke before he settled on her blue orbs. "Whatever your friend told you is true. Just last week I destroyed an entire village because I could not be bothered to travel around it." He stood straight.

301

"I destroyed my own palace because there were two people inside I didn't care for." He stepped toward her. "I killed my friend for sport." He smirked. "Now tell me I'm not fearsome and mean it. If you do then I'll let you go." Crescent dents dotted her palm but her mouth quivered with the rise of her chin. There were no words that would convey what he wanted. The man before her became more than Schylus' lacky; he became more than the attractive Kayei who warned her to run. He was a Ruler who allied himself with someone just as powerful. Said Ruler scoffed and walked behind her. She scrambled to keep her eyes on him but he kept his back to her as he walked to her side toward the window. "I'm sure Schylus already asked, but why did you try and steal the Princess?"

Farren replied, "like the two of you did? She's part of my job."

"You're not a King's Guard, that imbecile in the cells is but not you," he hummed with his hands in his pockets.

"I'm new."

Nero scoffed. The sound shot through her chest as she heard it from so many men over the years. She heard it from Argen when she originally asked for him to train her, from the other guards –Enrys, Ritrio- even from some of Lyla's cooks. Then there was the pity in his eyes as he glanced back at her. If she could grow claws and slash his face she would.

"No you're not, you are a sacrifice in return for the King of Altin's daughter."

"I'm only a sacrifice if I die." The second the words left her mouth she winced.

Suddenly, he was in front of her. Not once did he lay his hands on her but the smoke and the piercing nature of his gaze was enough to render her speechless. She remained still and waited as he crouched and tilted his head.

302

"You're the only person besides that solider who is stupid enough to travel across realms for a Princess you don't care for." She opened her mouth to protest but he raised his hand. "I saw the way you looked at her, no love was lost."

A smirk forced its way onto her face but it was more of a grimace. "No matter my personal feelings -which you know not of- I will bring that Princess back with me."

His eyes bore into hers for a long while. "That blind confidence might just keep you alive." For the first time since he entered the room she lowered her head. The dark strands of her hair cascaded around her. Her roots were oily, the ends in desperate need of a comb and those strands were moved to fall behind her shoulder by Nero's slow touch. That caught her attention and she raised her eyes while he brushed his hand across her shoulder. His ministrations paused when flesh met bandage. The pain was barely noticeable, if anything, the swelling on her face ached more.

"Maybe we have underestimated you if you managed to escape a Kuroguine." He sketched a brow.

"Two." He lifted a brow once again. "I escaped *two* Kuroguine."

"Did you really?" He actually looked impressed.

The door to the hall clicked open and he guided her hair back into place. Three guards stood in the doorway, hands on their swords and faces in permanent scowls. Nero was told to untie her and she swore flames raged behind his eyes as he followed their order. First the shackles then the smoke were removed from her body. In a second the dagger in her boot was in her hand and pressed against the blond's neck.

His throat bobbed against the thin blade. "Stay where you are," he ordered the guards who lurched forward.

Hooded eyes stared up at her body which loomed over his. Her foot was pressed between his legs as she knelt on the other. When she angled the blade closer to his jaw she straddled his thigh whilst his shirt was fisted in her free hand to steady herself. The shift of his weight beneath her had her teeth clenched; it was like he was settling down with his hands raised above his head, a universal sign of surrender. Despite the sweat on her palm, the knife remained steady in her grip. She should kill him, he would do the same in her position, and the King of Altin would expect no less from her; Rorke would do it, he would kill Nero without a second thought- but she wasn't Rorke. She was trained for combat, to defend herself and her comrades, to serve her country but she was not trained to kill an unarmed man –Kayei- though she supposed the King's Guard could never train her for that.

That unarmed Kayei stared up at her and despite his power he let her press the blade closer. A frustrated grunt escaped her and she moved her eyes from his to her hand. A pink line formed beneath the dagger as she pushed forward; any deeper and the blood would pool into her hand. Realisation flashed in his eyes and she hated him for it, she hated herself for it. She killed humans, she killed creatures who lurked in the dark so *why not him?* It was one flick of her wrist and he'd be dead then she would fight the guards, jailbreak Rorke and the Princess and get out of there. Her teeth clenched, it sounded better in theory.

"Guards! Grab the woman!"Schylus returned.

In contradiction to Nero's previous order the guards rushed forward and pulled her from him. The knife in her hand turned and she managed to slice it across the hand around her wrist. Quickly, she turned and sliced it across his shoulder. A yelp flew from the guard and he was replaced by the one at her back. Both her wrists were apprehended and she was pulled sharply backward. The weapon was thrown to the floor and kicked away from her struggling form.

"You cowards!" she spat. Nero's hands remained raised and his eyes never left her as she was dragged from the room. Her joints ached as she tugged and writhed against the guards; she continued to fight against their inhuman grips and screamed for a man that would not hear her. Her throat was dry and scratched as she screamed and screamed.

Schylus laughed as she was dragged past. "Save that energy, Farren, you will need it!"

Schylus' name was cursed which made him laugh more, but he knew, the guards knew, even Rorke knew that she did not retain the one thing every King's Guard needed: a taste for blood.

Perfume bottles, an elegant dress, silken bedspreads, and the smell of dust greeted Farren as she was shoved into the room. "bathe and get dressed!" Then the door was slammed loudly behind her and promptly locked. Dark bruises formed around her wrists and her face throbbed where Schylus hit her. Voices whispered behind the door, but she focused on the space before her. A large, circular tub sat beyond the four-poster bed next to an empty wardrobe. The room was painted a faded red, but there was a chip in the wood of the bed and dust covered the doors of the wardrobe. A large double-window sat on the opposite side of the room which she rushed to. The glass was flung open only to reveal a straight drop to the ground from five floors high. Below her was the entrance to the servant's quarter and she could see over the top of the high walls. Beyond them sat darkness, then the faint glow of the city.

Farren glanced behind her and grit her teeth. The sheets, duvet and pillow cases were not enough to tie together and clamber out of the window. It would likely reach half way and then she would have to drop two, maybe three floors to the ground. She did not need two broken legs to contend with. It also meant dragging the bed closer for a tether which the men outside would hear her move. Regardless, she kept the windows open if only to relieve the room of the musty smell and when she turned from the windowsill she rolled her shoulders. As the bandage pulled against her skin she winced and pressed her hand gently to the aggravated injury.

After her inspection of the window she opened every drawer and cabinet –of which there was one of each- for anything that might be mistaken for a weapon if wielded correctly. Dust mites were all that greeted her. The mattress was her final option but when she lifted it from the bed –a struggle- the door behind her opened to reveal one of the people that shoved her inside. "Hurry it up woman." His command turned sleazy, "if you don't start bathing we'll be forced to come in there and help."

She forced back her gag and dropped the mattress. "I'll get right on that then."

A disappointed frown was seen then the door was closed and locked. Warm water flowed after she glared at the wood and padded over to the tub. There were minimal tonics but ones that looked like they cost a fortune to acquire. A small feat for a Kayei King. A floor length mirror stood before the tub which revealed her dirt-covered, injury weathered body. The purple bloomed across her face and parts of the bruise were near-black. The light press of her fingers against it made her wince. It matched the bags beneath her eyes and she finally realised just how sleep deprived she was. The longer she stared at the mirror the more her face seemed to warp. *Her greyish skin was aglow, her features more prominent as though they were outlined by an invisible quill, and her eyes- They were no longer storm blue but a bright ocean blue with ripples of grey and navy as though a roiling sea sat beneath her iris. Her canines were longer, sharper.* She stumbled back as her hallucination started to take form in front of her.

Whatever Schylus planned he meant for her to dress up like his personal doll when all she wanted to do was be at home, sat by the fire with Baltar and Damera, book in hand whilst her mother cooked warming food. *Why did she ever want to leave?* Enrys' face flashed before her so she squeezed her eyes shut, and started to strip. The process of removing her clothes was quick and easy but by the time she was fully naked the water was high enough to reach her chest. The vial of poison which sat dutifully against her breasts was placed on the floor next to the tub with a frown. Warmth encompassed her battered body as she sunk beneath the water. Most of the filth fell from her the moment she hit the water. She blew out a shaking breath and kept her head against the rim of the tub. The bandage she wore peeled from her body with ease compared to the first time. It was flung with her clothes despite the blood stain. Carefully, she washed the crusted blood away from the stitches and scrubbed at the rest of her body with mint and sage bath tonic. The smell reminded her of Soter's wagon so, with that piece of her friend with her, she stepped from the tub feeling slightly more alive. Her hair remained unwashed and oily which was unpleasant but she would not risk submerging her head in a castle full of magic. The Oracle had shown her what water magic could do –would do- and Farren already nearly drowned twice in her life.

The towel beside the bed was quickly used before she grabbed the outfit that was crumpled on the mattress. Red fabric plunged to the middle of her chest whilst the sleeves slipped from her shoulders in red gauze. No pattern sat on the fabric but that didn't stop it from making a statement. There would be no way to hide her injury no matter how many times she or Nero moved her hair into place. Because of that, her hair was pulled into a braid with the three ruby pins she was granted; it was the only hairstyle she knew how to do. Her boots were replaced by fabric slippers which matched the dress. The shoes were comfortable but there would be no escaping through the woods with them: a house-shoe through and through. One glance in the mirror and she forced a smirk; she was a living ruby, a living forge.

With a final survey of the room she determined that there was nothing she could slip beneath her bodice as a weapon, so she opened the door with little care if someone stood directly beyond it. The lights behind her fizzed to nothing and the guards stood straight. Cuffs were clasped around her sore wrists and chained behind her back with the gentle nature of a raging bull. They closed the door behind her, but not without staring at her chest like she was in fact food. She swallowed, that *was* something the King warned her about. Their eyes never strayed from her body as they marched her down large staircases and into a brightly lit dining room.

A long, polished table of black wood stood vertical to the doors she walked through. It was not situated in the middle of the room but rather the

rest of the floor was left empty like a makeshift stage. Paintings of ambling
game and wildflowers decorated the walls. They were a nice reprieve from the
sight of humans brought to their lowest points. Her shackles were removed
and she was shoved forward with a stumble. Schylus sat at the head of the
table which she cast her eyes over when her eyes lifted from the shiny floor.
Beside him, chained to the table leg but sat on his right was Cyrille who
looked ready to stab Farren with a fork. The older woman looked at her the
same way. Rorke, with his chains looped around the arm of his chair sat
beside her with his injuries glowing beneath the lights. It did not escape her
knowledge that she was the only human without restrictions. She rubbed her
wrists to make sure she understood that correctly. Nero -who sat across from
Rorke, wine goblet in hand- scoffed at her actions. His positioning meant that
the seat to Schylus' left was free.

"Why is she here, Schylus? I thought this was supposed to be a nice
dinner," the Princess whined.

Farren rolled her eyes but Schylus replied, "it's fine my dear, I need
her here to answer some questions, you understand that don't you?" He placed
his hand on top of hers.

"But-" Cyrille scanned her from top to bottom,."She didn't even
bother to wash her hair."

"Forgive me, Princess," Farren spoke through a smile that was more
like bared teeth. "I did not have ample time to prune myself for your sake."

The lump that started to form in her throat was ignored as Rorke
looked between the two of them. Farren kept her sharpened glare on the
teenager but her steps were soft as she walked over to the empty chair. Four
sets of eyes followed her until she lowered herself onto the red-cushioned
chair. Rorke looked like he wanted to rip the chair he sat in to pieces and stab
Schylus and Nero with the splinters. But, as he looked at her, his eyes

softened. '*Are you alright?*' they seemed to say so she nodded and straightened her weary spine.

"As riveting as the two of you are," Schylus drawled, "I want to eat."

I want two hundred gold bars but you don't see me complaining. She nearly spit the words at him as she rested her welt covered wrists on the table. With her legs crossed beneath her and her shoulders back she stared forward which meant into the face of the girl who ruined their chance for an escape. She tilted her head ever so slightly and forced her eyes to slacken from their glare. The longer they sat, the more she found her eyes searching the table. Platters of food sat before them along with copious bottles of alcohol: some wine, some ale, some a colour that Farren did not wish to put in her body. With the silence she could almost picture her father at the end of the table as he laughed with Theron about their investors whilst her mother offered them more tea. Her chest ached at the sight but she was broken from it by tangible wine being poured into her empty glass. The pale liquid curled into the glass then into Schylus'. Once everyone's glass was filled Farren lifted it to her nose and sniffed in what she hoped was a subtle manner. She was not naive to think that there weren't undetectable poisons, she only hoped that Schylus would be dumb enough –like Janus suggested- to use one that *was* detectable.

Nero swallowed his own. "It's not poisoned."

"So you say." The glare she sent made him lean away slightly.

They weren't allowed to dish out their own food so two servants Farren recognised from the kitchen served them. The first course was small and full of leaves with the occasional tomato. It was nothing compared to Janus' spread and she pushed the plate away from her. Nero and Schylus dug into their food like three prisoners weren't sat with them and the Princess primly picked up her fork and chewed a tomato. Rorke did not touch his cutlery but his bad, roughly bandaged –with a piece of his shirt- hand twitched toward his knife. How many times had he pictured slitting their throats?

"Do the two of you have an aversion to salad?" Farren jumped ten miles in her skin as Cyrille spoke. It was the voice of a Princess and not the whiny, hysterical sound she heard before. That's when she noticed: her face was clear of dirt and tears, her dark curls –a deep brown with streaks of black- hung in ringlets past her shoulders. The tattered dress of a stolen prisoner was replaced by a long, lilac dress held up by shimmering straps across her bony shoulders. The dress synched at the waist but there was no corset to be seen, simply a diamond belt built into the dress. It seemed both she and Schylus liked to put on a show. Yet, there were bruises that littered her shoulders, some from her roughhousing in the cell and by the guards but others- Farren's hand clenched around her fork- those were teeth marks, love bites. She was seventeen for Griselda sake.

"It's the company I have an aversion to. Your Highness," Farren added as an afterthought. The Princess didn't deign to respond to Farren's words or her title; she kept eating. Farren did not miss the scowl on Rorke's face and the way he went to nudge her under the table, however he was not successful.

"That's my foot," Nero informed him.

The man's distaste and glare turned on Nero but was brought to the host when Schylus spoke, "if you don't eat you shant be allowed to leave the table." It sounded like he was scolding children.

Farren prayed her stomach was strong enough to withstand food in the presence of such heinous company. So, her fork was raised to her lips, filled with salad and she chewed slowly. It was salty but still edible. Rorke let out a short grunt as she chewed but instead of smiling or glaring she stared pointedly at his salad. It was obviously not poisoned as she swallowed another mouthful and she hoped her face conveyed as much.

"I'm impressed by your common sense, Farren." Schylus failed to notice Rorke had yet to pick up his fork. "Tell me," he looked between Rorke and Farren, "why did the King of Altin send the two of you after me and not a proper King's Guard?" She furrowed her brows and watched Rorke shift in his seat. The action made Schylus laugh. "He isn't a proper King's Guard, he fought with us, not against us."

"Pardon?"

Schylus smirked. "Oh, he hasn't told you? That's not very good spirited of you Rorkey-boy."

"What are you talking about?" She asked harshly.

Nero answered first, "there was a civil war in this Realm ten-ish years ago. The 'rebels'-"

"That was us," Schylus piped in.

Nero continued with a brief look at the long-haired man, "we asked the King of Altin for help and he sent a few hundred soldiers our way, the Accords were considered a good thing back then, and we worked harmoniously together."

"Until you attacked my Captain and demanded those soldiers leave," Rorke added.

Nero did not smirk. "You don't know what you are talking about."

"We wanted to help you win the war but the Kayei are too proud and too stubborn to let us humans have any say in what happens in war meetings."

Schylus laughed but there was nothing light in it. "You are full of shit Rorkey-boy."

Rorke lurched forward but Farren started, "wait, how does that make him any less of a King's Guard?"

Schylus chuckled and finished his salad. "The soldiers that crossed the Veil were tainted." He pressed a hand to his mouth to stifle his amusement. "And the King of Altin banished them from the Capital." He turned his attention to Rorke. "So how did you slip back into the ranks?"

"I proved my loyalty to my King which I know is a foreign subject for you creatures." Pure anger covered Rorke's face. Farren nearly choked on her wine and Cyrille gasped, but Rorke stared at Schylus with nothing short of contempt. Schylus leaned forward and grinned at the guard. A look was then shared between he and Nero who seemed just as amused.

"And why the woman?" Cyrille questioned.

"Maybe your father thought you would feel safer with a female presence," Farren's voice was clipped.

"My father would not care about such things." The Princess flipped her hair. "Which you should know."

Farren's eye twitched. "And *you* should know that we're it; nobody else is coming for you Princess so you should consider not pissing us off." All formalities flew out the window the moment Cyrille looked at her with such disdain. Farren didn't care that they spoke in front of their captors. Rorke, however, looked between the two of them with minutely widened eyes.

"So what you are saying," Schylus said slowly, "is that I only have the two of you to play with?"

"Yes." "No." Rorke and Farren spoke simultaneously. She sketched a brow at his denial and shoved another leaf into her mouth. Rorke looked at the pile of food on his plate but made no move to touch it. Cyrille scoffed at the end of the conversation and finished her own starter.

The conversation soon changed to the mission at hand. "Was your plan truly just to steal my Princess and run back home?"

Farren shrugged her good shoulder. "Yeah." Schylus blinked, caught off guard but nobody else spoke.

The sharp silence was interrupted by the servants dishing their second course onto their plates: rare beef and steamed vegetables. Her stomach rumbled and everybody but Rorke dug into the food. Whatever trance he put himself in was more stupid than it was noble but she admired his willpower; the apple she ate before no longer satisfied her system. She swallowed, it had to be well past one in the morning. How long had they searched for the Princess? When Schylus knocked her out had she been asleep for minutes, hours or days? Her thoughts were broken by Schylus, "Rorkey, does your mother still live in the Altin Capital? And you Farren, you're a small village girl, yes?"

The fork's handle bent in her grasp. "The niece of a merchant."

The "hey!" was automatic from her mouth.

"Hm, what kind?" Nero asked and when she furrowed her brows he said, "what kind of merchant is your uncle, or aunt?"

She swallowed her mouthful. "Medicinal."

"So you know a lot about poisons?" Schylus asked.

"No, I deal with the logs and schedules when I can."

Schylus scoffed, "you have no real place in the business?"

She ran her tongue along her teeth, the urge to plunge her knife into his hand growing by the second. "My uncle does not believe I am capable of such things."

A dramatic sigh left his lips, "there is no reason to threaten him then." He tapped a finger on his chin. "I assume there is a parent in the picture, perhaps a childhood friend back home. I shall have to dig deeper. It would be such a shame if I didn't get to torture one of your loved ones," he pouted. She was sick and tired of people threatening her family. First the King now the psychotic, power hungry, braid-wearing- A hand squeezed her knee tightly. Nero's fingers dug into each side of her bone hard enough that she let go of the fork and hissed quietly. As if her skin burned him he snatched his hand back. The anger that bubbled in her chest ebbed away to focus on the throb of her knee and her silent companion across the table. Throughout the second course she watched Nero from the corner of her eye. He ate and drank like it was normal, and he kept his hands to himself during it. "So, Rorkey." Said man lifted his eyes slowly from his plate and Farren looked between Schylus and Rorke. "How was your Veil crossing?"

"Quick."

"Aw is that all you have to tell me? Details, details."

"That's a bit personal isn't it?" Farren quipped.

Schylus shuffled in his seat, removed his attention from Rorke and settled it on her. It was amazing how much his irises resembled pools of blood. With both of his elbows braced on the table he rested his chin in his palm and tilted his head. Nero shifted behind her, his hands folded and head tilted on the back of the chair. "Then tell me about your crossing."

"Like I said," she spoke slowly, "that's a bit personal."

"Oh please, just tell them, who did you have to kill?" Cyrille snapped.

The anger that radiated from the freckle-skinned woman was near-palpable. Something in her eyes flashed and the blue seemed to turn darker in the light. The fingers she clasped together seconds before tightened. The wine rippled in the glasses, Rorke's throat bobbed, and Cyrille coughed. Farren didn't blink as she stared at the Princess who violently coughed against her palm. Excess spit filled her palm and it sounded like she was about to cough up a lung. All relaxed postures were gone as Farren tilted her head to the side like a contemplative wolf. Cyrille continued to cough and Schylus reached for her. He gently stroked his fingers down her back and offered her a glass of wine. She took the drink but continued to cough around the rim.

Nero looked between the couple and Farren who had yet to speak. The heat of his hand pressed against the hollow of her cheeks and he forcefully turned her to face him. His fingers squeezed beneath the formed injury under her eye and popped her mouth slightly open. The heat seared into her skin but she held his gaze. Gold seeped into blue as neither of them blinked. He breathed deeply; subconsciously Farren started to do the same. Cyrille quietened and Schylus sat back in his chair. Nero's eyes danced from hers, across her face and flickered to her parted lips.

"Get your hand off her," Rorke snarled. Nero smirked, squeezed her cheeks for emphasis and turned back to Rorke. Farren rubbed at the indents in her face and took a deep breath. Schylus grinned at her then at Nero like he just found the secret to ever-lasting riches. Cyrille rubbed at her throat and wiped the edge of her mouth with the napkin. That concluded the meal because after a sharp nod from Nero, Schylus stood, hands braced against the table and hair hung around him; he gestured toward the doors. A phantom wind pushed them open and in marched many more guards than escorted her. They divided in half and looped their arms around Farren's. She and Rorke were pulled from their seats and dragged over the threshold.

Each time they were called upon, the chairs were the same, the food was the same, and Schylus asked benign questions. Just like the first night, Nero's hand squeezed her knee when she spoke out of turn. Cyrille continued to scoff at Farren's presence and fawn over Schylus in any spare moment. He continued to threaten their families yet silence reigned. Farren didn't know whether he went after Argen or her parents. The only comfort she took was that nobody but Rorke knew who she was or where she came from; she remained a mystery to the Kayei. She would actually be impressed if they found Brentham on a map. Rorke was not so lucky but until he spoke, she remained uncharacteristically, uncomfortably quiet after that first night.

It was the third night that Schylus' question changed: "what is the King's plan?" *His plan for what?* The question must have been written on her face because he took a sip of his wine and answered, "what is his plan for my people? For me? This Realm? Why did he send the two of *you*?"

"You kidnapped his daughter, his plan is to have her back home," Farren spoke through a mouthful of greens.

Schylus waved his hand dismissively. "Yes I know that, but why send you?"

"Haven't we been over this?" Rorke snapped.

Farren kept her voice level, "multiple guards would have raised suspicion and broken the Accords, or whatever it is the Rulers call it." She shrugged. "Rorke knows the terrain and I know how to fight effectively." She glanced at Rorke. "You want to know something funny?" She paused. "A friend of mine actually said I should consider this my test. This damn mission is nothing more than a means to an end," Farren finished with her eyes directly on Cyrille.

"Is that right?" Schylus quipped, a hand under his chin. "A woman King's Guard?" He turned his attention on Rorke. "Is your King well? The last I spoke to him he despised the thought of our women in the army with his men."

Rorke scowled but did not argue with him yet Cyrille said, "hence why you should consider your test a failure because I am not going back home, I will not leave Schylus, *ever*. My father can maintain his men's-only club and you can go back and do... something else." Nero's hand had to squeeze incredibly tight to stop Farren from launching herself across the table. Rorke choked on his forkful of salad. The chains dug into his skin as he stared at the Princess with undiluted horror.

Cyrille turned to face him and folded her hands in her lap. "Why?" He breathed out.

"My father does not value women but I have been treated well here, this Realm is where I belong, with these Kayei." She turned to smile at Schylus who blew her a kiss in return. "I can never rule back home, my father would pawn me off to the highest bidder and that would be that. I choose a different life for myself." Farren placed her head in her hands and let out a disbelieving chuckle which brought Cyrille's attention to her. "Surely someone like you can understand."

A brief look at Rorke and she answered, "I understand wanting to be independent and wanting to be respected, believe me I do, but Princess, if you think that man," she gestured vaguely to Schylus who feigned offence with a hand on his chest, "has treated you well, you are very much mistaken. Your father may not appreciate women, but Schylus," she clicked her tongue and looked at him, "will give you honeyed words whilst he beat you to the ground."

Nero stifled his laugh. "She figured you out quickly."

318

"Oh yeah, what would you know? You're just a peasant girl who enjoys playing with swords," Cyrille mocked.

Farren's smirk was tight. "If you ever see me fight, you would not call it 'playing.'"

Rorke swallowed the rock in his throat. "Princess Cyrille, you are in no better hands than the two of us."

"What about Adrastos? He is still Captain isn't he?" The sharp nature of his Princess' eyes rendered him silent, so everyone ate their food –Rorke had a forkful of meat- and the dinner ended with Farren and Rorke in chains.

The Kayei guard screamed as the hot poker was thrust into his leg. The man was tied above the empty floor where his blood dripped and pooled. His skin was flayed away in parts and his face was so swollen Farren wasn't sure his own mother would recognise him. His eyes were swollen shut, his chest and back no more than slabs of raw meat. Schylus originally used a whip but became more creative the longer the night went on. There was no food touched as the horror unfolded.

"You should have told me there were two new humans in my castle," Schylus sang into the guard's ear. He coughed up blood until it dribbled into the large pool at his feet. Every muscle in Farren's body was clenched as she watched him butcher the man in front of her. Rorke and Cyrille's chairs were turned so that they could get a front row seat to the torture. She turned a sickly green. Nero –who sat silently next to her- stood from his chair and walked over the tortured soul. Schylus offered him the poker but he shook his head silently. He ran his hand through his hair and tilted the guard's face upward.

"You asshole! You asked us to do it! It should be you on these hooks! Asshole!" The globule of blood and mucus that was spat at Nero didn't make him flinch. He dropped the guards face so that the man's own blood was all that was visible to him.

"Are you finished, Schylus?" The black shirt Nero wore was rolled up beyond his elbows and he sucked in a deep breath.

The long-haired man shrugged and threw the poker to the floor. "I suppose."

Nero's back faced the humans so they missed how the gold of his eyes glowed with magic before he placed his hands on the guards face. A particularly awful scream ripped through the room and Farren flinched, eyes screwed shut and hands balled on her lap. The room went silent and the body held up by chains went limp. The taste of bile filled her mouth as she dared look back at the scene: the guard's entire face and neck were charcoal. A drip of blood from the body, then another yet Rorke stayed silent and she was too nauseous to speak.

Nero escorted her back to her room but she spied a line of servants mopping the blood from the wood and they removed the Kayei's mangled body from its confines. She waited until she reached her chambers to throw up and the blond left her in peace.

On the fifth night a servant died. Farren slept in her bed after another night of twisted socialising and threats when her door was pried open. She awoke to a knife above her chest but a quick roll and a thankfully slow servant, the knife plunged into her pillow. Farren rolled from the mattress into a crouched position but then the woman was in front of her, tears down her face. She apologised and sobbed through the whole ordeal. "He told me to, he threatened my sister, I have to kill you or he'll kill her." All she wanted was to protect the people she cared about. All she wanted was for Schylus to *stop*.

320

Farren paused at that, but as the woman made to swing her against the wall she grabbed the arm in her hair, twisted and slammed her face against the stone. Blood sprayed but she kept fighting, kept lunging at Farren with clawed hands and red-rimmed eyes. She pushed Farren again but this time she was prepared: her hand wrapped around the servant's hair and she thrust forward. Another crack against the stone. She swiped at Farren's face, her nails a hairsbreadth away from slicing her cheek so she pushed the servant again. That time she did not stand back up, she did not clutch at her face and wail. Instead, she sat in a slumped heap on Farren's floor, just like Emmett did in the cell. Her face and skull were cracked open, the wall and floor soaked in blood. Farren did not bother to wash it away or clean her hands of the mess; she crawled to the head of her bed, slipped the knife between the mattress and the wooden panel and stared at the woman.

Schylus truly thought I was so weak that a malnourished human would kill me.

The blood stain was there the next morning but Farren ignored the missing corpse and bathed as she normally would, a pink dress similar to her servant outfit shifted with her movements. The same red house-slippers cushioned her feet but her face remained bare save for the deep circles beneath them and she let the smell of mint coat her body, not any Kayei perfume. She hoped they suffocated on the scent.

"Say," Schylus started through a mouthful of bacon. "Do any of you know what happened to that short-haired servant girl? I heard she died." The water in Farren's goblet shook in her hand. Both Schylus and Nero's eyes were on her so she struggled through the sip then placed the goblet on the table. A chuckle escaped the dark-haired Kayei and he resumed eating. Her food remained untouched that night just as Rorke's did.

On the sixth night something changed. Another red dress was laid out but it was not like any other outfit she had been ordered to wear. It was soft with fitted sleeves, a curve-crushing corset, and slim-fitted. It shone in the light like silk but the skirt was made of three panels which were divided by two high-slits in front of her legs. What forced her brow to furrow was the exchange of shoes. No more house-slippers graced her feet, but instead knee-high red boots sat at the foot of her bed. She was to dress to kill it seemed, and Farren nearly smirked at the thought. Perhaps her bloodlust was hidden away all that time. The butterflies and churning of her stomach said otherwise. Yet, it wasn't the suspicious outfit that made her check every corner and slat in her room; it was the way the breeze outside shifted the thick air in the castle, the way the smell of smoke intensified, and the too quiet nature of the rooms around her. Farren spent a few minutes staring out of the window and debated the sheet idea once more. There were other people inside, there had been for the days she and Rorke had been prisoners but they stayed away the whole time. Either that was because they were ordered to or because they wanted to. It made her contemplate whether or not they knew what Schylus had planned for her and Rorke, or if Schylus himself knew what to do with them. *Why were they not dead?*

Once she donned the dress and braided her hair behind her –after she finally washed it beneath the running tap- a shiver ran down her spine. She grabbed the poison from where she camouflaged it among the tonics and tucked it beneath her corset. Farren thought about tucking the knife from the servant in the top of her boot, but realised there would be no way of hiding it; the dress slits were too revealing. Therefore, it remained tucked under the mattress.

The thickness in the air remained like a thunderstorm on the horizon and with a sudden thud behind her, Nero appeared. His trousers were a slate grey, fitted and tucked into grey boots. The overcoat he wore clasped at the top of his chest and moved behind him like a smoky-cape. It was a deep red and ended where the leather gloves started. One was the same red as his coat whilst -she cocked an eyebrow- one of them was blue. "You look good for a man who's been busy killing people," she said in greeting.

He chuckled and pushed his hair from his eyes in a swift motion as though he'd been doing it for hours and didn't know how to stop. "Thank you," he said sarcastically, "but I only killed one man this week. Anyway, there's no dinner tonight. I'm sorry if you were looking forward to it but there is another event on, so-" He pushed against his own mouth. "Big smiles."

She scoffed and straightened her skirts. One eye remained on the Kayei behind her in the mirror whilst he watched her just as she watched him; though, he looked bored out of his wits. He took a step toward her and she turned. "Why *are* you in my room?"

Like he was a twin flame to her raging storm he raked his eyes over her body slow enough to force her shoulders back and her chin high. Like a soldier ready for inspection. After his assessment of her person he shrugged. His eye snagged on her neck —no- her shoulder which made her press a hand to where a white bandage used to lay. There was no pain, no twinge of the stitches Rorke applied by the stream. All that was left were small, white lines of Kuroguine claw marks: a stark reminder of her time in the Kayei Realm.

Nero gestured toward the window as his eyes moved. "This is your last chance." Farren swallowed. "You could run, leave Rorke and his loyalty to Altin behind. You could go back home, whatever you want."

She tugged at the dark bruise on her face which no longer swelled her eye shut. "If I return without the Princess I will be hunted for the rest of my days. I either leave here with the Princess or I die here."

"Or you could stay in this Realm," he said with a blasé shrug.

"No. Thank you, but I would rather die." She braced her hands in front of her. "Not that that was an invitation to kill me." He looked incredibly unimpressed because he offered her a similar deal before. Yet it had been nearly a week and he sat there and watched as people were tortured and killed, as she and Rorke were abused. A growl nearly ripped from her throat.

"And what is so bad about this Realm?"

"Is that a joke? Do you have any idea how many things want to kill me in this Realm?"

"Probably no more than back in the Mortal Realm."

"We do not have Kuroguine in our Realm and they are terrifying enough."

He shrugged. "But we have Night Creatures, magic, beautiful sceneries, and men who actually know how to please a woman."

She quirked a brow. "Like you?"

"Would you like to find out?"

"You wouldn't fuck a human."

He clicked his tongue. "Such vulgarity, Farren, but you're wrong." The same look he gave her when she was caught by the dungeon door appeared on his face and she swallowed down the uncomfortable lump in her throat. His long body moved over to her bed where he lounged against her headboard, arms behind his head against the pillows. He wiggled for a moment and then reached under the thin mattress. *No.* She stepped forward and the knife she hid sat between his fingers. Raised, perfect, blond brows stared at her and she swallowed. Another shrug moved his shoulders and her windows slammed open. The wind carried small flurries of ash that settled on the windowsill. Seconds later the knife was flung from his hand and out of the window. Her feet sped toward it and the yelp of a servant sounded down below. The young boy looked up to find her franticly wide eyes. A curse was gifted her and he scooped the knife from the ground.

"That," she took a deep breath, "that was unnecessary."

"I disagree, love."

Her eye twitched at the nickname, and she turned from the window, arms folded across her chest. "Since you're here, can you tell me why I'm dressed like this?"

"You put the outfit on you tell me." He grinned cheekily.

"Somehow I don't think Schylus or his men would allow me to leave the room in anything but the red garments he sets out."

Nero leaned forward. "If it's any consolation, you look stunning."

Farren narrowed her eyes. "It's not." Their eyes locked and he dug into his trouser pockets. From it he pulled a small invitation with a red ribbon tied around it. He held it out for her to take, which she did. Once it was opened she found the same style of writing on the inside: *If you want your freedom you must earn it. Entertain me and my guests tonight and I will grant you passage from my lands. You first must find your way to me, don't take too long now.* There was no mention of Rorke or the Princess. No matter how many times she turned the parchment over in her hands or stared at the letters, that fact remained the same. Schylus wanted to play games. A map of the manor flashed in her eyes and even with the clear image in her mind, there were so many angles, too many blank spaces; they would be her downfall. She trailed her eyes from the invitation to the man on her bed. "Do you know where I will find Schylus?"

"Yes."

"Are you going to tell me?"

He looked at his nails. "No." Despite his denial, a feline smile crossed his lips. "But I can tell you what you have to do." She waited for him to continue which made him smile wider. "You have to fight your way through the castle. He won't settle for anything less."

Farren pinched the bridge of her nose. "Are you serious? So what, he is so determined to believe I'm not a King's Guard so he's testing my abilities?" He nodded and she nearly threw a fit. She was so *tired* of people testing her. For once, she just wanted someone to believe her and leave it at that. "Do I get a weapon?" He snorted at her question and she glared. "I do not plan on dying in this castle."

With no sight of his smirk he said. "You're going to."

"Is all you know how to do is warn me about death?" She turned back to the mirror, hands fiddled with the bottom of her corset.

A breath blew from his body and that bored, glazed expression fell atop his face. "Don't say I didn't offer you an out," there is a pause, "and don't start haunting me when you do die." A scoff and her hands dropped; his voice lowered as he looked her over once more, "are you ready?"

"Are you going to tell me what I'm going to face out there?"

"I'll see you out there." There was a duo of loud booms and he walked toward the door. She didn't have a chance to object before the door swung open and the dim light of the hallway was visible. Cheers and yells echoed around the building. Nero stepped out of the room and she glanced behind her and wondered if there truly was *nothing* she could use as a weapon. Nero didn't specifically say 'no' when she asked about a weapon so she stepped toward her bed.

"No you don't." Nero yanked on her collar and pulled her away from her room. She twisted in his grip and shoved him away, and he released her immediately, rolled his eyes and marched down the corridor. Nero disappeared before she could curse him out.

The dim light made Farren squint as she adjusted to the limited darkness. Nobody mingled on that floor, only closed doors and dehydrated plants kept her company. The signs of life she heard moments ago were nowhere to be seen or heard. With her only 'weapon' being the vial of poison against her chest she carefully manoeuvred across the wooden floors. The windows were open and for a moment –regardless of the peril she was likely in- she felt like she could breathe. The air was musty but lacked its usual smoke so she took in the deep breath. Thuds from her boots echoed in the empty space and her hands were slightly raised in the event of a surprise attack.

When she reached the end of the corridor she spied the stairs and paused at the top. Once she was on the lower levels she would have to decide whether to descend further and reach the dungeons or hunt for Schylus on her own. There was no way of knowing whether Rorke received the same note she did or whether he was in the dungeon, so she started down the stairs: the kitchen, that was where she would find a weapon and with no Nero to stop her, she quickened her pace. Once she reached the fourth, third, second, then first floor she jogged to the archway where she rebounded off of an invisible barrier. Rapid blinks and her arms out to the side steadied her disorientated form and she stared down the stairs. The servants huddled at the bottom, makeshift weapons in their hands: frying pans, knives, some held spatulas and rolling pins above their heads. A near-snarl lifted her lip but she controlled the urge to slam her fist against the barrier. Instead she backed away from the servants and toward the curve to the dungeon. The door was wide open so without a break in her step she plunged into the darkness and swiped a lit torch; she threw one of the unlit torches down the stairs where it clattered at the bottom then splashed. There was no whisper of clothing or breath, no thud or creak in the cells.

As soon as her boot hit the puddle at the bottom of the stairs a horn blasted through the manor. It was deep yet loud, like a hunting horn. That thought made her gulp and pick up the fallen torch.

"Who's there?" Something in Farren's chest stuttered at the sound of Rorke's voice. The sound of his voice ricocheted off the walls and once she was part-way down the aisle she lifted the torch higher. Movement caught the corner of her eye and she turned to the cell to her right. Rorke stood, pressed against the cell door. Bruises littered his face, his bandaged hand was tucked into his side, his hair wild on his head, and his once full face was sallow and sharp. Despite the obvious pain he was in, his good hand rose to cup her face through the bars.

"You smell like a sewer," she laughed as she pressed her hand to the top of his. He chuckled with her. They might have been covered in dirt, but the calluses on the pads of his fingers made her feel safe, made her strong.

"Did they hurt you?" Concern shone in his eyes.

She leaned into his touch. "No, no I'm fine." Not a lie. "Are you okay? I mean I know that's a silly question but are you? How is your hand?"

He shook his head. "It's fine. It doesn't matter, how did you get down here?" He scanned his eyes down her body. "What are you wearing?"

"You weren't given a note... Schylus wants to make a game out of our escape. I have to fight my way to him apparently. The note didn't mention you or the Princess but I'll be damned if I don't get all three of us out of this place."

Rorke's eyes widened and he cursed. "How reckless are you?! You should have run when you had the chance, found help!"

"Found help from who, Rorke? If I left they would have killed you the moment my boot hit the garden." The curse he spewed was impressive but his hand remained soft on her face. They gazed at each other for a moment longer. She wanted to map out the lines of his face in the torchlight no matter how many dark bruises covered his jaw. "We need to leverage the bars free," she muttered.

"They are rusty enough." He nodded and watched as she handed him the lit torch and flipped the unused one in her hand. It was just like one of her own knives, a flip in the air and a catch before she lodged the fat end under the gap between the bars and the floor. The metal groaned and flaked over the pressure as she used all of her weight to push down. A few more huffs from the woman and the door sprang free of its hinges. Rorke helped her lower it to the ground. They stood staring at that door and broke away too soon to look toward the end of the cells where the Princess laid.

Farren grabbed Rorke's arm before he walked toward her. "What are we supposed to do with a Princess that doesn't want to be rescued?"

"I will handle it." When she opened her mouth to protest he cut her off, "you need to play Schylus' game then find a way out. We will meet at the iron gate."

"When?"

There was no way to tell time. "Three hours. It should be enough time to convince Princess Cyrille that we need to leave." Farren nodded. "Make sure you survive. Now go." As she stepped around him and went to walk up the stairs, he called her name. She turned back to him with furrowed brows that shot to her hairline as his lips found hers in the darkness. He missed by a few centimetres but she tilted her head to adjust and sunk into him. The slight tang of blood filled her mouth as he kissed her, but with every swipe of his lips, every breath against her lips, the stress she carried in her shoulders melted away. They allowed themselves that moment to just *be* before he slowly detached himself from her. The warmth of his lips on hers remained and flooded through her face. "I'll see you soon."

With a final glance at Rorke she rushed up the stairs and back into the castle.

PLACE YOUR BETS

Up and up Farren climbed until she reached the fourth floor and opened the first room she found. She was meant to be hunting Schylus so every room – unfortunately for her- had to be checked. Her legs throbbed at the constant exercise. Rorke kept both torches so she had to find something else, anything that would fend off attackers that didn't mean resorting to hand-to-hand combat. It was the first thing Argen taught her, and the first exercise Adrastos forced her to show him yet those were human men and they could still put her on her ass on occasion. What the Kayei would do with their inhuman strength- a weapon would keep her alive. There was a lamp and a few piles of books but nothing she could swing around easily and cause damage so she creaked open a different door which revealed an empty bedroom. It was similar to her own, but all the furniture was covered in sheets and dust. No weapon caught her eye so she continued down the hall until a luxurious bedroom greeted her. It was filled with black fabrics and golden accents, the colour scheme of a dark God. Despite the luxury of the room the bed sheets were crumpled and covered a passed out form. The woman was beautiful and breathed deeply, her naked back faced the ceiling whilst her arms were star-fished across the mattress; she was completely unconscious. Farren chuckled, whoever owned the room, had a very eventful night.

Farren crept into the room; she took care not to step too heavily in case she disturbed the sleeping form and alerted the Kayei to her location. All those years sneaking from her house, around her dogs, avoiding every squeaky floorboard made her steps non-existent. She crouched to stare beneath the bed then through the drawers and finally the wardrobe where she found a trove of monochromatic clothes: black, grey, white with splashes of blue and red. Yet, there was still no sign of weapons. The trunk at the bottom of the bed held nothing but air so she slammed the lid and cursed. *What was the point in that?* The woman on the bed stirred –the motion froze Farren's body- but she was out like a light, and Farren thanked Griselda that she was too worn out to make a fuss.

Voices sounded down the hall and her head shot up from the plain, black trunk. The wardrobe stood tall behind her so she shot toward it, flung open the doors and pushed herself inside. She pulled the clothes in front of her and even shoved her arm inside one of the jackets. Anything to mask her scent from the Kayei beyond the door because if one more person sniffed her and mentioned it, she would become vexed very quickly.

"Absolutely not," one of the voices harshly whispered, "I am not trespassing into Nero's room."

"What if *she's* in there? That Malumrem's scent is all over the doors."

"I don't care if she's in there or not. I am not going in there."

Their footsteps faded until they were little more than a throb at the back of her head. A sigh of relief flew from her lips and rustled the clothes in front of her. The more she stared at the clothes the more it made sense they belonged to Nero: dark and sleek with an air of royalty. She pulled away from the fabric and sighed. Her elbow thumped against the back of the wardrobe where a click sounded. The wood behind her gave way and her feet stumbled with it. When she righted herself the space before her opened up. It was tall enough for her to walk through and wide enough to fit two men. *A secret passage, very nice.* Moonlight streamed through the grates above her which lit her way through the dark. They were too small to squeeze through and she was too high from the ground to risk dropping to safety if she did somehow manage to fit. The grates acted as markers for the curve of the passage. There was no dust, proof that the passage had been used frequently. The deeper she travelled the more frequent the moonlight became as though the bottom of the passage was built to be seen.

That theory was confirmed when the dead-end appeared. A large grate covered the ceiling, the shadows of the bars covered her hair and face as she stared upward. The light that broke between the bars revealed swirls and soft lines of a language she'd seen before. It was written in ink instead of the blood of half-breed Kayeis or Kuroguine, but the language was definitely Kayei, or rather the older Kayei. Those peculiar swirls were nearly identical to those in the books she borrowed before she and Rorke crossed Realms. One of the smaller runes was etched on the back of one of the objects Soter gifted her which she left with the horses- her eyes widened, if she got to the horses –if they were still outside the castle- then she could grab the weapons. Her eyes screwed shut. There was no point in thinking about objects and weapons she could not obtain. Her head pounded and her limbs shook. In the silence of the passageway she stood with her hands on her head, eyes shut and chest aching. A sniffle escaped but she forced it back. She would cry when it was all over, not until.

One breath, two and she opened her eyes. Experimentally she tapped the rune covered wall. Nothing, so she traced each symbol with great care. The same result and a sharp chuckle flew from her. They likely had to be read aloud which was the one thing she had no idea how to do. One more tap and she turned on her heel. The brush of parchment against her boot sounded and she looked down. Sat next to her heel was a small pile of letters each in beautiful handwriting. She picked up one and turned it over in her hands, untied the rope and read it:

Dear Nero,

You have been making a mess of the Realm, I hear your name spoken in hushed whispers amongst my men. Now my daughter has gone missing and I fear you may have something to do with it. You were supposed be done with your games but I received another letter from you informing me of your plans to stay and that your errand boy would also be staying put. You and I both know that is not what was agreed and that disappointing me will only make it worse for you. Instead of trying to play politics I expect you to focus on your work. I intend to read about improvements and progress in your next letter. Let's hope the Golden Harvest will clear your head.

    -V

    The more words she read, the wider her eyes became, but what truly made her sweat was the large King's seal on each envelope. Some of the letters were weathered with age but the one in her hand was less so. With a quick glance at the pile at her feet, she folded the letter into a small square and tucked it deep into the corset. The others were left to wither in the passage.

    She walked back the way she came and pressed her ear to the inside of the wardrobe door. The room beyond sat silent and hushed whispers no longer sounded from beyond the room's door. The wardrobe did not squeak as she carefully opened it, the bed was without the woman so she stepped out- her hair whipped around her as she ducked in time for an axe to glide over her head. The breath flew from her body as she crouched. Two Kayei, both decidedly larger than she, flanked the wardrobe. It seems they were not as frightened of Nero's room as the other two. Sharp weapons sat in their hands and once they glinted in the light of the bedroom she shot toward the hall door like a rabbit running from a sight hound. The sound of pierced wind and she moved, her left foot the purchase as she dodged to the side. The axe that was aimed at her back flew past her side and lodged itself into the wall. A smirk curled at her lips as she gripped the handle of said axe. They were not trained in combat it seemed or they would have grabbed her the moment she started to run. Schylus sent *amateurs* after her. The thought made her blood boil but with the axe's handle in her grasp she found that he did her a favour. She mentally chuckled: she'd be sure to tell him as such.

With the smirk still on her face she tugged at the axe. The wood of the doorframe splintered and groaned; due to the trajectory it landed in the wall at an odd angle meaning she had to use her whole body as leverage before she pulled. On her third tug the Kayei stomped toward her but as the axe thrower reached his hand toward her she fled, the weapon in hand and mood decidedly lighter. The thud of her feet beneath her matched the race of her heart as she rushed down the stairs. Footsteps did not follow her so she slowed her pace, but only until she reached the bottom, where she leapt off the step.

Schylus grinned as she rushed into view. Farren paused and the axe in her hand shifted along with her previously triumphant smirk. The Kayei stood tall and proud in a red shirt beneath a vest of onyx black, and his fingers were decorated with numerous rings. His hair cascaded down his shoulders and brushed against Cyrille's cheek while she stood beside him. Farren's eyes shifted from the long dark hair to the tight curls, then to the tufts of chocolate that peeked between the Princess' fingers. Rorke's unconscious face sat beneath her clenched fist, head pulled back and on his knees.

It had to be a joke. The Goddesses must have been playing tricks on her, because as she stared at the trio, she felt a laugh of disbelief bubble in her chest. A taste for cold-blooded murder may not have run in Farren's veins, but she was up to her limit of Princess Cyrille preventing the success of their mission, time and time again. It made her grip the axe tighter; she shifted the weapon so that it rested on her shoulder and narrowed her eyes on the Princess. The same expression that was etched onto Cyrille's face for days stared back her, hand clenched tightly in Rorke's hair and dress beautifully decorated.

"I thought I was supposed to come looking for you?" Farren stated to Schylus despite her gaze on Cyrille.

"I had to make sure..." He trailed off, eyes on the axe in her hand, "where did you get that?"

"It was supposed to land in my back but a poor door upstairs took the brunt of it. It's rather light actually." She demonstrated by twisting her wrist then placing the weapon back on her shoulder.

"How many have you killed with it?" Cyrille asked sharply.

"None." She tilted her head and looked the Princess up and down. "Yet." Her eyes then moved to Rorke. "Are you going to kill *him*?" The teen's eyes seemed to lose all colour as she swallowed. It was the same look Farren imagined Nero saw when she held the dagger to his throat. However, her grip tightened in Rorke's hair and she tugged the unconscious man closer to her. Farren heard the rapid approach of footsteps on the floor above and it broke her concentration for a moment.

"Come now Farren, you're supposed to be making this entertaining for me," Schylus pouted.

"Am I now? Aren't you supposed to be locked in a room somewhere *waiting* for me to find you?"

His grin was manic. "Touché." Yet, he made no indication that he would move.

Cyrille's gaze cast between the two adversaries which allowed her hold to loosen. There were no openings that didn't involve Farren's weapon swinging too close to Rorke, but she stepped back and removed the axe from her shoulder. Cyrille's eyes widened comically but Schylus laughed and braced a hand in front of her. "What are you..?" the Princess asked.

He didn't look at her when he said, "drag Rorkey-boy back to my room and keep him there. You know where my knives are don't you dear?"

She nodded rapidly. "Good, lock the door and don't answer unless it's myself or Nero," he spoke as though to a child, "I will make sure this horrid woman doesn't follow you."

"You really are an asshole, you know that?" Farren chimed in.

Cyrille looked once more between them then gripped the back of Rorke's shirt. She managed to tug him away from Farren whose mouth was slightly agape. She jerked forward to follow the abnormally-strong girl but Schylus manoeuvred his body to the middle of her line of sight. "You're welcome," Schylus sang, "to think you wanted to try and fight a girl with Kayei strength."

"Get the hell out of my way!" Farren didn't register what he said before she shot forward, axe high and eyes locked on his neck. Her human speed was her downfall as Schylus raised his hand to stop the blade slicing into his shoulder and across his throat. The axe instead carved through his hand, severing bone from flesh. Blood sprayed around them, the majority of it on their clothes. His roar rattled the floor and walls. Farren flipped the axe in her hand and slammed the handle against Schylus' temple which caused him to stumble backward with his good hand around the demolished one. She hopped around his stunned form and sprinted in the direction Cyrille dragged Rorke. She dodged a door that opened in front of her and kept her speed. Just as she turned a corner an arrow zipped past her head, inches from her ears. It lodged in a painting behind her. With a shake of her head she ventured deeper into the castle.

It was like the Princess disappeared without a trace, and Rorke with her. It was a matter of time before he awoke from his unconscious state. With Cyrille's new-found power and the state he was in, it was unlikely he was able to fight. As much as it pained him, as much as he longed to pick up a weapon and fight, he was in no condition to do so. His hand was wrapped shoddily and no-doubt hurt like hell. There was also the issue of a King's Guard raising a hand to the crown Princess. Down in the dungeon he told her he would handle the Princess and Farren dared not think about what happened between the two of them. She clicked her tongue and simply focused on finding him, Cyrille her secondary target. She had half-a-mind to turn back to Schylus and explain she completed her end of the deal so he had to let her go. That was likely never an honest deal so she rolled her eyes, swallowed the bout of fear that threatened to cripple her, and pushed her legs faster. The Oracle's test had not fazed her, she survived numerous attacks on her person, and she had the for-thought to pack magical options on a mission filled with magic. She stopped, hand braced on the wall.

"Has that guard been giving you trouble?" Soter asked as a greeting.

Farren chuckled and ran her hand down Elira's feathers. The bird nibbled at her fingers and hooted. She smiled sheepishly and faced the Magician who looked at her openly. "I need," she swallowed and her eyes darted to the door he stood next to, "I need to borrow some magic." His eyes widened fractionally. "Not a lot. I just need them in case, I don't know, I come across Nero."

Soter started to dig through his drawers. "Nero is a King." At the fear that shuttered across her eyes he added, "I thought you didn't like using magic?" It was purely inquisitive.

"Normally I don't." She pressed a hand to her ribs. "But I want every advantage I can have because like you said, he's a King."

He pulled three amulets from the top drawer and dangled them in front of him. "That's clever. These should do what you want. The smaller one is for speed, it should grant you an hour or so of a Kayei's power, the other two should give you enough strength and stamina to fight your way out." He looked from the stones to her. "These are a last resort, yes?"

"Yes, yes absolutely. Thank you."

He smiled widely at her. "You can wear them alongside your other necklace." He looked knowingly at her.

She chuckled and placed her hand over her chest where the red stone laid. "They will match nicely."

"Be careful, Farren. Kayei can sense bottled magic, do not take these where you wish to hide." He pooled them in her outstretched palm.

All four necklaces sat at the bottom of her saddle bag, hidden from anyone's view. The only reason the original necklace didn't sit between her breasts was because of Soter's warning.

She took that brief recollection to think of the castle map. From where she was on the second floor there was no other way to reach the horses save for the stairs at her back. There was a window next to her so she peaked through the glass to the ground below and cringed. There went her idea to jump out and clamber through the gardens toward the exit. The only route was forward so she steeled her shoulders, twisted her axe and threw it in front of her.

The axe crashed against the double-doors that blocked her path. No barrier posed a threat to the blade as it fractured wood. The sound of running water reached her ears through the gap the axe granted. She slammed through the doors, her shoulder used as her battering ram. Fluidly, her right hand pushed down on the axe's handle and the weapon was dislodged. The crash echoed through the castle but she paid it no mind as she continued forward.

Once she entered the room, the smell of fresh flowers and water attacked her senses. A large in-floor bath sat before her. Black tiles surrounded the clear water and lined the steps. Along the walls sat shelves-upon-shelves of bathing equipment. The moonlight from the large windows danced along the still water. Steam rippled through the room which added a heavy sense of humidity and her lungs pulled in watery air but it provided a moment of calm, of silence. Her chest rose rapidly with each breath and sweat coated her back and the sides of her neck.

There was a door in front of her that slowly opened. Two nobles entered the room which made her very aware of the fact that there were no tall structures –or structures at all- for her to hide behind. The sound of yells behind her stopped her from running to the double-doors. Farren stood on the other side of the steaming bath, clad in bright red clothing, with an axe in hand and no plan. The nobles grinned like the cats that caught the mouse and her fingers curled tightly around her weapon. One of them crooked a finger toward her and she slid one foot behind the other so that her torso was sideways-on with the bath. It was when the men stepped in different directions that she reacted. The axe catapulted toward the man on the left. The blade soared across the water, pierced through the steam, and clattered to the ground. The noble's hand was lifted like a shield. The weapon sat at his feet like it was forcefully pushed from the air. A metallic taste entered Farren's mouth and she swallowed.

"We've been looking for you," the one on the right crooned.

"So be a good human and surrender to us now," the other mimicked.

They moved slowly around the bath, an imitation of predator scouting its prey. Her heart thrummed, fingers tingled and the hairs on the back of her neck stood on end. The steam thickened the air so that the noble's faces were indistinguishable but their forms moved toward her. Their aim was to cage her in. Each time she glanced between them, her eyes snagged on the large pool of water in front of her. *The opportunity to see the water around her other self rise and curl. It danced like a living flame, and morphed into a wall behind her.* Oh she really was desperate. Just like the small bucket in her test and in

340

the dungeon hallway, Farren stared at the water. She blocked out the figures who stalked toward her, she blocked out the pound of her head and her missing partner, and focused solely on the hot liquid. Through her will and will alone, the water swirled violently in front of her. The blue of her eyes glowed in the moon's shadow and pure power, sharp and true shot against her bones and lifted her hair from her back. She was fluid and solid at the same time.

The nobles stopped their movements and stared at the swirling ball of water taken from the bath. They were only granted a second of shock before two strands of water whipped forward and flung the nobles in opposite directions. Their bodies spun in the air before they crashed into the shelves of tonics. Farren staggered backward. The water splashed downward and surged over the sides of the bath. She barely registered her wet hair and clothes, not as the water that covered her skin curled around her wrist and palm to lap at her fingertips. Dazed-eyes stared at the snake-like form. The sharp power against her bones faded to reveal shaking hands, the vibrations of adrenaline. Her hair lowered back into place and her cheeks were heated whilst the water dripped at her feet. She used magic... and won... she used magic... It was like her body knew what to do before her mind did. The triumph she felt turned into a hollow, cold dread that settled deep within her chest. She imagined Argen's face as he spoke to Soter in the throne room, as he met him in the market tent; she remembered Rorke's hatred for all things magical; Lyla's sharp eyes when she scolded Soter's behaviour, entered her mind. Part-way around the bath her knees hit the tile as she relieved herself of whatever was in her stomach. The trainee guard retched over the wet floor which had her tired muscles screaming. If that was the only price she would pay for using magic, then she would live with it. There was nothing that she would not give to not turn out like the bandits on the road to the Capital.

When her stomach was finally empty she gulped down mouthfuls of air. The back of her hand wiped against her mouth and she stared at the fallen Kayei. *Not a word*, she would not breathe a word of what happened to anyone. A fluke, that was all it was, a magical fluke that saved her life. Despite her determination to forget it ever happened, the Oracle appeared in the steam. Farren's eyes squeezed shut and she willed the image away. When she opened them, the image was gone and her eyes returned to their storm-blue; steely resolve settled in to hold back the tears.

One beat, two, three and she stood from the puke-covered floor and walked over to her discarded axe. She braced a hand against her chest and moved through the rest of the room. The thrum of magic echoed against her skin and urged her to retch again. The hand on her chest pressed to her mouth. There was another, shorter hall beyond the door that the Kayei nobles entered through hence why she surged through to the other side and picked up her pace. She had to find another set of stairs and find Schylus' room. It was not on the highest floor, nor on the bottom level. That only left four other floors for her to scour through.

The bright light that hit her made her realise just how dim the bathroom had been. She blinked past the sharp pain to her eyes and held her axe in front of her. A battle-cry sounded to her right. A brightly lit hand grabbed her arm then twisted. She jumped into the momentum and her head collided with the Kayei's nose. He reeled back but kept his grip on her. It was the guard from the dungeon who looked at her with such disdain. Blood gushed from his nose but it wasn't broken, until she turned in his grip, pulled his elbow over her shoulder and swung her head backwards. The crunch sounded in her ears and he finally released her. His eyes widened at something behind her and he moved swiftly through the door she entered.

"That was terrible," a silky voice floated toward her, "you should have broken his arm in that position."

Farren lifted her eyes and nearly cursed. Wearing the same outfit as Farren but in yellow, stood Amelie. Jaeger posed next to her. Farren nervously chuckled and raised her hands, though she supposed it was difficult to look innocent with her dress covered in blood and water. Amelie jutted her chin toward Farren and Jaeger moved. It was slow at first, like he didn't want to end up like the glowing guard, but then he ran at her with his insane speed.

There was no time before he swiped his foot under hers. She saw the ceiling in milliseconds then Jaeger's face above hers. He grinned evilly down at her, gripped the front of her dress and pulled her from the floor slightly. She gripped his wrist with her free hand but the wet skin slipped against his so she grappled for purchase.

"Prick," she ground out.

"Shh, it'll all be over soon." He moved his face closer to hers.

"Actually." The click of Amelie's heeled boots sounded behind Jaeger. "I would like to make this kill slow, intimate." Jaeger hummed his agreement.

Farren licked her lips to stop her from baring her teeth at him, and swung her axe-filled hand into his side. As she did so she curled her leg between them and kicked her foot upwards. With the nudge of her leg and the swing of the axe, the blade collided with his side. More blood pooled onto her dress from his open mouth but he remained on top of her. Amelie was the one to remove him with a disgusted scoff where Farren's thighs were covered in the red liquid. There was no time for Farren to rise from the floor because Amelie's boot slammed down against her breast bone. The pressure blew the air from her lungs despite her open mouth.

"Poor Jaeger," Farren coughed. "That's the second time you butted in. Are you that desperate for me?" Her forced laughter turned into another cough. Amelie's boot continued to bend her bone until she swiftly kicked the side of Farren's leg. The human cried out and curled upward. Amelie then kicked her across the face and Farren slumped back on the ground. She hissed through the pain, curled upward again and braced her hands around her thigh to massage the spasming muscle. The woman circled her just as Schylus did, her hands clasped in front of her and head slightly lowered to watch Farren's every move. Farren wasn't sure she would move for a long time. Amelie nudged the wrist around her thigh and Farren hissed louder. Her body felt hot and cold at the same time and she could not force her leg to work.

"Stop trying to stand, I've disabled your leg for at least a day, maybe more. I never know my own strength." She flicked her hair over her shoulder.

"Fuck." Farren felt the tears in the corner of her eyes. "What are you going to do with me?"

"Absolutely nothing," a voice like distant thunder rumbled through the room.

A bark of disbelief and Farren nearly smiled at Nero. His hands were shoved into his pockets with his head tilted to the side. Amelie stared at him the same way she stared at Jaeger. "She is my toy for the night, I caught her fair and square." If she were in different company, Amelie would have stomped her foot.

"Technically," Farren said, "Jaeger caught me."

"You bitch." Amelie lunged for her, hand outstretched to scratch across her face. A sigh sounded from Nero and he stepped forward. One second he was behind her, then he had Amelie by the throat and against the wall. His grip visibly tightened and she was lifted from the ground. The choking sounds brought a sense of satisfaction to Farren until Nero's wrist twisted and Amelie's neck was in the wrong direction.

"Oh Griselda," Farren muttered. She focused on her damaged muscle, head bowed, but Nero remained in her peripheral. He flexed his fingers and pushed the hair from his face. The intricate swirls on his back faced her as she whimpered into her knee.

"There are two unconscious men in the bathroom, how did that happen?" He asked, his eyes on Amelie.

"They slipped."

Farren leaned her head back and calmed her heart. The pain in her leg was uncomfortable, like somebody hit her funny-bone. She wiggled her toes in her boot which only flared the pain more. Next she tried her knee but her entire leg was incapacitated just as Amelie said. Not good.

"They are covered in water," Nero continued.

"Hence the slippage," she fired back.

He finally turned to face her, hands returned to his pockets and brow raised. "*How* did all that water get on the floor?" He scanned her body. "And over you?"

"You know," Farren chuckled humourlessly. "You and Schylus have the same questioning techniques. What I mean by that is, there is obviously something specific you want me to say, so just tell me what it is and I'll *parrot* it," she said through clenched teeth.

Nero's brow lowered and he rolled his eyes. "I just wondered if a Malumrem like yourself could use water magic." He shrugged. "But if you didn't see any-"

"That's it." She twisted her torso to squarely look at him. "What is a Malumrem and why do you all think I am one?"

He walked around her to lean against the other wall. "Malumrem translates in your language to 'wrong thing.' You smell off, that's all. No Kayei can figure you out..." he trailed off and scanned her again.

"Well you have spent a lot of time with me, if I can use water magic do you think I would be in this shitty position?"

He chuckled. "No, I suppose you wouldn't be." Yet, there was something in his eyes that told her he would not let it go.

She looked back down at her damaged leg and swallowed. There was no plan, no idea that swam through her head that would allow her to run; standing was already an issue. As though he read her mind, Nero offered his blue-gloved hand out to her. For a moment she hesitated, then plonked her hand in his and he tugged. He was strong enough that she barely registered that she was off the floor. Then she was spun in his arms and her back was pressed against his chest. The points of his canines grazed her ear as he growled. The sound was guttural and deep like his voice took on a demonic edge. Shivers wracked her body, and she took stock of her predicament: her bad leg was raised off the floor, one of her arms were trapped whilst the other hung at her side, and Nero's hand was pressed sharply to her abdomen. There was no use in bucking or thrashing, it would only injure her further and possibly break her arm.

"I thought we were having a civilised conversation?"

Nero breath washed over neck, "you were so focused on the other Kayei that you never perceived me as a threat."

"You really like to toot your own horn don't you?" The grip around her wrist tightened and she bit her lip to stop her cry of pain. *Breathe through your nose Farren.* He moved that wrist higher above them and dug his fingers into her stomach. She tried to hop away from the feeling but it only meant she was closer to his body. The feather-light strands of his hair tickled her shoulder and the tip of his nose brushed her skin. Another shiver ran down her spine.

"You got too comfortable," he commented. "I was never going to let you leave here with the Princess."

"Playing the waiting game, huh? I'm not going to lie to you but," another humourless chuckle jostled their bodies, "I thought you were mildly decent."

"Face it, Farren, you are nothing more than a piece of Kayei entertainment."

There was a moment where she breathed heavily against him. "Let me guess, you wanted the pleasure of killing me and those, what, lesser Kayei didn't deserve such a privilege?"

"Who's tooting their own horn now?" He leaned closer to her neck and smirked. "You think I'm going to kill you?"

The bob of her throat and she leaned as far from his mouth as possible. The hand on her moved further north and paused under her chest. His eyebrow quirked even though she couldn't see it and his hand dug down beneath her corset. An indignant cry left her throat as his slender fingers found purchase on an item. Her eyes closed slowly. She was unable to move as the blue vial was removed from her person. He shook it in front of her and they both watched as the liquid sloshed in the glass. "Ah, my liquid luck, I was looking for that," she said nervously.

He hummed and used two of his fingers to tilt her chin back against his shoulder. "I could save myself the hassle of sending you to Schylus and just pour this down your throat." For emphasis he trailed those fingers down the column of her neck and paused at the centre of her collarbone.

"You could, but wouldn't that be too *boring* for you?"

The vibration of his laugh started as a rumble, then it grew until he stepped away and doubled-over. He released her wrist and pressed both hands to his knees. Farren hobbled back, nearly fell over, and stared at him with furrowed brows. Laughter continued to flow from his body, the vial clenched

348

in his hand. The axe that was embedded in Jaeger's unconscious –possibly dead- body was clumsily removed: she stumbled and hobbled with each movement but with a sickening slurp of blood and flesh against metal, the weapon was freed. With a severe limp in her step she moved around the hysterical man toward the door at his back.

Farren returned to her search for Cyrille and Rorke, albeit in a less than speedy manner. However, she kept Nero's laughter at the side of her at all times. The walls were her purchase as she opened room after empty room. The sounds of nobles no longer assaulted her ears and Nero did not follow her. Farren was left to her own devices, she only hoped it was entertaining enough for Schylus to let her leave. Although, he was the least of her worries with Cyrille's newly visible powers guarding Rorke. *You know,* Farren thought, *I could still kick her ass with one leg.* The thought was her own bit of humour before she crashed through the final door in the hall before the stairs where two withered plants flanked the door and the handle was worn with use.

Immediately, the smell of mint and sage hit her. She blinked back against the golden light and braced a hand on the door. The familiarity of it forced her back straight and the grip on the axe's handle to loosen.

"Hello, Farren," the silken voice greeted her. Stood in the middle of the room, hands folded behind his back was Soter. He was dressed in his usual attire, green and white on his body and hair shaggy. The cufflinks were simple that night, unlike her dress which was once beautiful. His eyes did not snag on the blood and water, or on the axe in her hand, he simply kept them on hers, a small smile on his face. He was a man greeting his friend.

"Soter," she choked out.

Then she ran and flung herself toward him which was a lot better in theory because as she swung her leg forward, the other gave out. It didn't matter because his arms were around her in seconds. The axe was dropped at her side as the two of them fell to the floor. They knelt, arms cocooning the other. He didn't care that her dress soaked his clothes or that the blood would never be removed from his tunic. It was the first time she cried since she arrived in Kavan and it was like the floodgates had been unleashed. The vow she made to herself was broken but there was no stopping once she started. She cried and cried and cried because that was all she thought to do. Her leg hurt, Rorke was missing, everyone in the castle was after her; she had a right to cry, so Soter knelt there, with his hand moving in gentle motions across her back. When her sobs turned to sniffles he explained, "I came to help. The King of Altin expected your arrival two days ago."

"So he sent you?" She wiped her eyes. "Why you and not Adrastos?" She spied the water and blood she left on his clothes. "Sorry. I'll get you a new one, um, It's been-" She swallowed. "It's been nightmarish honestly."

"I can see that." There was something akin to worry in his eyes. "I thought I stood a fighting chance to get to you the quickest." At the disheartened look in her eyes he continued, "I'm sorry, I had no doubt that you were alive." He beamed. "Nero might be a King, but you are smarter than he is." He ran his hands down her arms and his mouth tightened. "Is any of the blood yours?"

Through glassy eyes she shook her head and explained. She told him everything, from the moment they arrived in Kavan to her collapsing in his arms. He held her hand when she started to rant, nodded when needed; he listened. What she didn't tell him, was about the two unconscious nobles that were taken down by *something* she did. After she finished her tale, Soter started to work on her leg. The soft skin of his hand glided up her thigh as he lifted the fabric of her dress. A large bruise of purple and black sat on the outside of her leg. He twisted and turned the muscles until she had the urge to kick him away. He raised his hands in surrender and gently moved her leg into his lap. She swore like a sailor but allowed him to do his work.

"I can heal this if you want me to?" It was a question and an offer.

"Please."

"It involves magic."

She sent him a pointed look. "I think I've been screwed over by enough magic that it owes me this time." He moved over to a small satchel in the corner of the room so she chuckled through her residue tears. "I don't think Schylus will appreciate me coming away from this little game unscathed."

The Magician peaked over his shoulder with a smirk. "All the more reason, yes?" She squawked out a laugh as he gathered a pestle and mortar, two bags of herbs and a skein of water. He lined them up beside where she leaned on her palms. Whilst he worked she watched his every movement; there was something different about him, or perhaps it had been so long since she saw him but he looked brighter, stronger. Yet, as he worked, her mood sobered.

"I need to find Cyrille and Rorke." She locked her eyes with his when he paused. "She has Kayei strength, Soter."

"What?"

"Cyrille, she dragged Rorke's body away with no effort. I don't know how he did it, but Schylus gave her magic."

Soter glanced to the side then hastily proceeded to grind the herbs. Farren followed his previous gaze to where a head of dark hair peaked over the bed. She did a double-take. Cyrille's curls were crazy on her head and her chest rose and fell in her sleep whilst she was slumped against the side of the mattress. "One down," Soter muttered.

Farren shot her head back to him. "Did you see Rorke?"

Soter nodded. "He's on his way to find you I think."

"Dammit, was he injured?"

Soter helped her onto the bed, hand wrapped in hers. "His hand and a headache. Nothing else seemed wrong. I offered a salve for his hand but I don't think he heard me before he ran to find you."

The fabric of her dress was hiked up again and Farren opened her legs to allow the red-head to kneel between them. He dipped his fingers into the paste he made –a sickly green colour- and rubbed it gently into her muscle. A few hisses escaped her but she let him do his work, the colour of her cheeks a bright red. After a while he shook his head and knelt on one knee. Her foot was guided to press on his thigh which made her groan but he was quick to continue his massage. The movement and the paste combined allowed a sigh to escape her. It was cool and slimy against her flushed skin.

She tilted her face skyward and took a breath. "I am so happy you're here." He smiled at her, his thumbs gently pressed into her thigh. "I could use some help getting the Princess out-" She shot her head forward. "Wait, how did you get in here?" His mouth twitched upward and he raised his hand between them. The air swirled to their left. Oranges, reds, yellows, and a spike of blue merged to form what looked like a miniature Veil. He threw a pillow from the bed at the magical swirl and it disappeared. Farren leaned forward for a closer look.

"I can only use this once more, any more than that and Nero will find me. It's safer this way."

"It will take four people, you included, out of this castle?" He nodded. "Okay, so you need to stay hidden from Nero and Schylus. I can distract them, find Rorke and meet you back here." Her head bobbed as she spoke.

"That is fine but Farren," he held her hand close to his chest, "are you alright, your eyes are glowing?"

A loud gasp escaped her and she covered her eyes with her free hand. He pressed against her wrist and she lowered it. Rapidly, she blinked and the glow dissipated back to its natural colour. At some point during her conversation with Nero the glow returned. Her hands shook, her entire body did, and the room seemed to spin around her. She braced her hand on Soter's shoulder to steady herself but the room continued to sway. A skein was pressed to her lips and she gulped the water down heartily. The room righted itself but she felt the sides of her face tingle.

"Thank you." She finished the drink. "I'm much better now."

He rolled his eyes playfully and helped her from the bed. The muscle of her leg remained tender but she was able to stand. A wobble was present in her steps but a cripple she was no longer. "That glow, has it happened before?"

Farren felt the urge to lie, to tell him that it was a trick of the light, but he was warm, and open, and kind, so she slowly nodded. "It has something to do with me being a Malum-something. Apparently my eyes glow now." She tried to shrug it off but the weight on her chest threatened to suffocate her.

"A Malum-something? I am not sure what you are trying to say, but when they glow how do you feel?"

Her eyes searched his. "Powerful, scared, overwhelmed maybe. It happened in my Veil crossing, when a version of me used... magic." She squeezed her eyes shut in realisation. The Oracle tried to tell her, she tried to warn her about the fluke, about the effects it would have on her body. As if on cue she started to shake.

"It's alright, Farren. It is. Every Magic User feels like that the first time."

"I didn't mean to use it."

"Then unless you call upon it again, it will likely leave you alone." He sent her a reassuring smile.

"You're sure?" He nodded but suddenly, the talk of magic brought her to another thought. "Those necklaces you gave me in the White Castle, do you have any more?"

"No, I am sorry. I did not want to risk anyone sensing my arrival." She ran a hand over her face but nodded in understanding, so he walked her to the door. "I will wait here."

"And guard the Princess?" Farren asked with her eyes on the tufts of hair beyond the bed.

"I will, but Farren, if it comes down to protecting you or Princess Cyrille, I will not choose her." She furrowed her brows. "Call for me when you wish to leave."

The rush of heat that encompassed her body made her cling onto him just that moment longer. Finally, she had a Kayei ally in the castle. A smile actually broke across her face. With a nod she stumbled, less than before, toward the door. That was when it slammed open. The young woman stepped back and dove for the axe on the floor. Everything ached —including her healed leg- but the weapon was in her hand. When she saw blond on the threshold she felt a shock through her. Deep breaths lifted her chest from the sudden surge of adrenaline and she looked between Soter and Nero. Golden eyes stared at Soter who stared back. Farren glided between them, her arms partially spread wide, her body a shield for Soter whose eyes moved between her and Nero.

"You look better," Nero spoke, eyes drifting over her.

"You don't."

Soter lifted his hand to grab her shoulder but she kept her stance strong, steel-like. Nero leaned on the doorframe, his arms crossed, brow raised as he turned his attention to the room. The pestle and mortar caught his eye but he quickly moved on until he saw the bed. "Hiding things are we?" Nero took a step into the room and Farren pointed the axe at him.

"You told me I underestimated you, not again," she snarled, "get out."

"Excuse me?"

"Get out, leave, Nero."

Soter smirked behind her. "You heard, Farren, *leave*." He gestured out the door. Nero looked like he debated the idea then stormed past both he and Farren. The woman swirled on her heel, remained in front of Soter, and the axe acted as a shield. The blond rolled his eyes and picked the Princess from the floor. She was slung over his shoulder like a sack of potatoes and was carried past the gobsmacked pair.

"She is not part of Schylus' deal," Nero said, his eyes bore into Farren's.

"Hey, no, no." She stepped forward, but Soter's hand was on her shoulder, his hushed whispers calm and collected. The blood in her veins boiled as they let Nero take the Princess. For good measure she threw the axe toward the back of his knee. It sliced through his fine trousers and clattered to the floor. A loud curse bellowed from his chest and he stumbled, hand braced against the door; he didn't drop the Princess. Blood trickled from his leg and then the door was shut and Farren was again without the King of Altin's daughter.

Sometimes self-preservation was an idea that was to be listened to. Farren and Soter could have left with the Princess and been at the Veil had she not stopped to heal her leg, had she not asked after Rorke. The thought of the human guard, battered, bruised and looking for her made her heart twinge. Self-preservation be damned, he was one of her own. She chanted that like a mantra in her mind. The blood that fell from Nero's leg lead her through and around corridors of the castle. It guided her down the main stairs and onto the first floor. The blood trail ended in a large foyer where she stopped on the bottom step. If she listened to her mind instead of the beat of her chest she would not have stared at Schylus' bloodied hand and sneer-covered face. A bandage had been haphazardly wrapped around his wrist as though he were on the move when it was seen to. How she hoped it hurt.

"Oh, you are still alive."

She angled the axe in front of her and said, "don't sound too disappointed, I'll start to think you don't like me."

He stood at the front of the foyer, like a man possessed. The lapels of his jacket and chest rose in large, deep breaths. His good hand rested atop a black vase, rings glinted in the light and parts of his suit were covered in blood. That included the side of his face where smudged red stained his cheekbones. His eyes flickered over her body, the way she leaned on her stronger leg, the water that drenched her clothes and hair. "My, my, how was your visit to my bathroom. Anything *interesting* happen there?" He smirked deviously up at her.

"Two of your friends became unconscious if that's what you mean."

She scanned her eyes around the room. The large chamber echoed their voices like a Goddess' temple and was brightly lit compared to the other halls and rooms decorated in shades of black and red. It was just the two of them and withered plants. There was no sign of Nero and Cyrille, or Rorke.

"You found me, Farren." He stepped forward. "And just as the note said I shall grant you passage."

She narrowed her eyes. "Really?"

That smirk remained. "Well," he elongated the word, "you were mildly entertaining, I found you the first time which I consider unfair for you; you hurt Nero badly so I hear and my bathroom is flooded. That warrants some praise, but-" He stepped forward again. "You didn't entertain my guests. Rumour has it Farren dear, that they barely saw you all night."

The far wall looked like a very good place for her to slam her head against. "What do you want me to do about that?"

He hopped. "I'm glad you asked! I have a few ideas, but I think my favourite involves Rorkey-boy too." He tapped his chin. "Maybe I should have you fight Cyrille... no, that's too on the nose, and you genuinely will kill her, so," he continued to mutter to himself about all the avenues he could take with her, and her new found entertainment job. "I have it!" He shot his head up and pointed his bloody hand at her. "Go back up those stairs, third door on your left."

"That's," she paused, "that's it? Are you seriously making this up as you go?" Her voice tilted between disbelief and outrage.

Blood ran down his wrist which he slowly licked from dripping onto the cuff of his shirt. Her eyes followed each of his movements like a fox about to pounce, but she wondered if she was the fox in that scenario.

"What are you going to do? Throw that axe at me and escape?" He laughed. "You can fight me, or you can go to the room third door on your left."

Schylus was different. He was calmer, more mature, but there was something in the way he looked at her that made her retreat a step. Option one was plausible, desirable, because he lost a lot of blood and was unstable on his feet. "Why would I not fight you?" She held up the axe for emphasis.

One moment she stared at him, the next there was a wind and a breath behind her ear, "because you would never win against me." The blood rushed quickly to her head and bile rose in her throat. *Not so unstable.* A quick nod and she turned, but the axe was not in her hand. Schylus waved it with a wiggle of his brows. The shuffle of his clothes and he moved to the side. Never had Farren ran up a set of stairs so fast before. The hem of her dress flew behind her and slapped against the banister as she turned sharply onto the landing. Her leg dragged behind her somewhat but the tingle that settled on the side of her face travelled to that thigh which brought on the urge to itch it. Soon she found the door he mentioned, a sliver of light peaked from beneath it and the sound of voices reached her. A shaky hand wrapped around the handle and twisted. The click of the door and she slowly opened it, her body hidden by the wood as she did so. All the voices stopped and she braced herself for an arrow, a dagger, an axe to be thrown through the open doorway, but it never came. She gave the door a wide berth and held her hands up to defend herself.

No furniture decorated the room but there were chains along the walls, some high and some low to the ground. Each of them ended with thick manacles and a large grate was embedded in the centre. What dragged her attention from those chains was the man who hung from the higher ones. His head was bowed and blood dripped from his mouth but he froze when the door opened. Nero stood in front of him, hand raised to press against his

358

cheek in a searing burn. The blond looked over at her with a mere tilt of his head. Just like her, he leaned on his good leg, the other with the trouser leg rolled up and bandaged around his calf.

"Where is she?"

"Who?" Nero lowered his hand.

"Princess Cyrille," she ground out.

"She's fine," the man in chains coughed out. Farren did not hesitate. She rushed toward Rorke who looked at her through his lashes. Nero stepped out of her way with a roll of his eyes. She brushed sweaty strands of hair away from Rorke's bruised face and gently traced his features. His smile was small but it was there.

"How did you get here? Did the nobles see you? Has Nero hurt you?" She fired off at him.

He turned his head to spit blood on the floor. "He was about to. I was looking for you when Schylus found me. Did you find S-?"

"Yeah I did, everything's going to be fine." She forced a smile. "You said Cyrille is fine?"

"She left to get changed."

"She left to-" She whipped her face to Nero. "You carried her from the bedroom so she could get changed?!"

Nero shrugged. "It was what she wanted to do, who was I to deny her?"

"Oh you know what." Farren stepped forward but Rorke called her name, his good hand stretched toward her. "You're a dick." She pointed at Nero before she turned back around.

"What happened to your leg?" Rorke asked.

"A friend of mine ruptured her muscle," Nero piped in, and as much as Farren wished it wasn't true, it was, so she lifted both brows in acknowledgement.

The chains that lifted Rorke's arms above his head were thick and heavy, his wrists hung limply and the attachments on the wall were as thick as the cuffs. Soft fingers glided up his arms and over those chains. A furrowed brow and an eye twitch and she lowered them again. She picked up the long chains beside his and used them like a whip. Metal hit metal. Only a scratch was made in both chains. Another swing and another clangour. She threw the chains against the wall and shuffled closer to Rorke, her voice a low whisper, "how am I going to get you out of these chains?"

"You're not," Nero replied another time.

"Was I talking to you?!" He lifted his hands in a bid to ease her.

"No need to be snappy, love, I thought you would appreciate some truth while you were here."

"Oh yes, because you have been entirely honest with me." She rolled her eyes.

"When have I lied to you? Hm?"

"You claim to do all these things because you're bored, when in fact you would do anything for Schylus if he asked. You're so far up his ass your hair should be brown." She turned her back on him, their conversation decidedly finished. Nero looked between the two, jerked a brow and moved to the back of the room. A bench dotted with small items missed her attention when she originally surveyed the room but upon a glance all that was there were clear bottles, a pile of ripped cloths and scissors. Nero walked over to the clear bottles and cloth, and uncorked a bottle. A sharp cough and he held it at arm length then placed it back on the bench. All the while, Farren and Rorke strategized. "There has to be a key for these cuffs somewhere in this room. Who chained you up?"

"Schylus."

She took a deep breath. "I only saw him moments ago, if I catch up to him I could strike a deal."

Rorke barked out a laugh. "We are in the middle of one of his deals." She shook her head in question and Rorke smiled at her sadly. "He offered you the deal to escape, but," he moved his eyes to her shoulder, no longer able to look her in the eye, "he offered me a different deal."

"What deal?" The man before her visibly shrunk. Rorke was her rock, her steady buoy in a roiling ocean. To see him move back from her gaze, from her touch, she felt her chest cave in.

"The Princess' survival, for my life."

If Farren didn't feel like ripping the room to shreds she would have commented on how cliché that offer was. The knot in her stomach tightened painfully; it was why Nero's attitude changed, why she had to be taken care of before she reached the Princess. It was why the nobles were nowhere to be seen, Schylus wanted her dazed and confused, injured and alone, so he could strike the deal. "Schylus can shove that deal up his ass. You are not going to die here, Rorke, and I swear to Griselda if you think otherwise I will kill you myself."

He laughed loudly and fully, his head on her shoulder. A smile spread across her face and she joined in his laughter. Once his glee died down to mere chuckles he tilted until his forehead pressed against hers. She cupped his face in her hands, gentle around his injuries. Together they were a kaleidoscope of purple, black, red, and white.

Their moment of bliss was broken suddenly, rudely, with a cloth over Farren's mouth and nose. She thrashed and clawed her hands down the flesh that held the fabric over her airways. Rorke jolted forward with a frown and a glare.

"Unhand her," Nero ordered from his place by the bench.

The man whose hand pressed down on her nose chuckled. "I don't take orders from you, traitor," he spat.

The blond marched forward; the smell of smoke encompassed the room and particles of ash floated in the air. Rorke continued to strain against his restraints whilst Farren behaved like a wild animal. Scratches and dents formed on the attacker's hands and arms but his hold was firm. Her heel caught the front of his shin, the top of his foot, and her elbow met his stomach numerous times but the world faded around the edges as the smell of medicinal chemicals filled her lungs.

"Do not interfere, Nero. This nice man is doing his job, and in a wonderfully efficient manner," Schylus' voice was the last thing Farren heard before the fade turned to black.

Everything blurred and a room ebbed in and out of her vision until it centred on a plush bed, the sheets silken and the smell of burnt sugar wafted over her. When the world around her continued to morph, more details became prominent such as the red light that lined the skirting of the room. Exotic

362

plants which decorated the corners and sat in ornate plant-pots, and the inky black sat beyond the open window. Farren stepped forward and a figure came to life. It was neither human nor Kayei but rather it was shadows solidified, with red, molten veins that crept up its arms and neck. The shadows seemed more like a cloak over a humanoid body. Tresses of shadowy hair fell across its face which consisted of a curved nose and sharp cheekbones. As the shadows danced they revealed pitch black skin –or skin like substance- that shaped a lean torso. More veins covered the expanse of its chest and curled around its wrists. Those veins stopped at what appeared to be a shadow-formed waistband. Farren could not keep her eyes from straying even further downwards. Then she blinked, it was just like her dream, and it was the same room she woke up in, the same silhouette that held out its hand to her. One leg was bent in front of it whilst the other stretched down the length of the bed. It was relaxed, open. Its elbow rested on its bent leg and it grinned at her, sharp white canines glowed in the light.

"Where am I?" She asked but it did not speak, instead it waved its hands out into the room. "Why am I here?" It shrugged and grinned toothily. "Am I the only one here? Where's Rorke? Nero? Schylus?" It shook its head and gestured to itself. "Yes, yes, I know you are here too but I was just," she turned and pointed over her shoulder where a large plant sat, "what...?"

After a moment of dumbfounded silence she returned her gaze to the figure. It crooked a finger for her to move forward. Just like on the balcony she did as it asked. She stood at the edge of the bed, her hand soon in its. The clawed tips of its hand brushed against the pulse in her wrist and her breath hitched.

"Farren," the voice was inside of her head and all around her. *"Can you hear me?"* She dazedly nodded and the figure beamed at her. *"You are safe here, Farren."*

"Where is 'here'?"

"Safe."

"Am I," her eyes widened, "am I dead?"

Her hand was brought up to its lips and hot skin pressed against her knuckles. Its head shook rapidly and it kissed lightly across her hand. Once it was done showering her with light kisses, it tugged on her hand and she crawled across the comforter, her motions slow as she scanned where its eyes were supposed to be. There was something intimate about the moment, like it was just the two of them in the whole world, but her brows were furrowed. Its grin widened and it pulled her ever closer. Fluidly, she swung her legs over its hips and its hand removed itself from hers to glide down her back and over her thighs. It used that leverage to pull her body even closer. They moulded together as her hands found purchase around the back of its neck.

"Not dead. Safe. With me," its voice soothed her tensed muscles.

She ran her fingers through the soft shadows at the base of its neck and it hummed melodically. The tips of its claws dug into the fabric of her dress as it gripped the material. Shadows licked against her skin like miniature flames. She swallowed and looked around the room; it was all so realistic, but- "Am I still in Schylus' castle?" The shadow-man nodded. "But I was just with Nero and," her eyes widened, "where's Rorke?" She scanned the room again but it squeezed her thighs which brought her attention back on it.

It only answered with, *"safe here, nobody else."*

"Where is everybody else, then?" It shook its head and leaned back on its hands. "Helpful, thank you." The sarcastic roll of her eyes made it grin. "And who are you? I've seen you before, in my dreams but you didn't speak to me." It shrugged but turned its face from hers like it was sheepish, embarrassed all of a sudden. "Are you here to warn me about something?"

"Keep you safe."

"How can you keep me safe if I am still in Schylus' castle?" A silence fell over them, Farren sat atop its thighs, hands on her own whilst it surveyed her with eerie precision. After it was bored of simply staring, it sat up, its hands returned to her back where it glided across her corset and to where the slit on her dress sat. She followed its movements with her eyes until it leaned forward, mouth a hairsbreadth away from hers. For a moment she hesitated, Rorke's face in her mind's eye, but then she noted the lack of doors, the slight shimmer on the bed and furniture that surrounded it. There was a phantom weight around her wrists so she lifted them between their bodies and twisted them. The weight shifted but only slightly. Her questioning eyes searched the figure's face for any answers but it shrugged. The grin permanently etched into the shadows faltered slightly and her stomach flipped. Her head was heavy but a buzz ran through her veins. Then she rested her hand on its warm cheek and smiled. "This is a dream right? I'm unconscious right now?" It audibly swallowed and slowly nodded.

Finally, after what felt like minutes of staring, their lips met. Her hands traced across its shoulders, but where shadows were supposed to meet her fingertips, lean muscle replaced it. The kiss was soft at first, nothing more than a caress of skin but then she shifted herself on its lap and the dark figure beneath her growled. The sound reverberated like a bee around her head. The grip it had on her thighs tightened as it rammed her against its chest. Her squeak of surprise was caught by the demanding press of its lips. Its tongue was hot against hers and it moved languidly in her mouth. The taste of the burnt sugar and something purely ethereal entered her senses. The two of them fell against the silk sheets, the figure's hold kept her secure against its chest. Hot breath hit her lips as they parted for air and its smile was feral as it moved from her mouth and attacked her neck, its body shifted above her. Her hands roamed the expanse of its chest, muscles she couldn't see clearly rippled and flexed against her fingers. The pale lengths were hidden by smoky shadows, but she didn't marvel for long as its teeth raked against every sensitive spot it found and its hands wandered just as hers did. They deftly undid the tie of her corset and slipped beneath the butter-flied item to massage her sides until she was putty in its hands. That was when it moved its hands higher, her bindings and dress nothing against the slice of its claws. Tatters of fabric were pushed to the floor with a flick of its wrist. It pushed her ripped dress higher and a mix between a growl and moan sounded from the creature above her. Its hands were rough against the flesh but she curved into his touch. With each squeeze and tweak she whimpered. Her own hands ran down its arms, desperate for a purchase. Once her hands were in its shadowy hair she pulled it back down toward her and there was no resistance as their lips glided against one another. It leaned back and gifted her another grin before it slowly ground its hips into hers. Another moan escaped her as she tried to match her hips with its. At the sultry sounds she made it trailed its hand across her body. Goosebumps rose on her skin as it lightly dragged its claws and fingertips down her sensitive stomach which made the muscles of her abdomen flutter at the caress. The heat of the room and from their actions caused a flush to spread across her body. Her skirts were removed; a swallow bobbed her throat as she kicked the fabric from her body.

"Okay?"

"Yes." She nodded quickly.

The figure knelt on the bed, its lips between its teeth as it roved its hands over her bare skin. After it had its fill of exploration it shimmied so that its shoulders sat comfortably under her thighs. Her eyes flashed and it paused, entwined its fingers —mindful of the claws- with hers and kissed the inside of her thigh. Wet, open-mouthed kisses pressed to her inner thighs, the figure swapped between the two legs as it settled into the mattress. Farren's core fluttered, she threw her head back and moaned. At the erotic sound the figure

366

dove forward to where she ached the most, but she did not feel its lips or the puff of its breath. Instead, cold water rushed over her which brought her screwed eyes to open. The shock of cold iced her veins and forced her mind to the present.

"Welcome back," Schylus sang and she could not stop the groan that sounded from her. "She's alive ladies and gents."

"Swallow a pinecone, Schylus," she snapped. The haze of the shadows against her skin started to fade to nothing the longer she breathed in Schylus' air. Her limbs trembled and the heat that coursed through her body, the pleasure she felt, was replaced by pure irritation. With water dripping from her lashes, she blinked and glared at the long-haired man who towered above her. Heavy metal cuffs sat around her wrists which were connected to a chain lower in the walls than Rorke's. It allowed her to be sat on the floor rather than suspended from it. The rest of the room then came into focus: Rorke's body chained against the wall to her right, Nero's hands in his pockets as he leant against the door with his jaw clenched, the table full of random bottles knocked over. Then Farren paused, because locked up next to that table, feet tucked daintily beneath her, was Cyrille.

He pursed his lips and looked at her, hands on his hips. "I will leave the three of you to mull over your mistakes. Then you," he pointed dramatically at Farren, "have another deal to accept."

"Why would I accept another one of your deals? In fact, I never actually accepted the first one, he," she nodded toward Nero, "forced me from the room. That's not compliance."

Schylus sighed and pouted. "Why do you take the fun out of everything? I have a final way for you to entertain me." She rolled her eyes and leaned back against the wet wall. "but we can discuss that later."

"Stop being a tease Schylus," Cyrille whined. The Kayei ignored her, scanned his eyes over the three humans and turned to Nero. Without words, the blond nodded and walked out the door, Schylus on his heels. The click of the door sealed the three of them in.

"Farren, are you okay? You were unconscious for a long time," Rorke's voice called over to her.

"I'm alright, I don't know what happened. How are you?"

"They were busy with you and Her Highness, so I'm fine."

"I feel special," she laughed.

"How can you be laughing right now?" Cyrille interjected.

"Because if I don't laugh, Cyrille, I'll try and strangle you with my chains." Rorke opened his mouth to scold Farren. "Why are you tied up with us *peasants*, anyway?"

Cyrille glared. "Because Schylus does not want me wandering around the castle."

"Your boyfriend really trusts you." Farren rolled her eyes. "So from what I've seen, Schylus stole you from the White Castle, made you his prisoner, and somehow trained you into loving him. At what point in that story did he give you Kayei strength?"

Cyrille's self-deprecating laugh made Farren's brows furrow. "He didn't steal me or ask for me. He was genuinely kind to me, he has never hurt me or tried to kill me." She flicked her eyes to Farren who looked more confused than she'd been in her whole life. "He did not give me Kayei strength either."

"Your Highness, please explain," Rorke spoke slowly.

"The morning I left the White Castle I was awoken by four guards knocking on my door. They said that my mother went for a ride through the forest and wanted me to meet her out there. We often did that, had tea out in the wildlife just to get away from the court. I got dressed in my riding dress and followed the men out the stables, then we all mounted our horses. It was not long before we were riding through the forest but one of the guards stopped. He dismounted as did the others and offered his hand out to me. I of course was confused because there was no sign of my mother and the guards had yet to properly speak to me. I demanded he tell me what was going on. They only spoke to each other in hushed tones, it was like I was not stood there!"

"Okay, so the men took you to the forest and ignored you, why?" Farren asked.

"The *why* is still unknown to me, but I will continue. One of the guards stared at a shimmering wall. It was very pretty and he was intently focused on it. When he turned back to me, the other guards grabbed me and then pushed me forward. I protested and demanded they explain themselves, but they said nothing. I met the shimmering wall and passed through it like a spirit. That was when I first met Schylus. He had-"

"Wait, wait, you passed through the Veil without a test? You just," Farren gestured with her hands what Cyrille described, "how is that possible?" She looked between Cyrille and Rorke.

"The Oracle obviously deemed me worthy enough to pass over without one."

Rorke shook his head, "Princess Cyrille, that is not how the creature thinks."

"Do not tarnish me with the same brush as you both. Anyway, I shall continue: Schylus took me into his arms and we rode to this castle. I was upset —obviously- but I knew they were Kayei so I kept quiet, I did not wish to anger them. They sent me to the dungeon the moment we reached the castle. For days I only saw Kayei guards who offered me food and drink and then he visited me. We had a long conversation about why I was here. That was when he told me the truth."

DEAL WITH HIM

"What truth?" Farren enquired with a quick glance at Rorke's frown.

Cyrille ran her tongue over her lips and chewed on them. "That my parents have been lying to me for my entire life." Her chin quivered. "I am under Schylus' protection because," she stuttered, "because I am not fully human." Stunned silence engulfed the room. "I am part Kayei and my parents never told me, they kept me from my powers and from my heritage, but Schylus, he never did. He allowed me to stay in his castle."

"And locked you in the dungeons rather than dealing with you," Rorke's voice was gruff.

"Schylus knew what I was the moment he met me, he likely knew before then as well. If I were him I would have killed me when I crossed through Realms. I am protected here and by being in this castle I can learn more about who I am and who my family is."

Rorke's eyes were wide. "Your family is the King and Queen."

"No!" She shot forward, tears in her eyes. "They lied to me! Family doesn't do that."

Farren swallowed back a sharp retort and instead opted for, "imagine if the King and Queen were Kayei themselves," she forced a chuckle but clamped her mouth shut at Rorke's beseeching look.

He turned his attention back to Cyrille. "What guards did you say took you from the White Castle?"

Cyrille shrugged with a sniffle. "I do not know many of the guards' names I'm afraid."

Farren swallowed the lump in her throat. "Do you think they – whoever they are- sent you here because you are part Kayei?" Cyrille nodded. "That means they are allies of Altin or they are Kayei themselves." She turned quickly to face the Princess. "And you didn't know? You never had a feeling that you weren't... fully human?"

"I never knew. I was sick for most of my childhood which is not conclusive to having magical powers." She rubbed a cuffed hand across her face. "I want to know the truth, that is all."

"Cyrille." The rattle of the doorknob meant there was no chance for Rorke to say more. Simultaneously, their heads turned and the door opened. Two servants entered, each with bruises across their faces. They ignored the two women and walked directly to Rorke. The guard strained against the chains and tried to morph with the wall behind him. The servants' facial expressions did not change as they un-looped the chains from the wall and pulled him roughly forward. Rorke stumbled in their grip as they guided him like cattle toward the door.

"Where are you taking him!? Hey, assholes answer me!" Farren thrashed in her own chains as she tried to get to him. Rorke looked back at her, a small, sad smile on his lips. She shook her head and yanked harder against the restraints. He nodded, cast his eyes to Cyrille then locked them with Farren's. Her head shook harder, the metal dug into her skin, and Rorke was gone.

It was a long while until more servants appeared in the doorway. A sliver of sunshine could be spied beneath the long curtains. Farren panted against her efforts to break free. Cyrille side-eyed her with disdain but kept her mouth shut. Farren tried so hard to reach Rorke, she attempted every trick she knew to try and break or unlock the cuffs around her wrists, but the iron held strong.

Sweat covered her brow and finally, after a loud yell, she slumped back against the wall. Cyrille's eyes strayed ever-so-often to the room but they always found their way back to the frustrated woman.

"Did Schylus tell you anything about Rorke's deal?" Farren asked through laboured breaths.

"No. I am a guest in this castle; I am not involved in such processes."

"A guest," Farren scoffed, "you are in chains just like I am, *Princess*."

"That may be the case now, but upon the end of this ridiculous game, Schylus promised to take me to an old Kayei archive. It shall hopefully contain information on my birth and my lineage."

Farren tilted her head. "If it doesn't?"

"Then I shall try another archive until I find the answers to my questions."

Farren's lips pulled into a thin line as she nodded. "Is there any chance Schylus is, um, *wrong* about you?"

Cyrille's eyes narrowed. "There is some chance, but he's not. You saw how I dragged Rorke from you, no human could do that alone."

"True, but he might have given the power to you."

Cyrille paused for a moment. "You have no idea how the Kayei magic system works do you?" Farren ran her tongue across her teeth. "You cannot give a human magic, their bodies would not be able to sustain it. A Kayei's strength would break my bones every time I try and lift something heavier than myself."

"There are trinkets, necklaces, potions. When was the last time you stepped foot out of the White Castle before your-" She formed air quotes. "Abduction? Humans have been using magic for a while in many different forms, so I would appreciate you not condescending me," she spoke through gritted teeth.

"Magic? In Altin?" Cyrille covered her laugh. "Schylus has hit you too many times."

Farren blinked. "Oh Griselda, you really don't know." Cyrille rolled her eyes and settled her gaze on the door. "Listen I don't know anything about your internal family politics but when you see your father again you have some questions you need to ask him."

"I do not plan to see my father in a long while."

"Unluckily for you, he sent me and I have far more to lose than you do. Consider yourself saved Princess, because Rorke and I are getting you out of here." She folded her arms for emphasis.

"How are you so confident?"

Farren smirked but her head shot forward at the sound of the door. Instead of the two servants from earlier, Nero stepped inside, two trays of food in his hands. The smirk gave way to narrowed eyes and a slight curl of her lip. Any time Nero was in her vicinity she felt like a wild animal prepared to pounce. He lifted a brow at her change in mood and crouched before them. On the trays sat two plates, each with chicken legs and string beans. The food was easy to pick up with their hands, which was lucky because they were granted no fork and especially no knife. "Are you honestly scared that I will stab you with a fork?" Farren asked.

Nero pushed one of the plates in front of the Princess who sheepishly picked up a green bean and nibbled on it. He offered Farren the other plate which she looked down at, then up at him. He remained crouched in front of them. They both watched as Cyrille picked up another vegetable and ate. However, Farren sat back and eyed the food in front of her.

"Should I take a bite of it to prove it isn't poison?" Nero asked.

Farren shook her head. "Aren't you technically a Prince or King or whatever? You likely will survive any poison they give me."

"When did you get so smart?" He popped a bean into his mouth and chewed around a smirk. When he swallowed he continued, "but you should eat. You have a big day ahead of you."

She leaned forward so that he could see her unimpressed glare. "I am so sick of Schylus feeding me, then offering no answers. The cryptic nature of you people needs to cease and desist."

"You people?" He chuckled. "You are sat in a room with a half-Kayei who didn't know she was half-Kayei a few weeks ago." His knowing look made her bite her tongue. "My advice is that you should take a long look in the mirror before you spit at me."

"Did I ask for your advice?"

His brows shot into his hairline and that obnoxious smirk prevailed. "Seriously, you should eat." He pushed the plate further toward her.

She glanced at the chicken. "Why not just kill me, Nero? All these games don't make any sense. Schylus is a Ruler right?" Something flashed in his eyes and he nodded. "Then why does he refuse to fight me himself? Or fight Rorke and I together?" Nero tensed at the mention of Rorke's name. "Something else is going on and I am not taking a bite of anything you offer me until I get some –any- information."

The smirk fell into a stern frown. "Fine. If you want to drift off into your dream world, feel free."

"My dream world isn't too bad actually," she quipped with a mental smirk. Nero manoeuvred from his crouched position to sit with his legs stretched out in front of him. He leaned back on his palms and tilted his head back like he was basking in sun rays. The tendons of his neck pulled against his skin and lengthened the golden stripes on his body. Cyrille ate silently and her eyes refused to meet Nero's when he glanced at her. Farren made herself as comfortable as possible, legs beneath her and arms folded across her chest. The metal cuffs dug into her sternum but the pressure allowed her to focus. Once Nero finished his inspection of the Princess he locked eyes with Farren. Neither blinked. "Giving up so easily?" She chuckled nervously.

"If you do not want to eat I can't make you." At her raised brow he added, "I don't care enough to make you."

"Then we shall sit here in silence until your boss returns."

He shook his head slowly, imperceptibly, then her stomach growled loudly. It echoed around the room and it vibrated through her whole body. She slammed a hand against her abdomen, face a light shade of pink. Nero bit his lip, his laughter stifled. "Are you sure you can last until then?" He snickered.

She glared. "Yes."

His eye twitched. "Eat the damn food, Farren."

"Why?"

"Because if you don't, you're going to die."

"And there it is!" She clutched harder onto her stomach as she laughed. "More cryptic lines."

He darted forward, hand around the bone of the chicken and thrust it in her face. His other hand grabbed her chained wrists and held them above her head. Crumbled stone fell into her hair from the dent in the wall caused by the manacles. One of his knees was braced on her skirts whilst the other –less injured- leg had its boot braced on the floor. It was the same position she was in when she threatened him with her knife. Wide eyes stared up at him then travelled to the chicken leg.

"I don't enjoy warning you about death, you know."

"Could have fooled me." Her taste-buds started to tingle at the smell of fresh chicken and her body was hollow. "But I am hungry." She looked quickly between the food and Nero. "So please tell me something about what Schylus wants from me?" The look she gave him was entirely open.

His strong jaw feathered, the hard lines of his face faltered. "You are a pain in the ass." She blinked and moved further away from the chicken with a glare. "But I suppose it will make the match more interesting if you are well informed." A quick nod toward the chicken and he leaned away from her personal space but his hand remained around her chain. Slowly, she opened her mouth, eyes locked with his, and bit the meat pressed close to her lips. She chewed and took another bite before she leaned back.

Once she swallowed she said, "continue."

"Schylus misjudged how well you would perform last night. It was supposed to be two hours of you getting beat before he intervened. He wanted you to be in his debt. When he found disgruntled and lost Kayei he sent me after you." He smirked. "We both know how that turned out. Schylus ran out of ideas soon after." He stopped talking and nodded at the chicken in his hand.

She opened her mouth for another bite; once she swallowed he continued, "now he thinks he has found a way to show off how powerful his court is whilst not having to fight a Malumrem." Farren wasn't sure she was prepared for what came next. "He wants you to fight a Kayei, one-on-one, arena style."

"Any chance I can just-" She swallowed. "Not?"

Nero scoffed and wiggled the chicken. Through their conversation Cyrille stayed silent, the food enough to occupy her. Farren finished the chicken, the meat cold by the time she did, and was about to barter information to eat the beans when the door swung open. She blinked against the light that spilled in from the corridor. The two servants who took Rorke walked into the room and moved over to Cyrille. Just as they did to him, they unchained her and guided her through the open door. Nero stood to his full height, wiped the chicken juice on the handkerchief from his trousers and turned his back on Farren. With furrowed brows she looked between his shoulders and Cyrille's disappearing form. Then a woman appeared. She was built like a brick wall, all muscle. She had no neck, and narrow eyes which zeroed in on the chained woman. Blonde hair was tied tightly behind her head and with each footfall, the ground shook.

Nero stepped to the side. "Be gentle with her, Mysie. Schylus needs her in fit, fighting condition." He glanced over his shoulder, looked Farren up and down, then left.

The large woman clomped forward, raised her hands and ripped the chains and their loops from the wall. More debris rained down on Farren but she merely flinched before she tugged upward. A brief stumble and she was corralled through the door.

378

Winter was ever present in Kavan. The previously mild air in the castle was replaced by a frosty ground and sharp wind. The metal around her wrists soon turned cold and bit her skin. The water that was thrown on her body made her shiver violently. Visible breaths puffed from Mysie and herself as they moved through the garden and out into the city beyond. The black walls loomed behind them like an omen. The sun was in the sky but the grey clouds above turned the vibrant city dull. The hustle and bustle had yet to start, the streets quiet and eerie. Some shutters were open to reveal families but the majority of them were clamped shut to keep the heat in.

"Why are we outside the castle?" Farren asked the silent woman in front of her.

No surprise, she did not answer. Farren stared down at the cuffs and chains she was forced into, then at the aforementioned woman. There were so many alleyways and side-streets for Farren to run down, but the weight around her wrists and the size difference alone made her balk at the thought. She mentally scoffed, there would be no eluding Schylus that time. However, a noise broke her from her defeated thoughts. A loud chatter and cheering sounded from down the street. The further they walked, the clearer that sound became. Men and women screamed at the top of their lungs in simultaneous joy, but it was not their screams that Farren found interesting, it was the circular structure that stood before her. A glass, domed roof arched into the sky and light poured out of the open double-doors. The rest of the building was a rose colour, with dark grey cobblestones that acted as the pathway. A few arched windows sat on the lower level and further around the side, but after that the only source of natural light came from the ceiling.

Mysie pulled her forward and she stumbled. The soles of her feet ached, blisters started to form on the back of each foot and the top of the boot chafed against the back of her knee. All of the pain and uncomfortable positions she was placed in caught up with her body in that moment. The

cheering and screaming continued, louder and they formed an echo inside
Farren's head. That brought upon a pounding at the back of her eyes and in
her temples.

The entrance they moved through was wide and short; another set of
doors sat at the far end of it but Mysie took a sharp right turn down a different
corridor that Farren struggled to regain balance. Once her feet were securely
beneath her they made their way around the side of the building and into a
small room with a long bar, table and empty shelves. Farren was pushed
inside and chained to the table; then the door slammed shut behind her. The
room was warm but it did little to heat the chill of her bones as she stood
shivering, arms crossed as best she could under her arms. The cheers could be
heard from her small room and each time they surged, she jumped out of her
skin. Eventually, the cheers stopped, and the building went silent.

"My esteemed guests!" Schylus voice rang out behind the walls, "it is
my pleasure to host you here on this cold morning. I know that the spree in
my castle was anticlimactic but this is bound to be a show!" He sang. "I have
an excellent tournament in store for you, but, but, but, there is a catch!" Farren
rolled her eyes. "One of these fighters is not only fighting for their life, but the
life of the person they love." Her heart thudded in her chest. "So when this is
all over, and if they are victorious, they leave here with their life and a
significant other. Isn't that nice?" A mumble echoed through the stadium and
Schylus placated them, "you will have time to make your wagers I promise,
but before you do, I shall go and fetch our champions." There was a silence
before he added, "or should I say *sacrifices*." Laughter erupted and Farren
clenched her fists. Moments later and her door swung open, Schylus' body in
the doorway. He wore a suit of black and his hair was pulled behind him in a
high, braided-ponytail. The brimstone crown was perched on his head. Farren
yanked against the chains in her attempt to reach him and he kissed his teeth.

"You said we were going to make a deal. I am not your prized fighter!" She sneered.

"No." He looked her up and down. "You most certainly are not, but you are what I have." He moved closer to her which is when she spied a saddlebag in his grip; after a double-take she realised it was *her* bag. "I thought to bring you your provisions." He threw the bag at her feet.

She knelt before it and started the rummage. "Where did you find this?"

"Where you left it, on your poor castle horses."

She paused. "What did you do to them?"

He straightened his hair. "Don't fret, I did not harm the creatures. They didn't choose to be stuck with two moronic humans. They make a beautiful addition to my stables."

She shook her head and dug through the satchel; everything was accounted for. "What's in it for me, you already broke your first deal, that isn't exactly motivation for me to agree again?"

"This deal is one you want to take." His grin was manic. "The other deal will be void and replaced by the one I'm about to tell you. If you win this tournament, you, Cyrille *and* Rorke will be allowed to escape Kavan. Nobody from my castle will chase you and you will be free to do what you want. Do we have a deal?"

Farren's heart pounded against her chest and she narrowed her eyes. "*All* I have to do is win the tournament?" She slumped back. "Against how many Kayei?"

Schylus pursed his lips. "Only one."

"Am I allowed a weapon?"

What he said next churned her stomach, "magic only I'm afraid. It's why I brought you those," he gestured to the bag under her hands.

"Why? There is nothing in this for you," she spoke as she pulled out item after item.

A dramatic sigh escaped him. "I don't mean to be rude, but you aren't going to win against my other man."

"Why not fight me yourself? Afraid of getting your hands dirty?"

"Oh darling I don't have to dirty my hands. My other fighter will do that for me. Only a suicidal man would offer to fight a Malumrem." She rolled her eyes and pulled out the necklaces. Each one was pooled beneath her corset, against her chest. They would not activate until she clasped them around a part of her body, whether that was her neck, wrist or ankle. Schylus watched as she then took a swig of her skein. The water quenched her dry throat but the shivers from earlier returned.

"You might be right," she chuckled without humour. "I'll freeze to death before I step foot into the ring."

Schylus raised both brows. "Perhaps you should not have let the water soak into your clothes in such a manner."

She deadpanned. "Water was thrown on my *unconscious* body, I wasn't *aware* of it soaking in."

"Not my problem," with that final, cold remark, he glided out of the room.

Farren sat there, dress clung to her body, hair frizzy and skin icy. The necklaces were a heavy weight between her breasts but she looked down. At the bottom of the bag, wrapped in her trousers was a red gem. The chain shone in the light as she pulled it from its confines. The red glowed like a miniature fire and something akin to triumph filled her chest. With numb fingers she clasped the necklace around her neck and took a deep breath. She willed the warmth into her bones but there was no movement, no flare of light, so she grasped desperately onto the stone and closed her eyes. A throb of power echoed around the room and the light –along with the sought after heat- flooded over her skin and deep into her bones. The aching muscles, tired body and chattering teeth ceased and made way for a more comfortable environment.

Farren felt clumsy and thick, like her limbs had a mind of their own. Mysie retrieved her from the small room –her body decidedly warmer- and pulled her to the edge of the arena. At the centre of the rose building was a sand covered floor where blood from a previous fight decorated the grains. What surrounded it were layers upon layers of seating, filled to the brim with nobles and their families. They were as multi-coloured as the city beyond but there was a vicious intent behind their gazes. Men wafted money at the stewards who shook like leaves, women demanded their drinks and entertainment in a timely manner. All the while, Schylus stood in the centre, gaze upon his people. Nero was at his side, hands in his pockets as usual and head tilted toward his boots. As though sensing her he lifted his eyes and blinked. She did not notice his intense stare, instead she focused on the dark archway at the opposite end of the circle. She tilted her head in a childlike manner. Not much could be seen from her position but the outline of large, defined muscles heaved in the shadows.

"Our sacrifices have arrived!" Schylus announced, his voice loud and nasally in her ears and his arms were thrown wide. Mysie's grip on her chains tightened so that the whites of her knuckles were prominent. A deep breath filled both women's lungs and the blonde looked at her. She did not speak but her look was enough. Kindness and confidence shone in her eyes, a sea of emotion for Farren to spy before she became the stone wall Schylus hired her for. That's why Farren nodded and offered her a small smile.

"Where are they?!" A woman from the higher levels shouted.

Schylus looked between the two dark archways and crooked his fingers. "They are here." Farren was nudged forward into the bright light along with the opposing fighter. "On my left is a man who has participated and won the Golden Harvest three years in a row, just because he could, he is all muscle and has been known to bite the heads off of geese for sustenance. His name is Killian." Schylus grinned, an evil spark to his gaze. "On my right is a woman who infiltrated my castle, fought off my men, and still managed to get caught, eh, Farren?"

Farren clenched her teeth. The bright light faded away and revealed the full seats and eager faces of the Kayei. There were three seats at the front of the crowd, one of them filled by Cyrille's shivering form. The Princess did not look at her, instead her eyes were on her opponent. Farren too trailed her attention to the man on Schylus' opposite side. If she thought Mysie was large, she was not prepared for the 6'5 man than marched into the ring. No shirt sat on his torso, a belt –no doubt with extra holes- held up charcoal trousers which, if they were to be unfurled, were the size of a boat sail. A shaved head already glistened with sweat as he turned from the cheering crowds to survey her, then he huffed. Farren stood a little taller.

A loud bell tolled and Schylus and Nero moved from between them. They walked up a long set of stairs to the two vacant seats next to Cyrille. Schylus of course was in the centre, fingers steeped on the ledge in front of him. Without the two overpowering Kayei, the arena looked larger. *More room for her to run from the large man in front of her*. Mysie walked up

384

behind her, a wide shadow cast on the sand, and reached around her body. Her thick fingers turned the manacle key in each lock. With a disappointingly, unsatisfying thud into the sand, Farren was chain free.

"Schylus!" A voice yelled from the stands. "Let me fight him, not her!" Everyone's heads turned to where Rorke stood at the edge of the front row. Two guards sat either side of him and attempted to pull him back into his seat. Farren's eyes widened as Rorke thrashed and pulled, the chains he wore stark against his skin. A grim smile sat on her lips because she knew, everyone knew, that there was no getting her out of the fight. Another bell tolled and he was held down in his seat, two hands clamped down on his mouth. Then Farren swallowed, turned her body to face Killian, and clenched her fists. Scars sliced over his arms and torso just like the faint white on Rorke's body. With her comrade's presence some feet above her, she steeled her nerves.

Freedom or death loomed over the next few moments of her life, but Schylus spoke, "remember to put on a good show you two," and he clapped his hands, so the worst fight of Farren's life began.

As expected by everyone in the crowd, Killian launched himself at her. Despite his size he was fast and knew what to do with his body. But so did she. For the first few moments of the fight she was on the defensive. Every which-way she bobbed and weaved to avoid his large, wide swings. Then she bounced up, the blisters on her feet forgotten as her knuckles collided with the underside of his jaw. He stumbled back, a hand on the bruising skin in shock. Quickly, he regained his balance and rushed at her. He was behind her, in front of her, at her sides. The blur that was Killian threatened to land her on her back, but he did not strike her. Instead, a glow eddied on different parts of her person. A bright line of blue sliced down her ribs and across her thigh, a few faint spots of white covered her bruised face, and another line circled her ankle.

What the fu-

Each light was a target for his palms, his fists, his head. First his skull collided with her cheekbone where an ugly bruise already sat; after that he curled his fist and plunged it into her open ribs. Once she was curled over, his boot-clad foot collided with the same muscle Amelie attacked. She was on the floor, gasping for breath in milliseconds. The crowd cheered and gasped and audibly winced. Farren tried to ignore it as she spit blood onto the sand.

"Stand up," Killian boomed from above her, but she shook her head.

The muscle of her thigh trembled from the kick, the shake of it moved through her body and into her arms. She swallowed down the discomfort and muddled to her feet. Killian gave her a wide berth. Sand stuck to her water-clad body and hair and specks of it flew in the air when she moved. Once her fists were in front of her, she did not give him the chance to lunge again. She swung, quick and short so that her sides were protected. One jab, dodge, two jab, dodge, three jab and she hit him. It was a graze of her skin against his but it took him off balance. Her hand throbbed where knuckle met bone. With each of her movements the dress swayed around her like wind-beckoned curtains.

He swiped for her ribs again but she jumped back, pushed down on his wrist and turned. "You're fast for your size," she spat out.

"Thank you," that polite response was followed by a punch to her face.

It brought something vicious and feral to the surface. The grin on her face was more of a baring of her teeth before she shot forward. Her foot seemed to pause for a moment before she sprung off the sand. Her knee met his palm when she aimed for his gut. With her other knee she did the same. Each time he pushed her leg back to the ground. Her arms moved in tandem with her legs but somehow, once he pushed her leg he blocked her punches with his arms. A frustrated yell flew from her mouth as she continued to barrage him with punches and kicks that never hit their mark. When her fist nearly collided with his jaw again he grabbed her wrist and twisted. She yelped, bent her shoulder with the twist to keep it in its socket and she lifted her foot high. The sole of her boot connected with his diaphragm and she pushed him away.

"Distance is your best friend, Farren," Argen informed her, his arms still raised in front of his face.

Farren panted, hands on her knees. "I thought you were my best friend."

He let out a chuckle before his arm curved and aimed for her temple. She dodged but only so that his fist grazed the tip of her nose instead. "If I grab your wrist," he did, "and twist, I want you to move with it and either side-kick me, or push me away with the sole of your foot. Okay?"

Farren nodded. As much as she teased Argen, she trusted his words and his experience just like she trusted herself. They practice those two moves over and over until they were engrained in her mind. When he stumbled back, hands raised, she did not give him time to grab her again because she ducked under his outstretched arm and wrapped both her arms around his waist and lifted with her knees. He did not budge so she tried again. A loud laugh rang through the room and his body shook above her. With a huff she released him and ran her tongue over her teeth.

"It's not funny! I've seen Enrys do the same to you." If Argen squinted he could almost see the pout on her lips.

After his laughter died down to the occasional snort. "You have seen Enrys do something similar." He snorted again and she narrowed her eyes. "Your arms were in the wrong place. Here, let me show you."

Farren ran head first toward the hulking Kayei, ducked under the arms that threatened to stop her and dug her head into his side. She curled her arms under his backside, bent her legs, and lifted. Despite the size and weight difference, Killian's feet lifted from the floor and she used her head and shoulders to follow the momentum. Gasps filled the arena when she let go and he thudded down. There was no spare second for her to bask in the success until he stood back up, so she jogged back a few paces. Distance was her best friend.

"Good," Killian grunted.

"I'm glad you approve," she sarcastically commented as her hands were braced in front of her face. Her body still ached and her feet started to rub painfully in her boots but she moved with a grace she thought impossible after her encounter with Amelie. She was quickly brought back to reality as the bright lines of light appeared on her body once again. Killian moved around her so she guarded her ribs and manoeuvred away from the swift kick to her thigh. However, that left her ankle open for him to stamp down upon. As she watched his foot descend upon her, the world seemed to flow in slow motion, and her eyes widened. The sand which fell from his boot did so slowly, so that she saw each grain individually fall onto the red leather of her own shoes. It gave her time to move and scramble on all fours then to her feet. By the time Killian's foot hit the ground she was stood in front him. Her chest rose and fell in rapid breaths and her brow was furrowed. Someone in her peripheral vision stood up, but she kept her eyes on her opponent. Crescent indents formed in her palm where she clenched her fists and tried to comprehend what transpired. Killian was equally as confused as he looked slowly from his boot to her face. With a click of his neck he brought down punches. Then a sadistic smile stretched his face.

"You can use magic, Malumrem?"

Farren's eye twitched at the name but she shook her head. "I don't think that was me."

That only made his smile grow. "What can you do?"

She cast her eyes to the necklaces beneath her corset, clasped them around her neck, and smirked up at Killian. Instantly, a glow of red and green eddied from her chest. It illuminated the underside of her chin, turning her smirk demonic. Killian curled his fists with unadulterated excitement in his eyes. Farren was suddenly struck with an overbearing throb of power. It coursed through her veins, suffocated her senses as she became nothing and everything at once. The magic tickled across her skin and nerves until it settled in her muscles. Every movement was like gliding through water and breathing in pure oxygen. She unfurled her fingers and held them in front of her. A laugh of disbelief sputtered from her and she locked her eyes with Killian's. A vibrant blue encased her irises; an ethereal glow radiated from them. "Let's find out," she said around another chuckle of disbelief.

That brought forth another rally of motion. With her new-found speed she dodged every punch he threw at her despite the slight falter of her body at the change in tempo. There was no more nose grazing, cheek hits or kicks to the side of her thigh. Instead she moved like lightning, sharp and dangerous. They fought like that for what seemed like half an hour, possibly more. It was like a dance, one that Farren was desperate to complete. She kicked him, then she swiped at him, then one of her punches knocked two of his teeth loose. A mild roar of elation came from the crowd when they spied the white teeth spat on the ground. That made her pause and she stared at her curled fist. *Mistake*. He tackled her just as she did him; that time his body followed hers so that his knees slammed to the ground either side of her. The large muscles of his thighs squeezed her hips and she felt the bones groan under their strength. One of her wrists was pinned to the side but she flexed her fingers to ensure blood still flowed to the appendage.

"Farren!" Her name was screamed from the stands, Rorke's bellow loud in her ears. "Farren damn it stand up!" He was jostled back into his seat and forcefully restrained.

The light of Killian's magic appeared but it circled her neck and that was where his eyes narrowed in. His hand followed suit. With the same speed she possessed, his hand wrapped around her throat and squeezed. She arched her back and lifted her hips in a meagre attempt to throw him off balance. He continued to sadistically smile and pressed her wrist further into the sand. Strands of her wet hair clung to the grains beneath her and collected in matted clusters. She stared at her free hand, mustered all of her acquired strength and pushed against his chest. He budged but then settled back onto her hips where she rasped out a cry.

"This is where you die, Malumrem. You were a worthy opponent." Farren didn't acknowledge him. Her hips bucked again but the sheer weight of him held her to the ground. Her windpipe was going to be dust, the sides of her throat were bruised badly and flesh was pinched between his fingers. The hand she used to push him away clawed down his chest and pushed up on his jaw. Red lined his skin and she even drew some blood, but he did. Not. Move.

The punch she threw next was awkward due to the angle but it hit his cheek, so blood pooled in his mouth and covered the inside of his lips. He swallowed the taste and pushed her further into the floor. The glow of her eyes remained but tears lined them and the lungs in her chest burned. Pressure unlike any other started to build in her head and chest like a dam about to burst. *You aren't going to win against my other man.* If she had room to think, she would have sneered at the voice in her head; instead she was only focused on the darkness that slid into her vision, the way the inside of her throat practically rubbed against the opposite side.

A sickening laugh floated around her and she realised it wasn't the man above her. The figure that stood up previously –Schylus- watched with glee as she struggled for breath. He was a tall blur but his long hair ebbed in and out of focus as she tried to look at him. Nero sat with his arms folded across his chest, head tilted to the side and pursed his lips. No-doubt boredom shone in his eyes. Cyrille's hand covered her mouth and tears ran freely down her face for a woman she hated, but her movements, Schylus' gleeful smile, they were sluggish. Once again her mind was murky and without oxygen. The crowd of people was silent, some shocked, some happy, others simply intrigued by the Malumrem getting beaten- *killed.* After a painful attempt of an intake of breath, her eyes weighed heavy and each blink was slower than the last.

A flash of striking orange caught her eye and Farren's world stopped. Soter paused at the top of the stairs, lowered his head in acknowledgement and disappeared out of view. She opened her mouth to call for him, a rasp or any sound, but nobody turned in his direction or noted his movements. It made her question if he was even there. There was no more room for thoughts as the world blurred and the glow of her eyes stuttered like a dying flame.

"Stay awake," a voice reached out to her. It was in her head or maybe it only felt like it was. The stamina from the necklace Soter gave her pushed forward but that only meant the pressure in her head was clearer, the pain around her neck was more prominent, and the rough sand was felt on the skin of her thighs. The necklace prolonged death. The tears ran down her face and fell onto Killian's fingers which only aided in making the world more blurry. "You can do this, get your ass up," that voice spoke again.

Farren sobbed and choked on her words, "I ca-can't."

"Bullshit, fight."

Was it Rorke, Soter, or Argen's old words that came back to haunt her? Whoever it was only brought more tears to her eyes. She had been certain, so certain that she bet her life on it, that she, Rorke and Cyrille would make it out of the Kayei Realm alive. But there she laid, the air no longer reached her lungs and the world tilted at an odd angle. The hand that pressed against Killian's torso fell to the sand, her fingers curled and filthy. A long streak of sand sat on the inside of her forearm, but next to that streak were droplets of water. They were small but they were there. The lack of oxygen made her delirious because parts of the Oracle's test rang through her mind:

"Hello? Mystical voice, are you there?" The silence reigned. "Can we talk about this?" There was a thick pause. "If not can you at least give me an idea what my test is because for Griselda's sake this is just water!"

Water trickled through her upheld glove for emphasis but her hand splashed into the liquid as the voice replied, "just water?"

One last chance- A sharp panic shot through her chest as her eyelids closed for a lengthy amount of time. Then she focused on those droplets. She didn't care that Schylus was there or Cyrille, or Rorke who she knew would be sick at the sight of magic on her skin. Normally, she would have swallowed but Killian pressed just that bit harder and she focused. Each droplet trembled on her arm, and she became aware of the water in her hair and on her other arm, and even the water that clung to the inside of her corset. Like an earthquake, the droplets shook, but then they rose from her skin, from her dress and levitated above her. Schylus leaned further over the ledge with the breath caught in his throat. Every little distraction made the droplets drop a centimetre or two until she focused on them again. Yet, her vision was almost gone, her head felt like it would explode, and her muscles were tired, so, so tired. Then she caught sight of Rorke as he ripped away from the guards and fought his way to where Schylus stood. Her eyelids fluttered and Killian squeezed. Then she looked at her hand and curled it into a fist. The water shot forward, the liquid quick enough to pierce skin.

Then her body arched off the sand with her eyes wide and aglow.

And she took in oxygen.

"Did anybody see what just happened!?" Schylus was frantic as he leaned further forward.

A chorus of 'what do you mean?' and 'water' swirled around the arena. Farren glanced to where her opponent gripped his chest. Killian groaned from where the water pierced him and blood seeped from certain spots on his body, but not each droplet was strong enough, just as she wasn't. Deep lung-fulls of air became her priority as she rubbed a hand across her bruised neck. The roar of the arena stand entered her ears and the pressure in her head made way for a headache from hell. The next obstacle was to get her limbs to move. The heavy feeling she felt at the beginning of the fight hit her full force but with the Kayei strength that continued to thrum in her veins, she staggered to her feet. Killian opened his mouth to speak but she was in front of him, her fist against his throat. He coughed before she kicked him in the genitals. The large man doubled over, blood spat to the ground but he rammed against her as she went to knock the side of his leg. Ragged breaths flew from both of them and the sound of her heart pounded between Farren's ears.

Yells erupted from them. Bruises bloomed across both their bodies and blood covered their faces. Whose blood it belonged to, they didn't notice. They were like two wild animals grappling for their lives. More breaks were given to the other as they huffed and puffed. An unpleasant metallic taste filled Farren's mouth and the room swayed beneath her feet.

"Just end it!" a Kayei heckled from their seat.

Killian and Farren locked eyes and he nodded. They shot toward each other with speed. The bones in her forearms creaked as his fist collided with it. They each spat blood to the floor and fought off the urge to throw up. The light from his power shone along her leg and chest where he slammed his palm. The muscle of her thigh balked under the blow and she fell to one knee. He stepped forward to aim for her sternum, but an immense pressure filled her, the limited liquid around them rose and the drops hit Killian in the chest. He stumbled back then grabbed his own throat. Her eyes were solely on him, the people around them blocked out. Killian's mouth ran dry and he coughed. Farren stood and hobbled back as the large man fell to his knees. The glow of her gaze and the slight lift to her hair were ignored, instead she furrowed her brow and clenched her hands at her side.

"How are you-?" Killian was cut off by a raspy cough. His fingernails clawed at his neck and he started to bleed, but he didn't stop, not as he gurgled on the liquid in his mouth, gasping for breath just as she had. He never begged her to stop, only his eyes were bloodshot as he looked at her. Then it was over; he fell forward, bloodied hands around his neck and eyes stuck wide open. His face hit the sand and caused a mound of it to land on his head.

Deafening silence covered the building, but after a minute of Farren's wide eyed stare, Nero stood up and cleared his throat, "the winner of the match, is Farren." It took a moment for his words to sink in but soon enough the crowd jeered. Money passed hands, some screamed expletives and others high-fived and hugged. Rorke slumped back in his chair, a sigh of relief fell from his lips. Schylus was stunned into silence with his body half-way over the railing. Cyrille reached for him but her other hand was on her mouth, the tear-tracks prominent on her face.

Farren stared at the dead body before her then at her hands. The metallic taste made way for bile as her limbs shook. The adrenaline began to wear off and her head still swam in a haze from the strangulation. Her wet eyes blinked down at herself as she replayed the match in her head. She knew she hit his throat but not to the extent that she ruptured his arteries. There was a vague recollection of moving water but none hit above the breast-bone. She stumbled backward only to hit a solid chest. She jumped out of her skin and spun around, the Kayei speed still in her veins. Mysie stood behind her with her arms folded and Farren squinted up at her with a tilt to her head. The action hurt more than she realised and she pressed a hand to the bruises on her neck. The blonde woman reached for her arm and Farren stepped back. Mysie did not try again but she made sure to keep her eyes on the victor. The chains hung limply in her grip.

"Settle down!" Schylus screamed at the crowd and they did as he commanded. "I told you all that one of these fighters not only fought for themselves, but for the person they loved. That fighter was our dear Malumrem, Farren." Shocked murmurs rippled through the Kayei. "It seems we all get a happy ending." Schylus looked Farren in the eye and ordered, "bring the soldier into the ring!" Rorke was pushed and shoved and manhandled, down a set of stairs, and brought to stand in the sandy circle. He struggled against each pull but his face was a mess, his hand still broken, and his shirt was torn in random places. Schylus departed from his position, but not before he clicked at Nero and pointed at Cyrille. If she had the energy, Farren would have rolled her eyes. Once Schylus was in the ring with them, he stood in front of Rorke and bent down to look into his eyes. A swift kick was delivered to the back of Rorke's knees. He cursed as he went down, his arms still held by the guards.

"What are you doing?" Farren asked, her voice rough in her ears.

Schylus grinned down at Rorke like he was about to devour him. The guards twisted his arms tighter behind him; if they pressed any harder both his shoulders would have dislocated but the human only glared hatefully up at the brunet. Farren took a step forward just as Schylus did, only to crash into a barrier. His laughter sounded in her ears just like before. The magic was numb beneath her skin as she pressed her palm flat against the invisible wall. Cyrille stood abruptly from her chair and pressed her chained hands to the ledge. Nero was at her side, a hand braced on her shoulder.

"I have been waiting a long time to do what I'm about to." Schylus' hand slid toward Rorke.

Farren swallowed and pressed closer to the barrier, her gaze torn between Rorke and Nero who flicked his eyes to her in that moment. As gold clashed with blue she pushed every ounce of desperation and pleading into her eyes, but there was nothing; there was no light or flicker in the gold. Nero's mask remained intact, because he was simply bored with the game. With the smoothness of silk he moved his eyes from her to Rorke to Schylus where they remained. Instead of focusing her efforts on a Kayei who wouldn't help, she slammed against the barrier. It shuddered against her fist. One more obstacle for her to defeat before she could go back to Altin. Her eyes drifted toward her legs: speed, maybe she could destroy the barrier with sheer force. An hour, that was what Soter told her, that was how long the magic lived in her system before burnout. So, she took a few steps back, bent her knees and ran full force into the barrier. Her injured leg barked under the movement but the slam of her body covered the slap of Schylus' hand on Rorke's face. It started as slaps but then he curled his fists and rained them down on Rorke's already bruised skin. Soon enough he switched to his polished shoes and pushed Rorke against the floor like a roach beneath a boot. The guards released his arms and stepped back, hands folded behind their backs. *Obedient servants*. The crunch of bones met her ears.

"Schylus you prick!" Farren screamed. "We had a deal! I won your tournament, I entertained your guests!" She sneered up at the masses of people "You said, Cyrille, Rorke and I would be allowed to leave, that we would not be killed!"

"Do not," Schylus snarled, "disrespect me. The deal was to allow you, Cyrille and Rorke to escape Kavan. Nobody from my castle will chase you. I never said I would not rough him up a little bit."

"You slimy-"

"Careful," he warned her, "or I will turn my attention on you."

"You sure you want to fight a Malumrem, Schylus?" He stepped toward her, teeth bared, but Rorke ground out his name. "Rorke, please." She didn't know what she pleaded him for.

The angry look on Schylus' face morphed into something sadistic. He kicked Rorke in the side with all of his force. Ribs snapped beneath his shoe. Farren slammed against the barrier again, her eyes fixed on Rorke's bleeding body. His eyes were already on her, the green bright against his dark hair which was plastered across his face. His arm stretched toward her as though he would hold her hand through the horror that played before her. Then she was crying, hot tears streamed down her face and a broken sob spilled from her chest. Rorke coughed out her name, blood spilled from his open mouth but he kept his eyes on her. The pain in that one word –the name he whispered in the middle of the night- made her heart break in two.

So she started to beg.

Farren begged to be by Rorke's side; she begged for Schylus to lower the barrier. When he laughed for the umpteenth time she dipped her head, then with a broken look on her face she looked back at Nero and she begged once more: she begged for him to move, to do something instead of sitting there, she begged him not to let a decent man die. An inhuman scream was aimed at him as Nero simply stared at Rorke, and she pounded against the barrier. For a split second she thought he would do something but he only stared, a slight bob to his throat. And she hated him for it. She wanted him dead, she wished she killed him when she had the chance, wish she had been strong enough to slit his throat and move on. When he looked back, her face full of fury she knew he read it all on her.

That fury turned to shock as the barrier fell and Schylus stood back from Rorke's broken body.

There was no-doubt that Schylus had only been startled one or two moments in his life, but the way his mouth slightly gaped brought a sick sense of satisfaction to her chest. It told her one thing: he was not the one to release the barrier; someone broke it, but she didn't care who, all she cared about was scrambling to Rorke's side. Sand flew everywhere as her knees slammed down and hands ghosted over his face and chest. The heat of his palm caressed her cheek which brought a watery smile to her face as he stared up at her. Blood fell onto her dress as he coughed. Neither of them cared. No words were exchanged and she kissed the back of his hand over and over. Rorke's breathing was too slow, his torso was twisted in odd angles and his face bled. The lashes of his eyes fluttered open and closed so she called his name, kissed his hand again, and then his lips gently as she cried. Everything in her honed in on the shallow breaths against her lips; he kissed her back, the taste of his blood and their tears mingled together.

"Farren," it was a prayer on his lips. It was all he could say because in truth he was afraid. He was afraid that if he didn't cling to her as tightly as possible he would die. It would not be the broken bones or destroyed organs but the fading of her warmth that would kill him. They had so much left to do together: he wanted to tell her about his battles, show her the home he grew up in, wanted her to meet his mother and talk her ear off; he wanted to listen to her talk about missions and life and he wanted her to call out his name in happiness and pleasure. Loving Farren would have been his future.

Yet, he leaned his head backwards, his hand slack in hers and he stopped breathing. *Rorke stopped breathing.* Low mutters engulfed the arena, Farren's tears were hot against her face but no sound escaped as she stared at his body. Warmth still covered her lips from where he kissed her. It was funny what a person remembers after they watched someone die. It's especially odd when that person had only been a part of their life for a short period. Farren remembered the way he looked first thing on a morning, his shoulders stooped and face in his porridge; she remembered how gentle he was with her wound despite the grunts of irritation. What she remembered the most was the way he looked at her, how he trusted her. She never thought of his life as a King's Guard or what he left behind, she just thought of *him*.

"Well, that is that," the silence was broken by Schylus.

Farren kissed Rorke's palm before she laid it gently on his chest, "goodbye, Rorke." His eyes were closed as she brushed a finger down his face, let a broken sob escape her, then she stood.

Mysie, who watched the entire ordeal unfold, moved toward the back of the ring. The aura surrounding the dark-haired woman changed and there was something about it that sent shivers down her spine, and brought something she supposed was fear, into her bones. When Farren moved, she took the opportunity to leave, chains in her hands and back to Schylus, even as Farren walked over to one of the guards who originally held him. They kept their hands behind their back and even flinched slightly as she gripped the hilt of one of their swords to unsheathe it. It seemed they were just as afraid.

"What do you think you are doing?" Schylus asked with a sigh.

"You think this is over?" Her smile was lethal when she turned to face him, nothing kind nor human beneath it.

The sword twisted in her hand once, twice, and she sprung forward like a jungle cat. Screeches came from the crowd above and chaos ensued. They started to run to every available exit. The only two who remained still were Nero and Cyrille. Farren didn't look over at them, not as Nero watched her, not as Cyrille cried for Rorke. Every move Adrastos and Argen taught her came to life: a swooping swipe, a sharp stab toward the jugular, the uppercut of the blade. Her speed mixed with her training made for an unhappy Schylus but he dodged each one. The fight from before weighed on her, but she left no opening for his attacks. She was too fast, too precise, so much so that his magic stuttered as he tried to fight back; he barely touched her. Each time she aimed for vital organs he defended them. Scratches and bruises on his body faded as quickly as they happened.

"What stolen magic have you used?" He growled.

"Scared?" As soon as the word left her mouth her movements slowed, the magic faded but Farren did not stop. Jabs and swipes at Schylus ached her arm and one of his blocks snapped the blade so that it looked like a jagged dagger. The Kayei who ran screamed at him to fight back as she jabbed at him again.

Suddenly, his back was against the wall. Her movements pushed him beneath the ledge he once sat behind just as Rorke's advancements pushed her against the tree in the Aureum forest. It was a poor place to be in a fight. With his hands held at his sides she pointed the blade at his throat. All the while tears continued to run down her face. *Hooded eyes stared up at her body which loomed over his. Her foot was pressed between his legs as she knelt on the other. She straddled his thigh as she angled the blade closer to his jaw.* Her teeth grit, it was different, because that was Rorke's blood on her dress, his life gone, and it was Schylus' smug, manic face that stared at her.

"You should have kept to your end of the deal, Schylus."

"I upheld my bargain you bitch." His laugh was crazy. "I will allow the three of you to leave Kavan, Rorke was the one who died from his injuries."

"You killed him," her voice slipped into a growl.

"My hand was not on him when his heart stopped."

"That statement is bull and you know it."

"There is no court of law here to judge that." He leaned his head back for emphasis.

Farren slipped the blade along the side of his neck like a soft caress. "Lucky me."

The Kayei in front of her sighed with a raised brow. The glow of her eyes seemed to flare and she teetered on the edge like one breath would send her over. The once frustrated look in his stare faded when she paused, blade at his throat. He'd known about her inability to kill Nero, she supposed he thought it would be the same. All she had to do was plunge the knife into-

"Nero," Schylus drawled, "dispose of Rorkey-boy's body."

Nero tugged on his jacket and rolled his eyes. "It will ruin my suit."

Schylus scowled. "I will buy you a new suit, just get it done."

Farren's eyes moved to where Rorke's body laid bloodied and beaten. Nero shifted around the side of the wall and down the stairs onto the ground. He screwed his nose up as his shoes hit the sand. Nero or Schylus, she had to choose, who would she plunge her knife into. *Rorke is already dead,* but then she thought of all the horrible things magic users could do with a corpse and her limbs interlocked. Then a flash of orange entered her vision and she knew he wasn't a figment of her imagination. Soter ran into the arena, his still blood-stained clothes billowed around him. He braced a hand on Nero's chest, a decorated knife against his jugular. Soter flicked his gaze to her and gave her a short nod. He would hold off Nero whilst she did what she had to.

The red of Schylus' eyes darkened as realisation shuttered across his face, "I know y-" He made to move but Cyrille's small hands grabbed the sides of his head. With his good hand he gripped Cyrille's wrist tightly but with the Kayei steadied, Farren took the opportunity to plunge the knife into his throat. Hard. An uncontrollable yell ripped from her. Blood poured onto her hand, down her sleeves, onto the skirts and bodice of her dress. Without hesitation she used every ounce of strength she had to pull down. His chest cavity opened like she was gutting a pig whilst his hands wrapped around her wrists in a feeble attempt to stop her. Blood and guts spilled to the floor and the arena was covered in the smell of it. The shock in his eyes remained until it faded to nothing. No arrogance, no mania, no sneer, no life.

Cyrille removed her hands to throw up behind the ledge. The sound of her wretches were ignored as Farren removed the broken blade and flicked blood to the sand. She took a deep breath and turned her glassy eyes to Nero. His mouth was parted and his eyes were wide as they locked with hers –the first true emotion she saw on his face- but then he vanished into smoke. *Coward.* The magic in her veins finally simmered to nothing which left something hollow and dark behind. The frantic guests stopped and looked down at the blood-covered woman then at their Ruler whose body slumped to the floor with his arms at his side like a puppet. Once she was satisfied with her work she looked up at the crowd. She must have been a sight: jagged blade, dark bruises around her neck and tears on her cheeks. However, that did not deter two guards –one of whom lost their sword at her hand- from rushing at Princess Cyrille in a final attempt to honour their boss. They hauled her from the floor, her screams loud enough to rattle Farren's ears, and dragged her up the large flight of stairs between the seats.

"No!" On unstable legs she stumbled toward the stairs but then she looked back at Soter.

"I will guard his body," Soter told her as he stepped in front of Rorke.

She swallowed. "Thank you."

The crowd of people practically threw themselves from her path as she followed the guards. They weaved in and out of the guests until they disappeared around a corner. Without the Kayei speed she struggled to keep her eyes on the target but the building was built purely circular so there were limited avenues the guards could take, until they reached the exit. She shook her head and pumped her legs faster.

"Farren!" The Princess' scream echoed off the walls.

"Cyrille!" She called back and swerved around a corner.

But they were gone, the guards and Cyrille were nowhere to be seen.

The cold no longer registered on Farren's skin and the water in her clothes and hair no longer plastered them to her body. She marched up the same hill she was escorted down and held the broken sword close to her chest. Every face she walked past was glanced at but nobody made a move against her. It made the walk to the castle uneventful. What made her brow lift in contemplation was that no guards stood by the iron gate, so she stepped through, braced herself for the sharp pressure against her lungs that never came and stormed up the garden path.

"You are stronger than I thought," a woman said. Like a guard-dog the Head stood in the castle doorway. Her arms were crossed over her chest, eyes narrowed. No weapon sat on her person and she seemed to be the only one at the entrance.

"Did a couple of guards and a Princess walk past here?" Farren craned her neck to look beyond the woman.

The Head shook her head, "I would not tell you even if they had," and looked her up and down. "That is a lot of blood on you."

Farren bared her teeth. "Thanks, it's Schylus'."

404

That made the Head pause. "Pardon?"

"Schylus is dead." Farren slipped her eyes back to hers.

The servant looked Farren over from head to toe and back again. The tear streaks, the blood, the broken sword all painted a picture. One that made her lunge. Farren cursed and dodged the woman's grip. She slipped her feet into a defensive position and hit her shoulder with the hilt of the sword. She went down with a thud but stood moments later. "You have no idea what you have done!" The Head clawed at Farren's face but she ducked under each swipe.

"I killed a tyrant, a murderer."

"He protected us, our families, you idiotic girl!"

Farren kept her body steady as she evaded each hit. "I don't want to kill you too." After one of the Head's nails scratched her face she added, "but I will if I have to." The words tasted like sewage in her mouth, but she needed to find Cyrille; she needed to get Rorke and Soter out of Kavan, out of the Kayei Realm. The Head did not stop her onslaught so Farren counted the beats of her heart and dove forward with her blade. Metal met flesh as she plunged the jagged edge into her stomach. Bile and the taste of blood filled Farren's mouth but she watched as the older woman spluttered and choked then fell onto the floor. That was where Farren left her.

The castle was just as before: black and red and empty. There were a few sounds deep within the structure but no way to find from which direction so she aimlessly walked, a deep limp in her step and ragged breaths shuttered from her chest and scratched her throat. The blade in her hand weighed heavy but she kept it in front of her. For what felt like hours but in reality were only minutes, Farren creaked open the door to the room with the grate and the chains. The two guards struggled to chain a wild Cyrille to the wall. Farren had not known that the Princess had such a fight in her.

"How much do you think we can get?" One of the guards whispered.

"Thirty thousand at least, we might have to rough her up a bit, so twenty?" The other replied as Cyrille struggled against them.

Ransom money, it was not loyalty or fulfilling their master's wish, the guards simply wanted to use Cyrille. She did not have the luxury of dwelling on it as she blasted forward. The first guard went down easily, the sheer surprise of her entry enough to throw him off. The other pushed Cyrille harshly into the wall and turned on Farren. She braced her weapon in front of her but he never made it to her person. A bright light that forced her to duck into her shoulder squeeze her eyes shut, filled the room. Her eyelids turned red and then ebbed away to the normal lighting. Farren blinked away the change in light. The first thing she saw was the guard on the floor, his eyes burned out of their sockets and a soft whimpering sound that came from his throat. Then she trailed her eyes up to Cyrille who stood against the wall with one arm outstretched. Long breaths lifted her chest and her limbs shook. Slowly, she lowered her arm and looked at Farren. "What did I do?" She asked.

It took Farren a moment to respond then she carefully grabbed her hand and tugged her away from the guard. "You saved my life. We can deal with the specifics later I promise, but just, we have to go."

"I burned him."

"No, no, you aren't Nero, you didn't burn anyone. You technically blinded him." When Cyrille sniffled behind her she added, "but it's fine. We wouldn't have made it out otherwise." Cyrille nodded as she dragged her down the corridor. "We need to get back to the arena okay? Then Soter will get us out of here."

"Wait!" Cyrille tugged back. "Where are we going to go?"

Farren's step faltered as she thought about it. "I have a friend outside of this Kingdom that can house us before we get to the Veil. Hopefully he will let us in."

"Hopefully?" She snapped.

"Do you have any better ideas?"

"Schylus is *dead*," she choked on the word, "we are now safe here."

Farren stopped, her hand tight around Cyrille's. "You cannot be serious? You want to stay in Kavan? I killed their Ruler, Cyrille, and you helped! We will be hunted down and killed which is the only ending if we stay here."

"But I made allies-"

"Who? Where are they? Because I would very much like to meet them right about now."

Cyrille pouted. "There is no need to be so rude about everything."

Farren blinked. "Yes, Your Highness, I'm sorry, when I'm running for my life I should remember my manners I do apologise."

Cyrille huffed, rolled her eyes, and Farren pulled her back onto the path to the garden. There were no more obstacles between them and the castle exit. Just like when she and Rorke entered the gardens, she did not take the time to appreciate the environment. They half jogged, half stumbled out of the gate, down the street and back to the arena. Everything went by in a blur and before her brain caught up with her body, Farren was stood in the sandy circle, hand in Cyrille's. Rorke's lifeless body was at Soter's feet. There were one or two Kayei left in the stands but they mainly kept their focus on Schylus, paying their respects or some such malarkey. The corpse against the wall was practically unrecognisable save for the crown that fell from his head and rolled into the blood. Farren merely flicked her gaze to the dead Ruler and automatically her lip lifted in a sneer. The smell of puke and blood hit her in the face the moment she took a step toward Soter.

"Are you ready?" He asked and Farren nodded. Cyrille's hand tightened around hers and she squeezed back if only to make sure the Princess did not run from her grip. Farren handed Cyrille to Soter like a gift and the green-eyed man made sure to keep his grasp on her. Cyrille opened her mouth to object, but it faltered as Farren fell to her knees beside Rorke. All of her fight was gone, the energy sucked from her as she placed her forehead on his chest. More blood soaked into her hair but she ignored it as she tried to soak in what was left of his scent. When a set of feet moved forward her head sprung up and something primal stared back at Soter: wide-eyed and hands tight around Rorke's arm, a lioness prepared to protect her own.

"Farren we should go," Soter whispered, "I can take you and Cyrille to Ja-"

"I will not *leave* him in this hellhole!" She nearly bit at him the moment he suggested it.

With a curt nod, more for himself than anyone else, he lowered his free hand toward her. Instead of her own hand, she placed Rorke's in his and stood by herself. Whilst Soter hefted Rorke over his shoulders, Farren slipped her hand in Cyrille's and the Princess held on for dear life, her eyes screwed tightly shut. A swirling portal of magic appeared in the centre of the sandy ring. Soter's eyes were aglow when they landed on the new opening. They all shifted toward the portal but that time it was him who paused. With his eyes on the remaining nobles, he spoke, "you should tell the world the story of the woman who saved Kavan and who finally put Schylus in his place. She deserves to be recognised for her strength and her sacrifices. It is a story that needs to be told."

Because they would remember her whether they wanted to or not.

With a sharp look, Soter stepped through the portal.

The rust-coloured leaves of the Aureum territory brought a weary sort of pain to Farren's heart but with each breath she felt like she had a new pair of lungs. The Golden Harvest was over, so traipsing through the forest was less dangerous. That did not stop the muscles in her back from being tense, shoulders hunched ready to fight. The broken sword she used against Schylus had not fallen from her grip. They landed just inside Aureum which meant another day of travel, possibly more. Once Soter opened the portal and they all stepped through, Cyrille threw up nothing but bile against a tree, her hand still in Farren's.

"I can transport us again after some rest," Soter informed her.

So they set up camp. Luckily, the Magician packed his own provisions with some to spare. It was those provisions that he dug through. Cyrille was released from Farren's grip once he placed a warning barrier around their small camp because nobody would get in or out without Soter's permission; that knowledge made Farren's shoulders relax a little. The Princess spent her time sat against a tree, her arms wrapped around her knees, eyes on Rorke's dead body against the opposite foliage.

Once Soter found what he looked for –a skein of water- he offered it to Farren who sipped around the bruising and cuts on her lips, then he took a swig. The Princess refused his offer and sunk further into herself. Farren looked between the two and crouched to make a fire ring. The air was chilled but whether it was the atmosphere or the come-down from the magic, Farren shivered then winced as her muscles spasmed.

"Do you want me to heal you? It will not be a full recovery but it will take away the more severe injuries," Soter asked.

Farren swallowed back a chuckle. "I feel like you are always saving me."

Soter held his hand out to her which she took with a heavy grip. "It's my pleasure to do it, but you are not a woman who often needs saving."

She bit the inside of her cheek. "Something happened, twice I think, that helped me survive and I'm not sure it was all me."

"The water droplets?" Soter sat her on a mossy rock.

"No," she said too quickly, "no not them." She shook her head. "Time slowed, or I mean, it seemed to slow. There was a moment where he nearly broke my ankle but I was able to move it before he did."

"You were imagining things," Cyrille piped up. "Killian stumbled before he aimed for your foot; that is why you were able to get away."

Farren sluggishly rolled her eyes whilst Soter traced his hands over her face then moved down to her neck where he paused. Sadness flickered across his eyes. "May I?" He gestured toward her and she tilted her head gently in answer. The inside of her throat burned like a pulled muscle but soon ebbed back into an uncomfortable bruise. The dark fingerprints on each side remained, a stark reminder of what happened. She was glad for no mirrors.

"Can I ask?" She shifted on the rock and he stopped his movements to look at her face. "You are Kayei but you have done nothing but help me, heal me." He smiled softly and she continued, "why bother? Even when you knew what my mission was, you came and-" She gestured generally to his person.

He slipped a chuckle. "Your time in this Realm has been terrible, but I promise you Farren, not all Kayei think so ill of humans or Mal-"

"Please," she sighed, "please don't call me that."

He brushed a strand of sandy hair from her face. "Alright. Do you have any other injuries you need me to heal?" She gingerly prodded against her ribs and his hand followed hers.

"Is this your power then, healing?"

"Sort of. I learned about medicine and potions as a child but I do not have the power to mend a wound back together."

"You could definitely make a career as a Healer." But she paused with her hand over her corset, like she remembered something important. She dug beneath the fabric and tugged on a sharp corner. Between her fingers sat a sodden letter –Nero's letter- and with delicate fingers she opened the square. The ink ran in every direction, the words no longer legible. The King's seal was the only recognisable feature.

"Where did that come from?" Soter enquired.

"I found it in a secret passageway, would you believe. It was addressed to Nero talking about his duties and how he needed to do better, I can't really remember now. That was why I kept the letter, the King's seal was stamped on each one."

"There was more than one?" Both his brows rose and she nodded.

Whilst Farren stared dejectedly at the parchment Soter stood. He offered to gather firewood and ventured into the patch of trees behind them. A sigh that shook her soul sounded from her. She flexed her fingers in front of her face and found they no longer shook but once she focused on her hand, her eyes slipped from the blood coated skin to the stained sleeves and skirts of her dress. *There was so. Much. Blood.* The way it gushed from Schylus' neck like she popped the cork of a fizzy wine bottle or opened a dam, caused the majority of it to fall onto her. It mixed with Killian's, her own, Rorke's.

"Is any of it yours?" Cyrille's voice made Farren jump.

"Some, not a lot. Most of my injuries were bruises and ruptured muscles." She looked up at the Princess whose sideward gaze was on her. "I wasn't sure I'd be able to go through with it, the kill I mean." She casted her eyes to Rorke's body. "But I saw the life leave his eyes and I was an entirely different person."

Cyrille blinked slowly. "He was why I helped you. I never thought Schylus would renege on a deal in such a way."

"Yes, well, he doesn't have that luxury anymore."

Cyrille shot to her feet and Farren did also. "You callous-" Farren took a step back and curled her fists. The blood roiled in her veins at the prospect of another fight but before Cyrille launched herself at the dark-haired woman, Soter dropped the large pile of wood in his arms and sat the Princess down on the grass. With her dress tucked beneath her and her glare on Farren, she looked like someone whose peaceful lunch had been interrupted, not a prisoner who had been freed from her abuser. Instead of explaining such a thing, how heinous and horrendous the things Schylus made them endure was, how Cyrille deserved a life without him, Farren kept her mouth shut and sat down on her rock.

Farren watched Soter's every move, the delicate way he laid the logs down and piled them to build a fire, and the way he gave the two of them space. The moment the fire flared and the smoke hit her she felt her stomach churn. Her feet swiftly moved into the patch of trees where she proceeded to hurl up everything left in her stomach, so much so that she thought her stomach came with it. She sank to her knees with a broken breath: she was successful, she retrieved the Princess from the castle but at too high of a cost. Rorke was dead, Nero went missing and the people of Kavan were left without a leader. Farren felt her lip twitch at the thought of Schylus dead against the wall. He could no longer hurt anybody, she killed him... she killed him... *she killed him*. More bile rose and was deposited on the ground. Somehow it felt different from the Brentham guards; she killed those men out of self-defence, survival, but Schylus, she wanted him truly, fully, dead. The broken sound of a twig and she whirled around to where Soter offered her a rag, "killing him was a good thing." It was like he read her mind.

"That's not why I did it." She wiped her mouth with the rag.

"It does not matter why you did it, you should just know that the world is better off without him." A slow nod and she knew he was correct, but why did she feel so empty about it?

WHAT IT MEANS TO WIN

Everything was the same: the gardens, the golden palace, the gargoyles that guarded Janus' gardens. Not one thing changed since she and Rorke left his company. That acknowledgement made her roll her shoulders as she stepped from Soter's portal. Cyrille's hand was tight in hers as Farren dragged her forward on unsteady feet. The Princess sniffled every now-and-then, her tears kept at bay by the need for rest. There was no better person to ask that from, than Janus.

The gargoyles that stood proud next to his palace gates stared down at her, flared their eyes and settled back on their haunches. When the gate swung open, Farren was the first one through, followed by Cyrille and then Soter who carried Rorke's body on his shoulders. Farren previously offered to help carry him but the Magician insisted she focused on the Princess. The shock on Janus' face when they appeared in his gardens was ingrained in her mind for the rest of her life. It was like he saw a ghost stood between his flowers. He casted his eyes across Farren first. She was always covered in blood when she saw him, he might have thought she had a killing problem. Like a worried mother hen he rushed down the stairs and stood before her.

"Janus," Farren breathed, "it's good to see you."

"Likewise lass, I-" He shook his head. "I'm glad you're alive." He did not expect her to return as such.

"This is Cyrille." She pulled the Princess to her side. "Do you mind if we rest here for the night?"

He nodded. "Of course, of course. My servants have returned from the Golden Harvest so everything is in tip-top shape. Where is..." He trailed off as his eyes slid past the two females. Soter shuffled on his feet, the full

414

weight of Rorke on his back and Janus stumbled, his hand pressed to his chest.

The flames crackled loudly in the large fireplace. The servants fluttered about for a moment more before they left their master and his guest to their private conversation. Janus sat —as usual- with a glass of wine in his hand. His legs were stretched leisurely in front of him, the velvet seat his purchase. Rorke sipped on his own glass of alcohol with his back straight and eyes on the Kayei.

"Will you relax, Rorke, make yourself comfortable, please."

With a stiff nod he settled back into the couch cushions and took another sip. "Thank you for inviting me."

Janus grinned. "Of course! We are only a few days away from victory, we just need to hold our positions until Nero calls for us." Janus drastically craned his body over the lip of the couch to spy a clock. "Which should be any day now."

"Then you will have your masquerade ball?"Rorke asked.

"Yes and I hope you will attend?" He chuckled.

Rorke looked into his glass but nodded with a small smile on his face. Janus sat closer, his hand on the lower part of Rorke's thigh. A shiver ran up the soldier's spine and the light creeping of a blush adorned his neck and face. It had been two years of Janus being a flirt and Rorke had not rid himself of the fluttery feeling he got in his chest when the Kayei touched him, or spoke to him, or simply looked in his general direction. It made him want to roll his eyes. He was no longer a child: he knew what sex was, what a kiss was supposed to feel like, what his body craved from his friend, yet any time he wanted to tell him he froze. So, just as every other time, he swallowed the thick lump in his throat and smiled. "Yes that will be fun."

Janus stared into his eyes for what seemed like an eternity then cracked an award winning smile. "Yes I imagine it will be." He looked at Rorke from beneath his lashes. "Do you think we make good comrades Rorke?"

Like a startled deer he turned. "Yes." He cleared his throat. "You are one of the few friends I made in this Realm. You are nice."

Janus scoffed but moved forward, his hand just that bit higher on his thigh. "I'm 'nice'?" Rorke nodded. "Well thank you." A chuckle reverberated from his chest. "You are nice too and you have been a good friend to our little group."

A slow, almost absent nod from Rorke. "Good, but is that what we are?"

"Friends?" Janus drawled, "is that what you want us to be?"

It was an opening, an offer, something to give Rorke the confidence to finally speak his mind. "I want to be your friend," he swallowed, "I think that is what I want."

"Really?" Janus raised a brow and slid his hand back to its original position. That brought a panic to Rorke's chest. His heart stopped more times in Janus' presence than on the battlefield. "Then that is what we shall be!"

Rorke stuttered, "but, is that what you want?" Janus smirked around the rim of his glass. "You put your hand on my thigh, you ask me questions like that. I just thought-" Rorke's eyes went wide when Janus shuffled closer to him, the aforementioned hand on the inside of his thigh.

"I want to be your friend." The crack of Rorke's heart might as well have been audible. "I want to be the friend that you confide in. The one that you come home to and tell about your day. I want to be the friend that you let

416

into that thick skull of yours and you do so because you want to. I want to be the friend who makes you moan in bed, the friend you kiss deeply and passionately until there is nothing left but our," he choked on his smirk, "friendship."

The blush that originally crept up on Rorke hit him with full force. The white irises that stared back at him sparkled in the light and with mischief. Yet, there was a sincerity that wasn't there before, because what Rorke didn't realise was that Janus was serious about the soldier, serious about how he felt. That was why Rorke lunged and cupped his large hands against Janus' face for leverage. He did not pause before he pressed his lips against the Kayei's. Janus pulled his thigh closer so that he was flush against the soldier's chest. Their tongues played together slowly and his other hand grabbed Rorke's collar. The young man pressed further forward then they parted. Soft pants and pink faces sat between them.

Janus shook his head; that was not the memory he thought would surface if he found him dead. Nor did he expect not to cry because 'friends' was not what they had been. "It was Schylus he-" The Kayei held up a hand and Farren stopped.

"I don't need to know. Please, please come inside. I can place Rorke in your room if you would like?" He asked her and she nodded, though her eyes were firmly on the guard. "He will be safe in my care lass, I give you my word." The last time she trusted a Kayei's word, Rorke died. However, he was handed to two servants who seemed to appear out of nowhere. Farren lunged forward but Cyrille held her back along with Soter's arm that was braced in front of her. Her heart beat dangerously hard in her chest as she watched them haul Rorke's body away. Then Soter stepped forward so that he stood side-by-side with Farren and successfully blocked her view. Broken from her staring she gestured between the two Kayei in greeting. Her mouth opened to introduce them but Janus held out his hand, a look of awe on his face. "Soter," he breathed, his hand clasped tightly around his forearm, a comrades' greeting. "By the Goddess." The two embraced tightly when Soter smirked. "What are you doing here?"

"I was tasked with helping Farren return home."

Janus leaned back and glanced at the woman in statement, a slight 'o' to his mouth. "Really?" Soter nodded and flicked his eyes between Janus and Farren. "Well, now that you are here. Are you hungry?"

A trio of nods and they followed Janus into the heated palace; Farren took that moment to stare at the two Kayei. Shared looks danced between the two and she nearly asked how they knew each other but with the stench of blood in her nostrils she had bigger priorities. Once Farren was comfortably in the foyer she was attacked with licks and paws bigger that her head. She allowed the Night Creature to smother her in love even if her body protested at the assault, and she sunk to her haunches to gift it with belly rubs. Cyrille leapt back with a yelp and let go of Farren's hand. Soter kept close to her side, hands folded behind his back. "This is the Night Creature I told you about," Farren spoke over her shoulder, "it was the one who found its way into Brentham."

Soter tilted his head as he listened and held his hand out for the creature to lick. It sniffed tentatively then nuzzled against his palm. "He is very pretty." He smiled down at it. Farren watched them for another second before she turned her attention to the bustling palace in front of her. Janus' servants all wore white suits and dresses whilst they cleaned and carried miscellaneous items through the halls. She rose just as Janus called her from upstairs.

"Cyrille." The girl turned a furrowed face to her. "Stay with Soter, please. I need to wash all of this blood off of me. Unless you want to watch me bathe you can stay with him."

The Princess' limbs shook just as her head did. She removed her eyes from Farren and looked at Soter who raised a brow at the attention, then gifted her a charming smile. A curt nod and Farren removed herself to traipse upstairs. With each step she winced, the shooting pain in her leg enough to make her cry out. Janus met her on the top step and helped her hobble to the bathroom. It was perfectly clean, made of white porcelain with golden accents. He left her with a fluffy white towel which she held between them awkwardly.

"I have plenty more, don't worry about the blood stains."

"Thank you."

The door clicked shut behind him. She turned the shower knobs and hot water streamed from the curved head above her. Slowly and with sharp breaths, Farren removed the corset and then slipped the dress from her skin. She tugged at the places where blood stuck it to her skin. It slopped to the floor so she gingerly stepped out of it. The boots were next to go. Her gaze snagged on her reflection in the mirror above the sink: bloodshot eyes, dark purple fingerprints across her neck, matted hair, bruising on her side and across her thigh. Quickly, she turned from her reflection and gingerly moved into the shower. Hot water cascaded across her back and shoulders which she rolled under the steam. Sand and blood swirled at her feet and down the plughole. She let the water pound against her leg and back. The numb, emptiness from earlier that day started to creep up on her again so she ducked her head under the water and let the pressure pound on her head. A deep breath filled her lungs and she squeezed her eyes shut until she pushed the feeling further and further down.

An hour passed and she found fresh clothes on the padded chair in the bathroom. Janus found her a shirt and trousers that would loosely fit. The shirt

419

hung from her slim shoulders and the trousers needed to be tugged at constantly but they were clean and dry. Once she was fully dressed there was a knock on the door and a servant guided her down for dinner. With slothful feet she followed the servant into the dining room and sat in the chair next to Soter -who wore a new change of clothes- but despite the delicious food that was placed before her she poked and prodded it.

"Are you not hungry?" Soter tilted his head. She shrugged; a few mouthfuls were all she could stomach. Cyrille however ate her fill of potatoes but with the dainty nature she always did. Janus watched her with a glass of wine in his hand and a minor furrow to his brow. Water was all Farren drank to wash down the mouthfuls she managed. The inside of her throat was raw and she found herself pressing her fingers to either side every time she swallowed.

It wasn't until Soter and Cyrille's plates were clean that Janus asked, "what happened?"

Farren ran a finger around the rim of her glass. "You were right, it wasn't Nero who started all of this, it was Schylus." She nearly choked on his name as his wicked smile and long hair flashed in her mind. "Everything was fine, Rorke and I had been undetected and I found Cyrille in the dungeons. I was in the process of breaking her free when-" Farren suddenly stopped and glared at Cyrille. "When Cyrille screamed at the top of her lungs for Schylus to help her." The Princess avoided their hot gazes. "So Rorke and I were captured and kept in the castle. There were weird dinners and I had to fight my way through the castle."

"That could not have been easy," Janus commented.

She shrugged again, her finger stilled on her glass. "Even though I completed his stupid game, Schylus locked Rorke and I up until he thought of something better. That was when he came up with the fighting match."

420

Janus sat forward, forearms braced on the table. "He had Rorke fight a Kayei?"

She shook her head. "Not Rorke, no." Realisation hit his face like a carriage. "I was promised that if I won the fight Cyrille, Rorke and I would be allowed to escape Kavan and nobody would chase us." Janus' brows furrowed further. "But then Schylus attacked Rorke." Tears sprung to her eyes and she dipped her head. "And I tried to stop him but there was a barrier and," a deep swallow and she faltered on her words.

"And what of Schylus?"

"Dead," Soter answered for her, "she killed him."

Janus nodded. "Well, one less horrible person in this Realm I suppose." He turned to Soter. "Do we know who will rule Kavan in his place?"

"Surely Nero?" Cyrille said.

Janus blinked between her and Farren. "Nero was there also?"

"He was so deep in Schylus' pockets it was difficult to tell the difference between the two," Farren told him.

Soter stiffened beside her. "He disappeared after Schylus was killed." There was a long, knowing look shared between the Kayei. Telepathy or another form of understanding flittered between them.

Janus ran a hand through his hair and sighed, brought back to the conversation. "What is happening in this Realm?" He asked more to himself then, louder, he said, "I was under the assumption that Nero was working on his own, I never dreamed he would do another Kayei's bidding. "

"Working on his own to do what?" Soter sipped at his drink.

"Who knows, there was always a trick up that man's sleeve, even before the rebellion. He's the smartest one of us and he certainly liked to show that off. He likely wants to start another war and Schylus was his way of doing so." Janus' eyes twinkled when they locked with Soter's. "Because I am not certain that it was Schylus who pulled the strings in Kavan."

"Because Kavan is Nero's territory?" Farren interjected.

"No, Kavan has been one of the territories –cities- that has been passed between many Rulers. Ropik is Nero's territory and has been quiet for some time." He tapped his chin. "Although, now that there is no Ruler in Kavan I suspect Nero will make a bid for it, if he hasn't already."

She turned her attention to Soter. "Then why does the King of Altin think that Kavan is already Nero's?"

"I'm sorry but I do not know."

"My father's men are traitors, I would not be surprised if his scouts feed him false information as well," Cyrille added.

"What do you mean?"

"The men that took me," she reminded Farren, "they were my Father's men. They were the ones that handed me over to Schylus."

Farren held back her scoff. "You say his name with such disgust but a mere day ago you were pledging your undying love for him."

"Listen," Cyrille spat, "I cared about him for what he did for me, how he treated me when you and Rorke were not around. That does not excuse him for what he did to Rorke."

"Ah." Farren slowly leaned back in her chair. "So if Rorke was," she swallowed, "if he was here, you would still be fawning over Schylus?"

Cyrille stood abruptly. "I am getting very tired of you being bitter about my relationship with Schylus."

"That was not a relationship. You were his captive who he simply decided not to kill. Cyrille-"

"Princess Cyrille, if you please."

"Princess," Farren ground out because she still had to live in Altin. "Someone who cares for you would not have forced you to watch your old friend die, he would not have chained you in a dungeon or in a room with his prisoners, he would not have forced you to watch as Nero burned those guards alive. I am sorry, truly, but you need to let him go."

"I am going to have to, considering you killed him."

"Don't forget that you helped." They stared at each other for a beat then Cyrille sat back into her chair and took a large gulp of water. Silence reigned as servants cleared their plates and brought in an array of cheeses and nuts and fresh bread.

"How was the journey back from Kavan?" Janus asked after he swallowed a small chunk of cheese.

"A lot quicker than travelling to it, Soter helped us escape with a," Farren's brows furrowed and she looked at the red-head for confirmation.

"A portal. I used it to get the four of us out of the arena and into your forests."

"Steal that from Nero did you?" He smirked and leaned forward to explain, "when the rebellion started I gifted my leading comrades some portals. It's my speciality you see. It takes a lot of magical control to be able to use them, hence why the leaders were the only ones to have them." He smirked at Soter again. "And apparently so does Soter." The Magician had the decency to look sheepish as he slipped a nut into his mouth.

Their host clapped his hands loudly and a servant rushed in, hands folded in front of their apron. He ordered tea for the table then continued to eat.

"Will you not try and secure Kavan for yourself, Janus?" It was a risky question but one that snagged in Farren's mind.

"Goddess no." He looked up at his grand ceiling. "I have everything I need in Aureum. It is my home and my sanctuary. I would not want to leave my people stranded whilst I hunted for territories elsewhere. The Oracle would have my head!"

Her face paled at the mention of the ethereal woman. "Do I am really not looking forward to taking another test on the way back through."

Soter shook his head. "You will not have to. It is only those who wish to enter the Realm. Although she does like to change the rules from time-to-time. If you were a Kayei desperate to travel through she might have you take a test." He shrugged and ate another nut. "It will be safe for the two of you to cross."

With that said, the smell of fennel and lavender hit them as the tea arrived. It was easier to stomach than the food so Farren drank her fill. Soter kept to his own drink and Janus focused on the wine. It was just Farren and Cyrille who sipped on the hot liquid. The heat somewhat eased the ache in Farren's throat and warmed her chest. The day's activities caught up with both of them and each let out a loud yawn hidden behind their hands. They excused themselves from the table and Janus' servants lead them both to their respective rooms. They were adjacent to each other and an extremely large servant stood outside Cyrille's door.

Farren was in the same room Janus granted her the first time she stayed and it was just as clean. However, Rorke's body was nowhere to be found. She casted her eyes over the bed, the floor, she went so far as to check behind the curtains, but he was not in there. The sound of her heart thrummed in her ears and she felt it thud against her ribcage. She shot to the closed door and slammed it open with a force she did not mean to use. The guard outside Cyrille's room jumped in his skin and stared at her with wide eyes. She shook her head and shot back down the stairs. Her limbs were heavy but she forced them to move into the dining room where Soter and Janus remained. Both men looked at her owlishly as she panted against the doorframe, "where is he?"

"Who, lass?"

"Rorke! He was supposed to be placed in my room but he isn't there."

Janus' eyes softened. "There was a lot of blood on him so I asked my servants to wash him before they put him in your room." He quickly glanced at Soter whose eyes never left Farren. "But there is not a lot of room in there, and I cannot have you sleep next to a corpse." At the hopeless, desperate look in her eyes he sighed and added, "I can wrap him for you, and have him on the floor, if that is what you want?" She shook as she nodded, "Then that is what we will do."

The longer she stood in the doorway, the heavier her lids became. Suddenly, it took all of her energy to stay standing. Soter rose from his seat as she swayed. He looped his arm around her back and scooped her legs into his arms. "Why am I so tired?" She muttered into his neck.

"You have had a trying day, Farren," Soter replied.

"I can't sleep yet... Rorke..."

"He shall be in your room by the time you get there," Janus said as he clicked for his servant to do just that.

Lazily, she hung her arms over Soter's shoulders and breathed in his scent. She willed her eyes to open but they were heavier than any stone. The warmth of his body and the tea lead her into a forced slumber; she missed the way he held her tighter and whispered a quick 'sleep well' into her ear. Janus only watched over the rim of his glass, another bottle ready to be opened in front of him.

Farren awoke twenty-four hours later, her head light and limbs in working condition. Sunlight streamed between the curtains and formed shadows on the sheets. What she focused on was not the light or the comfortable bed; she watched the still body of her travel companion, of her lover as he laid wrapped in white silk like a decorative sword. His face was visible, the sharp nature of his jaw and his soft hair. The lump in her throat tightened as she scanned the deep bruises and cuts along his cheekbones and around his eyes. Her fingers glided softly down his grey face and trailed over the silk.

"I am so sorry, Rorke." Her lip quivered. "I should have killed Schylus before he touched you, better yet I should have," she swallowed as a couple of tears escaped, "I should have insisted I be the only person to go on this mission."

"... Not your fault, Farren." She whipped around to where the voice echoed. The curtains billowed on a phantom breeze and stood in the corner, next to the sink, against the wall was Rorke. He was clean, his hair perfectly styled, and he wore a white tunic tucked into charcoal trousers. His shoulder guard –the one with the King of Altin's emblem- sat proudly on his left arm. The green of his eyes were soft as he smiled at her. Farren's eyes had never been so wide and she braced her hands on the bed to push herself forward.

426

"Rorke?" She gasped.

That was when the door slammed open and rattled the sconces on the walls. Her heart skipped a beat and she turned her head to the servant. "I apologise for the intrusion, my lady, but she's gone."

Farren shook the haze from her mind. "Who is?"

"The Princess Cyrille."

Farren jumped out of bed, tied her hair behind her and followed the frantic servant from her room. Janus appeared a second later with more servants by his side while Soter exited Cyrille's room with a frown.

"Your Princess is missing?" A nod from both her and Soter. "How?"

"You tell me Janus, she slipped out of your palace under your guards."

"The only guard here is Pep." He gestured toward the Night Creature who was half-way up the stairs. Farren's eyes were ablaze as she stared down the owner of said palace. Soter placed a hand on her shoulder in what was supposed to be a comforting manner but she shook it off with a quick glance over her shoulder.

"Janus, may we search your grounds?" She kept her voice level as she stared at the golden-robe-clad man.

A shrug and a gesture down the stairs. "Be my guest lass."

The servants helped her and Soter search. Farren was given a weapon to use, a dagger the length of her forearm. How a seventeen year old girl escaped from her room without anybody noticing was something Farren could not wrap her head around. The man who was stationed outside of her room was nowhere to be seen either. She thumped around on bare feet and skidded out of the back doors. More Aureum forest sat beyond the palace and she only hoped that the Princess had some form of a weapon with her. That hope was dashed when, twenty minutes after the initial shock, Cyrille was found. She was not the most efficient runaway, nor the smartest because she was without a weapon and still dressed in the glittery clothes Schylus gave her. It was Farren who found her pressed against a dirt mound as a small herd –four-Kuroguine loomed over her. The mound acted as a solid wall which prevented

Cyrille's escape. Her dress was filthy, her hair plastered to her face with sweat and one of her shoes were missing. Pleas fell from her lips in a chant and she looked like any other fugitive. It was weird for Farren to run without the Kayei speed she used in the fight but she pushed her legs forward and used the dagger to slice the throat of the closest Kuroguine. The others screamed and the sound reverberated through her skull.

When they rounded on the woman in the forest they paused, recognition on their faces. "Malumrem," they hissed in unison. The old language was used by all creatures it seemed. Once they spoke, one of them lunged so she slid to the left, her bare feet scratched against pebbles and mud. It was slower than the first two she encountered so it fell beneath her blow like any human would. The other Kuroguine pounced, its heavy body on top of her in seconds. Farren's head collided with the ground and rattled her brain in her skull. Cyrille whimpered and stood on shaky legs.

"Stay where you are!" Farren screamed.

"I do not take orders from the likes of you."

The roll of her eyes was involuntary and she continued to struggle against the Kuroguine who remained too quick, too strong for her. Despite the Princess' harsh words, the Royal remained pressed against the dirt mound like she asked. The creature above her drooled and dipped its face closer. The last Kuroguine stalked toward Cyrille with its black teeth bared.

"Farren!" Soter called as his footsteps came to a halt. The world slowed, the Kuroguine's drool hung from its open mouth and the claw that was prepared to slash open her throat barely moved. That granted her the opportunity to kick the creature in the gut and use that momentum to slide away from it. As soon as she found her feet she flung the knife at the Kuroguine above Cyrille. It was the only action that was not slowed around her, and the blade hit its mark. The Kuroguine went down before the world sped back up again. The last creature –the one that pushed her to the ground- stumbled back, glanced at Soter and escaped through the trees. There was no time wasted before Farren marched over to Cyrille and pulled her from the ground. Soter helped guide her back toward the palace. Two servants who followed Soter trailed behind with awe and fear in their eyes.

"Let me go! I do not wish to return to Altin!" Cyrille protested, "I do not belong there!"

Farren's face twitched with the effort not to curse. "I will not have Rorke's death mean nothing just because you are having an identity crisis." Farren sucked in what was supposed to be a calming breath. "Janus!"

The Kayei met them at the open doorway to his conservatory, a mug of something in his hand, hip jutted out to the side. "Yes?"

"Do you have any rope I can use, please?"

His brows shot up at the request but his servants went to fetch it. "I see nobody was harmed except." Janus looked at the black liquid –blood from the Kuroguine- and chuckled, "for some Kuroguine."

A servant spoke up, "three dead in the forest, My King."

"That reminds me," Farren changed the subject, "does the Kuroguine's blood have any magical properties? What I mean is, would there be any use for it?"

Janus and Soter shared another look and Aureum's Ruler shrugged. "It can be used as a thickening substance in some spells." He ran a hand over his chin. "People thought it was a good liquid to write with but I have never heard of it being used in a spell."

"It can mask smells as well," Soter added.

That made Farren stop. "Like the smell of half-Kayei blood?" Soter nodded with a furrow to his brow. "And it could slow the flow of liquid too?" Another nod, that time from them both. "Would a location spell need a thickening substance?"

Janus' eyes were wide when he said, "an advanced one."

"Advanced? What makes it advanced?"

It was Soter who answered, "how far it has to travel."

"Like across Realms?" Farren's head started to spin. There was too much to think about when she returned. She didn't know whether or not she wanted the inky substance Emmett used to be Kuroguine blood or not. During her mental struggle, the servants brought the rope. Soter took it from them and tied it around Cyrille's wrists, but not before one of the servants handed her the missing slipper and she placed it on with a struggled huff. An indignant cry sounded from her but she simply gaped at him as he looped the rope through. He kept a hold of the rope as they made their way inside.

"So," Farren looked up at Soter. "It was you in the match." He hid his smirk behind a cough. "You were why my ankle didn't get crushed."

"I wanted to help you survive."

"You did, you really did, thank you. Is that your main power then, time manipulation?"

He smiled. "Yes. I can play with time. I make things appear as if they are moving slower or faster."

She pursed her lips. "That's rather impressive," but there was a pit in her stomach. It wasn't that she survived Schylus that tumbled through her head, but the fact that the King of Altin likely knew that Soter possessed such abilities and he sent them into a Realm without him, on their own, with no magic. *You're not a King's Guard, that imbecile in the cells is but not you. You are a sacrifice in return for the King of Altin's daughter.* The King of Altin never wanted her to return alive. The urge to scream, to rip her hair out filled her soul but she never showed them how angry she was, she had no reason to be because she made it out alive; she completed his mission and she lost a comrade along the way. That is what it meant to be a soldier. Yet anger was what fuelled her. It was better than tears, better than grief, better than the guilt that lived in her chest.

Cyrille scoffed and Farren was brought back to the present. "Maybe you should go back in time and kill Schylus before he kills Rorke."

Soter replied with his furrowed brow pointed at her, "I can only reverse or fast forward a single entity three minutes."

With the roll of Farren's shoulders and a deep breath she moved through the building. Three minutes was not enough to save Rorke, and even if it was, there was no longer a way to rectify it. Rorke was dead and no amount of time tampering would change that.

They reached the horses Janus gifted them and Soter helped Cyrille clamber onto her steed. The rope connected to her wrists was handed to Farren who swung her leg over the saddle. That was when Soter nodded toward the end of Janus' garden. Sat like a beacon of light was the wagon Soter healed her in over a month ago. Cyrille looked between Farren and the wagon. "Are we to travel on horseback whilst he-" Her eyes flicked to Soter. "Travels in luxury?"

Soter spoke, "of course not. You will ride the horses to the wagon so I can tack them on the front. We will travel across the Veil together and we can tie Rorke's body to the bed whilst we do."

Farren nodded but Janus caught her attention, "Farren, if you ever need someone this side of the Realm," he dipped his head again, "I will be here."

"Thank you. I hope if we ever meet again," *unlikely*, she thought, "I will be attending your masquerade ball, I heard you are the best at throwing them."

Something glimmered in his eyes and his throat bobbed, so he turned on his heel and entered his palace, Pep at his side. The door swung closed and Farren stared at the magnificent building in front of her. The window to her room was thrown open to let in air and the curtains parted slightly. In that window, like a shadow, stood Rorke, hands braced on the ledge and the same smile on his face. She shook her head and forced her horse forward, Cyrille at her side. Just as he said, Soter tacked the horses to the wagon, checked the wheels, and opened the door for Farren and Cyrille. The rope remained around the girl's wrists and they sat at the dining table by the window. Soter carried Rorke's silk-wrapped body over to the bed after the servants placed him at the foot of the stairs, and placed him on the duvet to be secured with the spare rope he had in his cupboard.

"I will guide the horses through the forest. You two can stay in here," he said as he climbed out of the wagon. Farren nodded absently and watched the Princess like a hawk. She leaned back with folded arms whilst the Princess' legs were folded primly beneath her.

No more Kuroguine, no more Faeries, no more Kayei trying to kill them, nor human servants to do their bidding. The ride through Aureum was arguably peaceful. It was smooth and quiet, the occasional rock of the wagon wobbled the females but Soter kept to the path with no diversion into the smaller forest nooks and crannies. Farren's attention was split between Cyrille and Rorke's

433

body. Every muscle in her was tensed and the dagger sat at her side glinted in the sunlight.

"We should talk." Cyrille shifted in her seat when she spoke. "About what I told you in Schylus' castle."

"Which part?"

Cyrille folded her bound hands on the table. "About what I am, what I can do. I am not silly enough to try and escape you a third time. I will be seeing my parents, and I will continue my duties as the Princess of Altin, for Rorke," she clarified with a slight narrow of her eyes, "but that means there needs to be-" She looked up as she thought of the word. "Discretion."

"You changed your mind quickly." Farren tilted her head. "But I do find it funny, how you let Schylus beat and abuse Rorke, yet there you sit and say you will finally do your duty *for* him?" *I will not have Rorke's death mean nothing just because you are having an identity crisis,* understanding nudged against the mistrust in her gaze.

Cyrille clicked her tongue. "Rorke and I knew each other well before you came into the picture. He was my friend, a man who never judged me, so it is for him."

"Then why let Schylus-"

"I cared for him!" She swallowed down the yell. "Each night I asked him to release Rorke, but he never listened." Her eyes became silver lined.

"I cannot say that I believe you. However, I am sorry that being the Princess is your only option." There was a sharp edge to her voice when she proceeded to ask, "do you truly believe that your parents don't know that you are part Kayei?

"I do, I might be their daughter but if they knew," she shook her head with a sad chuckle, "I would not be allowed to live."

"I did not intend to tell the King every detail of this mission. If you will not either." Cyrille's eyes narrowed further. "You watched the fight between myself and Killian, you saw that I used borrowed magic to do so. What I am asking, Princess, is that you please do not mention any use of magic to His Majesty or his wife."

Cyrille searched her eyes for a moment and recalled the bright blue, the ethereal glow that seemed to shine from within. "Not all of that magic was borrowed was it?" Farren's jaw clenched. "Is that why they call you that awful name?"

"Malumrem? Yes, I suppose it is." The taste of the words in her mouth were foul.

"Then we have an understanding: you will not inform my parents or anybody of my condition, and I shan't utter a word of yours in return." She held out a soft hand.

Farren took it. "We can stay out of each other's way and merely cross paths in the hall."

They shook and Cyrille said, "sounds perfect," there was a pause, "but what shall we tell my father?"

Farren groaned and leaned her head back with a wince. "Parts of the truth? He can know about Schylus and his games and tournaments, he can know about the dinner, and the fact that you were kept in the dungeon and-"

"Do you intend to tell him that I did not want you to rescue me from those dungeons?"

Farren tapped her fingers against her leg. It was a thought that crossed her mind more than once, and if Cyrille had run again she just might have. That was not what decision she fell upon, however. "I see no need for that." Cyrille nodded.

"We are here!" Soter called from the seat of his wagon.

Both Cyrille and Farren rushed to the window only to spy the colourful ripples of the Veil. Soter was stood in front of the horses, his hand pressed against the barrier. Every touch made colours appear beneath his palm. Farren nearly snatched his hand back but he looked so concentrated that she stopped herself. He knocked on it like a door and a shadow appeared beyond the Veil.

"It's just like in Brentham," Farren whispered and Soter turned to face her; she looked up at him before she stared at the figure beyond. "The first time I saw the Veil up close, there was a person on the other side. We tried to communicate but they couldn't hear me."

"The fact that you saw someone at all is incredible."

"What do you mean?"

"The Veil is only thin at certain points, but it looks like it is beginning to thin everywhere."

"You mentioned that in your tent; you said you came to Brentham because the Veil thinned. Does that make it easier to cross?"

He chuckled, "unfortunately no, it does mean that the Oracle can hear us clearer."

"Oh this is ridiculous," Cyrille huffed before she opened her mouth to scream. She screamed for the Oracle, for the being to show herself and let them cross. The sound rang in Farren and Soter's ears but then the smell of rain filtered through the Veil, along with a much colder wind. The Veil itself thinned and like a pool's reflection, the Oracle faded into view. Her beautiful features glared at Cyrille but she casted her eyes over Soter then tilted her head when she spied Farren. From the edge of the dead grass, where the shadow once stood, the Oracle surveyed them like a hawk would survey its prey. With a visible snort she waved her hand and the colours rippled before them. The Veil parted like curtains in the wind so Soter climbed back into his seat.

"I need the two of you to close the window and curtains." He looked over his shoulder. "The human eye cannot see the inside of the Veil. The Oracle is granting us passage for our loss. She mentioned," he paused as though listening to a sound neither female could hear. "Something about Rorke being the most noble of the guards that have passed through."

"You are joking?" Farren asked with her brow furrowed.

"Would you like to question her yourself? I can let her know," genuine and open he asked, but she shook her head.

"Thank you though." She did as he asked and the Veil was hidden from their view.

Soter dipped his head to the Oracle when they passed but she did not smile. The Veil caused a sort of rocking motion to move the wagon and a low growl rumbled through the floorboards. Yet, the Oracle never left her post, eyes too busy tracking the wagon across the clearing. The molten gaze followed them until they broke through the tree-line, "welcome back," she seemed to sing to all three and then the lock of her hut sounded behind them, her final deed for the day complete.

"You can open it up now," Soter called over the pound of the rain.

Cyrille shook her head but Farren flung open the window and stuck her head out. He beamed at her, the waves of his hair stuck to him. There was something that writhed under her skin once the freezing rain hit her. It was Winter in Altin and the shirt and trousers Janus offered did nothing to prevent the shivers and goose-pimples that rose on her skin. Her bare feet curled in on themselves to try and seek warmth, as she ignored the fact that she was in the carriage where the Princess looked so sad, and Rorke's body laid on the bed. No, the rain was good, the cold was welcomed. The forest that surrounded them was both similar yet remarkably different from the one they were in minutes before. The world around her seemed dull and grey in comparison to the bright oranges and reds of the Aureum land. There was no layer of magic in Altin which left the brightness and the shimmer behind them.

A hoot sounded above them which brought Farren from her daze. A tawny owl flew above them through the gap in the trees: Elira. A hoot and the flap of her wings and she was out of sight. "She followed us from Janus' palace," Soter told her.

She smiled up at where the owl was. "I didn't see her."

He too looked up. "She is very good at being stealthy."

"Can animals cross the Veil at will?" She tilted her head in question.

He blinked and thought for a moment. "Elira has never had a problem, I suppose they can. I have never thought about it."

"Soter, how often do you cross Realms?" She directed her eyes to watch the rain hit the horses.

"That was the first time in ten years, or perhaps it was eleven."

That was not the answer she expected. "Do you miss it?"

"Sometimes, but I want to return to a Realm without civil war and division. It has nothing for me at the moment."

Farren bit the inside of her cheek. "I don't know if it helped, but I hope with Schylus out of the way, you are one step closer to living in such a place."

The White Castle stood stark against the dull buildings that surrounded it. The entire Capital looked grungy but a busy city it remained as people bustled around the streets and continued with their days. It had not changed but the guards at the castle gates gaped when they saw the wagon approach. The Princess sat tall beside Soter from where, on the edge of the city, she clambered next to him, her face a sign that they were permitted through. Her chin was raised and her hair was haphazardly pulled behind her. The guards that gaped so openly stopped the carriage as the horses stepped onto the bridge and one of them rushed into the castle. Mere moments later the doors swung open and Adrastos and Argen stood on the threshold as though they awaited their return that exact day. The Captain of the King's Guard ushered Soter forward; the horses made their way over the bridge, whilst Argen shifted on his feet, his neck craned to spy his best friend.

"Help the Princess down!" Adrastos ordered. A gaggle of guards rushed from behind him and helped Cyrille from her seat. She was swept into a group of handmaidens who surrounded her like a human shield. Soter also dismounted and opened the wagon door. Farren swallowed as the smell of the city hit her and the castle walkway sat beneath the wagon's wheels.

"It's time."

"I know." She looked back at Rorke's body. "Can you give me a minute before you reveal him, please?" Soter nodded and she stepped from the wagon.

Her eyes were on her feet when she found the ground. Slowly, she lifted her head, her injuries stark in the light, and she locked her eyes with Argen's. He didn't blink, not as he took her all in. A breath that she didn't know she was holding was loosed, then she sprinted toward him. The pain in her leg was nothing, not as the gap between them was closed when she flung herself at him, her arms tight around his frame as a sob escaped her. He was knocked back a few steps but his arms were firm around her, his chin on the crown of her head as she gripped onto him. "You're back, you made it." Argen leaned back and scanned her face.

"I'm back," she rasped, "I'm back, Argen." His fingers reached for the bruises on her neck but she flinched back just as silence reigned among the men. One look over her shoulder and she knew why. Soter brought Rorke's wrapped body from his wagon and she made her way over to help him. Her arms burned as she held his weight on her side and shoulders. Farren was suddenly hit with the thought of never seeing him again. She wanted to ask Soter to erect a barrier around them just so she would not have to face Adrastos and his men. She was so desperate to hold onto Rorke that she felt her knees buckle and Soter knelt to the floor with her, his hand around hers on Rorke's back.

"You brought him home?" Adrastos took a step forward. Everyone was frozen around her as she fixed her bloodshot eyes on him. Her slow nod made him move. Along with two other guards, he removed his Second from Soter's grip and pulled the body away from Farren, but her hand continued to grip onto the silk. That made the men pause. "Farren," the Captain whispered gently, "you have to let him go." Her grip did not loosen. "We are just taking him to the infirmary. You can see him later."

"He's dead," she said.

The blond closed his eyes for a moment. "I know, but we need to prepare him for the burning ceremony, okay?" He looked to Soter for assistance.

"Farren," Argen walked over to where she knelt and coaxed her hand from the sheets. It was difficult to pry her fingers open but once he did, the guards hauled Rorke up onto their shoulders as though he were in a casket and marched him into the castle. Farren's hand was clenched tight like the wrapping was still between her fingers but her eyes stared into nothing as Rorke was taken from her. The burning ceremony, that was what they had to do, because he was their soldier and that was what you did with fallen soldiers. He fell in battle, in the fight against Schylus.

The haze faded from her eyes. "I need to see the King."

Argen and Soter's arms hovered around her when she stood. Both men nodded despite the unsure glare Argen gifted Soter, and they walked through the open double doors to the White Castle. Pure determination shone in her gaze as she marched forward. Behind them, the horses and wagon were ushered off of the bridge and into the courtyard where they would be tidied away.

It was not just the look of the Human Realm, even the air was different, it seemed denser, like a heavy fog covered her chest. It wasn't the same pressure she felt from Nero's –Schylus'- barriers, it was like a cold or the start of a fever. She cleared her throat which made her wince; a fever was not something she needed at that time. Ignoring the negative thoughts that flittered through her mind, and her hand empty without Rorke's, she yearned to see the marble floors and walls of the White Castle. She longed to see the guard's uniforms and the harmless nobles that stuck their nose up each time she appeared. Instead of the nobles, the guards lined the walls, wide-eyed and

441

gaping as they bowed their heads when she walked past, but something was dark in their gazes. She shook it off. Word travelled quickly in a castle, just like in Brentham, because that was the King and Queen stood before the throne room doors. They were dressed immaculately, both of them all in white and covered in diamond jewellery.

"My hero!" The King held his arms out wide, a large smile on his face. His polar opposite stood solid next to him in the form of his wife. She harboured the same stillness Schylus prided himself with. The observation made Farren's brow twitch. The Queen looked anything but happy that she returned in one piece, that she returned her daughter; the scowl etched onto her face was cold, permanent and her eyes betrayed no emotion. The three of them were ushered into the throne room by the King who had a large grin on his face. The Rulers looked at the people before them: each of them with their hands behind their backs and chins tilted high.

"You found them, Soter," the Queen's voice sounded like a void.

"Indeed I did. Not that Farren truly needed my assistance."

"Is that correct?" The Queen's chin lifted higher so that she could look at the woman down her nose. "Regardless, she should bow before her King."

Not my King. Farren's eyes widened fractionally at the intrusive thought and she bent at the waist. It was on the King's order that they rose but it was not her, nor Soter and Argen that he had his eyes on, rather he gazed at the figure between the ballroom doors. Farren twisted; Cyrille stood with her eyes on the floor. When she lifted them the King beamed. Adoration, plain and simple radiated from him when his daughter looked at him. A man with no idea what his daughter actually was. There was a look shared between Farren and Cyrille, that exact thought resonated and then she bowed before her parents.

"Tell me everything," the King demanded as he settled on his throne.

Farren did. It was a filtered story filled with hidden facts and diversions, but he knew that they went through hell, that Schylus was the man he wanted and not Nero, and that he was dead by her hand. She told them of how she found Cyrille –she made sure to call her *Princess Cyrille*- and how Schylus treated her. Soter added the gory details of Farren's fight against Killian which brought Argen's widened eyes to the side of her face. A strangled noise fell from his lips and Farren flicked her eyes to him. Soter made it sound like what she did was noble instead of the inherently selfish act that it was. By the end of the tale, the King's smile vanished and his face was stone. What she wanted to mention, to question him about were the letters she found in Nero's passage. They had his emblem, and his signature on them. Was Nero under the thumb of not one, but two tyrants, a double-agent for the King Altin? From what she remembered of the letters, Nero was under orders and had yet to please the King. She went so far as to part her lips to discuss it, but Adrastos stepped forward, the cologne he wore infiltrated her nose and she held her tongue. There were too many people, it would be a question for the King when he was alone –she looked around the room- if he was ever alone.

"I expected no less from the King's choice of saviour," Adrastos commented from behind her.

"Yes." The King stroked his beard and gave her a once-over. "Now that I know the truth it is time I offer you my thanks."

FAREWELL

The tension in the room was thick enough to cut with a knife. Farren ensured that her feet were planted shoulder-width apart and that her back was straightened. Every time she stood in front of the King there always seemed to be an injury on her body, first it was her ribs and then it was her throat. She only hoped he noticed what she endured just to be recognised by her country.

"Farren, you have far exceeded my expectations: you not only did as I asked and brought my daughter home, but you defeated a threat to these lands, to this throne. My daughter is safe and alive and you stand before me fully intact. It is beyond what I thought possible and I am glad," the King spoke. There were many points in his speech that made her want to correct him. He never asked her to bring Cyrille back, he threatened her family and livelihood; she was not fully intact, she was battered, bruised, and slowly started to heal by magic; she wanted to ask him just how far he intended her to get before she died, but she clamped her lips closed and simply blinked.

"His Majesty and I must reward you for your valiant behaviour." There was no pleasantry in the Queen's voice.

The King's smile returned. "You did this for your country, position, and family, and for that reason I shall grant your father and uncle the Royal Seal so that they will be known as Altin merchants, with Altin ships."

The world shifted around her. A Royal Seal was more than just a symbol stamped on pieces of parchment, or by the names of men, it showed any foreign traders that they were legitimate, that they had money and resources behind them. It was an incentive for them to stop trading across the Dark Sea. She swallowed the laugh of disbelief that surged in her chest. There wasn't more to say than a short, "thank you."

It was a reward, yes, and it helped her father pay off his debts, but there was something deep within her that wished Theron never saw the fruits of her near-death mission- of Rorke's death. The King's eyes remained on hers as she pushed that gloomy thought deep into her gut and plastered a smile on her face. After a moment he waved to Adrastos who –throughout the entire conversation- stood tall behind her. He did not speak as he walked around her and Soter, and proceeded to unsheathe his sword. The sound rang out across the room but faded once he was knelt before the King. The weapon was held out to him with a smile and the lift of his arms. The King rose from his throne and removed the sword from Adrastos' hands. Farren took a small step back with a stutter to her heart. Surely the King was not about to- The Captain stood and moved beside the King as he stepped toward a pale-faced Farren. It was the King's turn to lift the sword above his head, but she didn't know where to look; did she look at the sword? The King? Adrastos? Her own feet? She internally cringed at the filthy toes she glanced down at but instead she lifted her eyes to the throne he descended.

"Farren, you have completed your test and your training, you have a spotless recommendation from the Commander of Brentham, and you have proven yourself to your King. Therefore, I wish for you to kneel and I shall swear you in as one of my guards."

When her body moved of its own accord her head caught up with what happened. The King opened his mouth as her knee hit the marble. The ancient words of the Prayer of Protection rolled off the King's tongue. It was something that haunted Farren's dreams since she was a child, it was what every King's Guard was blessed with when they ascended to the position from trainee to a lower-level guard. The words were spoken loudly which was a harsh contrast to the delicate wording of each syllable. The prayer used to be delivered in the Old Language but since the First Great War it had been translated, yet it sounded as beautiful as it once had. She had to push back the

445

tears. The moment he finished it, the King used Adrastos' sword to draw a symbol above her head. It was the same entwining symbol that adorned the guards' uniforms. Twirling circles and curves that formed a knot at its base then numerous swooping lines above it. There was no way to know where it started and ended. The second he finished drawing, something beneath her ribs roiled, something heavy and dark that slithered beneath her bones that recoiled at the symbol, at the words, at the cold floor against her trousers. She ignored it, the feeling amassed to that of indigestion.

"Welcome to the guard, Farren, "Adrastos congratulated once the King stood back and handed him his sword.

The King's smile constantly shone at her as she rose to her feet, hands a trembling mess. Every guard in the room clapped but as she turned her attention past Argen and Soter to where the men either side of the throne room doors stood, she noted they were not the smiles of those who wished her well. Each clap was strained and loud whilst their faces were filled with acid and grime, something sour that had the darkness inside of her begging to be released. Subtly she turned away from the unpleasant men only to be clapped on the shoulder by Argen. He grinned at her, chest puffed and his stance steady, so she smiled back. Soter held a softer smile but one that had the red of his brows turned slightly downward. Adrastos, despite his congratulations looked like he wanted to tell her to run back home, his smile impressed but also sad. It was not the face she imagined when she thought of her ceremony.

"Adrastos, Argen, your work for the day is far from over so I suggest you return to it," the King ordered.

"Yes, Your Majesty, we have a funeral to prepare for."

That brought the mood down a few a notches. "A funeral, whose?" It seemed the guards had not informed him of Rorke's death.

It was Adrastos who replied, "Rorke's funeral, Your Majesty."

A shadow crossed over the Ruler's face and he looked down at Farren for confirmation. She only dipped her head and swallowed deeply. Soter's hand was on her wrist, fingers tight around her muscle. It was for comfort, for strength, just something that would keep her emotions in check. "Schylus killed him," Cyrille spoke from her place at the back, "Farren did everything she could but he still died."

Farren glanced at the Princess but the King asked, "is this true?"

"Yes, Your Majesty, the fighting match Soter told you about was to save Rorke. I won and he was killed in front of my eyes." She cursed herself for choking on her words.

"And you sat by and watched?" The Queen asked.

That made Farren's head shoot up. "No," the sound was nearly that of a growl so she took a moment and focused on Soter's tight grip. "The Kayei erected a barrier that could not be broken."

"So you were powerless against them?" The Queen dug the knife in harder.

"Obviously," Farren bit out; the darkness reared.

The King clapped his hands, the tension worse than when they began. "A burning funeral shall be held tonight, then. After that I grant you four days of rest. A ball will be thrown in your honour of course at the end of it. Do try and sleep off the awful injuries you have acquired, Farren." Thus, they were dismissed and she followed Argen, Adrastos and Soter out of the throne room.

447

By the time night fell, the castle was quiet. No celebration or gathering was held that day. Farren tried to sleep through most of it, through the ache in her chest and the roar in her ears, but all she had been successful at was lying on her bed to stare at the ceiling. Argen had not come by, his attention on Adrastos and the preparations for the funeral. Before she retired to her chambers she visited the infirmary but just as she had been lied to before, they lied to her again. She was not permitted to see his body, to hold his hand whilst they dressed him. She was locked out: 'family only' they told her. The wall took the brunt of her anger and she was escorted out of the medical wing.

Adrastos tried to speak to her as she was shoved up the stairs but she plainly stared at him, glanced back down the stairs to the white-clad Healers, and walked to her room. What good was being a member of the King's Guard if she was still locked out?

A loud bell echoed through the castle and the castle moved. Farren climbed from her coffin-like position and pulled on a pair of boots that remained where she left them over a month ago. She brushed her hair and tied it back, grabbed a spare sword she found on her bed and buckled it to her waist. The jacket she donned was plain. Many of the candles went unlit so she braced a palm along the walls and guided herself toward the farthest courtyard. It was on the opposite side of the castle to where she and Adrastos trained. Argen met her at the top of the stairs and they walked together. It wasn't until they reached the opening to the gardens that Farren stopped. Soter was pushed further and further back by three guards. His hands were raised and he allowed them to move him. Argen pulled on her wrist in the opposite direction.

"Hey!" Farren shucked off his hand. "What do you think you are doing? Do not handle him in such a way!"

The guards –with their hands on Soter- looked at her with disinterest, but one of them spoke, "he is not permitted beyond this point."

"What you mean to say is he is not invited to the funeral. On whose orders?"

One of them smirked. "The King's."

Farren glared and gestured wildly. "This man carried Rorke's body over Realms to ensure that he returned home so that his body could be burned properly, so that his comrades have a chance to say goodbye, but there you stand corralling him like he was no better than an urchin boy trying to steal bread from your pockets. Let him through!"

Soter looked between the red faced woman and the guards. "Farren it is alright." She opened her mouth to inform him it was most definitely not alright and the men before her enjoyed their position just a bit too much. "I understand. He was their commanding officer, a friend so to speak. I am fine with watching from a different level of the castle."

Farren balled her hands into fists. "It's not right."

"No." Soter shrugged. "But it is what it is." The guards released him and the Magician walked away with a final glance at Farren. She said nothing more to the guards and let Argen guide her forward. Torches lit the walkway into the courtyard and trees flanked them. Any guard who could be there, was, their armour glistened in the torchlight. That was when she noticed Argen wore his own armour, polished and shiny for the occasion. The partners of the guards stood in their best dresses, arms linked with white metal. Farren shook her head at Argen's outstretched arm.

Beyond the crowd of people the pyre was built high into the sky. Copious logs and grass and kindling formed a platform where Rorke's body would be laid to rest. The King and Queen stood beyond the pyre, their eyes on their guards and hands clasped in front of them. Cyrille stood at her mother's side, her dress a dark grey and hair piled on top of her head. It would not be them who lit the wood, but rather a sobbing woman who stood next to the pyre's ladder. She wore a black dress, her hair pulled from her strong face and when she lifted her head from her hands Farren's stomach dropped: she was the spitting image of Rorke. *His mother*, with a handkerchief in her grip and a quiver to her lip. Each line of her face was visible but she had the same broad shoulders and square jaw as her son, handsome and full of strength, something Farren hoped to live up to one day.

Another loud bell rang out and the crowd quietened. A cold wind whipped around them. Women gasped as their skirts billowed and the men held them closer to their sides. Argen held his own hair to his head but Farren barely noticed the cold, her jacket undone and her face bare to the weather. The rain dried on her skin from her travel to the White Castle so the chill was purely from the wind. Words were exchanged. They went in one ear and out the other. She was solely focused on the cloth-wrapped body a quartet of guards carried from inside the castle. He looked so much smaller on their shoulders. His broad muscles, strong face, large hands, none of it was visible as they climbed up the ladder and placed him on the podium. The white silk was replaced with black cloth tied with oil-stained rope. More pretty words, ones she heard when the guard died on the road to the Capital. Rorke's mother raised the torch and everyone took in a deep breath. They loosed it when the torch was dug beneath the wood where the flames caught immediately.

Rorke would have hated the spectacle of it all, but he would have appreciated the tradition, the loyalty of his men as they cried for their fallen soldier. Soter stood high in the castle, Elira on his shoulder as he stared out of a large window. His head was bowed in respect but soon enough his eyes trailed to where Farren and Argen stood between gaps in the crowd. They were in their own bubble.

450

The King then rose to make a speech and Farren smiled to herself at the thought of Rorke's flustered face. She turned to her right to dry her eyes only to find a large, tall body stood close to hers. Half-way with her sleeve to her face she stopped and drifted her eyes to look at the man beside her. His face looked sharp in the firelight, hair perfectly combed. Farren swallowed and quickly looked at the guards in front of her then at Argen who stared sadly at the body on the pyre. "Rorke," she muttered. Argen did not twitch at the sound of her voice, nor did he notice her attention no longer on the fire. The other man at her side turned and smiled. His scarred hand reached for hers and their fingers entwined. The spirit's skin was warm and felt so very real, so real that Farren found herself leaning into his side. His body held still, the same clothes from when she saw him at Janus' on his frame. The sharp thud of her heart in her chest, the heat from the fire, the suffocating smell of a bonfire, were all ignored, because Rorke's hand was in hers, his smile addictive. Then, just as the smoke dissipated into the sky, he started to fade from her hold. For a moment longer she clung to him and let the tears flow freely.

"Please don't leave me," she cried softly.

"It's okay Farren, we won, I have to go."

Alive or not, she was thankful for his presence and it truly made her realise: if love could have saved him, Rorke Alliard would have lived forever.

The next day and the White Castle returned to normal. The large wall of names in the National Gardens was where Rorke's name would be etched for everyone to know he fell in service to his country. There were many slabs dotted around those gardens with too many names written on them. Farren told herself she would visit once his name was there, a tombstone for those who burned their bodies. It was to be done by the end of the week, so in the spare four days the King gave her, she went for the occasional walk in the castle grounds. It strengthened her leg and brought fresh air to her lungs. At breakfast she chewed sheepishly on her porridge but after a few mouthfuls she found her spoon in the bowl and that bowl passed to Argen who had not left her side since the funeral. He spent the mornings with her and sometimes until she slept. Not, that sleeping was a sanctuary. Nightmares of thick blood and a brimstone crown clouded her mind. The sweat which covered her body stuck her nightshirt to her back so her window was flung open and she curled into her side. When she roamed the castle and Argen had other duties to attend, she and Adrastos returned polite small talk and each smile she sent him or any other guard was tight against her mouth. They were her comrades, comrades who she had to risk her life for, comrades who shivered at the thought of her near them. That was what she guessed by the daggers thrown her way whenever she looked at them.

What unsettled her the most was the weird energy that surrounded her and Argen. He was protective and often asked how she was, but there was always an apologetic twinge behind it. It was her wish that the sympathy and lingering shock would fade from his gaze in time because it was as though he saw the missing part of her, or the darkness that lived beneath her skin. It was something she had to become used to, the way she walked on eggshells around the people she left behind for her mission. What helped ease her mind and her soul were her visits with Soter.

"How are you?" He asked as he handed her a mug of tea.

She sniffed her cup and smirked. "This isn't going to put me to sleep is it?" Soter faltered and she snorted. "Not that I couldn't use that right now."

He tilted his head. "Nightmares?"

As she brought the cup to her lips she shrugged. "Sometimes it's Schylus, sometimes it is Rorke." She swallowed the hot liquid. "Other times I dream of a black figure."

"Black figure?"

The original meaning of her visit was to return the magical necklaces that saved her life. She pooled them into his outstretched hands and he placed them in their original drawer. The small red one he gifted her in his tent sat under her shirt, in its permanent place.

"He's shadows made flesh, or at least, he is majority shadows. Red veins climb up his arms and face." She drank. "He has no eyes however. The first time I saw him was when I fell asleep in the bath here." She nodded toward his door. "And then again in Kavan."

"Are they all nightmares?" Her face flared at the question but she shook her head. "Are you ever afraid of this figure?"

"No, intrigued is probably a better term."

Soter nodded and hid a cheeky smile behind his mug. "Maybe he is trying to tell you something."

Farren smirked. "Oh I don't think there is any hidden meaning in our last encounter." Soter's eyes widened and after a beat, he erupted into laughter. When their mirth died down she swallowed the tightness in her throat and locked eyes with him. He continued to sip his tea as he waited for her to speak. It wasn't until half her cup was drained that she spoke again, "do you think dreams follow us into the light?"

He quirked his brows. "Into the light?"

"When we aren't asleep," she clarified. When he remained silent she pursed her lips and focused on Elira who slept in the sunshine. "I feel like I am going crazy."

"What have you seen?" He shuffled closer to her.

"Rorke, I saw him at Janus' then at the funeral."

The shine of Soter's eyes nearly made her sniffle but there were no harsh words for her. "You saw his spirit?"

"Do those even exist?" She chuckled in disbelief.

"For some." He leaned back in his chair. "Have you seen him since the funeral?" She shook her head. "Then his spirit has passed on, I am sorry."

"It's not your fault. I just wish he was..." She finished her tea and looked at the remnants at the bottom of her mug.

"Is there anything I can do?"

"No, but thank you. I can't hope for anything more than him at peace," the words were true but the strain to her voice spoke volumes.

Steam rippled from the tub where Farren's hands were braced on the porcelain. The water's reflection stared back at her with the same frown on her face. The smell of lemon verbena encompassed her and the scent clung to the strands of her hair that dipped into the water. It was that night she decided that she would submerge her head beneath the water. She was tired of water being poured over the floor and fresh towels, so she thought, after what she endured in Kavan, a bath would not end her existence. Naked, she sank into the water. The groan she let out was near erotic as the heat soothed her muscles. She settled into the tub and breathed deeply before she sunk to her shoulders. The water lapped against her skin, then she took the plunge.

Everything was muffled, a dull pressure in her head and on her shoulders. The heat of her body was a stark contrast to the snow beneath her feet and the Brentham river in front of her. A body laid face-first in the running water and she rushed toward it, the brown strands and large shoulders familiar. A blond figure formed above the body. With Rorke's chest pressed to the cold ground she couldn't see the skin that fell from his torso but the blood that seeped from his wounds turned the snow pink. At the shaky in-take of breath, Nero —who stood tall above Rorke- smirked, his foot on the back of the soldier's head. She was so focused on them that the corpse against a tree, which had been a mangled mess of limbs and blood, was able to twitch without her knowledge. The corpse soon gained a full form: Schylus' form. It all happened too fast: Rorke's eyes flew open, his mouth followed suit whilst water filled the orifice. Farren turned and then there was a ruby dagger plunged into her stomach. Storm blue eyes locked with red and the dagger twisted. Schylus smiled as she fell to her knees. The pain forced a scream and a surge of water to slam into the corpse. Nero and Schylus stumbled back with the blow.

Water slammed over the side of the tub and hit the bedroom wall as Farren emerged. The liquid dripped onto the floor as she gasped for air. One minute, maybe two she was under the water but that vision was clear as if she was there. She clambered from the tub and grabbed the nearest towel. Once it was wrapped securely around her torso she perched on the edge of her bed. The flush that covered her skin ebbed away to a pale complexion, eyes wide and limbs stiff.

"Dammit," she breathed as her concentration moved to the dark stain on the wall. Eight feet, that was how far the water shot from the bath. A few cracks formed in the wall where the water dripped. The wood beneath her toes was dry so the sheer power propelled it forward at such a speed that there was no time for it to fall onto the floor. Farren looked between the bath and the wall and ran a hand through her hair. Water slid down the bridge of her nose and fell onto the towel. Deep breaths lifted her shoulders and she wrapped her arms around herself. Her lower lip quivered as she stared at the water stain. The longer she stared the sharper her breaths became. She was not entirely human, the waves that surged beneath her skin were a stark reminder of that. Twenty-two years, she had gone twenty-two years without a whiff of magic on or near her person, but there she sat, in the White Castle, her position earned, with that *thing* within her. A King's Guard with magic, the one thing that guaranteed her death with no trial, no discussion, simply 'Off with her head!' So she screamed. It was raw and loud. It pulled against the damaged muscles of her throat but she screamed and thrashed on the bed.

Exhaustion found her, the cold of the window hit the tear tracks on her face. With each rise and fall of her chest she tried to even her breathing. The length of her arms covered the bed as she spread out. The darkness filled the room, the moonlight a sliver against her skin, she stretched her legs just to feel something. The remnants of her screams reminded her of Nero, about how he told her to run, how she begged him to help, for Schylus to stop. With eyes screwed shut, she raised her hand and felt the hairs on her arm rise at the memory of the barrier against her skin. She flexed her fingers against the moonlight. Schylus' words flew around her head: 'because you would never win against me.' *Arrogant bastard.*

With a quiet sniff she sat up and stared at the dress hung on the wardrobe. Another note from Soter sat on her desk; she could not attend her own ball without a formal dress. It was a sleeveless, high neck, cerulean gown with beaded bluebells at the hem and around the waist. It took a lot of willpower to stand from the bed and pat herself dry. A gold pin held her twisted hair in place which added to her pale face, but she walked to the door on blue-heeled feet. There was nothing to be done about her red-rimmed eyes. Beyond the door was Argen, dressed in a light grey, sharp-lined suit. A wide smile covered his face and he held out his arm for her. With his eyes on her she ran her tongue across her teeth and raised a brow.

Argen slowed his pace so that they had time to speak, "Are you going back to the village tomorrow?"

She faltered. "Am I allowed to?"

Argen chuckled. "You can travel with me if you like, I haven't been back since you left and I think Princess Cyrille's saviour deserves some time with her family. Even if all you do is give your father the Royal Seal." A nod from her and they continued toward the ballroom, side-by-side.

EPILOGUE

Colourful streamers hung from every light fixture and table in the ballroom. It coincided with the cheerful music that filtered through the room from the grand piano in the far corner. The tables that lined the right wall were littered with foods similar to that of Farren's first ball and her stomach growled loudly at the sight. In the few days since she arrived, a few bites of anything was all she could stomach before it turned bland and settled like steel in her stomach. Before she was able to inspect the smaller food items, the King's voice boomed through the room, announcing her presence. The piano stopped and all eyes turned to where she and Argen stood. She shifted on her feet, eyes wide and her hand awkwardly flexed at her side. The cheers that followed nearly split open her ears. Her own grin —one she reminded herself how to make- followed that of the King's. The Princess stood beside her father, hands in front of her and eyes on the pianist. The swaying of bodies and chatter resumed whilst across the room the Queen whispered in the ear of a dark-haired, narrow-eyed gentleman. His hands were folded behind his back but those eyes —a blue that almost shone through the crowd- were fixed on Farren. She blinked and his eyes were on the Queen. A simple trick of the light, or perhaps her sleep deprivation caught up to her.

A piece of cheese covered pastry sat between her teeth as she stood with her eyes on the crowd. The colours that danced in the candle-light reminded her so much of the tent she found erected in her village square. The beautiful scarves she spied in the rafters brought her mind back to Soter and his beautiful collection. She searched the sea of people for the Magician, and went so far as to stand on her tip-toes to find his bright orange hair. He had not mentioned attending the ball, perhaps he was holed up in his room or outside with Elira. On cue, a hoot sounded above the chatter and music. Farren craned her neck to find the tawny bird perched in the rafters surrounded by colourful scarves. The smile that crept onto her face felt slightly less forced than those previous, strained, sharp smiles she gave her friends. She was so caught up by the owl's playful flap of wings that she barely noticed the change in atmosphere. The music shifted from light, joyful music to something slower, something that glided through the air and across her skin like a whisper of wind. Once she returned her gaze to the party she blinked. Soter's hand was outstretched before her whilst he bowed at the waist.

"May I have this dance?" So she took Soter's hand with a lighter chest and he pulled her onto the newly-polished dance floor. He spun her into his arms effortlessly; the skirts of her dress shifted around her ankles. With his hand in hers, the other respectfully on her back she allowed the music to wash over her. All they did was dance until a new song reached their ears, one just as soft as the last. That was when Soter asked, "have you thought of what you will do now?

She shook the daze from her mind and swallowed. "What do you mean?"

"Now that Schylus is dead and you have these new po-" Farren gently placed her fingers against his lips with a pointed look, he apologised. "Do you intend to remain the King of Altin's guard?" He spun her.

"I did not work this hard to *not* be." She curled back into his chest. "That mission was my test, you know that. I cannot go back to being a merchant's daughter." She roved her eyes to the Royals on their right. They watched each move she and Soter made with the flick of their gazes. She blinked her attention back to Soter before they noticed her stare.

"What about being an ambassador to the Kayei Realm? You have been there, understood our customs and cultures quickly. Mainly, you did not balk at the Night Creature that attacked your village."

Farren stopped him dead on the dance floor. "That is literally your job. I am not Kayei which means I do not qualify. I may have saved that creature but that does not mean I condone one being in Brentham." She felt slightly ill when Pep's happy face entered her mind. "I serve my King and country and that is that," she ground out and moved her eyes back and forth between the King of Altin and Soter. Some guards moved minutely closer to where they danced. *Understand, Soter, please.*

The green of his eyes flashed whilst his grip on her hand tightened. "A King's Guard is where you think you will be happy?" A sharp nod from her. "Then I find myself staying as the ambassador a bit longer." He smiled, grabbed her waist and brought her into another dance. "Your leg seems healed." His eyes ghosted where dark purple contrasted against her freckled skin. "But how are you, any more visions of Rorke?"

Farren clicked her tongue. "I am fine." She bowed at the waist as the dance demanded. "I haven't seen or heard from him. My mind is obviously pre-occupied with the nightmares."

The smile he gave her was soft but calculating and he squeezed her hand. "I think Argen would like your next dance."

Farren looked over her shoulder and there Argen stood: his hands behind his back and his eyes bore into hers. She turned back to Soter who was engulfed in the crowd, then held out her hand to her friend. Argen rushed to her side and enveloped her hand in his. The music increased in tempo but they kept each other close as they danced. Their steps flew with the music and they just let themselves move.

The National Gardens were as grand as they sounded. Plant life imported from across the world lined the pathways. Beautiful men and women, children and babies filled the gardens with happy smiles and laughter. A cool breeze ruffled Farren's hair as she walked down the well-kept paths. The winter sunlight meant families were inclined to visit because the sun tried to warm the ground and the air around them. It was a reincarnated summer in winter. A small map sat in her pocket that she pulled in front of her face. Adrastos' writing sat alongside sketched lines and descriptions. If he were not the Captain, she would have recommended he work as an artist. The lines were clear, the flowers he sketched perfect replicas. She turned left at the daisies just like the map said and as though it appeared out of nowhere, a large, black, marbled wall stood tall. A man sat hunched near the base, a bag of tools next to him. From where she stood the names were dents in the structure but once she moved around a patch of flowers and pushed her hands into her pockets, she was able to read the names. There were too many to count, but each one was etched delicately, perfectly, into the marble.

The man at her feet did not look up from his work but he said, "a nice day for a walk."

"Yes." Farren tilted her head to the sun. The tendons in her neck stretched and the bruises smarted but the warmth on her skin was worth it. "It is." She lowered her head back into position and read some more names. However, there was only one name she went to say goodbye to. Farren stared at the man with the chisel as the letters formed into the wall. Pieces of marble fell to the ground whilst the man worked. Soon enough he sat back, placed his chisel in his bag of tools and stared at his work. It was simple, no 'in remembrance' or 'rest in peace', there were no words other than his name, but it was fitting and it almost brought a smile to her face:

Rorke Alliard

The ride to Brentham was filled with heightened nerves. Farren's heart had yet to calm down the entire journey but when they reached the edge of the village it felt like it would explode. Argen offered words of encouragement but he was just as nervous; their horses trotted side-by-side. It wasn't long before they saw people, most of whom had to do a double take when they spied Farren. The baker paused in his haggling, washer-women let their clothes drip onto the cobblestones and children whispered reverently to each other. The villagers had not changed. There was no more snow on the ground but the icy wind reminded her that Spring had not yet sprung. It levelled her head and gave her a moment to focus on the clear air and the wind in her hair. Then she was forced to notice the rose-guarded house that stood proudly at the end of the gravel pathway.

With a squeeze of the reins she dismounted, the crunch of stones sounded beneath her boots. They secured the horses to wooden posts that once held up her mother's tomato crop but in the cold sat empty. Farren trailed her eyes from the horses, up the pathway to the open doorway where her family stood and paused. Eydis stood at Theron's side, a small smile on her face and her hand in his. They looked- a shocked chuckle escaped her- they looked happy. Argen stepped forward which brought her from her staring and they walked toward the warmth of the house.

"Theron," she spat, "what are you doing here?"

He rolled his eyes. "As polite as always, Farren." He did not bother to look at her when she stepped forward.

"I was polite to you many times."

The dislike that rose to the surface simmered down and a smile curled her lip upward when her parents unceremoniously shoved Theron aside and ran to her. Each parent hugged her tightly with large smiles on their faces. Her mother fussed with her face, the cuts and bruises faded to nothing. She lightly pulled at her daughter's clothes –riding leathers with the King's emblem on the back- and commented on how skinny she became. "Did they feed you out there? Were you able to eat their food?" Jessibelle asked as she synched Farren's shirt at the waist.

"Leave her be, dear," her father cut in. When Jessibelle removed her hands, Farren waited for her father to clasp Argen's hand with an uncertain glare, and returned to her mother's side before she pulled the King's letter from her jacket pocket. She gripped the edge of the letter and Theron finally looked at her. He *really* looked at her. There was no limp in her step; the shirt she wore covered the bruises on her neck, and her shoulders were pushed back, chin held high. Her brow raised in response and she stared back only to find his complexion slightly green.

"What's the matter Theron, did you expect me to return with missing limbs?"

Questions swam in his eyes; they nearly escaped his mouth until he cleared his throat and sneered when he turned to Argen. "What made the King decide to trust her with the Princess' life?"

Argen's mask of polite calm did not break. "She is determined."

After a beat of silence where her uncle thought more explanation followed he rolled his eyes. "About the wrong things, you will find, Commander."

The twitch to her eye was justified when he removed his hand from Eydis' and clasped them behind his back, but she replied, "do you want this seal or not, Theron?"

"Would you be so petty that you would punish your father to spite me?"

"Do not, try and bluff me. I have dealt with scarier things than you."

"And I suppose you think you are one of those scary things?" He scoffed.

"My position says yes." Her grin was wicked.

Eydis patted his arm before he retorted. There was no side-long glance at Eydis, no scornful look sent Argen's way, nor did he bother to invite the conversation inside when he turned and stormed into the house. Why he was at her parents' house was a mystery but she assumed he wanted money, whatever her reward for saving the Princess was. To see Theron again was no blessing. What was a blessing, was the way her father's eyes lit up when he read the King's letter. His lips on the crown of her head broke her from glaring a hole into Theron's blazer. "Thank you Farren, we can finally make headway on our orders." He skipped away like a school boy with the biggest grin on his face she had ever seen. "Theron! Theron you need to read this!"

Jessibelle chuckled as her husband ran after Theron like a puppy with a new chew toy. With a deep breath she announced, "I shall start cooking. I have made roast, you still eat that don't you?"

"Yes, yes I do." Farren nodded.

Before she slipped through the doorway where her husband ran through she said, "Lyla wanted to be here but she was called home. Her father had some news for her that he wished to deliver in person, something quite serious it seemed."

Farren nodded absently and wrapped her arms around herself. While she was in the other Realm, people's lives carried on, they lived, and laughed, and loved, and received letters from across the country. She only wished she could have been there for her friend when she saw her father's writing. With a hum from Argen, he followed Jessibelle with an offer of assistance. That left

464

Farren with Eydis who took the moment to grip Farren gently by the shoulders. Her hands were bony and incapable of a harsh grip but they sat on the cold leather of her jacket. There was no haze in Eydis' vision or perhaps it had been too long since she last saw her aunt, but the older woman steadied herself on the gravel and brushed the back of her hand against Farren's cheek. It took every muscle in her body not to flinch from the kind, soft touch. The tense nature of her muscles made her insides roil just as the internal darkness swirled low in her stomach. It licked at the back of her mind but she clenched the hands in her pockets and swallowed.

"You have seen so much my darling survivor, my roaring ocean," Eydis cooed.

Another nickname from her aunt, "what do you mean Eydis?"

An answer to a completely different question flowed from her mouth, "the Flame, Farren, it watches over you, it is drawn to the water."

"Aunt Eydis I'm not sure I understand. Fire is repelled by water?"

Instead of replying, Eydis stared at a spot over her shoulder, eyes glazed and her smile was lopsided. The minute Farren glanced in that direction Eydis released her and she followed the chatter inside. It allowed for a moment to herself. The need for a sliver of food and sleep was deep rooted, but Farren took a long breath in. A sharp wind blew her hair in front of her face and she turned fully. With her back to the house she was able to see the edge of the woods where piles of mud lined the evergreen trees whose leaves darkened in the damp air. As her eyes scanned the trees they snagged on a flash of gold.

"No," she said aloud. Her eyes lowered from the green leaves to the blond hair and golden eyes that accompanied the flash. Against a tree on the edge of the forest was a smirk she wanted to tear apart, crossed ankles and a purple shirt that contrasted with the gold on his bare forearms, leant Nero. Steam rippled from his skin and his smirk widened into a feline grin as her eyes locked with his. An animalistic growl reverberated from her chest. He straightened from the tree and held up a small bucket. It was a clone of the one in the Kavan castle. He shook it like a baby rattle. The action opened up the pit in her stomach.

Bastard.

She removed her hands from her pockets and marched down the path. Once her foot met the threshold of her parents' land Nero sent her a wink and he looked to his left. A swirl of a magical portal formed, he waved, and stepped through it. In one swift motion she turned on her heel, grabbed the handle of her parents' door, and stepped into her family home. She plastered a large smile on her face. She smiled as Argen looked up from his place by the fire, she smiled as Damera and Baltar covered her in kisses, and the smell of damp dog hit her; she smiled as an ache forced its way wider and deeper into her chest. Her smile never faltered as she pushed the image of Nero's smirk from her mind. Instead she focused on her family; she focused on her future and kept her smile in place.